I0550249

FOREVER MY LOVE

By

Riette Suzzette Ormond

SUNSET COVER PHOTOGRAPH
By
Riette Suzzette Ormond

All of the names and characters portrayed in this novel are fictitious, the product of the author's imagination, and any resemblance to actual persons living or dead is purely coincidental. However, the sites, places, and cities are factual and most are historical.

Riette Suzzette Ormond   Forever My Love

Published by: Suzzette Exclusives, San Diego County, California

ISBN: 0-9620518-6-1

Front and Back Cover Designs and Photography by Riette Suzzette Ormond

Manufactured in the United States of America

I DEDICATE THIS BOOK TO:

My Darling Husband, George Ormond,
Sweetheart, you have been there with your
love, support,
inspiration, and motivation.

Always there to encourage with your love
and affection.

You have always been my love and filled our
marriage
With love, fun, and happiness.

We will never be married long enough.

**ALL MY LOVE, FOREVER and EVER and
ALWAYS
MY SWEETHEART**

A Special Thanks to Treasured Friends
Who have been there with their Love
and Friendship:
Kimberly - Sylvia – Darlene

And in Memoriam: Jennie 1923 - 2012

OTHER EXCITING WONDEROUS BOOKS

By
Riette Suzzette Ormond, B.A.
And
George Ormond, B.S., M.S.

Cuddles Helps Santa Claus Save Christmas(c)

A Fun Loving Story that will keep you in Suspense!
An Enjoyable Book For Children of All Ages 2 to 102

Colorfully Illustrated By
Riette Suzzette Ormond

A Great Gift!
HO! HO! HO!

Unique Program for Staying Healthy, Young, and Trim(c)

For All Those Serious Health Conscious
Individuals.

ABOUT THE AUTHOR

Riette Suzzette Ormond, B.A., a former fashion and television model, resides in San Diego County, California, with her husband, George Ormond, and their adorable pets: Cuddles, the laughing. talking, funtastic goose, and Yammy Yogurt, a cocker-spaniel poodle, they rescued.

She is an accomplished professional photographer, entertainer, ballroom dancer, and stand-up comedian who enjoys delivering singing telegrams with her darling husband, George Ormond.

Mrs. Ormond attended the University of Southern California and earned a B.A. Degree in Journalism from San Diego State University.

In addition to a major in journalism, she has strong minors in photography and public relations.

She was tapped and became a member of the Chimes Honorary Society and Phrateres.

Mrs. Ormond is a professional photographer and artist, specializing in oils and watercolors. She is being urged to have a one-woman show of her paintings and photographs. The sunset photograph on the front cover is one of her creations.

Among her passions are writing, interviewing, nutrition, and researching.

Mrs. Ormond loves bringing characters and situations to life in the pages of her books.

FOREVER MY LOVE
By
Riette Suzzette Ormond

I was highly motivated to write this book to bring forth the concept that families can live happily and in harmony despite tragedies.

In my book, *FOREVER MY LOVE,* one can relate and follow what happens to my main character, Cliff Camden, a happily married man with two children: 4-year-old Gabriella known as Ra Ra and her 18-month-old brother Jacques, when their mother, Julia, is unfortunately struck down and killed by a drunk driver.

The earth-shaken situation deeply affects Cliff Camden and his in-laws, Gordon and Grace Deveaux, causing Cliff, an attorney, to move from Manhattan, New York, to San Diego, California--new surroundings and open the firm's west coast law office.

Jane, Cliff's secretary, now feels she has a chance to be the next Mrs. Cliff Camden and offers to drive with him and his children to California. A trip, that in her imaginative day dreams, will make him realize that he loves and wants to marry her.

The events as they unfold are dramatic and fulfilling for Cliff when he meets Claudette on the beach in San Diego, CA.

She is helping his daughter, Ra Ra, build a sand castle who repeatedly asks Claudette to get more pails of water—Ra Ra never has enough water.

Cliff purchases a home for his family and invites his in-laws to move in. He makes his hired help members of his family. Monique, the French cook, the Svensens, housekeeper and grounds maintenance, Nancy, the au pair, also become a member of his family circle and is welcomed at all family functions and events.

There are events throughout that require the strength and love of each as in most families.

It is the story of three-generations who love, nurture each other, and live happily together.

CHAPTER ONE

It was a beautiful sun shiny day. The kind of day Claudette Dubois loved as she walked barefoot on the beach, feeling the soft, warm sand beneath her feet. Walking barefoot made her feel good as the grains of sand sifted in and out between her toes. What a great day! Waves were splashing against the shore. The sky was the bluest she had ever seen. She couldn't resist looking up at the fluffy white clouds that seemed to take on a myriad of unique swirls and patch patterns.

It was gratifying to see singles and families enjoying the day. Everywhere you looked, children were running back and forth with their pails, getting more water to make their sand castles. Bikini-clad teenagers were joining in the fun, braving the ocean waves, while parents were playing with their children who were using their tiny fingers to write names in the sand then standing back to survey and admire their art work.

She was so deep in thought that she didn't see a sand castle directly in her path and was suddenly brought back from her dream state as she looked down and saw the cutest little girl with red curly hair and the biggest most expressive blue eyes, holding two pails and asking in a soft sweet voice, "Will you please help me get some water for my sand castle?"

Together they walked to the water's edge and filled the pails with water. It was fun and brought back a flood of happy childhood memories. Claudette always loved coming to the beach to look at the waves, play with the sea kelp, and work on her tan. It was enjoyable sitting here helping this adorable little girl make her sand castle.

The little girl looked up and said, "My name is Gabriella, but my baby brother, Jacques, calls me Ra Ra because he can't say my name, Gabriella."

Ra Ra was happily smiling, giggling, and incessantly talking to Claudette who was having an equally good time. It was fun helping this tike.

They were busy laughing while molding sand for their castle as they dipped their hands in and out of the pail of water. When for some unknown reason she couldn't fathom, she felt a pair of eyes staring down at her. Upon raising her gaze, she saw a pair of legs. As her eyes moved upward, she saw a tall handsome man smiling broadly as he stood looking down at the two of them.

He had the girth of a lifeguard, huge broad shoulders, strong biceps, looked as though he lifted weights, and worked out to keep in shape.

Ra Ra proudly announced in her sing-song fashion as she pointed, "He's my daddy!"

"Hi," he said, smiling as he introduced himself, "I'm Cliff Camden. I'm happy to meet you and glad Ra Ra has such a great sand castle architect to assist her with building a sand castle complete with moat," and they all laughed. His laugh was much the same as Ra Ra's as little specks of sunlight bounced off his hazel eyes.

Ra Ra was such an endearing, outgoing child who loved to chat with everyone. Her parents had always been concerned because she was constantly talking to strangers and making friends, requiring that they had to closely watch her.

Her mother had always been vigilant, watching her adorable daughter with the naturally red curly hair and bright sparkling eyes. It was indeed a challenge to keep her safe.

Ra Ra was very inquisitive, and when they went shopping, she had the unnerving habit of wanting to touch and feel the texture of everything. Whenever she saw a fabric, she would press it to her lips and cheeks to enjoy the soft texture, causing her mother to inwardly smile, but she didn't dare let her little one see fearing it would encourage the child even more.

CHAPTER TWO

Cliff missed his wife, Julia, and the good times they had together. He needed a confidant, someone he could talk to about every day things and now, most especially, with this move and the myriad of details.

How would he be able to do it all by himself? He had no one to help him. He was beginning to wonder if taking on this new responsibility of opening the west coast office was really advisable.

Cliff liked Ra Ra's new "play mate" who immediately gave the impression that she enjoyed making "mud pies" reminiscent of the days when she was Ra Ra's age.

He had never seen anyone with such superbly exquisite skin that seemed to glow, a perfectly shaped pair of lips; and he couldn't help wondering how many times she had been kissed. He tried not to but couldn't help staring at this beautiful young woman whose raven hair highlighted by the sun brought out the natural red streaks in her hair that fell carelessly down around her shoulders in soft curls. He was also mesmerized by her violet eyes.

Claudette said that she was very happy to meet him and wondered if he was going to join them. She was having a wonderful time. She had always loved the beach; it was so much fun but was very cautious about going in the water and especially if her face were to get wet, she'd run out to grab a towel.

It stemmed back to the time when she was visiting in New York and her aunt took her for a day at the beach. The Atlantic Ocean was much rougher than the Pacific. Her aunt was very good to her, having taken her shopping for a new bathing suit, beach jacket, dresses, and water shoes.

Why would she need water shoes? It was a whole new concept for Claudette who couldn't understand why she needed shoes to go in the water.

Claudette was very excited to be going with her aunt to the beach. It was going to be a really big adventure. She got up early, put on her new swimsuit, beach jacket, and the water shoes her aunt had purchased and they were on their way.

She was amazed and somewhat perplexed that the ocean swimming area was roped off. There were posts in the water and ropes.

Her aunt said, "Remember, you must hold tight to the rope, and when the wave comes in lift your legs and the wave will go underneath you. It will be so much fun!

Claudette didn't fully comprehend, and being just a little girl, she had difficulty holding on to the rope. The waves were very strong, she inadvertently let go, and was consequently swept away by the undertow much to her aunt's chagrin.

A man, swimming nearby, saw what had happened and rescued little Claudette.

Her family was so thankful that they made him a member of their family. He was welcomed into their home, however the down side was that each time he was invited to dinner or came over to visit, the story of her near drowning experience and ocean rescue was constantly relieved and the event became indelibly etched deep in her memory bank, resulting in her being so frightened that she would only go in the ocean knee deep, and if any water splashed on her face, she would immediately run out to towel dry.

She had a wonderful childhood with caring, loving parents who enjoyed making her happy, and the times they spent at the beach were truly memorable despite the unfortunate Atlantic Ocean incident.

Beach goers, who walked by stopped, smiled and some even offered to join in, and the first thing Ra Ra would do is smile and hand them a pail because she always seemed to need more water.

Cliff loved watching his little one having such a good time and had by this time whole heartedly joined in making great structural recommendations to the delight of his daughter, Ra Ra, and Claudette, whose face expressed joy and happiness as evidenced by her smile. He loved looking at her, focusing on her shiny dancing eyes and her curly locks bouncing around with each movement of her head.

Claudette tried hard not to stare at this very handsome man and became rather pensive as she wondered if they were visitors from out-of-town and why had this little girl been down by the shore alone, why wasn't he more concerned about his daughter's safety and began mentally questioning, "Who is taking care of Ra Ra and her little brother, Jacques?"

Cliff seemed to know what Claudette was thinking and volunteered, "We just moved here from New York and are glad to be in the sunshine."

He had been given several places to choose from for his job transfer, and he excitedly chose San Diego with all its historical sites but primarily for Ra Ra. He wanted her to have the opportunity to enjoy the beaches to learn to swim, play in the sand, and run along the water's edge.

Claudette wanted him to know that the beach is a great place to play in the sand, gather sea shells, swim in on the ocean waves, and have great picnics and barbecues.

She had fond memories of her mother's annual 4th of July beach picnic and barbecue arrangements that included several families who planned and talked incessantly about who would make what dishes resulting in making it a grand affair. Everyone looked forward to the morning of Independence Day especially the kids who were so excited that they hardly slept and were up early, putting their clothes on top of their bathing suits, grabbing their towels, and running to get in the car. They were all ready to go.

There were always several cars in the driveway, everyone scurrying about, and, finally, it was time to leave. The caravan of revelers was singing as they backed out of the driveway and headed for the open road. Claudette had a beautiful soprano voice and always sang whenever they went anywhere which her parents enjoyed, making it a happy time for all.

Finally, they would arrive at the beach, and it was time to carry the beach chairs, card tables, umbrellas, ice chests, charcoal briquettes, and all the necessary paraphernalia. It was quite a time consuming task, and Claudette always wondered when everything would finally be in place as her parents and the other adults made countless trips back and forth to bring everything from their cars.

Up went the beach umbrellas, the blankets carefully laid out on the sand, the beach towels stacked up, coolers, and baskets of food all ready for when the time was right for cooking and serving.

After everything was arranged under the umbrellas, her mother would nod, and with loud shouts of joy, off came their outer clothes revealing colorful swim suits, and they all ran screaming, jumping, and splashing into the waves.

CHAPTER THREE

Claudette was interested in knowing more about this soft spoken man with the dreamy eyes, blondish red hair, and great muscular body.

Although, they had just met and Cliff wasn't physically close to her, but he felt Claudette's warmth and wanted to know what she thought, suddenly her opinion was very important to him.

Cliff hadn't felt this way for a very long time since the unexpected loss of his dear wife, Julia, who had been killed by a drunk driver. It wasn't the first time a driver had been up on charges for being drunk, but the system always let him go with just a fine, and consequently he was back on the road to injure or kill another; and this time it was his beloved Julia, the mother of his children, who were now without their mother.

It was a horrendous ordeal that he had spent countless hours trying to disregard that became especially vivid when he was in the area where it occurred. He would never forget that day when the phone rang in his office, and his secretary, Jane Simms, ran in to tell him that it was a phone call he should take.

He tried to explain to her that he was on a conference call and a client was waiting to see him. But, she kept anxiously pointing to the phone in an insisting manner that he take the call. He couldn't understand. She had been with him and the law firm for a long time and had never acted that way before.

Finally, he put his conference call on hold and as quietly as possible, asked what could possibly be so important, but before he could finish the sentence, two uniformed police officers came in, and he suddenly realized that this was a matter he had to attend to immediately.

He walked over to the officers, shook their hands, and asked them to be seated. He couldn't understand why they had come to see him as he anxiously asked how he could assist them and noted the sad look in their eyes as first one and then the other tried to speak.

Realizing there was no easy way to put it, they told Cliff that his Julia had been tragically killed by a drunk driver. By this time Jane was standing on one side of him and a police officer on the other side, concerned that he might collapse, which he almost did.

It seemed like an interminable amount of time before Cliff could speak. It was hard to comprehend what they were saying. It couldn't be. He had just spoken to Julia a few minutes earlier when she called him on her cell phone and everything was fine. She was going to the hair dresser and to shop for a special new dress to wear for their intimate anniversary party. Now she was gone. It wasn't possible.

Cliff had so many questions, but his brain was moving a thousand miles an hour; and for a man of his advanced education and extensive vocabulary, he was having difficulty expressing himself. He felt as though his brain was mired in quick sand. What was he to do now? Jane was holding a glass of water in front of him but he couldn't drink it.

His perfect life had been shattered, came to a standstill. Now, he was all alone. So many decisions to make. What to do? How had others coped? For the first time in his life, he was crying unashamedly as rivers of tears were cascading down his face

His mind, in an effort to avoid reality of the dreaded news, could only think about his beautiful bride as they stood before the altar reciting their vows. She looked so radiantly beautiful in her exquisite lace beaded wedding gown and veil that caressed her long flowing hair, sparkling eyes, soft white skin, and full red lips that he would passionately kiss when they were pronounced, "Man and Wife."

His attention was focused on the tall, muscular, commiserate, empathetic police officers who never wanted this type of duty and were at a loss as to how to say the words, and what to say or do to console the survivor.

They asked Cliff if they could do something as each handed him their business card and said to call if he had any questions or needed any information.

Cliff tried desperately to utter words of thanks as the gentlemen were leaving. Jane, his secretary, was hesitant to leave the room. She wanted in some way to comfort him, but how? She was only his secretary, and although she had worked for him a number of years, she didn't know how to proceed. Who should she call? What should she do? She wondered who was caring for his children.

This wonderful man whom everyone had always said had the perfect marriage was now desolate. They were always happily dancing, engaging in fun conversation, and the life of all the parties.

She always looked beautiful in whatever gown she wore. Everyone loved being with them because they were so happy. His wife was always the perfect hostess, gracious, and made everyone feel welcome. Business associates and employees always looked forward to the firm's parties because they knew she would be present with her sparkling personality--and now she was gone. Whatever would he do? He had two children who were now motherless, what about them? How would he manage? It was a terrifying thought.

Cliff looked up at Jane with the most sorrowful eyes she had ever seen that were filled with tears uncontrollably rolling down his cheeks that made her want to do something, but what? She, herself was also fighting back tears.

Finally, he was endeavoring to speak and asked her to call his wife's parents. He was in no condition to talk to anyone but needed to communicate with his in-laws. "Please call my wife's parents and tell them to come to my home and bring my children."

Furthermore, he emphatically instructed Jane not to answer any questions, just make it sound urgent and that they were desperately needed. He then motioned to his phone, indicating that he wanted her to make the call on his phone.

She walked over to the other side of his desk, picked up the receiver, and dialed. She knew the number because she had called on prior occasions. His father-in-law answered. Jane identified herself and asked if he, his wife, and the children could please go immediately to Cliff's home. She was silently hoping he wouldn't ask any questions and was relieved when he said that they would be arriving as quickly as possible.

She called to have one of the firm's limousines drive him home. Usually, he would drive or call a cab, but now he was thankful that limousines were available for the firm's law partners.

He was looking around in a daze, not really functioning on all cylinders. Jane called the garage and requested a limousine and driver to be in front of the building to take Mr. Camden to his residence.

Cliff heard her conversation and stood up trying to figure out how he would tell his wife's parents. Jane took him by the arm, guided him to the door, and into the elevator. Their offices were on the top floor but they were down in the lobby in a matter of moments.

The driver opened the limo door as Cliff turned to Jane and asked her to please tell his law partners what had happened, thanked her for all she had done, how much he appreciated her, and as he spoke the tears flowed more freely.

He settled down in the limo trying not to think of the recent events. The driver seemed to understand and said nothing for which Cliff was most grateful as he sat sinking into the luxurious black leather seat impossible to comprehend all that had happened; the implications were too overwhelming.

He had always been a man who kept his composure but now in view of what had happened tears were uncontrollably rolling down his cheeks. He had lost his wife, his soul mate, his friend, his sweetheart, the mother of his children, and was in total disbelief at what had transpired.

This morning and even this afternoon his life was serene and wonderful. He had his wife and his marriage; all was complete. He kept remembering that awful moment when the officers told him he had lost his beloved. He was a lawyer and heard of this type of thing happening to others, but that was to others.

All their plans were now gone. He would now have to start over as a single dad--how could he do that? He knew family members would be willing to help but that would be short lived.

He leaned his head back against the soft cushions as he in vain endeavored to compose himself. How would he tell his wife's parents? They were up in years and a jolt like this could send them to the emergency room with heart problems, a situation that would be even more disastrous for his children who adored their grandparents. They were so good and loving with them. It would be even more fatal if his children didn't have them and all the love they so freely gave.

The driver slowed down and stopped. Cliff looked out the window and saw his in-laws' car and his children standing in front of his house awaiting his arrival. How was he going to pull himself together? He wasn't very religious, but he did believe in God and thought he should have stopped at a church to pray but, for now, he bowed his head and said a silent prayer for guidance, hope, strength, the right words, and comfort for those two adults waiting for him to get out of the car. How could he do that to them? How could God have done this?

He wished that it had all been a dream, and he would wake up in a minute, thereby escaping this hideous nightmare. Unfortunately, it was not a dream, it was reality. He was going to be breaking the hearts of two of the nicest and most loving people he had ever known.

CHAPTER FOUR

He recalled Jane saying that he needed to make arrangements, and she would be happy to help. He didn't know what she was talking about--arrangements for what? He couldn't understand. Everything was rushing at him all at once like a torrential tidal wave inundating him.

The limo had stopped. The driver, in deep respect, remained silent. He could see that Cliff was in tremendous emotional pain. His tearful ravaged eyes told all those who saw him that he was suffering.

He looked out the window and took a deep breath wondering how much time it would take to get the words out. He took out his handkerchief dabbing at his eyes, fully realizing he wouldn't be able to hide his sorrow.

The limo driver opened the door. Cliff hesitated for a moment, and then reluctantly moved one foot in an effort to delay the inevitable. How could he be the bearer of such horrendous news? His children ran over and gave him a big hug which made what he was going to say all the harder.

His in-laws were at his side and couldn't conceive what was going on. Cliff looked terrible. His eyes were red and swollen, he seemed to have difficulty speaking, and when he finally did say, "Hello," after the hugs, it started all over. He couldn't help it. Tears filled his eyes and were literally pouring down his cheeks the same as when he heard what the police officers had told him, only now it was worse because it involved others and he began shaking with grief as shock set in.

His mother-in-law, Grace Deveaux, tried to comfort him to no avail. His father-in-law, Gordon Deveaux, asked for the keys and walked up the steps to open the front door, and they all went into the living room.

Grace took the children upstairs to their playroom, and when she had them settled, she came back down. Grace and

Gordon Deveaux didn't know what to think as they sat on either side of Cliff, each with an arm around him.

Grace had a habit of softly humming which she now did in an effort to try to calm a situation, not realizing that shortly she too would also be in tears.

Finally, Cliff could stand it no longer and decided to plunge forward. He said, trying desperately to control his tears, that there had been an accident.

Grace began screaming, "No, No, No." Cliff was already experiencing great difficulty; after all how do you tell parents they will never see their child again?

Grace turned Cliff's face toward her and begged him to tell them what he was talking about.

Cliff had never been an outwardly emotional man. He had never cried in front of others and now for the second time that day, he was crying like a child unashamedly in front of others as rivers of tears rolled down his face as he recounted what happened that afternoon when two police officers came to his office to tell him that there had been a tragic accident caused by a drunk driver.

Grace cried and emitted more screams as Gordon groaned the way men do during times of crisis. They guessed that it wasn't a simple injury otherwise they would be at the hospital and not in Cliff and Julie's home.

Gordon eyes were also filled with tears. All three of them sat as though in a stupor, unable to believe what they had been told.

Gordon was worried that Grace would faint and Cliff was worried about both of them.

They heard the door bell chime. It was Jane. She came offering to help in any way she could.

He was really glad to see her, asked if she could make some coffee, and check on the children which she was happy to do. She inquired if she should call a doctor.

Cliff said, "I will let you know."

Gordon and Grace were too drained to go home. They spent the night in the guest room. The next morning Cliff was lying in the king-size bed he had shared with his wife.

When they purchased their home, she went window shopping to select the furniture she felt would be most appropriate for them and when Cliff came home from the office, she would have brochures and pamphlets of all the furniture she had seen that day, and they would "pour" over them, making their selections. Saturday morning they would arise early to make their selections. She wanted everything to be perfect for them; each room was decorated to reflect her personality.

Cliff, still in a sleep state, reached out to caress Julia, his beloved wife, when all of a sudden it hit him, she wasn't there; he was all alone. The events of the previous day began to engulf him. He was desolate as to how he would cope. He had two children dependent upon him and his wife's parents were also looking for moral support. How could he offer them anything; he had nothing to give. He wondered what time it was and hoped that it was still early when he heard a light knock at the door. He called out.

Jane cautiously opened the door and asked if she could get him something. He thanked her and asked for a cup of strong black coffee. It was unusual for him to drink black coffee, but she theorized that he needed to wake up to face the fateful day. Jane was back in what seemed like moments with a cup of hot coffee. She said that she had bathed, dressed, fed the children, and they were playing. They were still oblivious as to what had happened the day before.

He asked about his in-laws.

Jane was quick to tell him that she had also brought them a cup of coffee. It was all they wanted even though she was willing to make them a full breakfast.

The phone started ringing. Jane said that people were already coming to call. Everyone was shocked about what had happened and wanted to help.

"What should I tell them?" Jane asked.

Cliff was still in shock.

She suggested that he take a long shower to help clear his head and left to answer the door.

More and more people were coming to the house. The newspapers were running the story about the socialite wife of a law partner, who was killed by a drunk driver.

Jane made sure that the children had not turned on the television, and she also removed the newspapers. She hoped that her boss would tell the children before they heard it from someone else.

Cliff took a long hot then cold shower as he tried to collect his thoughts. He needed desperately to find the strength to get through the day. He dried off and proceeded to get dressed. He put on a clean white shirt with French cuffs and a dark suit. He was particular about his shirts and suits that he had tailor-made in London. He selected a dark tie and a pair of simple gold etched cuff links a birthday present from his wife. He recalled that she had impeccably good taste. As he put in the cuff links, he glanced down at his wedding ring inscribed, "We'll be together forever and ever."

He then looked in the mirror and said a silent prayer for fortitude and guidance to make the right decisions that would have made Julia proud. He wanted everything to be perfect for her.

This was his last gesture to care for her as her husband, and he wanted it to be right and in the very best taste.

He opened the bedroom door just as Jane was coming up the winding staircase. He asked, "Have you called our minister?"

She said, "Yes. He will be over shortly."

Jane was extremely efficient and highly organized. She had been with him for a number of years, and he had always appreciated her attributes.

She said that his in-laws were sitting in the kitchen. She made them some breakfast but didn't know if they were up to eating it. Jane had also gone to their home and packed a suitcase for them, not knowing how long they would be staying.

He thanked her and went downstairs to the kitchen. He saw Gordon and Grace seated at the table. They were appropriately attired. Gordon was wearing a white long sleeve shirt, dark suit and tie. Grace was wearing a smart black dress that had a matching coat and hat with a veil.

Cliff walked in, put his arm around Grace, kissed her gently on the cheek, and put his hand on Gordon's shoulder as he said how glad he was that they had stayed and were welcome to stay as long as they wanted. He was happy they would be staying not only for him but for the sake of his children who would need their grandparents. They were wonderful people and he dearly loved them.

He hesitantly spoke the words no one wanted to hear that the children had to be told.

Grace suggested that they call them into the kitchen.

Jane had prepared hot cocoa and French toast which they loved, and after they have eaten, they could all go to the playroom, sit on the floor, and cuddle them as he told them about their mother's accident with the help of their grandparents. They all agreed that it was an excellent idea.

Four-year-old Ra Ra and eighteen-month old Jacques came into the kitchen, sat down, and enjoyed the food Jane had prepared.

After they finished, their father said, "Let's go the playroom," and they each took one of his hands.

They walked into the playroom. Cliff sat down on the floor and asked them to come over and sit on his lap. He held them tightly with their grandparents looking on as he hesitantly said that he had something to tell them.

Ra Ra got very excited thinking it was something happy. He had to tell her that this was very sad, and it would be all right if she cried. It tore his heart out to have to tell them that they would never see their mother again.

"Mama isn't coming home to see me dance at my ballet recital?"

Reluctantly, tears filling his eyes, he had to tell this adorable little girl, "Mama has gone up to heaven."

"Is God taking care of her?"

Cliff answered, "Yes, darling, God is taking good care of her."

Ra Ra quickly asked, "With Boots, our pet turtle?"

"Yes, with Boots and they are all probably playing together."

She accepted her father's explanation that God would take care of her mother.

Jane came in to say that the minister and his law partners had arrived.

Grace and Gordon held out their outstretched arms to envelope the children. Cliff excused himself and went to meet the gentlemen. Making the arrangements was the most difficult thing he would ever have to do.

They went into his study where they wouldn't be disturbed. Jane brought in a pot of hot coffee and an assorted tray of Danish. The minister and his law partners were giving their condolences which were very much appreciated, but made Cliff even sadder. They observed that Cliff's eyes were red, and as they talked tears were rolling down his cheeks.

Cliff asked Jane to join them and said that he wanted a simple ceremony with lots of white flowers. Julia loved gardenias, and he thought that orchids and roses would also be in keeping with what would make her happy. He hoped they could make the arrangements inasmuch as he didn't think he could, it would be too depressing.

Cliff looked at Jane and said, "You knew my wife and I would be most appreciative if you would please help with the arrangements. I will help with the music selections." Jane and his partners assured him that they would do everything possible.

He recalled when as a child he "lost" his beloved grandmother who used to bake cookies, took him to the park, and put him on the swings. They would go to the zoo every Saturday and had a happy time feeding peanuts to the elephants and laughing at the monkeys antics.

All day well-wishers were at the door, expressing their regret at what had happened. Like everyone else, they couldn't believe that Julia wouldn't be coming into the room with her sparkling personality, greeting everyone, and making sure they were all comfortable. She had been the perfect hostess always knowing what foods her guests liked and the bar was always well-stocked. But, Julia would never be coming in again; they were all trying desperately to cope.

The next morning highly polished limousines were parked outside, waiting. Jane was a tremendous help preparing and serving a delicious breakfast. She also bathed and dressed the children. Gordon and Grace were sitting in the library, holding hands. They were a very affectionate couple, envied by all who knew them for their close loving relationship.

Cliff came downstairs appropriately attired in a white freshly laundered shirt, black suit. shoes, and tie. He asked his in-laws to join him for breakfast, and they all sat down together trying to relax.

After breakfast, they said in unison, "We are ready to go to the church," and went outside. The limo driver opened the door for the family and Jane. They were trying not to think about the events that would shortly unfold. How would they get through it?

They all arrived at the church and were amazed at the hundreds of well-wishers. They got out of the limo as people began rushing over to embrace, speak words of condolence, and shake their hands.

Cliff's law partners were suddenly at his side ushering him, his children, and in-laws into the church beautifully adorned with white orchids, gardenias, and roses. Jane had done a magnificent job arranging it all.

There was a large photo of Julia with her beautiful smile and sparkling violet eyes. She was indeed a very radiantly, beautiful woman. They finally were seated as music filled the church with Julia's favorite selections.

The minister's sermon followed by the 23rd Psalm was awe inspiring and was accented by each person speaking in glowing terms about Julia's attributes. Cliff felt Julia's presence and that she truly approved.

CHAPTER FIVE

Cliff was back in his office going through the files in his briefcase and checking phone messages in an effort to catch up and block out the past events. Jane came in and he profusely thanked her for her assistance and said that there would be a bonus in her pay envelope. She advised him that it wasn't necessary. She did it because she wanted to help during those difficult days.

"My in-laws will be taking care of my children, but I still need a housekeeper and would appreciate your interviewing candidates," he said.

Jane was happy to do so and advised him of the partners' meeting in fifteen minutes. He thanked her again.

This was not going to be an ordinary partners' meeting, and he was rather reluctant to go. His mind was still racing as he went into the meeting. There were rounds of handshakes and putting an arm around his shoulder to let him know how much they cared; but they had to get down to business.

They were planning to open a west coast office and wanted Cliff to manage the operation. He had known that this was in the works and was excited to go but that was before, how could he do it now; move across the country?

They told him how much faith they had in him; he was the ideal partner to head up their west coast office. The more he analyzed it, the more he thought that perhaps this was an excellent idea. San Diego was a beautiful place even though it was 3,000 miles from New York.

He thanked them and said that he would be taking some of his staff with him for which they all approved. He really wanted Jane and a few other members of his staff that he had worked with and knew they were reliable.

When he got back to his desk after the meeting, he asked Jane and a number of preferred staff members how they would feel about moving to San Diego. They were all excited and began planning to move.

When he got home that night, he told his in-laws who were still living with him and taking care of his children, he would be moving to open and manage the west coast office.

Grace asked, "Where precisely?"

Cliff said, "San Diego, California."

"Cliff," Grace whaled, "That's all the way across the country, 3,000 miles!"

"Yes, I know," he acknowledged but wanted her to know that they could come with him and his children and that it would be great for all of them--a whole new experience.

Grace and Gordon were shocked. Would it really be a good idea for them to move considering that Gordon is a test pilot, and Grace is busy with her charitable work?

Cliff quickly added that they could always come out to visit. They told him they would have to give it considerable thought. He reminded them that he loved them. They would always be welcome, and he'd be sure to have a home large enough with a room for them or perhaps a cottage on the property. Grace came over and hugged him. He was the ideal son-in-law. They knew he would always make a place for them.

Grace offered to assist with the packing and would do everything possible to make the move as smooth as possible. She was hesitant to bring it up but felt that now might be the most appropriate time to ask if he wanted help with Julia's things.

It was another subject that Cliff was avoiding, but with the move so imminent, he had no choice and said he would appreciate her help.

The next day they went through Julia's things, making several piles; one for Grace's charities, another to be boxed and saved for the kids, and an extremely small pile of items he wanted as remembrances. They finally finished and felt better for it was one more difficult aspect completed.

They needed to go room by room and decide what would be moved and what would be in put in storage. All the while he kept reminding Grace that she could have whatever she wanted. She did select a few pieces, but for the most part, it was either to be saved for the kids or to one of her charities.

He selected the pieces of furniture, books in the library, music, figurines, etc., to be shipped.

Suddenly everything was decided and Grace said that the movers would be called with the understanding that nothing was to be shipped until Cliff had found a place to rent or purchase. He said, "I'll call when I find a suitable home."

Next on the moving agenda, one more depressing point, a real estate agent would have to be called to put the house up for sale. Grace offered to assist in that area as well. She was more than a mother-in-law; she was a dear friend--a mother to him. A real lady to whom he owed a great deal and loved as though she were his mother.

Cliff decided to drive rather than fly. The corporation had a company jet, but that would be far too quick, whereas a drive across country with stops at historical sites, fun parks for his children, and exploring would allow time for relaxation and give him the opportunity to gain a new perspective.

When Jane asked if he wanted her to make reservations or reserve the company jet, he said, "I have decided to make it a road trip," and asked her to contact their travel agent for maps, locations of historical sites, restaurants, perhaps a few bed and breakfasts, and places of interest. He and Julia had always loved to go on ferries and hoped they could be included.

One of his majors was in history. It was always exciting to visit Civil War Battlefields, museums, and homes of presidents and generals. He wanted the trip to be both interesting, educational, and of course fun for his children which meant that coloring books, talking books, and games were needed to be in the car for them.

Jane looked at Cliff amidst all his preparations and with great hesitation, cleared her throat and tried to form the words. Cliff looked up as she lowered her head feeling embarrassed to ask, but after clearing her throat several times, said that she was all packed for the move and wondered if it would be all right if she went with them as she quickly added that she could also help drive and take care of the children.

If he wanted to go somewhere with the children, she could take care of the car. She also told him that she was taking a number of novels that she had wanted to read and books on California, especially San Diego.

Cliff looked at her and said that would be fine; he would enjoy her company. As she started to leave his office, she turned her attention toward him and said she would be getting the maps and all the pertinent information including items to keep the children entertained.

Cliff thought, "It would be nice to have Jane along. She would be good company and could help take care of his children."

Everything was set in motion. Cliff had one final meeting with his law partners prior to leaving, and much to his amazement, he was really looking forward to the trip.

His partners asked if he wanted to take the limo. He thanked them but felt that he would like to drive; and when he found a nice place for a picnic or where they could stop and explore, he could park the car, and have an enjoyable lunch with his children right out of a picnic basket, and play ball with his children.

He knew Jane was very flexible and would be a good companion.

CHAPTER SIX

Gordon and Grace spent the day and evening with Cliff and his children. They had a nice dinner and played games with the little ones. Ra Ra had her grandma pack all her dolls, stuffed animals, favorite books, music, and games. Grace then filled a suitcase with Jacques' toys.

The children were dancing all around the room. Ra Ra was very specific about which outfit she would wear for the first day of their trip and wanted her grandma to please wash and starch her dress the way her mother used to.

Grace offered to help Cliff pack and he was happy to accept her offer. They opened drawers, closets, and began packing. She asked him if there was anything he wanted to donate to her favorite charity and those items were put aside in a pile.

He was a meticulous dresser and always wore a white cotton T-shirt under his long sleeve white shirts. He placed his ties and belts on the bed, opened drawers putting his socks and underwear in a suitcase and filled another with shoes. Grace opened another closet and carefully began packing his suits.

Grace didn't want to say anything but wondered how everything would fit in the car and still leave room for them to be comfortable.

Cliff realized there might be a space problem and arranged to purchase a brand new Mercedes that would provide comfort and still have sufficient space for their luggage, the children's stuffed animals, toys, games, books, c.d.'s, etc.

They spent an enjoyable evening playing with the children, and then it was bedtime. This time grandma and grandpa read to them. After Ra Ra and Jacques were "cradled" in lullaby land; Cliff sat with Grace and Gordon. There was so much he wanted to say to them, but it was difficult to get the words out.

Finally, Grace put her arm around him and said that they knew how he felt and they wished all the best for him and his little family in their new home.

"After you find a home and the furniture was shipped, we will be out. And, she said, "Don't forget there is always the telephone. I am going to be looking forward to hearing from you and our beautiful, beloved grandchildren.""

Cliff hugged her as tears were welling up in his eyes and Gordon put an arm around him and said, "We love you and know you will do the right thing. And, if you ever need us or need anything at all, we want you to call and let us know. We can fly out at a moment's notice. We know that we will be able to use the company jet."

Cliff knew he really lucked out when he was blessed with them as in-laws. They were sweet, loving, kind, and wanted only the best for him. He realized how hard it would be for them tomorrow to wave good-bye to Julia's children.

The next morning Jane came over with her suitcase and briefcase full of maps, places of interest for them to visit, explore, c.d.'s, and games. She was very excited and felt that it would be a very enjoyable trip.

Cliff's in-laws were very special people. He felt truly blessed that they had accepted him from the beginning and were always supportive of everything that he and Julia did. Now, he had to say a temporary good-bye to them as they stood next to his new Mercedes.

His children were comfortably settled in their car seats and Jane already had her seat belt on. One more hug and Cliff walked around to the driver's side, got in, waved one more time, and they were off on their momentous journey.

CHAPTER SEVEN

Cliff was excited about the road trip and decided to make driving cross country both enjoyable and educational for his children. He knew that it would be extraordinary to see how the vegetation and flora changed as they crossed from one state into another and thought it would be a great idea to take a photo with his children next to the welcoming sign as they crossed each state line. He wanted them to know how wonderful America is and what it has to offer. He planned visits to parks, lakes, historical sites, museums, ferries, battlefields, etc.

The highlight of the trip would probably be driving until they came to a park with a lake with boats for rent, a grassy area under a huge shade tree where he would put down a blanket, enjoy a picnic lunch with his children, and rent a motor boat. His children would be very excited as they enjoyed their first "trip" in a boat as he would caution them to sit very still.

He announced, "The first stop of our journey will be the drive to Philadelphia, Pennsylvania, Independence Hall the principal meeting place of the Second Continental Congress from 1775 to 1783, where we'll be greeted by men and women in colonial garb. They will show us both the Declaration of Independence that made our country free and the United States Constitution that tells the American people how the country should be run."

Ra Ra pointing asked, "Daddy what does that say?"

"It's the Preamble of our Constitution. It starts out: 'We the People of the United States of America...'

"Now, we'll go across the street to the Liberty Bell Center to see the original Liberty Bell with its distinctive crack."

On the way back to the car, Jane hesitatingly asked, "Have you mapped out the whole trip?"

"Yes, I have delineated places to visit that will be entertaining, enjoyable, and educational for Ra Ra and Jacques."

Jane was visibly disappointed. She wasn't interested in visiting a chocolate factory or going on any amusement rides. She wanted to plan their itinerary.

Cliff said to Ra Ra and Jacques, "You know how much you love Hershey bars?"

"Yes, yes, we do like that candy. Grandma and grandpa buy it for us."

"How would you like to go to Hershey Park and see how the chocolate candy is made and go on some rides?"

"Yes, Yes," Ra Ra said as she waved her arms around for emphasis. "Let's go there."

Jacques getting all excited asked, "Daddy will I get some chocolate?"

"Yes, you will both enjoy some chocolates."

Cliff was pleased that his children were enjoying the park and made reservations to spend the night at the hotel.

Jane, becoming more interested, asked, "Where are we going tomorrow?"

"We're off to the beautiful state of Virginia. It's about a five-hour-drive. We'll spend the night here and be off in the morning for more exciting adventures."

Ra Ra was thrilled as she sat in her car seat, singing to her dolly, and Jacques, holding tightly to Cuddles the goose doll.

"Here we go back to the 18th Century Colonial Williamsburg where one can visit a number of museums including a hands-on museum providing activities for children."

"Daddy, the people are wearing funny clothes," Ra Ra said.

"Yes, it is traditional colonial, which is what they wore during that time, and those houses are of the same time period."

"Daddy, look at the houses. They're not like ours."

"No, during that time the houses were different than ours."'

"Can we go in?"

"Yes. These homes are different than ours. The homes and gardens are from the same period as the garb of the people. Remember don't touch anything, it's all very old."

Both Ra Ra and Jacques promised that they wouldn't touch anything.

"Can I take my dolly with me?" Ra Ra asked.

Jacques, not wanting to be excluded, asked to take his Cuddles   doll.

"Yes, of course you can take your dolls," their father said.

Now, they were back in the car and off to Jamestown, once the capitol of Virginia.

Costumed historical guides led them into the past.

"This is where the first people lived when they came to America, 400 years ago and built James Fort. They have preserved a copy of a 1620's building made mostly out of mud and over there are wine bottles from 1620. The seal of Governor,

Francis Nicholson, is stamped on one of the bottles.

"There's the Powhatan Village. See their reed-covered houses, ceremonial circle of carved wooden posts, and crops. Would you like to grind some corn?"

Ra Ra and Jacques thought it was fun helping their daddy grind corn. But they wondered, "What good is it? What will we do with it?"

"Use it to make food."

"We can go over here and do some gardening the way you help grandma in our garden."

Cliff and Jane tried their hand at playing a game of corncob darts, but weren't very successful.

"Daddy, I'm hungry," Ra Ra said, pulling on her daddy's sleeve. Jacques, not wanting to be left out and always watching Ra Ra, walked over and pulled on his daddy's other sleeve.

Cliff looked down into the faces of his two beloved little ones, smiled, and asked, "What would you like for dinner?"

Ra Ra was quick to respond, "Lamb chop."

"Let's have dinner and spend the night here in historic Jamestown. Would you like to call grandma and tell her what you've been doing?"

"Yes," they said.

Early the next morning they were on their way to Charleston, South Carolina, home of the Confederacy. They visited Fort Sumter, the Maritime Center, and Marion Square Park with its number of historic monuments.

Cliff decided that the park would be an ideal setting for a picnic under one of the huge shade trees. They stopped at a local store and purchased a picnic basket complete with fried chicken, mashed potatoes, green peas, a salad, thinly sliced French bread, and milk. He didn't purchase dessert knowing that his darlings preferred ice cream.

Everything went as planned and soon with Jacques in his arms fast asleep and Ra Ra holding on tightly to his hand for fear of getting lost, they were registering at the hotel.

The next morning after a swim with his children and a nutritious breakfast, Cliff said, "Let's go. We're on our way to Kennesaw, Georgia, to visit the Southern Museum of the Civil War and Locomotive History. How does that sound?"

"Will it be a lot of fun, Daddy?"

"When you see it, you will like it."

"Okay daddy, I'm going to like it," she said hugging her doll.

He decided that they should have an early night for the next day's activities. "Jane, can you find a hotel or motel in Kennesaw?"

She looked and looked but couldn't find the Georgia tour book. She was becoming more and more flustered because it seemed that she had no say in anything.

Finally, Cliff pulled over, parked, took out his cell phone, and phoned the Kennesaw Chamber of Commerce.

The next morning after breakfast, they were on their way to the museum that housed the Georgia Civil War artifacts, exhibits, and memorabilia of the soldiers' lives during the Civil War.

"Look at the locomotive factory."

"Daddy, what is a locomotive?"

"It's a train engine,' he said while pointing to the locomotive.

"What does it do?"

'It pulls the cars. Remember when you see a train, it has a large number of cars all attached together?"

"Yes."

"The locomotive pulls the train."
"Oh, yes daddy, I remember. It's like in my book grandma gave me, *The Little Engine that Could*."

"That's right."

They then noticed the display cases and Ra Ra pointed as she asked, "What are those things?"

"These are all from the days of the Civil War. See the medical instruments, guns, uniforms, and over here is the *General*, a locomotive involved in the Great Locomotive Case of 1862."

Jane hadn't been that interested in history and surprised herself that she was enjoying the exhibits.

They left the museum and started crossing the street when Ra Ra exclaimed, "Look daddy, ice cream!"

Jacques chimed in, "Yes, daddy, ice cream. I like ice cream."

Cliff happily smiled as they walked across the street.

Ra Ra immediately sat down at a table by the window, picked up a napkin and announced that she was ready for her ice cream.

Cliff asked Jane what she would like and ordered for everyone.

The next morning after the group had a refreshing swim in the heated pool, ate a good breakfast, and was on their way to Kentucky, the horse capital of the world.

"Look. See the state line, we're entering Kentucky. All out for our photo."

"Can I take my dolly, daddy?"

"Yes."

"Can I take my Cuddles, daddy?"

"Yes."

Cliff stood with his children and their dolls in front of the "Welcome to Kentucky" sign while Jane took their picture.

Jane asked, "What's next on the agenda?"

"We're going to a horse farm," Cliff answered.

"Real horses?" Ra Ra asked.

"Yes, real horses. "We'll take a tour and see race horses that have finished their racing careers, horses having babies, yearlings, hopefully there'll be some newborns, and walk through modern barns."

"What's a tour?"

"It means that a man will show us around, answer questions, and we will learn about the thoroughbred horses."

Their guide came over and said that they also had some ponies and would be all right to put his children on a pony.

Cliff was delighted.

"Ra Ra would you like to sit on top of a horse and take a ride?"

"Yes, Yes, Yes, daddy. I really, really would."

"Me too, " Jacques said emphatically.

They were put on ponies with the guide insuring their safety.

Ra Ra and Jacques laughing, kept saying, "It's fun!" It's fun!"

Jane with camera in hand obligingly took photos.

Cliff said, "It's another ten-hour drive to our next stop. We'll spend the night here and get an early start."

The next morning, Cliff, full of enthusiasm, said, "We're now off to the state of Mississippi where we'll ride on a showboat and see the mighty Mississippi River."

The weather was pleasant. He was making great time as Jane was checking the maps to ensure no more wrong turns.

Finally, they saw the mighty Mississippi River. "Look kids, we're driving on the bridge over the Mississippi River. Isn't this great?"

"Yes, daddy, we like it."

The ride over the bridge was all that Cliff hoped it would be.

He bought tickets, they boarded the beautifully restored showboat, walked around the ship, drank lemonade, met the captain, and Jane took more photos

When they got off the boat, Ra Ra excitedly asked, "Where are we going now, daddy?"

"We're going to a historical site, the Battle of Vicksburg. It's where a Civil War cannon is still aimed over the hotels and casinos along the river. The Battle of Vicksburg was a very important Civil War Battle. It was during the late spring and early summer of 1863 that the Confederate and Union armies battled for control of the city," he explained to his children.

Afterwards, he drove around and showed them: forts, historic homes, period structures, and an ironclad Civil War wreck,

"Where to now, daddy?"

"The state of Louisiana, where we'll see Louisiana's Civil War Museum, formerly known as the Confederate Museum. It has the largest collection of Confederacy related artifacts and memorabilia in the United States including a Civil War cannon dating back to 1864."

"Jacques, how would you like to have your picture taken on top of that cannon?"

"Yes, yes, yes," Daddy.

"Here let me help you up."

"Daddy, I want to have my picture taken on the cannon, too."

"I have an idea, why don't you both sit on the cannon and I'll stand next to you. Would you like that?"

They both said, "Yes," and Jane took their picture.

Memorial Hall was the site of the city's farewell to Jefferson Davis, the only Confederate States president. "We'll be able to see Civil War uniforms, guns, bullets, shells, swords, mess kits, battle flags, the Louisiana secessionist flag, paintings, photographs, and documents. Look, a statute of General Robert E. Lee."

"Louisiana is noted for fine cuisine. Shall we have dinner here?"

"Yes. Do they have lamb chops?"

"We'll find out."

After dinner they took a walk in the French Quarter and down Bourbon Street.

"New Orleans became a French colony way back in the 1690's. Shall we go in this shop and buy presents for grandma and grandpa?"

Ra Ra let go of her father's hand as she was rushing inside the store. She loved it when her grandmother took her shopping. They selected a number of items, had them gift wrapped, and walked back to the car. Cliff could see that his babies were getting tired. It was time to find a hotel.

The next day they were driving to what many say is the great state of Texas.

Suddenly, Ra Ra called out, "Stop Daddy!"
Cliff pulled over to the side of the road and stopped.

Ra Ra pointed, "Look daddy, you almost forgot to stop at the sign."

"You're right little one. Thank you for being alert. Let me help you and Jacques out of your car seats and we'll ask Jane to please take our photograph in front of the Texas sign."

Look Cliff announced. "We are now in Houston, named for Sam Houston who was responsible for making Texas a state in 1845. Shall we have a picnic and rent a boat for a ride on the lake. It's also a great day to fly a kit. Do you think we should do that?"

Ra Ra excitedly was waving her hands and enthusiastically saying, "Yes! Yes, daddy, let's do that."

Not to be left out, Jacques was also waving his hands and shouting, "Yes! Yes, daddy."

Cliff turned and asked Jane, "Would you like to join us?"

"No, I think I'll get a sandwich, sit in the car, and read." She was realizing that the trip was not going to make Cliff fall in love with her and wondered what she could have done differently. It all seemed so futile.

"If that's what you prefer, but you are welcome to join us."

She shook her head indicating that she wasn't interested.

They purchased the picnic supplies and asked directions to a park with a lake.

Cliff couldn't wait to get them settled, he knew they were hungry, and he was as anxious as his children to fly the kite he had just purchased for them.

They enjoyed sitting on the blanket under the big oak tree, eating fried chicken, French fries, carrot sticks, tomato wedges, bread sticks, and milk.

Ra Ra squealed, "Daddy, you forgot dessert."

"No, I didn't. The desk clerk said there's a superb ice cream shop nearby."

"Ice cream. You know, daddy that's my favorite," she said while singing, dancing, and waving her arms.

Jacques got up and joined his sister. Daddy was smiling as he watched his two little darlings.

Cliff took out the kite, opened it up, put on the tail, tied it to a ball of string, stood up, and said, "Come on you two, let's fly our kite."

Ra Ra and Jacques began repeating, 'Let's fly our kite, then off to the ice cream shop."

On the way back Ra Ra saw some swings and ran over as she loudly called out, "Daddy, please come and push me I want to go high, high, high up to the sky."

Ra Ra and Jacques enjoyed going on the swings, down the slide, and in and out of a cute plastic play house.

Cliff enjoyed watching his little ones enjoy their ice cream as he proceeded to wipe off the amount that landed on Jacques face instead of in his mouth.

"Shall we find a hotel, take a bath; and when you two are all cozy in your pajamas; we can call grandma and you can tell her all about your day."

"Yes," Ra Ra said as she was being secured in her car seat.

Jacques was really getting sleepy as they drove up to the hotel entrance.

Cliff asked Jane if she was all right.

"Yes, I'm fine," she said.
Cliff carried his sleepy little boy in his arms as Ra Ra tightly held her daddy's hand. She was unsure of new places.

Cliff told Jane that he would call her in the morning.

She nodded and went into the elevator with the bellboy. She didn't even ask if he would like her to help bathe or take care of the children. It was as though she was a nonentity.

After their bath and there were all warm and cozy in their pajamas, as promised, Cliff called Grace who was anxious to hear about their trip and to talk to her grandchildren.

Ra Ra, clutching her doll, rushed over to speak to her grandma. She had a lot to tell. Her chatter was adorable. It was cute the way Jacques would take the phone from his sister to talk.

The next morning Cliff announced that they were going to the Space Center that had a four-story "Kid's Space Place" where children could enjoy learning about physics as they flew through the exhibit .on their Journey to Mars aboard the *Curiosity*. Then the highlight--lunch with an astronaut.

Cliff, while driving, talked about "New Mexico, their next stop, home of Indian tribes and cowboys. We're going to see the Puye Cliff Dwellings, which were home to ancestral Indians".

"Daddy, what is an Indian?" Ra Ra asked.

"Indian people were here before the first settlers came to America."

"What do they look like?"

"They are people like us; it's just that they have a slightly darker skin tone."

"Will we get to see some?"

"You probably will."
"Today, there are many Indian tribes living in America."

"Arizona, the next stop on our "voyage" is the last state before reaching our California destination."

"Where are we, daddy?"

"We're on our way to Arizona."

"Don't forget to watch for the sign. You forgot last time."

Ra Ra was being very vigilant looking through the window, watching for the sign, "Welcome to Arizona."

Cliff was glad they went to bed early and were on the road at seven as he calculated, it would be an eight-hour drive to the Grand Canyon Railway, Arizona, where he wanted his children to enjoy a ride on the train, then take them to the petting zoo, and stop over to show them the Grand Canyon.

Finally, Ra Ra exclaimed, "There it is daddy," she said waving her dolly. "We have to stop!"

Jane was graciously taking photos of the trio in front of the sign.

"Would you like to go to the zoo and pet the animals?"

"Yes! Daddy, it's been a long time since I had a balloon?"

"Me, too," Jacques said.

"Have you been good?" Do you deserve a balloon?"

"Yes," both children said.

"I know you've both been very good. We'll look for a balloon store, but it's getting late. We need to find a place to spend the night. Jane, do you have any suggestions?"

By this time, Jane was at a loss. She felt as though she was sort of a "throw-in" included because she was there. Most of the time, she felt invisible, but since she was also getting tired from the long drive, decided to comply.

The hotel was perfect. Cliff suggested a swim before dinner in the heated pool. His children were rapid learners. Jane didn't join in the swimming activities. She went straight to her room.

After their swim, Cliff and his darlings had dinner in their suite, and played a few games.

Ra Ra stood up and said, "Let's call grandma."

"Good idea. I'll dial the number and you two can talk"

"Daddy, grandma wants to talk to you."

"Hello Grace. We're spending the night in Arizona. Tomorrow, I'm taking our darlings for a train ride, petting zoo, and then we'll go for a look at the Grand Canyon. We'll be spending one more night in Arizona and be on our way to California the following morning. It's about a ten-hour drive not including stops along the way. I figure that we should be arriving in San Diego in a few days; we'll call to keep you appraised; your grandchildren keep reminding me. You do know that we all love you very much. Give our best to Gordon; we're looking forward to talking to you in person."

The next morning Cliff asked the concierge where he could purchase balloons for his children.

She said, "You don't need to do that. We have balloons. I'll get some and have them blown up." She came back with the balloons and asked Cliff if it would be all right if she gave them to his children.

He said, "Yes," and thanked her.

Both Ra Ra and Jacques were thrilled with their balloons and thanked the lady.

Cliff was glad to be back on the road again, this time to the last state on their agenda, California. He was anxious to finally be situated in San Diego where he'd find a home to purchase and a suite for their west coast law office.

"Daddy, there it is," Ra Ra said pointing to the California sign. "My dolly and I are ready for our picture."

The drive, across America, was uneventful. It was extraordinary how the vegetation and flora changed as they crossed each state line. They had fun visiting historical sites. The highlight of the trip, according to his children, was sitting under a big tree and enjoying their picnic lunches.

Upon checking a map, he noted that Blythe, California, was some five miles west of the Arizona state line. The hotel was classified as a three diamond hotel by the auto club. Cliff scanned the amenities and was delighted because it had a whirlpool and an indoor heated pool that would be ideal for his children.

Putting the car in gear, they proceeded on highway ten to spend their first night in California. Tomorrow they would travel the approximately 290 miles to Pacific Beach.

The next morning, after an early swim and a hearty breakfast, they were ready for the final part of their trip.

Cliff said, "I have a surprise for my darlings. How would you like to see the world's biggest dinosaurs? They have replicas in Cabazon, Riverside County. Shall we go?"

Jacques was quick to answer, "Yes. Cuddles and I are ready to go."

"Would you like to ride a dinosaur?"

"Yes," Ra Ra and Jacques simultaneously said.

"Next stop to ride a dinosaur." Cliff said.

Jacques and Ra Ra enjoyed the dinosaur ride and trip to the museum.

Now back on the "trail" to San Diego; a two-hour drive.

"Shall we sing as we go?"

Ra Ra started singing *Row Row Your Boat*; Jacques chimed in, then Cliff, but not Jane.

They were on their way.

It was all that Cliff had hoped for. Ra Ra and Jacques enjoyed it but were disappointed when he said that it wasn't practical to take home a dinosaur. After all how would it fit in the car? The head would be sticking out one window and the tail out the other and they all laughed.

Ra Ra asked, "Where to now daddy?"

"We're on our way to San Diego where we will live. You will be able to go to the beach play in the sand, build sand castles, and enjoy swimming in the Pacific Ocean. How does that sound?"

"Great daddy, we can hardly wait."

"Yeah," Jacques said, "We can hardly wait."

Jane, "Please get out the map of San Diego County and a list of motels," Cliff said. Normally he only stayed in four-star hotels but wanted a motel on the beach as close as possible to the sand.

He had visions of them getting up in the morning, putting on their swim suits, running out the door with his children, and racing across the sand toward the water's edge.

He was surprised when Jane said that there were hotels on the beach and one was a four-star with a pool.

"Call and make reservations for a suite with bedrooms for the children, a living room, and kitchenette with a microwave and refrigerator. Also reserve a room across the hall for yourself."

Jane picked up the cell phone. She spoke with the front desk reservation clerk, advising him that they were on their way from Blythe. The clerk affirmed their reservations, stating that the suite and room would be ready upon their arrival.

Jane started giving directions to the hotel and set the GPS. They were going to be staying at a motel in Pacific Beach, San Diego County, California, which was adjacent to Mission Beach. Jane suggested that location because Mission Beach had an amusement park with a historic Roller Coaster.

Cliff registered for the suite for himself and his children and a separate room for Jane, across the hall. He requested a bed with side-rails for his baby son who was sound asleep in his arms. Ra Ra was tightly holding her father's hand. This was another strange new place, and she didn't want to get lost.

The clerk asked, "Is there anything else, sir?"

Cliff quickly responded, "Yes, I will be requiring the services of a highly competent au pair. Can you take care of that or should I speak with the concierge?"

The clerk said, "I will obtain that information for you. Is there anything else?"

"Yes, please send up a dinner menu."

Cliff thanked the clerk and turned as the bellman had their luggage arranged on a luggage cart and guided them toward the elevator.

The suite was beautifully appointed and spacious with a balcony, a bowl of fresh fruit, and flowers in each room, compliments of the hotel management.

The bellman realizing that Cliff was anxious to put his baby son to bed quickly opened the door to the boy's bedroom. A bed with side rails was already in place.

Ra Ra was happily jumping up and down, her curls bouncing as she was tugging her father's sleeve. She was anxious to see her room. It, too, was beautifully furnished in shades of pale pink--her favorite color. She was ecstatic. Cliff took off her coat and indicated which suitcases he wanted brought to her room.

Cliff opened the suitcase with her toys and plush animals, and then explained to Ra Ra that she could put them on the shelves that were sufficiently low enough for her to reach. He

also told her she could put some of them on one of the two
overstuffed chairs.

She immediately took out her favorite doll and put it on her
bed, smiling as she asked her daddy "Is it all right if I put her
there?"

"That's a good idea," he said with a big smile on his face
and reached down to lovingly hug and kiss her. Seeing that she
was adjusting to their new environment, he felt that he could
leave her alone for a few moments and went out to the living
room to give a huge tip to the bellman after asking him to please
see that Jane, his secretary, was comfortably settled in her
accommodations.

He noted that a member of the staff was standing in the
doorway with a menu. Cliff thanked both of them and said he
would check the menu and call to place his order.

Jane walked to her room followed by the bellman who
was carrying her luggage. It was a lovely room with all the
amenities one would expect of a quality establishment. She was
anxious to take a long leisurely bubble bath in the huge Jacuzzi
tub, order dinner, and relax with a good book prior to going to
bed. She knew that Cliff needed to relax and enjoy being with
his children and wanted to give him that space.

Cliff, after checking again that Ra Ra was happily playing
and Jacques, was sound asleep, went into the luxurious hotel
bathroom off his bedroom. He shaved and debated whether to
bathe in the oversized Jacuzzi tub or take a shower. He opted for
a long leisurely shower. It felt good having all that warm water
spilling over him as he soaped up. He was wonderfully refreshed
and donned a golf shirt, pair of shorts, and sandals.

He immediately went in to check on his children and asked
Ra Ra what she would like to eat.

She answered, "Daddy, I would like a lamb chop, please."

He called in his order: two lamb chop dinners, a large green salad, green beans, two glasses of milk, and a chocolate eclair for dessert. They assured him that dinner would be brought up to his room in about twenty minutes, thereby allowing him sufficient time to make a few phone calls.

He left a message on Jane's machine that he was eating in, suggested that she order whatever she wanted, and he would be speaking with her in the morning. He wanted to spend time with his children.

He suddenly realized he needed a high chair and called to ask if one could be brought up. They told him that was no problem, and prior to hanging up, he also requested a playpen.

Next, he called Grace. She answered almost before the phone rang. She was looking forward to his phone call. He brought her up-to-date and gave her the name of the hotel, room, and telephone number.

They discussed a variety of issues then she asked to speak with the children. He said, "Just a minute," and went to Ra Ra's room. She was sitting in the small rocker the hotel provided, singing to her doll. It was an adorable scene.

"Sweetheart, would you like to come over and say, 'Hello' to grandma?"

She ran for the phone, carrying her dolly.

"Hello grandma," she said and continued chatting while he went to get her baby brother. When he came back, she handed him the phone, and he said to Jacques, "Here, say hello to grandma."

Ra Ra spoke again and handed the phone back to her father who said that they would be going to the beach tomorrow. He was planning to engage an au pair for those times when he would be busy.

He then called one of his law partners, regarding his whereabouts and said that he would be working with real estate agents to find a location for their law offices and a permanent residence for himself and his children.

CHAPTER EIGHT

They all had a good night's sleep. They were happy to have spent their first night in San Diego. He decided it would be best for them to have breakfast in their suite that had a mini kitchen and dining room. He called room service to send up a breakfast menu.

When the waiter arrived with the menu, Cliff invited him to come in and asked Ra Ra what she would like for breakfast. She loved waffles with lots of pure maple syrup. He ordered orange juice, waffles, scrambled eggs, toast, jam, coffee, and milk.

The children had been bathed and were dressed for the day. Ra Ra had her sand toys. She was walking around waving her pail in one hand and shovel in the other.

The three of them sat down and enjoyed breakfast amidst Ra Ra's cute chatter and Jacques waving his spoon in one hand, a piece of waffle in the other, and maple syrup all over his face. Cliff picked up a napkin, went to the sink, dampened it, and fatherly wiped the maple syrup off his boy's face. He really loved his children and enjoyed eating breakfast with them.

He called Jane to advise her that they were going to the beach and she was welcome to join them. She said that she would like that and would arrive shortly.

When Jane arrived, Cliff and the children were ready to leave. He had the foresight to request an umbrella, blanket, towels, and a cooler filled with cold drinks, milk, and water. They had their sand toys, sunscreen, sun glasses, hats, and were on their way to enjoy a glorious day at the beach.

Cliff stopped at the concierge's desk to inquire about the procedure for engaging a fully qualified, responsible, and dependable au pair. The concierge said that she had a list of several and would check them out for him.

They walked across the luxurious lobby and out onto the beach. It was a beautiful day; the sun was brightly shining. Cliff selected a spot a few yards from the water's edge, set up the umbrella, put down the blanket, and cooler. He stacked the towels on top of the cooler and proceeded to put sun screen all over Ra Ra and her brother. It was hard to apply the sun screen on Ra Ra. She was focused on making a sand castle while still waving her pail and shovel.

Finally, Cliff said, "All right, you can go down there," pointing to the water's edge, "and start building your work of art." She hugged her father, said, "Thank you, daddy," and ran smiling toward the Pacific Ocean. Jane and Cliff began applying sun screen on each other to prevent getting sun burned. Jane offered to sit with Jacques so that Cliff could check on Ra Ra.

Cliff was convinced more than ever that he had made the right decision to move his family to San Diego. Here he was watching his little girl having so much fun playing at the beach, fascinated by the waves, sea gulls and sand pipers.

They were all transfixed as a sea gull suddenly swooped down and picked up a pair of socks from a bather's towel. They wondered what he would think when he came back and his socks had been "stolen."

Cliff hurriedly decided to bring Jacques to join in the fun and have an opportunity to play in the sand and ocean waves.

Jacques thought all this was wonderful. He liked having his daddy pick him up each time a wave came in. It was fun "jumping" the waves. Then he saw something that he had never seen before and pointed asking his daddy, "What is that?"

He answered, "It's a sea shell. You can pick it up and keep it if you want to"

Jacques bent down, picked up the shell, and with his chubby little hand handed it to his daddy for safe keeping.

Jane came down to tell Cliff that she was going back to the hotel to call real estate agents and check with the concierge regarding the employment of an au pair.

Cliff thanked her as he walked toward Ra Ra who was busily engaged in building her sand castle.

Claudette enjoyed watching him playing with his son in the water as she sat on the sand helping Ra Ra build her sand castle and carrying buckets of water for the little girl who never seemed to have enough water.

However, she was looking somewhat puzzled as to who the lady was with Cliff and wondered what part the woman played in Cliff's life. Claudette instinctively liked him but didn't want to intrude if he was having a relationship with or perhaps she was his wife.

Cliff approached and asked Claudette if she would like a cold drink? She nodded. He left and came back with a soda for her and milk for Ra Ra and Jacques.

He said that they had just arrived in San Diego from Manhattan, New York, and were temporarily staying at a motel here in Pacific Beach.

Claudette asked if he had any idea where he would like to live, perhaps she could help.

He said, "I am still uncertain but need a home large enough for a staff, especially an au pair." Although it still hurt, he said that since he had recently lost his wife, he needed someone to take care of his children when he is at the office.

Cautiously, holding her breath, and uncertain as to whether she should ask, she finally very softly asked, "Did the lady come with you from New York?"

"Yes," he said, "Jane is my secretary and was extremely helpful after the loss of my wife and in helping me to coordinate the move. She'll be my secretary and personal assistant here. I'm very fortunate inasmuch as she is a very organized and competent employee. I have a hotel suite adjacent to the beach and Jane has a room down the hall.

"The hotel has been most accommodating for which I am very appreciative. We'll be taking some vacation time prior to my opening the office."

Claudette felt relieved. She was just beginning to realize that although she had just met this man, he made her head spin. How could this happen so fast--in just a few hours? She wasn't prepared for a serious relationship. Her life was just beginning to crystallize She had so many career decisions to make.

She was in the process of completing the required courses for her law degree, would be graduating in a few months from Stanford, and wanted to practice law. There was nothing in her schedule for a ready-made family although she adored Ra Ra and Jacques. She glanced at Cliff--her heart melted. He was very tall, extremely handsome, soft spoken, and well-mannered. She brushed those thoughts aside, besides maybe there is something between him and Jane. Claudette saw the way Jane looked at him-- in a very adoring way.

It was getting late. Claudette stood up and brushed herself off. She told Ra Ra how enjoyable it was making the sand castle with her, when suddenly Ra Ra ran over, grabbed her legs and looked up into Claudette's face, wanting to be picked up. She was such a darling child that Claudette couldn't resist.

Cliff asked if she would like to join them for dinner. They could eat at the hotel or one of the cute restaurants on the boardwalk. He looked at her with intensely hazel eyes. She wondered how it would be if he took her in his strong arms and kissed her passionately.

Claudette hesitated for a moment, stopped day dreaming, and accepted his dinner invitation. .

He asked, "Have you eaten in any of those restaurants? Is there one in particular that you would you recommend?" as all four of them walked on the sand up toward the boardwalk.

She nodded and indicated the one on the corner, "The Blue Ocean Cafe," would be the most ideal. It has a play area for children," she said.

They walked in and a waiter directed them to a window table which was perfect as they could spend more time enjoying the beauty of the ocean while watching the sail boats with brightly colorful sails; one red, the other blue.

Cliff was amazed at how much he was enjoying her company. He told her he had graduated from Harvard and was a senior partner in his law firm. He really loved the law, and when she told him she would be taking the "bar," he became so excited because they had so much more in common to talk about. Her father had his own law firm. Her grandfather had also been a lawyer. Law ran in the family. He asked what area of law she planned to specialize in, and she replied, "Corporation."

"That's uncanny," he said. "My specialty is corporate law." They laughed as their eyes met, and Cliff was surprised at how she made him feel, the dormant feelings she arose within him. He didn't think he could ever feel that way again. Julia had been his whole life. They had a very unique marriage from the very beginning. It was perfect. And, now she was gone, and here he was three thousand miles away in a strange city, having dinner with this enchanting exquisite vision. It was inconceivable that she would also be a lawyer--a wonderful coincidence.

At that moment, Ra Ra interrupted, asking for a drink of water. Cliff was glad for the interruption.

When they finished eating, Claudette told him about the Mission Beach amusement park, the proud home of the "Big Dipper," a 73-foot-high wooden 1925 historic roller coaster, refurbished in 1990. There is also a merry-go-round at which point Ra Ra jumped up and excitedly said, "Daddy, I am ready to go!"

"How far is it?" Cliff asked. "It's at the other end of the boardwalk where Pacific and Mission Beach intersect," and added, "There is a stand that rents carriages, with two seats and a canopy. It is pedaled like a bicycle. It will be ideal for the kids."

They rented one, buckled in the kids, and pedaled to the Mission Beach Amusement Park adjacent to the beach. Ra Ra loved to sing and they sang songs as they rolled along. Claudette had a beautiful soprano voice. It was a lot of fun.

They parked the carriage, walked over and watched those riding the roller coaster. Ra Ra couldn't wait. She wanted to go on the merry-go-round. Cliff purchased tickets. Ra Ra wanted a horse that went up-and- down. Claudette climbed on one and Cliff put Ra Ra down in front of her. He held Jacques on one of the stationary horses.

Ra Ra couldn't contain her enthusiasm as the merry-go-round started. She squealed with glee. When it stopped, her daddy came over to take her off but she wouldn't move.

"Please, daddy, can we go again?" Claudette nodded and round and round they went. After several more times Ra Ra allowed her daddy to take her off but not until he promised that they would come back the next day.

"How would you like an ice cream cone?" he asked. Ra Ra and Jacques liked that idea and they walked around, enjoying their ice cream and watching people riding and screaming on the roller coaster.

The sun was slowly slinking below the horizon, and as night began covering the park, they decided to head back and return the carriage. Ra Ra and Jacques were falling asleep, it was past their bedtime.

Claudette thanked Cliff for the dinner, said that she had a great time, and that they should do it again. He really didn't want to let her go. They returned the rental and he invited her to his suite. She didn't want the day to end either and agreed.

When they returned, the concierge saw him come in and walked over to tell him that she had found the ideal au pair who was readily available and lived in the area. She gave him a slip of paper with the nanny's name, address, phone number, and a list of references. The concierge further stated that she had been employed by other hotel guests who had all given her glowing recommendations. He thanked her as they headed for the elevator.

He saw Jane as they arrived at their floor and told her that the concierge had an au pair for the children. Jane nodded. She didn't speak because she was very upset when she saw the young woman from the beach.
Cliff told Jane that he would speak with her in the morning and she again nodded as she quickly turned around to hide her disappointment as tears were filling her eyes and flowing down her cheeks.

When Cliff, Claudette, and the children entered his suite, he planned to call the au pair. He dialed the number provided by the concierge. A man answered. Cliff, assuming it might be her father, introduced himself and asked to speak with Nancy Stewart. She came to the phone and Cliff once again introduced himself.

Nancy said that she had been waiting for his call and was available 24/7. He asked if she lived nearby and could come over. She agreed, saying that she was on her way.

Cliff looked around for Ra Ra and Jacques who were nowhere in sight. He heard sounds of water splashing and laughter emanating from the kids bathroom.

He went over and saw that Claudette had already bathed Jacques and was giving Ra Ra a bath and shampooing her curly hair. Claudette rinsed the bubbles off Ra Ra and wrapped her in a large soft terry cloth towel, while fluffing the child's bright red curls with her finger.

Jacques already had his pajamas on.

Cliff picked him up and put him in bed after giving him a big hug and kiss. He pulled the covers up and gave him his favorite toy, a plush goose, named "Cuddles" that was wearing her red and white polka dot dress. Cliff sat on the edge of the bed and sang to him. His favorite song "The Wheels on The Bus," and when the boy heard the words "The Driver on the Bus says," Jacques said, "beep, beep" and repeated the last line of the song. It was very cute.

Claudette brought in Ra Ra. Her daddy picked her up, carried her to her room, and put her in bed with her favorite doll. She was very tired; it had been a long day.

Cliff took Claudette's hand leading her into the living room. They sat down on the luxurious couch. It was a beautifully decorated room enriched with antiques, oil paintings, and water colors by well-known and local artists.

"Would you like a drink?" he asked.

"I would really like a tall glass of ice cold lemonade," she said.

He ordered a pitcher of ice cold lemonade, ice tea, crackers, cheese, and chocolate dipped strawberries.

Claudette watched him as he ordered. He was an extraordinary man. How did he know what she would like? It was uncanny. After the food arrived, they sat looking at each other. Claudette was not ready for a relationship. She had too many plans, too much to accomplish.

CHAPTER NINE

There was an interrupting knock at the door. It was the au pair, Nancy Stewart, somewhat out of breath, carrying an overnight bag. She was a pretty petite girl in her twenties. Cliff invited her to come in and they sat as he interviewed her. He was impressed and understood why the concierge had recommended her.

She said that she could stay the night and asked to see the children.

"They are both asleep," he said as he motioned for her to follow him. First, he opened the door to Jacques room, and she very quietly stepped inside. There was a warm smile on Nancy's face; her expressive eyes told him that she was a very compassionate person. Jacques had kicked off the covers. She bent over, and very carefully, so as not to wake him, arranged the covers to keep him warm.

He showed Nancy the way to Ra Ra's room. She entered the room and saw the little girl who was also sound asleep, her arms wrapped around her favorite doll. Nancy pulled the covers up to keep the little girl warm.

Cliff felt that she would be perfect, and he could trust her with his treasures. They sat down in the living room, and he asked her about herself and the man who answered the phone.

She said that it was her father and he would probably be stopping over to meet Cliff. A few minutes later, Mr. Steward knocked on the door. Cliff invited him in and offered them a glass of lemonade or ice tea.

Cliff told Mr. Stewart that they had just moved from Manhattan and were in the process of looking for a home to purchase that would be large enough for his children, an au pair, cook, and housekeeper. He also said that he was hoping to find a home with a cottage on the property for his in-laws when they came to visit.

Furthermore, he told Mr. Stewart that he would be welcome any time and his daughter, Nancy, would be an excellent au pair for Jacques and Ra Ra.

Nancy's father was very interested. He reached into his jacket pocket, took out one of his business cards, and handed it to Cliff as he advised him that he was a real estate agent, in fact he was the president and C.E.O. of his own company.

Cliff was delighted. This was good news.

He immediately liked Mr. Stewart and told him that he was also looking for offices for the west coast branch of his law firm. He went on to explain that he was a senior partner and had just moved from New York to open their west coast law office here in San Diego County.

Mr. Stewart stood up and extended his hand. Cliff was quick to grasp it; everything was beginning to fall into place. Mr. Steward said, "Call me Alan," thanked him for the refreshments, and said that he would call the next day with possibilities. He asked if his daughter would be spending the night. Cliff said that wasn't necessary, but he would appreciate it if she would call in the morning. She agreed.

After they left, Claudette said that she had a wonderful time and appreciated the thoughtfulness of the chocolate dipped strawberries as they were her favorite. He asked for her phone number and if she was available.

She said, "I'll call in the morning.

He really wanted to take her in his arms and kiss her but felt it might be too soon; he didn't know that Claudette was thinking about how much she wanted this gorgeous man to wrap his arms around her. She knew it was somewhat premature but she was "falling" hard. They shook hands and she left.

As she walked out, she saw Jane and said, "Hello," however Jane acted as though she hadn't heard Claudette.

Cliff, hearing a knock at the door, thought Claudette had forgotten something and was disappointed to see Jane. He asked if she needed something and that he had engaged a real estate agent and an au pair.

Jane was again disappointed. She wanted him to be dependent on her, and it didn't look as though that was going to happen. She had always been in love with him and hoped that he might feel the same way about her. She rationalized that perhaps if she did more to ingratiated herself that he might love her as much as she loved him.

The next morning Claudette called and Cliff asked if she would like to join them for a day at the zoo. He had heard that the San Diego had a world famous zoo with pandas from China. She accepted and said, "I will be over shortly."

Cliff then called Alan to ask if any properties would meet his needs.

Alan told him that he was working on it and expected to have something to report later that day. He asked, "Should Nancy come over?"

Cliff said, "Not now, we are going to the zoo," but said that he would call her later. He still wanted her to be the children's au pair but knew he would be busy and wanted to spend as much time with the children as he could. He needed to have his furniture shipped but first he needed to find a suitable home.

Claudette arrived and the four of them were off to the San Diego Zoo. She offered to take her car but didn't have car seats for the children. Cliff told her that it was all right, they could take his car. It was equipped with car seats. Ra Ra had her favorite doll and Jacques his favorite plush toy "Cuddles", the goose, wearing her red and white polka dot dress.

The zoo was all they expected it to be. They spent an enjoyable day, taking photographs, watching and feeding the animals, and having a picnic. By 6:00 they were back at the hotel suite. Ra Ra and Jacques had been bathed, read to, and were sound asleep.

Cliff and Claudette were happy to sit down and relax. It had been a whirlwind day. The children had been very excited requiring that they had to be watched closely to ensure they wouldn't get too close to the animals or lost.

They ordered dinner to be sent up and were ready for a relaxing evening. Claudette was somewhat nervous because soon she would have to leave for Stanford to finish the term. She found herself deeply attracted to Cliff. He was unlike any man she had ever known. A gentleman she appreciated. He was an impeccable dresser, hair neatly combed, and shoes shined. She just sat there looking at him. He looked so appealing in a powder blue shirt and perfectly pressed navy blue slacks. She had never felt this way before and it both excited and terrified her. She kept telling herself that she wasn't ready for a long term relationship and definitely wasn't interested in getting married.

It was an enjoyable dinner; Cliff put on some music and asked her to dance. He couldn't wait to get his arms around her and theorized that dancing would be a good starting point. It was incredible that so soon after the loss of his wife, he could feel like this. He never thought he could feel like this again. What would his in-laws think? Would they be upset and chastise him, or would they be happy that he had found someone?

Claudette loved being in his arms as they "floated" around the living room of his suite, it was magical but getting late. She said that she would have to leave. He wanted everything to continue going smoothly. He walked over and turned off the music as he opened the door for her. He said that he hoped he would be able to see her the next day.

She was noncommittal saying, "Let's touch base in the morning" as she picked up her pink cashmere sweater. He didn't want to do anything that would make her back off. She smiled and walked down the hall toward the elevator.

It was only then he saw Jane by his door. He was startled and wondered how long she had been standing there and what did she want.

She asked if she could do something for him, anything he wanted her to do.

He was baffled and replied that he didn't at which point he noted her disappointment as she turned and walked toward her room.

CHAPTER TEN

The next morning Cliff phoned Alan to inquire whether he had any suitable properties.

Alan said, "Yes, I was just getting ready to call you. What time shall I pick you up?"

Cliff advised him that ten o'clock would be ideal and said, "I will need Nancy's services. Would it be possible for her to come over now? If she hasn't had breakfast, she can eat with my children."

Nancy's father handed her the phone and she said that she was on her way and would enjoy having breakfast with Ra Ra and Jacques.

Cliff ordered breakfast. He heard Ra Ra and went over to check on her. She was sitting in the little rocker singing to her dolly. He checked on Jacques who was just waking up and extended his arms to be picked up. A scene Cliff always enjoyed. He was such a sweet, lovable baby. Cliff was blessed with his two wonderful children.

Nancy arrived and they all had breakfast.

Alan arrived with listings to go over with Cliff.

Nancy asked if she could take the children to the park adjacent to the hotel.

Cliff approved and suggested that she take a bag with sun screen, water, juice, baby wipes, towels, and a blanket. He said, "I made arrangements for you to order room service."

She thanked him, put Jacques in his stroller, took Ra Ra's hand, and they were off.

Alan reiterated that he had several properties that he could go over with Cliff, or they could drive to each location. He had the keys. Cliff said, "Let's go!"

The first property was not acceptable, nor was the second, but the third was ideal. It was a three-story brick house with eight bedrooms, quarters for the household staff, a huge living room, dining room that could seat twenty, ballroom, library, den, huge pantry adjacent to the kitchen, and a room that would be perfect for the children's playroom. It was ideal because it was light and airy with French doors that opened on to an enclosed garden area with a beautiful mini-lawn and flowers. The master bedroom was complete with a sitting room, balcony, and a bathroom with a Jacuzzi the size of a small swimming pool, and two dressing rooms with closets. Outside there was an Olympic size swimming pool, tennis court, pool house with a table tennis setup, and pool table.

Cliff was thinking about how happy Grace and Gordon would be when Alan showed him the quaint cottage reminiscent of one he had once seen during one of his trips to England. He couldn't wait to see the interior. It would be perfect for Gordon and Grace. It had a spacious living room, dining area, kitchen, two bedrooms, spacious bath with a Jacuzzi, and a studio that could be used for any number of purposes. The property was perfect. He was already picturing how Gordon would setup his study and library. He had hundreds of books, many were rare first editions.

Everything he saw pleased him. He wanted to negotiate the price but didn't want to seem too eager. Alan saw by the look on Cliff's face that it was ideal for his personal needs and entertaining clients. "What is the asking price?" Alan jotted down a figure; Cliff counter offered.

The property was vacant; the owners were now residing in Europe and would need to be contacted. Cliff said that if they reached an agreement, he would like to move in immediately His furniture would have to be shipped.

Alan said, "All furnishing in the house are included in the purchase price."   Cliff smiled. There were some beautiful antiques and the draperies looked as though there were new and would be perfect accents for the furnishings he was having shipped from New York.

Alan stood up and said that he would contact the owners. "I have several office suites that might be suitable for your law offices; would you like to drive over now?"

Cliff said that would be fine, but first he wanted to call Nancy to check on his children.   There was no reason for concern; Nancy and the children were playing in the park and had enjoyed a picnic lunch. Cliff thanked her, turned to Alan and said, "I'm ready, shall we go now?"

The downtown area of San Diego was bustling with multistory buildings many of which were already occupied by top law firms. Cliff was excited.

Alan pointed out as they drove through different sections why he felt that this area would be ideal. La Jolla could conceivably be another choice, but being centrally located in downtown San Diego adjacent to the Lindbergh International Airport, heliport, and hotels with great views of the Pacific Ocean and bay would, in his professional opinion, be an ideal location.

Alan had a great deal of experience. It had always been his goal to provide the best possible service. He always listened to what his clients had to say, and more importantly, how the property would be used. He was extremely conscientious and knew how important it was for Cliff to have the best possible and easily accessible location.

The downtown area was in the proximity of the Gas Lamp District.   Many buildings, dating back a century, had been refurbished. It was a lively place with four-star hotels, great restaurants, and all the amenities out-of-town clients would require, appreciate, and enjoy.

Alan told him about three buildings, but Cliff was not pleased with any of the offices and said that perhaps he had not made his requirements clear. He would require at least the building's top three floors and asked if that was a possibility.

Alan apologized profusely. He said that he was sorry he had misunderstood but had such an office space available.

Cliff said, "Great, let's go there now."

This suite of offices was perfect. He inquired about leasing arrangements and was pleased with what Alan told him. This looked like the perfect location and the offices were ideal. He made a counter offer. Alan advised him that he would make the necessary contacts and call him in the morning. Cliff reminded him that he also needed an answer concerning the residential property he had been shown that morning.

Everything seemed to be shaping up. Cliff was pleased and asked Alan if he'd like to stop for a cup of coffee or wait until they got to his hotel suite.

Once again, he called Nancy this time to advise her that he was on his way back and asked about his children.

Nancy said that everything was fine and they would head back to the hotel.

Realizing the time difference, Cliff called Grace. He was anxious to tell her he had found the perfect home and was waiting for the owners to accept his offer. "I will call when the purchase has been finalized, then we can ship the furniture, and I hope you and Gordon will also be on your way as soon as the furniture is shipped," he said.

She was very excited but reminded him that Gordon met with his regiment once a month after which they would leave.

Cliff admired and had always respected Gordon who served as a pilot during the Vietnam War. He was a highly decorated officer having been awarded the Congressional Medal of Honor. He retired with the rank of Brigadier General and always enjoyed meeting with his fellow officers and crew to renew their friendships and relive the days when they flew for the United States Air Force. The squadron he commanded saw a lot of action and was the most highly decorated of that war.

The next day Alan called to say that the owners had accepted Cliff's offer, and upon receiving a check, escrow would be opened, and his family could move in immediately even before escrow closed.

"Yes, I told them you had two small children, were opening a west coast law office, and would like to move in immediately," Alan said.

"What about the three-floor suite of law offices? Was my offer accepted?"

Alan said that one of the owners who had been out-of-town was returning the next day.

Cliff hung up and immediately called Grace. He asked her to please have his furniture shipped and hoped she and possibly Gordon would also be coming out. He said, "I have a surprise for you and Gordon that will make you both very happy."

He didn't want to tell her that they would have their own private fully equipped cottage on the property which would provide them with "their own home;" and yet be close enough to see their grandchildren and enjoy the numerous amenities.

Grace was ecstatic and said that as soon as the furniture was shipped she would make plane reservations and let him know the date and day of their arrival.

Cliff couldn't be happier. They were such wonderful people and had accepted him from the very beginning. He couldn't wait for their arrival as he knew they would surely enjoy San Diego, but more importantly it would be good for Ra Ra and Jacques to have their grandparents visit.

Cliff called Nancy and asked if she would be willing to be a live-in au pair. She was thrilled. She loved the children and Cliff was a nice man to work for. He then asked to speak with her father. "Alan, do you have any recommendations and references for a cook and housekeeper?"

Alan said that he would check his book and get back to him.

"Everything was falling into shape." Cliff thought as he sat in the living room of his hotel suite. He was very anxious to get his family settled and looking forward to Grace and Gordon's arrival.

The phone rang, it was Alan. He had the names of several prospects who had excellent references. Cliff jotted down the names and proceeded to make calls. He liked the idea of having a French cook and immediately called Miss Monique. Alan told him that her surname was both difficult to pronounce and spell, therefore everyone calls her Miss Monique.

The phone was ringing. Cliff was very excited. Miss Monique's recommendations and references were impeccable and he believed she would be the ideal person for his household. Not only did he want her to cook but also be willing and happy to have his children come into the kitchen to snack and have milk and cookies. He knew that Ra Ra loved to bake with her grandmother and hoped that Miss Monique would have the temperament to let his little girl bake and help with simple things in the kitchen.

He heard a very distinct French accent when the phone was answered and inquired whether Miss Monique was available.

The voice replied, "Oui, Monique, and how can I help."

After introducing himself and explaining the reason for his call, he heard a loud gasp and wondered if something were wrong and inquired.

"Everything is fine in fact, it's wonderful," she said further explaining that her former employer was now residing abroad, and she was praying for an exceptional position with a good family.

Cliff was thrilled. Could it be this simple to find someone? He asked if they could meet.

She offered to have him come to her home and bring his children. He couldn't have been happier when she ecstatically said, "Yes," and that she would have cookies and milk for his children and some other goodies for them to enjoy during their visit.

Cliff was happy beyond his wildest expectations. Monique sounded like a wonderfully warm hearted woman and felt his children would be very safe with her. She had mentioned that her last employer had five children and they all had a good time in the kitchen.

Next, Cliff called Katrine Svensen for the housekeeper position and her husband, Hilmar Svensen, as grounds keeper. Mrs. Svensen answered the phone, and even before he finished explaining the reason for his call, she said a resounding, "Yes" for both she and her husband and they set a time to meet the next day after he saw Miss Monique.

CHAPTER ELEVEN

The next day Cliff, Ra Ra, and Jacques went to visit Miss Monique. She hugged Ra Ra and Jacques and the four of them sat down in her warm cozy kitchen. As she was about to serve refreshments, the door bell rang, and she excused herself to answer. It was Mr. and Mrs. Svensen who lived close by and stopped by often to visit.

Unbeknown to Cliff, they had all worked together for the same employer and were very good friends. Cliff felt that he was truly blessed. They were such charming people and good friends. When Mrs. Svensen saw Ra Ra and Jacques, she was thrilled and kept talking about what adorable children he had.

What he thought would be a job interview turned out to be much more. They were like wonderful new treasured friends, more like family.

Miss Monique had a beautiful garden and asked Ra Ra and Jacques if they would like to go outside and play. She gave them a ball, some other toys, and showed them the way.

Cliff knew that they must have questions about their mother but he didn't want to bring up the subject with the children in the room. He was quietly working to keep his composure as he told them what had happened and the reason for their move from Manhattan to San Diego. He also told them about his opening the west coast law office for his firm.

Miss Monique came over to Cliff and said, "I know how difficult it is to lose the one you love. "I left France because I was broken hearted. I was engaged to a wonderful man, a jeweler, who suddenly and without any warning disappeared. It was very disheartening, I was extremely distraught, and decided to immigrate to America and start a new life.

"I have been happy in America and your being here to offer me a position in your household with your adorable children, your in-laws, and others, I feel as though my life has new meaning. I know that I can also speak for the Svensens, who also feel fortunate indeed to become a part of your happy home and we most humbly thank you."

Cliff was overwhelmed and very pleased that his household would now be complete as Miss Monique bent down to wipe away his tears and give him a hug.

Cliff felt further obligated to explain that his furniture was now on its way and his in-laws, Grace and Gordon, would be coming out for extended visits. "There is a cottage on the property; it will be their home when they are in town."

He wanted them to know the full story. Also, he had engaged an au pair, Nancy Stewart, whose father, Alan, was the real estate agent who found the property he had purchased and recommended them.

He advised the Swenson's and Miss Monique that they would have their own quarters and days off could be arranged. They would also have access to the swimming pool, tennis courts, and all the amenities. He asked if they had any questions. The smiles on their faces told it all. They said that they already loved his children and were looking forward to doing all in their power to make them happy.

He could see that there would be plenty of hugs and felt that these three would be a delightful addition to his family.

Miss Monique asked if she could call the children to come in. He nodded. She called and gave each of them a great big hug.

Mrs. Svensen was also very loving and asked Jacques if he would like to sit on her lap. He ran over as Cliff sat watching, tears once again were welling up in his eyes. Before he knew it, his cheeks were wet with tears. Miss Monique walked over with a tissue and hugged him.

"How lucky can you get?" Cliff asked himself.

CHAPTER TWELVE

Grace called the next morning to tell Cliff, "We will be arriving today at 4:30, gate 732."

Cliff had offered to fly them down in the company jet, but one of Gordon's friends had his own plane.

He told her that he would come down in a limo to pick them up.

Previously that morning, Cliff had spoken with Alan who was bringing over the keys and reassured him that everything was set at the house. Cliff thanked him and said that his in-laws were flying in this afternoon and he would be bringing them to the house. Alan said, "Nancy and I will be there to welcome them.

Grace looked wonderful. She was still a beautiful woman who cared a great deal about her appearance. She was wearing a pale blue two-piece suit with a pearl choker, earrings, and a beautiful gold leaf lapel pin. She had a girlish figure and long shapely legs. Gordon looked very handsome in a navy blue suit, a perfectly pressed shirt, and burgundy tie. They were a beautiful couple, and as they walked, everyone looked at them admiringly.

When Ra Ra saw her grandparents, she ran full speed ahead and Cliff who was carrying Jacques put him down and watched smiling, tears filling his eyes as he saw that they couldn't get enough hugs and kisses from their grandparents. It was a beautiful sight!

Cliff put his arms around Grace and told her how much he appreciated all she had done and was so glad that she and Gordon had come. He also hugged Gordon. The three of them weren't just related, they were also good friends--had a very good relationship.

Cliff was enjoying the ride to their new home. Ra Ra as usual was talking a mile-a-minute her curls bouncing up and down and Jacques was showing his grandpa the new toy plane his daddy had purchased at the airport. Suddenly they asked, "Any presents?" and everyone laughed.

They were approaching the gated house, Cliff punched in the code, and the gate opened to a wide expanse of greenery and a long curved driveway lined with tree roses that led them to the front door. Cliff looked at Grace, he wanted to see her facial expression and saw that she was pleased.

It was a beautiful brick structure set back with lovely front and side gardens. She remarked at the beautifully carved exquisite renaissance double doors with the huge brass knocker.

Grace couldn't wait to see the interior, the grounds, and the surprise. She kept wondering what it might be. Just then Alan and Nancy drove up, Cliff introduced them, and they all went inside.

Grace was thrilled. It was a magnificent structure in keeping with Cliff's position. They walked through the glass French doors, out to the garden, past the swimming pool, pool house, and tennis courts.

Cliff asked Grace, "Do you know what your surprise will be?" She replied, "No, but I have been excited and know that since you picked it out, it will be wonderful."

Cliff gently asked Grace as they approached the cottage, "Now, close your eyes and be surprised." When they were standing directly in front of the cottage, Cliff said, "Open your eyes and look at your surprise." Grace was overwhelmed.

"Cliff," she said, as she threw up her arms to express her delight, "What a wonderful surprise. It's perfect! It's beautiful! I know that Gordon and I will be very happy here."

"Grace and Gordon, this is your cottage to enjoy," Cliff said. "You will have privacy when you want it, be close by to enjoy your grandchildren, and join in family festivities. I want you to make this cottage and the main house your home." Grace hugged him and Gordon put his arm around Cliff.

Gordon had spent time in England during the war and was enthralled with the cottages, and when he saw this one, he was visibly happy that it would be theirs. Grace was excited, knowing Gordon's penchant for the Irish style cottages. He couldn't wait to go inside, but first he reached down, picked Grace up in his arms to carry her across the threshold, as had been their ritual, when they had a new home, and kissed her gently before putting her down. They were very much in love and stood in each other's arms, and then he gently ran his hand down her hair and carefully caressed her cheek.

The children rushed in wanting to see everything and to be close to their grandparents. Grace and Gordon looked around. It was beautifully furnished down to the linens, silver, china, and utensils. Nancy, unknown to Cliff, had the kitchen stocked; it was ready to be enjoyed.

Nancy came over to tell Cliff that the rental furnishings had arrived and he thanked her profusely for taking care to stock the kitchen. .

Cliff had ordered rental furniture for a few days until theirs arrived. He wanted them to feel at home. He advised Nancy which rooms would be occupied by Ra Ra, Jacques, and herself, have the beds and other furnishing moved in. "Please let me know when it has been accomplished and tell the men from the rental company that I would like to speak with them before they leave," Cliff requested.

Miss Monique and the Svensens arrived and Cliff showed them their rooms that were already furnished and said that they should advise him if they need anything else.

Nancy had also stocked the pantry but some other items might be needed and to let him know. He introduced them to his in-laws and immediately saw that everything was going to work out sublimely. They all seemed to like each other, which was extremely important to Cliff. He wanted his home to be filled with love and harmony.

Jane had been feeling left out. She didn't know Cliff had purchased a house and his in-laws were arriving. It was Nancy who brought her up-to-date giving her Cliff's address. Jane really loved Cliff and desperately wanted to be the next Mrs. Camden, but it didn't seem to be turning out as she had hoped. What could she do to win him over? She was desolate as she sat on her bed with her head in her hands. Why did she ever think that moving would make him love her?

She cried for a long time fingering the paper Nancy had given her with Cliff's new address. Then abruptly she stood up, decided to take a shower, wash her hair, put on a cute outfit, and go to his house.

Jane was amazed when she saw the house. It was huge. The grounds were immense and beautifully manicured. She used the brass knocker to announce her arrival and was startled when someone she didn't know answered the door. It was Mrs. Svensen, the housekeeper.

Jane introduced herself and said that she had come to see Mr. Cliff Camden.

Mrs. Svensen said with a Swedish accent, "Just a minute. I go see where he is."

Cliff came to the door and said that he was really busy getting everyone settled, would call her in the morning, and closed the door.

Jane stood dejected. She couldn't believe what had just happened. No greeting. No glad you are here. She was shocked and how would she get back to the hotel. Should she walk or should she knock again and ask them to call her a cab? No, she decided to use her cell phone and called a cab. She just couldn't believe what had just happened; she felt used and unwanted.

The next morning Cliff called Alan to check on the office suites.

Alan said that he was about to call and tell him that the owners had accepted his offer to purchase the top three floors including all the furnishings and Cliff would be able to start moving in that afternoon.

Cliff called his law partners. They were pleased that the deal had gone through and they could begin planning the next step of their operation. Cliff had already opened a business checking account; money would be wired into that account. He also advised them that he had purchased a home and they were welcome anytime.

Cliff called Jane. She sounded very distant and cold.

He said. "The deal has gone through. We have purchased the top three floors of an exclusive office building in downtown San Diego."

Cliff asked Jane, "Are you available to conduct an inventory and let me know as soon as possible what additional furnishings and office equipment will be needed."

He wanted to start making appointments with clients as soon as possible.

She said, "I'm not sure when I can get it done."

"Is there a problem?" he asked.

"I don't know," she continued, "I'm beginning to wonder if I made the right decision to move."

Cliff was shocked and wondered why her attitude had changed. He thought she was anxious to move and be instrumental in getting the west coast office set up. She was familiar with the firm's operation and would be a terrific asset, but if she felt that she had made a mistake, he would have to inquire if someone else in the New York office would like to relocate, or he would have to hire a local secretary.

This wasn't like Jane, she was always so solid. He liked the way she conducted herself and handled clients. To say the least, he was speechless--at a loss as to what to do. Could he change her mind? Should he or would it be in the best interest of the firm to pay her way back to New York? He decided to give it one more try. He had to leave; it was time to open the office. He didn't have time for histrionics.

Jane's knocking on the door surprised him. He looked at her, trying to restrain himself. He kept his voice low key. He asked what she would like to do and what could he do to change her mind as he would really like her to stay. She was efficient and organized--more like a personal assistant. He had relied on her and hoped she would want to stay to be an integral part of the office team.

She looked at him trying desperately to control her tears. He had complimented her. She wanted to stay but what could she expect. Maybe, if she went slowly and didn't make any demands, perhaps, he would fall in love with her. But if she left, there would be no chance at all.

She loved him, and he looked so manly. She wanted to throw her arms around him but knew she shouldn't.

"Cliff, I have decided to stay. I'll help you establish and run the office," she said haltingly and then continued, "Guess I was a little bit homesick. Sorry."

Cliff felt relieved and told her it was all right. "If you are looking for an apartment or house to rent or purchase Alan Stewart, Nancy's father, would be willing to work with you."

She thanked him, asked for the office address, and a key. He handed her a key and wrote down the address.

She said. "I will go early tomorrow morning and call you after I complete the inventory."

He also asked her to find out what business licenses were required, thanked her, and said that he was glad she decided to stay, and walked her back to her hotel room.

Cliff decided he no longer needed to stay at the hotel. Although the moving van had not yet arrived from New York, he was anxious to move into their new San Diego home. He realized that he had not ordered sufficient furnishings and called the rental company to order additional pieces until theirs arrived.

He decided to check out of the hotel, but there was one more thing he wanted to do: purchase the rocker Ra Ra liked. He went to the lobby and asked to speak with the manager who was concerned that something was wrong when he saw Cliff approaching.

The manager wasn't in the mood for any complaints and usually didn't encounter any, but this could be the exception. He walked over extending his hand as he greeted Cliff and asked how he could be of service. Cliff was very complimentary telling him they enjoyed their stay, was appreciative, and the staff was to be congratulated for a superlative job.

The manager was overwhelmed. This was fine praise indeed coming from the man who was to head the west coast office of the highly acclaimed prestigious law firm.

Cliff continued, "I have purchased a house and am now proud to call San Diego my home."

The manager had a look of relief; these were truly fine praises.

Cliff then told him how much his little girl loved the rocker and was hoping he could purchase it for her. Cliff said, "She loved to sit in the rocker while holding and singing to her doll."

The hotel manager excused himself for a few minutes and went to check on the cost of the rocker. He knew Cliff had rented a suite of rooms, a room for his secretary, and wondered what he could do. It would be great public relations. The manager spoke with a member of his staff who returned to the lobby with the rocker.

"The hotel has appreciated your patronage and we would like to make the rocker a gift to your little girl."

Cliff was surprised not having expected to be given the rocker.

The manager said, "My clerk will carry the rocker out and put it in your car. Perhaps you could take a photo of your little girl rocking her doll and present it to the hotel."

Cliff readily agreed as he stood totally amazed. He reached in his pocket to give the manager a tip, but was told it wasn't necessary. Cliff thanked him and walked to his car with the clerk who was carrying the rocker.

It was a happy afternoon when Cliff arrived home with the rocker. He stuck his head in the door and asked Mrs. Svensen where Ra Ra was.

"She's in the garden," Mrs. Svensen said with a quizzical look on her face.

Cliff came in with the rocker and dashed to the playroom with it as Mrs. Svensen was smiling, and then Cliff went outside to find Ra Ra. She and Jacques were playing with their grandparents

When she saw her daddy, she ran fast into his arms; and he motioned for everyone to follow him.

They went into the playroom, and when Ra Ra saw the rocker, she was very excited. She grabbed her doll and began to rock her. It was adorable; Jacques then looked at his father who was pointing to two little chairs and Jacques eyes opened as wide as saucers as he immediately picked up CUDDLES, his plush goose, put her on one chair, and he sat on the other.

Cliff knew if he gave something to Ra Ra, he should give a gift to her brother.

He grabbed his camera and as he had promised the hotel manager, took a picture of Ra Ra and then Jacques. He would have the photos enlarged and delivered to the hotel. Cliff was a man who always kept his promises.

The children were very excited. They wanted to eat dinner in their playroom. Nancy said that she would make the arrangements, bring their food, and have dinner with them.

Grace thought it would be cozy for the three of them to have dinner in the cottage and she was right. It was a perfect evening. Gordon had lit a fire in the fire place and soft music was playing as they sat drinking another goblet of champagne to celebrate and, in essence, christen their new home as they talked about the children, Cliff's new law offices, and the plane Gordon was purchasing.

Gordon was an ace pilot having flown in the Vietnam War and now flies jet planes for a top rated aero space company. He really enjoys flying and has flown many times with Cliff, also a licensed pilot.

The next morning Cliff called Jane for the inventory results. She advised him that she had completed the inventory and made a list of furniture, filing cabinets, chairs, and other furnishings to purchase for the offices, conference rooms, and waiting areas. She also said that she made a list of electronic equipment, phones, stationery, office supplies, and printing they would need.

Cliff was very pleased and asked if it would be convenient for her to meet him in an hour. She said, "I'll be there."

A great deal had to be done to get the offices ready for clients. A contractor was needed to assist with putting up walls and installing doors and wood floors. He called Alan to inquire if he had a recommendation for a contractor, office furniture, window coverings, carpets, etc.

Alan as usual had the information Cliff needed and proceeded to fax the list. Alan also offered to call the contractor and make calls to the various companies on Cliff's behalf.

Progress was being made. The walls were going up, floors and carpets installed on the top floor. Cliff needed his office and Jane's ready as he wanted to begin seeing clients. The lower two floors wouldn't be needed for a few months.

Cliff invited Grace and Gordon to have lunch with him in the historical Gas Lamp District at a great little Italian restaurant he had found. They enjoyed a large green salad and pasta. The owner was a delightful old world gentleman who with his wife operated the quaint restaurant. After lunch Cliff showed them around the law offices and they congratulated him on a magnificent job.

Finally, Cliff could start to relax: furniture arrived, his offices were set up, children were happy, and Gordon and Grace were at home to oversee the running of his household. Now, he would have some free time to spend with Claudette who would be graduating from Stanford with her law degree in a few weeks.

He took his cell phone out of his pocket and called her. He couldn't wait to hear her voice. It seemed an eternity since they sat on the beach, helping Ra Ra build a sand castle, the evenings they walked on the sand, and enjoyed having a cup of coffee in one of the quaint cafes that had tables on the boardwalk.

He wondered if she was ever going to answer, each millisecond seemed like hours and finally he heard her soft melodious voice. He could exist on that "Hello," forever. "How is everything?" Cliff asked not really being sure of how to start the conversation.

There was a pause at the other end, and with an exuberance that was about to burst his ear drum, she said, "Hello it's so good to hear from you, it must be mental telepathy. I was just getting ready to call you with some really good news, I'll be graduating in two weeks and you can, she laughed call me a lady lawyer which is what my Daddy says jokingly."

Cliff congratulated her. She had finally earned her degree after three arduous years in law school. He was anxious to have her back in San Diego but didn't know how he could wait. Two weeks can be a life time!

She thanked him and hesitatingly asked if he would like to see her graduate.

He really wanted to go and was mentally trying to figure out how he could arrange his schedule. The house was now harmoniously staffed, and with Gordon and Grace on the premises, he felt confident they could handle any situation that might arise. Could he really get away from the office though? Throwing all caution aside, if he continued to rationalize, he could talk himself out of it, took a deep breath and enthusiastically said, "I'll be there. Just provide me with the date and time."

Claudette had difficulty controlling her excitement. She had never felt this way before and couldn't wait until he arrived. She was picturing him walking up to her and ever so gently gathering her up in his strong masculine arms. "I'll call you when I have all the details," she said. They stayed on the phone for several hours, drinking in the essence of each other. It was so beautiful. She never knew anyone could make her feel this way. It was glorious.

Cliff was also in a state of ecstasy but how could he be moved so soon after losing his Julia. What would his in-laws think? He feared they would be displeased, and how could he cope with that? "I can't let their feelings interfere with my plans," he rationalized.

Later that day, Claudette called with the date, time, and address where the graduation ceremonies would be held. He thanked her and asked after the ceremony, "Would you be ready to return to San Diego?" He hoped she would accompany him.

"I would love to return with you after we attend the various parties that I am certain you will enjoy. You will be my escort, won't you?"

Cliff was thrilled and answered a resounding, "Yes!" He asked if she would like him to pick her up and take her to the ceremony. "

Yes," she said.

Cliff, in a questionable tone, said, "I was just wondering, what is the color of your outfit?"

She couldn't figure out why he was asking her that but answered, "A demure pink."

"That sounds beautiful and will truly complement your beautiful tresses," Cliff remarked. They spoke for about an hour. Cliff said, "I will make the reservations." He was close to saying those magic words, "I love you," but knew it was premature. He theorized that if he didn't want her to back-off, he should soft-pedal it.

Cliff was going to make reservations but then thought better of that and called Jane to have the company jet fueled, ready to take off on the appointed day, and asked her to call their florist. He wanted a corsage comprised of three exquisitely large purple orchids delivered to him as he boarded the plane.

Jane was amazed at what he was doing. She kept wondering who the corsage was for and why was he going out-of-town when they were still in the process of establishing the west coast office. She was totally perplexed, but picked up the phone to reserve the jet and ordered the corsage.

Jane felt as though she was losing, tears were filling her eyes again and rolling dramatically down her cheeks. How was she going to cope? She wanted to be the one Cliff was showering with attention. She had been in love with him for a long time but never thought she had a chance because he and his wife were happily married. But, now with the turn of events, she thought she had a chance. She had been ingratiating herself to him with the hope that he would really look at her, realize she was special, and could make him happy. There had to be something she could do and called a top hair stylist. She made an appointment for that afternoon.

Jane walked into the beauty salon telling herself this was the first step to a new and better Jane. She felt like an article she once read in a magazine about a "plain Jane" transformation that ran through her mind as she was directed to a booth. She sat in the chair, looking dismally at her reflection in the mirror as a large towel was draped across her shoulders to protect her clothes.

A man came in smiling as he introduced himself with a strong French accent, "My name is 'enri, and I shall endeavor to fulfill your dreams, mademoiselle. What is it precisely you would like to see when you look in zee mirror?" he asked as he was examining her hair.

She smiled bashfully which was really out of character for her as she replied, "I desperately want the man I love to look at me and in that magical moment realize he loves me with all his heart."

Henri was taken aback. That was huge--a really tall order. He could give her a fantastic hair style that would make her look more attractive and have his makeup artistic show her a few tricks that would enhance her beauty. She had an acceptable figure and the right clothes would add to her overall look.

Jane gave him "carte blanche" as she sat back in the chair, avoiding all eye contact with the mirror. She didn't want to look until Henri had worked his magic. He had quite a reputation as being a "miracle worker" and right now she felt as though she needed him to use all the tricks he had ever learned.

Hours later, Henri, after putting one more curl in place and smoothing out the back, he asked her to come over to the makeup department where Denise was waiting to do her makeup. He was a very fast walker and had a very large shop.

He introduced Jane to Denise who asked her to sit down in the chair and began studying her face as she reached for one jar then another and a large brush as though she were brushing off flies. Finally Denise swirled the chair around and stepped back to look at her handiwork. She nodded, highly satisfied. She had accomplished the unbelievable--a real work of art. She called Henri over who was smiling and nodding that he approved.

Jane had avoided looking at her reflection in the mirror. She was scared; so much was riding on this. Henri and Denise said in unison that they had some outfits brought over for her to try on as they led her to an area with a dressing room. They suggested she first try on the red cashmere suit with the matching red silk blouse. Denise put the outfit in the dressing room and closed the curtain.

Jane looked stunning as she walked out of the dressing room. Henri and Denise looked at the total picture and were very pleased.

Henri said, "Part of the problem was that you've been wearing clothes that were too big. They hid your slender figure." The hair style Henri created was magnificent. Her auburn hair shone and the makeup Denise created made Jane's large dark eyes shine. It was quite a transformation, she looked ravishing. It was all she wanted and wondered if she still had a chance or was it too late.

She tried on the rest of the dresses, suits, evening dresses, sport clothes, and decided she wanted them all. They loved seeing her model them and insisted that she let them take her picture. They wanted to frame and hang it up in the reception area.

Jane couldn't wait for Cliff to see her. She kept contemplating the look on his face. Would he be transfixed, immediately gather her up in his arms, and tell her how much she meant to him?

It was all too exhilarating. She had all these mental pictures, then suddenly breaking into her train of thought the cab driver said, "Here we are lady," and she looked up to see they were in front of the office building.

She asked the cab driver to please help carry her purchases: the clothes and shoes that looked so great on her. He carried her packages to the top floor. She was surprised that the door was locked. Why? Cliff was supposed to be working late prior to going to Stanford.

She took the key out of her purse, opened the door, turned on the lights, and paid the cab driver. She walked over to Cliff's office then to hers and saw he had scribbled a note that he was leaving for Stanford and if she had an emergency to call his cell phone, but only if it was an emergency, something she couldn't handle.

She was crushed as she tried to brush away the tears. She didn't want to cry and ruin her beautiful makeup, but what difference did it make now, Cliff wasn't around. He was the only reason she was at the beauty shop all day and spent all that money.

CHAPTER THIRTEEN

Cliff left that night. He decided not to wait. He wanted to spend time with Claudette prior to her graduation. He phoned to tell her that he was on his way. She was pleased that he was coming earlier than planned and offered to meet him at the airport.

He was excited as he sat on the plane, fingering the corsage box, hoping it would still be fresh for her to wear on her big day. He had planned everything down to the clothes he packed. Grace didn't seem at all upset, in fact she told him to have a good time and that she would take care of everything on the home front. She had his cell phone number if she really needed him but felt that everything would be fine as she hugged and kissed him.

Cliff was a wonderful son-in-law. They had loved him from the first time Julia brought him home and Grace was glad that they had such a good relationship because it afforded her the opportunity to live here and see her grandchildren whenever she wanted to. She couldn't comprehend why more families couldn't get along.

The pilot announced that they had reached their destination and Cliff should fasten his seat belt. He looked out the window to see if he could catch a glimpse of Claudette as the plane taxied in; then he saw her waving. She was jumping up and down while waving her arms. She was so adorable, and if he ever had any doubts about how he felt about her, they all evaporated.

"She was the one," Cliff said to himself as he watched her excitedly waiting for the plane to land. Her dark hair with the natural reddish streaks was accented by the sunlight while a soft breeze was blowing in several directions. He was captivated by her large expressive violet eyes with the longest eye lashes he had ever seen. Her skin was soft and clear highlighted by soft accents of color at her cheek bones and lips. Oh! Her lips, they were perfectly shaped, he couldn't wait to kiss them.

The cabin door opened and Claudette, in all her exuberance, ran up into the plane. He felt as though his world was perfect as she literally fell into his arms. They stood gazing into each other's eyes for a long time, holding each other, and then he kissed her. It was everything as he knew it would be. He wanted to pick her up, get back in the plane, and fly off to a deserted island--just the two of them.

They walked over to where she had parked her car, handed him the keys, asked if he was hungry, and proceeded to tell him about a really charming restaurant with a spectacular view of the Pacific Ocean. "It's only a thirty-minute drive," she said. He guessed that she had planned for them to go there; they were on their way with her giving directions.

Cliff was driving with his arm around her even though somewhat encumbered by the seat belt. He just couldn't get enough of her. She was so beautiful, the sweetest thing he had ever seen, and he wanted to believe she was all his. What a beautiful thought!

The view of the Pacific Ocean was breathtaking almost as beautiful as Claudette sitting next to him with her head on his shoulder. She pointed out where they should turn into the restaurant parking lot. It was charming from the outside and the inside offered so much with a waterfall and aquariums filled with fish of all sizes and colors. It was magical.

It didn't matter what they ate, they only had eyes for each other, and food was secondary. It was a quiet, serene atmosphere as they sat drinking in each other. They were oblivious as to how long they had been in the restaurant until the waitress came over and announced that they would be closing soon and wondered if they would like to order dessert.

The waitress realizing that they weren't comprehending what she was saying because they were so much into each other decided to bring over a dessert tray and let them make their own selections.

Cliff noticed once again as he was holding her hand that she had very small delicate hands and wrists. He asked, "Have you ever done any hand modeling? You have such lovely hands and slender fingers. It must be difficult to purchase a bracelet or ring."

She said. "I do have difficulty finding a bracelet that fits. They are usually too big and slide off. Rings can also present a problem, and it's interesting because my ring size is the same as my shoe size--five. Isn't that amazing? I also have difficulty finding shoes because they don't seem to make many in my size."

It was entrancing sitting with her, lost in their own inimitable world, oblivious to all around them. All they could think of was each other, enraptured.

Suddenly, they were brought back to reality when they saw the dessert tray delicacies. Cliff asked Claudette which one she would like. She suggested taking two different ones, cut them in half, that way they can have the pleasure of eating two different selections.

Claudette chose the chocolate mousse, she loved chocolate, Cliff decided on the chocolate dipped strawberry because he thought Claudette would enjoy it. They were very appreciative and thanked the waitress who paused to fill their coffee cups.

They reluctantly got up and went outside their arms entwined around each other. It was all so magical. Claudette suggested that they walk toward the water and sit down on one of the benches. They weren't anxious to leave just yet. They just wanted to be together.

Finally, Cliff hesitantly suggested that they drive back after all tomorrow is a very important day and she would want to get a good night's sleep.

They slowly drove back. Cliff had left in such a hurry that he didn't make reservations. He needed to find a hotel and expressed that to Claudette. She quickly answered that it wasn't necessary because they had rooms especially for guests who would be coming for the graduation exercises. Rooms were available in her dorm; she had the foresight to reserve one for him, and suggested they drive over so he could get settled.

Cliff knew the history of Stanford University. It was the vision of Leland Stanford. It meant a great deal to him and his wife Jane. It was a beautiful campus about one hour south of San Francisco, encompassing over eight thousand acres of open space maintained for the students' enjoyment.

The next morning Cliff arose excited, he felt this was in essence the first day of the rest of his life. He shaved, showered, and took his suit out of the closet. He put on a freshly starched white long sleeve shirt with French cuffs, his dark blue suit that was hand made by a London tailor, burgundy tie, and made-to-order impeccably shined shoes.

He picked up his cell phone and called Claudette who answered on the first ring. He asked if she wanted to meet him in the dorm lobby, she responded positively. He put a handkerchief that matched his tie in his suit breast pocket, picked up his wallet, and was ready to meet his...and then caught himself, he almost said "bride" that was the way he was beginning to think of her.

He was standing in the lobby when Claudette came in. She looked stunning, in a pink two-piece outfit with a swirling skirt and full billowing sleeves that accented his corsage. A single strand pearl choker encircled her swan like neck and dangling pearl earrings completed the picture. What a doll! Her skin was soft, her hair flowing down around her shoulders. He noted the tastefully matching high heel shoes with small bows.

Cliff felt proud escorting Claudette, what a happy day! He helped her into her cap and gown. She was a vision especially after changing to black heels. He couldn't wait for the ceremony, the parties, and for them to be on their way back to San Diego.

"I'll be up front watching the most beautiful young woman handed her degree, Dr. Claudette," Cliff said smiling broadly.

He left her in the line and walked in to find a seat. An usher came up and asked if he could assist. Cliff said that he was looking for a seat. The usher asked his name, then said, "Mr. Cliff Camden, there is a special seat reserved for you in the front row."

Cliff was startled and found himself repeating what the usher had said, "A special seat reserved for me, are you sure? Why?" The usher assured him that it was correct. Cliff was still perplexed but sat down and unzipped his camera bag. He wanted to be ready and set his camera for when the graduates would march in.

The orchestra was tuning up and started playing the renowned graduation march, "Pomp and Circumstance." Cliff was surprised when he saw Claudette at the head of the line, she smiled when she saw him, and he took her picture. They all filed in and were seated. Cliff took more photos and waited.

Cliff didn't know any of the other graduates, therefore he wasn't paying particular attention when it was announced that the graduates names would be announced in the order of their grade point average until he heard the university president say that only one candidate had a straight "A" average and he saw Claudette get up and walk forward to stand next to the university president as he announced her name, "Miss Claudette Dubois, you have excelled in all your classes and the moot court."

She hadn't told him. Cliff was astounded, very proud, and couldn't help himself, he stood up, loudly applauded, and Claudette beamed.

The president continued, "Ladies and gentlemen, I, hereby, present your valedictorian, Miss Claudette Dubois."

Claudette walked to the podium, started speaking as everyone listened in awe as she spoke.   Her speech was magnificent, her voice crystal clear as she perfectly enunciated each word.   Her speech was phenomenal and she received a standing ovation.

The college president stepped forward and said, "I, on behalf of our faculty congratulate you, want you to know how proud we are, hereby hand you your diploma and confer upon you the title, Dr. of Jurisprudence." He shook her hand and said, "Congratulations Dr. Dubois."

Cliff couldn't be prouder and felt sad that her parents didn't attend to see their daughter highly honored; therefore, in addition to taking still photos, he also recorded the proceedings on video tape.   He didn't want them to miss out on such an auspicious occasion--their daughter's law school graduation.

Cliff waited for the graduates to "march" out.   He walked toward Claudette who was impatiently waiting for him as evidenced by her expression and smile.   He quickly walked toward her and before they knew it, they were in each other arms. He was passionately kissing her amid   congratulations all around.

Cliff reached into his pocket, took out a small box as he guided her toward a bench, and suggested that they sit down for a few moments.   She looked at him rather quizzically because she was anxious for them to attend the parties.   He had his arm around her and drew her closer to him as he handed her the beautifully wrapped gold foil box.

She looked at it in amazement.   She didn't expect anything. He wanted to give her a gift to commemorate this very special day. She began taking off the ribbon as she carefully unwrapped it. She looked up at him as she took off the box cover and removed the cotton to reveal the most beautifully engraved gold locket she had ever seen. Tears were welling up in her eyes as she reached up, putting her hand behind Cliff's neck to bring his head down as she looked into his soft smoldering hazel eyes to tell him how much the gift meant to her.

He smiled, put his hand under her chin, kissed her, and asked if she would like him to put it on. Her eyes were filled with tears that were spilling down her cheeks. She carefully took the locket out of the box when Cliff suggested that she look on the back. He had it engraved, "Forever My Love." Claudette read the inscription that made the tears flow even faster down her checks.

Cliff enjoyed looking at her and smiled as he took out his handkerchief to wipe away her tears. He suggested that she open the locket and when she did the tears flowed even more profusely as she opened it and saw his picture on the left and hers on the right. She sat looking at it transfixed. A gift she would forever treasure. She held up her soft shoulder-length raven hair as he fastened the clasp. It looked beautiful nestled between her cleavage.

Claudette told Cliff about the number of parties she hoped he would want to attend. Secretly, she wanted to show him off. He was a very handsome man and looked very dashing in his dark blue suit, white shirt with the gold cuff links, and burgundy tie. His blondish red hair was perfectly combed, and when he looked at her with those dreamy hazel eyes, she melted. She loved to hear him talk, his voice was soft, dreamy, and she could listen to him talk for hours.

Cliff didn't know where the parties were being held and asked Claudette whether they should drive or walk. "All the parties are being held on campus, therefore we'll walk," she said.

"I like that, it's a beautiful night, there's a full moon--a perfect night to commemorate your special day," Cliff said.

First, they walked side-by-side, then holding hands, and by the time they arrived at the first party, their arms were entwined around each other. She introduced him and he enjoyed meeting her friends.

It was a lively group, everyone seemingly talking at once while standing around the punch bowl, toasting each other. The fact that they were finally finished--they were free, they had graduated and now they could party and have fun prior to thinking about taking the bar and fulfilling their lifelong dream about being an attorney. Shouts of happiness emanated throughout the university.

They walked around the campus, attending parties, having fun together. She didn't know she could feel this good. Just being near him sent her mind on a wild ride and her heart pounding. It was a great feeling! She felt a sense of pride introducing him and seeing how envious the other graduates were.

It was a whirlwind of parties, all very festive whether they were being held inside or outside. The couple found themselves in a garden setting with colored lanterns, candles, and brightly colored balloons creating a fantastic ambiance. Cliff was enjoying them all because he was with Claudette; she was a fabulous date whether they were laughing or joking at the punch bowl or on the dance floor. She was a superb dancer, fitting so beautifully into his arms. He loved whirling her around the floor.

She introduced him to faculty members, and to his surprise he knew a number of the professors who were pleased to learn that he had just opened a branch of his law firm in San Diego. They were interested and asked about positions for Stanford law graduates?

Claudette was a lot of fun. He loved her laugh. They were having a good time but he really wanted some alone time with her and was beginning to wonder how many more parties they would be attending.

Claudette, looking up at him with those exquisitely beautiful violet eyes and seemingly reading his thought, asked if he was ready to leave. Cliff was thrilled as her held her close under the stars. The full moon shone brightly making the night full of magic. He told her again how proud he was and what a pleasure it was meeting her friends, the college president, and members of the faculty. He knew that Stanford had an excellent reputation and the faculty was of the highest caliber, but they were more personable than he had expected.

It had been an absolutely perfect day. They said their good-byes and waved to the party revelers as they walked away their arms around each other, walking so close together that a ruler couldn't be slid between them.

It couldn't have been better if she had written the script for her memorable graduation day. After all Cliff was sweet, agreeing to attend all those parties, and surprising her with the engraved locket with their photographs. It was a perfect accent to her special day.

CHAPTER FOURTEEN

Now, Cliff's attention was being directed toward planning their trip back to San Diego and wondered if Claudette had any suggestions or had made any plans.

She seemed to know what he was thinking and said, "I have been collecting maps and checking a variety of routes for a driving trip via a picturesque coastal route. A beautiful drive closely parallels the Pacific Ocean. Are you interested in our taking that route?"

Cliff said a resounding, "Yes! That sounds wonderful. We both love the ocean, therefore taking a highway that is close enough for us to see the waves, watch a sunrise or sunset, and stop for a walk, swim, or picnic on the beach sounds ideal."

Claudette invited him into her room where she showed him the multitude of maps and tour books she had collected and suggested that taking Highway 101 for three miles, then Highway 85 south, then switch over to Highway 17 south which joins California State Highway 1. She further explained that Highway 1 is very picturesque.

"We will be able to stop at Moro Bay, Carmel, and Monterey where there are restaurants specializing in superb sea food dishes."

Cliff liked her suggestions and jokingly said, "I appoint you the navigator since you have all the maps and tour books. It will be a lot of fun!"

The next step was to decide whether they should leave tonight or in the morning. Cliff suggested they leave tomorrow morning as they will feel refreshed after a good night's sleep. Claudette agreed and he offered to help her pack.

Cliff called Jane to ask if any issues needed his attention. She said that everything was under control and wondered when he would be returning. He said that he was on his way and would keep her appraised of his expected date of arrival.

Next, he called his law partner in Manhattan and then Grace. He needed to check on his children.

Grace told him that everything was running smoothly. Nancy was fantastic with the children; Monique was happily cooking and also great with the little ones. Many times they all sat at the kitchen table and enjoyed Monique's good humor and food. The Svensens were also a great addition to the household. Alan checked in regularly which they all appreciated. Grace did not expect any difficulties and told him to have a good time, enjoy himself.

The next morning, the car was loaded with all Claudette's luggage, Cliff's suitcase, cameras, and an ice chest filled with cold drinks. They were ready to roll. Cliff opened the door for Claudette attired in a cute pair of white fitted sporty shorts and matching scoop-neck sleeveless top that showed off her great figure and long legs.

She got in with an armful of the navigational maps and tour books. He fastened her seat belt, kissed her, closed her door, walked around to the driver's side of the car, opened the door, seated himself, fastened his seat belt, switched on the ignition, turned on the radio, and they were off on their "safari."

Cliff looked at her smiling face as she was busily arranging her side of the car, finding a place for their water bottle, hand sanitizer, c.d.'s, tapes, and the multitude of maps she had to have.

"It's always more fun when you have lots of maps and tour books," Claudette said as Cliff glanced over at her smiling at how beautifully adorable she looked in what he called "her nest," in the most loving way.

They hadn't gone one mile when she had maps spread out all over her lap.   They were singing as they sped down the highway to the first stop on their journey.

The ocean was as beautiful as they anticipated.   They stopped along the way to sit on the sand, take a run, have a picnic, and swim. Claudette did a great job selecting restaurants, motels, and a bed and breakfast along their route.

They visited museums, rented a motor boat, stopped at a few art galleries, and rented a tandem bicycle. It was going to be an even greater "trip" than Cliff had anticipated.   It was enjoyable being with her. They had the same taste in foods, art, politics, and it seemed just everything. She was so well-versed that they talked on a number of subjects from astronomy to botany, to oceanography, to space, music to sports, it was unbelievable. She had a great mind and seemed constantly willing to learn as much as he.

They didn't want the trip to end.   They were having a wonderful time. It was glorious. When they realized they had passed Los Angeles and were on their way to Orange County, the home of Disneyland, she suggested they stop and meet Mickey, Minnie, Donald, and Goofy. She directed Cliff where to turn off the freeway and soon they were enjoying the rides and exhibits.

Then they were back on the road heading to Oceanside, the first city in San Diego County; their trip was ending much too quickly. Cliff wanted it extend but had no idea how to do that.

Claudette was still pouring over the maps, checking to see if there was anything special they might want to stop and see, but when she looked up through the windshield and saw they had passed a La Jolla off-ramp, she knew it would be a short time before they were home.

They were both disappointed their trip was ending. She wondered what next. She knew she would have to spend long arduous hours studying for the bar, but what about the locket. What did it mean? So many unanswered questions, she was probably being too impatient.

He asked if she would like to stop first at his home. He had met her on the beach; she always came to his hotel suite. He suddenly realized he didn't know where she lived or where her parents lived--so many unknowns. He was not the kind of man to ask a multitude of questions unless it was in the course of his profession as an attorney.

"I think it might be better if you drop me at my apartment. I really need to freshen up," she said as she gave him her address. She lived near the beach. As they turned down her street, the ocean was in full view complimented by the blue sky, puffy white clouds, and a bright yellow sun slowly sinking below the horizon.

He saw a quaint beach-type cottage with blue awnings and a few blooming flowers as he pulled into the driveway. He unbuckled his seat belt, went around opened her door, and helped her out. She had maps all over her lap and some had "spilled" on to the floor. He was picking up her map collection when she suddenly reached up and stroked his face. They gazed into each other eyes, hers were like sparkling sapphires that transported him to a state of ecstasy he had never before known.

He unbuckled her seat belt, helped her up, and brought her close to him; she felt good as he wrapped his arms around her. He loved the way she always put her hand behind his neck, it felt so warm and soft. No one had ever done that before. It helped to create a very intense feeling that he found enjoyable as it encircled his total being.

It was as though they had been transported, were floating in free space, another state of ecstasy, until they heard a voice say, "Hi, Claudette. We've missed you, how was your graduation? Do we now call you, Madame Attorney?" she asked laughing at her own joke.

It took a moment for Claudette to catch her breath as she turned in the direction of the voice. "Hi Clarisse, we just got back from Stanford." She realized that momentarily she forgot her manners to introduce Cliff.

"Clarisse is one of my four roommates," Claudette explained.

Clarisse offered to help carry her luggage, Cliff thanked her but said that he could handle it and she waved as she walked away saying that she had to shop for groceries--nothing in the refrigerator. They smiled and waved back.

Cliff and Claudette busied themselves with getting her luggage out of the car. She walked ahead and opened the door. Soon everything was out of the car with the exception of his cameras and suitcase.

He wanted to know if she wanted him to wait while she showered and changed but at that moment the phone rang. It was her father. She paused and signaled to Cliff to take her car and would call him later. He blew her a kiss and reluctantly walked out the door.

He was undecided as to whether he should check in at his law office or go home and decided on the latter. The office could wait until tomorrow. Jane had not called, meaning that everything was obviously running smoothly. She was extremely competent and he felt that she would have contacted him if a client, issue, or case needed his attention.

Cliff was experiencing a tremendous let down. He felt as though someone had punctured his balloon. It had been a spectacular two weeks with Claudette and took every bit of strength when he had to leave because her father called. Cliff understood how important it was for her to speak with her father which was not even a point of contention.

Claudette had become very important to him. She was the embodiment of everything he could ever want. She was so beautiful both inside and out from the top of her head down to her tiny toes. Her petite figure accented by her tiny waist which is what every woman considers ideal and wants.

He was trying to keep his mind on his driving but kept drifting back to the events of the last two weeks as he remembered her beautiful soft dark hair that cascaded down to her shoulders and the way that he could get lost in her eyes that sparkled like the bluest sapphires he had ever seen. He couldn't believe the way she could mesmerize him unwittingly, totally enveloping him. It was a magic that he couldn't explain and really didn't want to. She was that special someone that everyone looks for but few ever find.

The sound of a passerby's horn brought him back to the present and he realized that he better keep his mind on the road and not drift off to thoughts of Claudette. He knew he should concentrate more on his driving and put all thoughts of her aside.

He suddenly was in front of his gate. He turned into the winding driveway and saw the garden was a blaze of color. The flowers were beautiful and the grounds meticulously maintained. Mr. Svensen was doing a terrific job. Cliff wanted to be sure to thank him and give him a bonus. He decided to have Miss Monique make a picnic lunch. He wanted to sit on a blanket under the big shade tree with Ra Ra and Jacques. It would be a great place to play ball with them and hoped that Gordon and Grace would have time to join them. His children needed time with their father.

The carved door was looming before him; he stopped the car, opened the door, grabbed his cameras, suitcase, and ran. He couldn't wait to see everyone. Suddenly, the massive door opened. They witnessed his arrival and couldn't wait to see and hug him. They were showering him with hugs, kisses, and everyone speaking at once.

Grace said, "Let's go into the kitchen. Miss Monique made some fresh cookies in honor of your arrival." He didn't realize how much he had missed his home even though they hadn't lived in the house that long.

Miss Monique ran over to give him a hug. She was such a special person and he was thankful she agreed to be a member of his household. She took his face in her hands and told him how much he had been missed, and they were all glad he was back home. Then she picked up one of her freshly baked cookies, put it in his mouth, and they both laughed.

They all sat down at the table with Ra Ra on one knee and Jacques on the other. They were both talking to him at once. Ra Ra put a hand on his cheek and turned his head toward her. She wanted to be sure he was listening to every word she excitedly had to say. And, then Jacques, having seen what his sister did to get her father's attention, took his small hand, put it on his father's cheek to turn his daddy to look directly at his son who had so much to tell him. It was adorable. Grace and Gordon were smiling, enjoying the family picture--all of them together.

Mr. and Mrs. Svensen came in and were welcomed. Cliff was listening to all the happy chatter. It was wonderful. He told Mr. Svensen what a beautiful job he had done maintaining and planting the grounds. "I was hoping we could plant more fruit trees. We all enjoy eating fruit and picking our own would be fun, especially for the children. Also, let's plant some nut trees: an almond, walnut, and pecan. It would also be fun to have a mini vineyard: concord, red, and green grapes. Perhaps, you could check with a nursery to purchase large fruit trees. I don't want to wait years for them to bear fruit," Cliff said.

Mr. Svensen said that he was delighted, anxious to get started on the project, and would check in the morning about availability.

"Mrs. Svensen," Cliff said, "You've done a magnificent job on the house, and Miss Monique you are the queen of the culinary arts." They all laughed as Nancy walked in. She had been on some errands, wanted him to know how much he had been missed, and was glad he was back.

Cliff thanked her for taking such good care of his children and invited her to join the group. Now his household was complete with loving, caring people--a very homogenous group. He was indeed a blessed man.

They sat for hours in the homey, warm, and inviting kitchen painted in soft shades of yellows with a touch of orange reacting with the sunlight. Miss Monique arranged the pots and pans on a hanging rack and knick knacks on the small corner shelves, a focal point. Eyes were directed to that corner and then would move left and right.

Miss Monique was very organized, everything was conveniently arranged. Other shelves were equally set-up with attractiveness being her goal.

Grace pointed to the shelf with tea pots and matching tea cups, saucers, and plates.

Mr. Svensen installed a greenhouse window with several glass shelves. It was a great place to grow herbs, garlic, and spices that added to the ambiance.

Miss Monique started serving dinner. She thought a typical American hamburger with French fries, and a large green tossed salad with tomatoes, garlic, onion, broccoli, celery, cucumber, and croutons would be enjoyed by all. She also made a fresh pot of coffee, tea, and poured glasses of milk for the children. For dessert, she made a luscious chocolate cake with mounds of chocolate icing which she knew would delight everyone.

It was the culmination of a wonderful day. He thanked Miss Monique and she hugged him. She was a very warm motherly type person who loved having everybody come into "her" kitchen. He suggested they all take a walk around the grounds; it would be good to get some exercise after that wonderful meal.

Ra Ra and Jacques were thrilled that their daddy was home. Ra Ra held one of his hands and Jacques the other, but then Jacques wanted to ride piggyback and off they went.

Grace was looking at Cliff. How well-rested he looked. She was interested in hearing all about his trip to Stanford, the graduation ceremonies, and the reason he went. She hoped that in a few moments he would volunteer the information. She waited as they casually walked, then he suggested they sit down as they approached the area that she decided would be ideal for a playground, and had ordered a slide, swings, sand box, merry-go-round, and monkey bars. Mr. Svensen offered to install the equipment.

Cliff slid Jacques off his shoulders and gently urged his children to go play, and as they ran the short distance, he looked at Grace and proceeded to tell her about the events of the previous two weeks.

She listened very intently as he talked about the Stanford law school graduation ceremony, the numerous parties, and then mentioned Claudette. He was being very careful about how he phrased the information. He observed Grace's keen interest by her demeanor and suddenly sitting up much straighter, Cliff continued, "She is a very special young woman, graduated summa cum laude, and was valedictorian."

"We met the first day I took the children to the beach. Ra Ra was making a sand castle. Claudette was walking by and stopped to admire the child's creativity when Ra Ra asked for her help. She gave Claudette a pail to get her more water. Ra Ra never had enough water.

"When I walked over the two of them were busily making the sand castle. Jacques and I joined in the fun. We had dinner with the children a few times in my hotel suite. After I engaged Nancy, we took long walks on the beach and had coffee at the outdoor cafes on the boardwalk. She is very beautiful and well-read.

"Claudette was going back to Stanford to finish her last semester and graduate with a law degree. We hadn't seen each other because I was busy setting up my law offices. I called and she invited me to attend her graduation. I flew up in the company jet. It was so good to see her again,"

"Grace, I loved Julia with all my heart. She was special and I will always love her, but she isn't here. I didn't plan to fall in love with Claudette, it just happened. I don't want to hurt you or Gordon. I hope you don't think badly of me."

Before he could continue, Grace reached out and touched his hands that were folded in his lap and he looked at her. She was smiling and said, "I am happy for you." She was certain since he felt strongly, it was right. Tears started filling his eyes and flowed down his cheeks. Grace put her arms around him and wiped away his tears with a handkerchief she took from her sweater pocket.

"It's all right Cliff, I really understand. You don't have to feel uncomfortable because you fell in love, it's beautiful, and I am happy for you. Gordon and I sort of suspected and are pleased," she said.

Cliff, choking back his tears, said that he wanted her to know, it wouldn't change anything between them. He wanted them to stay and live in the cottage. Grace said, "Shh! Shh! It's all right, we know that. We know you and the kind of man you are, we admire you. You've had a tragedy, a very difficult experience, and have come through it admirably. We love you and always will. We know you will make the right decision, and if we can be of help, Gordon and I are here for you, nothing will change. You have made a wonderful home here and today was just perfect, all of us in the kitchen eating and talking. It's a rare togetherness that most wish for but never attain."

Cliff felt blessed, he had a wonderful family, and here was a unique woman, his beloved understanding mother-in-law, with whom he could confide without any reservations or recriminations. He wanted her to know that she and Gordon would always be an integral part of his family. He and his kids needed her. He loved, appreciated, and treasured her friendship.

They exchanged a few more pleasantries, hugged, and got up to join the others. It was a beautiful night. The stars were shining brightly, and even though Cliff didn't believe in such things, it was a good omen.

Later that night, Cliff called Claudette who sounded refreshed, made plans to meet, and have dinner together.

The next morning, Cliff was up bright and early. He wanted to get down to his law office, check his calendar, confer with his law partners, check with his office manager, and Jane who still wasn't at her desk which surprised him. He remembered she used to be at her desk at dawn and here it was already 11:00 and she still had not come in. He called for another secretary to come in and gave her a list of phone calls, appointments to schedule, and a stack of papers to be copied.

Jane finally came in at 12:30 looking disheveled. Cliff couldn't believe what he saw and before he could stop himself said, "What happened to you?" His first thought was she had been in an accident and then wondered if she were drunk. She had always been a meticulous dresser, totally well groomed.

He was waiting for her to speak, but she didn't. She just stood transfixed; her face flushed, and eyes red. Finally, he got up and went over to her, and wondered when she had last bathed. "What's wrong?" he asked keeping his voice soft. She just stared past him. He said as compassionately as possible, "I think you need a doctor. I can either call the paramedics or have someone take you to the hospital." She finally lifted her head a trifle, looked at him through blurred eyes, and said that she was fine. He went back to his desk, called security, and asked for a guard to come to his office, to take Jane to the emergency room to be checked out, and have the doctor on duty call him.

Cliff was dumbfounded. Jane had always been such a solid together person whom he had always admired. What could have happened to her? She had always been a very valued employee.

Hours passed, he couldn't wait any longer. He called the hospital emergency room and asked to speak with the attending physician on duty.

Dr. Matlock came to the phone; Cliff introduced himself and stated that he was inquiring about Jane Simms prognosis. The doctor was hesitant until Cliff provided information about his relationship to the patient.

Miss Simms is suffering from depression. She seems to be having difficulty coping with a set of circumstances. I am recommending that she be held overnight for observation and during that time a psychologist will do a work-up.

Cliff agreed to the terms and said that he would try to contact her mother who lived in another state. Cliff contacted Jane's mother who said she would let him know her arrival date. He was glad she was coming and made every effort not to answer any questions about how Jane looked.

When Jane's mother arrived, he immediately took her to the hospital and they both went in to see Jane's doctor who was very optimistic. He said that Jane had a shock that she didn't know how to handle but he felt with a few therapy sessions and some mild medication; she would be able to resume her life.

Mrs. Simms asked what kind of shock as she looked at the doctor with sorrowful eyes filling with tears, the doctor lowered his head avoiding her gaze as he answered her.

Jane knew you were coming and said that I should answer your questions honestly without breaking any confidences. He said that Jane was madly in love and hoped she had a chance with the man in question, but it turned out he wasn't interested in her. She went all out with a total makeover including a new wardrobe but he never saw the new her, which caused her mild depression. She will be all right and seems to have accepted that he's not interested in her and she should look elsewhere. Jane can go home today and go back to work which will probably be best.

Cliff drove them to Jane's apartment and said, "Jane, come back to the office when you are ready. You are missed."

CHAPTER FIFTEEN

Cliff called for Claudette. She looked ravishing in a red knit dress that accented her slender figure, red heels, and a red clutch bag, her raven hair falling freely in soft curls on her shoulders, and her violet eyes sparkling like two sapphires. She got into his convertible and was thrilled as he reached over, brought her close, and kissed her passionately. Then reluctantly he put his hands back on the steering wheel and drove to the restaurant he had chosen.

They had a superb dinner: a tossed green salad, filet mignon, baked potato, asparagus, coffee, and were now enjoying a glass of champagne. He really wanted to toast their future but thought it might be premature. At that moment the band started playing and he asked her to dance. They hadn't danced since her graduation, far too long ago even though it had only been a few weeks. It was wonderful holding her in his arms. They seemed to have become one as they glided across the dance floor.

He asked if she wanted anything from the dessert cart, he knew she loved chocolate, and offered to order a chocolate delicacy. He reached across the table and they held hands as he suggested they walk on the beach.

The night was full of stars with a full moon shining down on them as they took off their shoes and walked along the water's edge. He took off his jacket, and they sat down on the sand. It was an absolutely perfect warm night as he carefully reached out for her, pulling her close wrapping his arms around her, and kissed her with the greatest passion he had ever felt. It was magical. They sat for hours under the moonlit sky enjoying the pleasure and closeness of each other.

"I am going to be leaving in a few days to see a client in New York, who has been in ill health. I have been taking care of his affairs. He wants me to come because unfortunately he needs to have peace of mind--everything in order for his family," Cliff said.

Claudette was disappointed but realized it was something he had to do. She said, "I will miss you, but I totally understand."

"I want to do something before leaving, introduce you to my family, will you?" Cliff asked.

"Of course, I'd love to meet your family. You've told me so much about them. Just let me know the day and time." Claudette said.

"Perhaps tomorrow night for dinner, but first I would like us to go swimming in the afternoon. Will you go?"

Smiling she said, "There is something you don't know about me. It'll make you laugh. . Yes, I love the beach, but don't go into the water. I don't know how to swim."

"Then I will teach you. It will be fun," He said.

She was apprehensive but enthusiastic.

The next day he went to the office and was surprised to see Jane at her desk, looking more like herself. She was wearing a beige two-piece suit and was totally well-groomed. He found himself looking more closely and saw that she looked more attractive. What had she done to herself and her suit was different than what she had previously worn. It was as though she somehow had herself transformed.

She was as efficient as ever, everything went smoothly. He told her about the business trip to see Mr. Hartley in New York and asked her to get everything ready pertaining to him.

"I will want to review the entire file."

Later that afternoon as promised, he called Claudette and made a date to pick her up to go swimming. It would be fun teaching her to swim. He called a local tire store asking to purchase two large classical inner tubes of yesteryear.

When he arrived, they asked why he wanted them. Obviously, they weren't for his car.

"No," he said, "I am going to teach my girl friend how to swim in the ocean." They were still perplexed.

He picked up Claudette who looked as lovely as ever wearing a pastel pink beach jacket, straw hat with one pink poppy, and carrying a picnic basket, she looked so young, he was a lucky guy.

They drove the short distance to the beach, and he took out the inner tubes.

"What are you going to do with those?" she asked.

"You are going to put one around your waist and I am going to put one around mine and I'm going to teach you how to swim," he said.

"Oh no, you're not," she said emphatically.

"Come on," he said, let's find a nice spot on the sand." She followed him having frightful thoughts about those inner tubes. He put down the blanket and she took off her beach jacket, she had a fabulous figure. The pink bikini fit her perfectly in all the right places. She was a vision.

He carried the inner tubes to the beach as she reluctantly followed. He handed her one and asked her to put her head through the donut opening. She backed off unwilling but did offer a suggestion. "Let's put the inner tube between us, stretch out our arms, and hold hands." He agreed and they floated. She was really beginning to enjoy herself, and eventually did "wear" the inner tube.

She kept asking him if he had seen any jelly fish. He said that he hadn't and wondered why she asked. She told about the time one had bitten her big toe. She couldn't even get her sandal on. It was so badly swollen that the life guard insisted on her soaking it and told her to get a tetanus shot. What a nightmare that was! She had to go home and soak it for several days. One man was bitten and his arm swelled up like a balloon.

He could tell she was scared and tried to reassure her. I don't see any jelly fish and he continued with her swimming lesson.

She was beginning to enjoy the whole experience of bouncing up and down on the waves and then going out further holding on to the inner tube and riding the waves into shore. She couldn't believe how much fun she was having. She got so brave and trusted Cliff so much that she let him toss her into the waves and they rode them in together. She had never felt such exhilaration. It was fabulous. "I'm really enjoying this," she said as she reached out to him and he pulled her toward him as she felt the waves gently rush past them.

She never thought she would feel brave enough to enjoy playing in the ocean. Her past encounter with the ocean had been so frightening that she became very apprehensive and never felt as though she would have fun swimming and jumping the waves. But, Cliff was so kind and gentle. He didn't rush or pressure her, their intense love for each other, and the fact that she trusted him implicitly gave her the courage.

He said, "Let me throw you into the next wave."

She wanted to but was still somewhat reluctant. He asked her several times and assured her that he would be beside her.

Claudette still had some misgivings, but finally acquiesced, and it felt good riding the wave that propelled her toward shore with Cliff right beside her as he promised. She kept saying over and over, "Let's do it again, let's do it again."

They did, and then sat on the sand entwined in each other's arms, watching a glorious sunset.

That night he told Gordon and Grace he needed to see an ill client in New York. Gordon said, "That's a coincidence, there's a business meeting, I am obligated to attend on the east coast. I'll be flying my plane."

Grace, who was listening intently, suggested they go together. It had been awhile since they had flown together and Cliff liked flying as Gordon's co-pilot. "I'll file a flight plan," Gordon said. They talked more about the flight as Cliff broached another subject.

At breakfast, Cliff mentioned that he had invited Claudette for dinner and hoped it wouldn't be an inconvenience.

Grace said, "Yes, of course, it's all right. We are anxious to meet her. I will help Miss Monique make a delicious dinner." Just then Nancy came in with the children. Ra Ra rushed over and put her arms around her daddy's neck. Jacques who mimicked his sister, pushed in to get his share of hugs and kisses.

Cliff was a very thoughtful and caring father. He loved his children and considered himself lucky. His home was filled to the brim with love and devotion. Gordon and Grace were a tremendous asset and with Miss Monique and the Svensens life was idyllic.

They enjoyed a hearty breakfast of orange juice, bacon, sausage, eggs, and coffee, while the children had a bowl of oatmeal and a glass of milk. Jacques was making great strides in learning how to use a spoon, and in between bites, he would waive his spoon around like an orchestra conductor while making gurgling sounds.

They all laughed. It was something seeing him eat oatmeal but more importantly the cereal that missed his mouth was spread all over his chubby cheeks that everyone liked to squeeze. He was so cute that Grace couldn't resist and suddenly reached over, picked him up, and put him on her lap spoon and all.

Cliff thoroughly enjoyed meal time with his family, but the clock was ticking and he needed to leave for his law office. He stood up, put his napkin on the table, kissed his children and Grace, pressed his hand on Gordon's shoulder, thanked Miss Monique and Nancy, and walked out the door, looking as though he just stepped out of a fashion magazine, wearing a navy blue suit he had made in London, white silk shirt accented by a pair of gold designer diamond cuff links, burgundy tie, and black custom made shoes.

Jane arrived early that morning beautifully attired in a red knit suit that showed off her slender figure with matching three-inch heels, a treasured heirloom gold locket around her neck, and gold earrings.

She had put a picture of Cliff and herself in the locket. It made her feel good to have him close to her heart. She just had to find a way to make him realize that she was the only one who could make him happy.

Earlier that morning she talked Henri into opening his salon early for a facial, hair style, and makeup. She just had to look her best, the salon staff complimented her, and she walked out of the shop feeling as though she was walking on air.

She passed a jewelry shop, felt compelled to look in the windows, and saw a beautiful pin she couldn't resist. She went into the store. A kindly older gentleman greeted her and thought to himself, "She is a doll. Wonder if she'd consider having dinner with me even though I am a few decades older than she?"

He smiled and inquired as to how he could assist her. Jane walked over to the window and indicated the piece of jewelry she was interested in purchasing. He carefully picked up the designer broach, walked over to the counter, put the exclusive one-of-a-kind pin, his creation, on a square of black velvet, and turned on a small antique burnished gold lamp.

Jane looked at the intricately designed gold pin encrusted with tiny pearls that would artistically accessorize her outfit. She asked if it would be all right for her to pick it up and the clerk nodded. It was exquisite. She held it up against her red suit, looked at her reflection in the mirror, and smiled. She also caught a glimpse of the clerk in the mirror. He was smiling and nodding. He couldn't help himself; she was a vision of loveliness.

Jane pinned it on her outfit, took out her wallet, and paid for her newest acquisition. She extended her hand and thanked him. He wished that he had the courage to ask her for a date and decided to forge ahead and asked if she would consider having dinner with him.

She smiled and said, "Perhaps. Why don't you give me your phone number and I'll let you know."

He picked up a business card, wrote the number of his cell and residence numbers on the back, and handed it to her. She looked at the back, then the front and read that he was the owner, Pierre Bouchard. She thanked him, smiled, and walked out feeling very elegant.

She couldn't help thinking about Pierre Bouchard, the jeweler. He was tall, handsome, very distinguished with a perfectly combed thick mane of gray hair, and the bluest eyes she had ever seen. "I really should call him. He was very nice to me and I think I would have a good time going out with him; I am in love with Cliff, although he doesn't know it. I think he will look at me differently with my new coiffeur, makeup, and smart designer clothes that accent my figure. I didn't realize I had a great figure or even looked beautiful until Henri worked his magic. I'll put the jeweler's card in my purse and as I told him, 'Perhaps.'"

She planned to arrive at the office ahead of Cliff. "I am anxious to have him see the new me." She was at her desk when Cliff came in. She waited for him to get settled at his desk and then went in on the pretext of arranging his travel arrangements.

Cliff was busy reading some briefs and making notes in the margin when he realized someone was standing in front of his desk. He looked up and saw Jane smiling. She was waiting for him to really notice her. She wanted him to stand up, come over to her, tell her how beautiful she looked, put his arms around her, and pull her toward him, but that wasn't happening. It was a day dream she was tired of reliving. Nothing she did to transform herself worked. She was slowly disintegrating and worked hard not to let her feelings show.

She kept smiling while asking if he wanted her to make reservations for his trip to New York or anything else.

He shook his head, "No," as he continued poring over the papers that needed to be updated. His Manhattan client was in poor health, the legal papers had to be keyed into the computer, copies made, affidavits, and a power of attorney prepared. He told Jane what was required and he would buzz her when he was finished.

Jane left his office feeling dejected. She didn't want anyone to see her eyes filling with tears as she crossed the threshold of her office. Her eyes were brimming with tears that were spilling onto her cheeks, and before she could wipe them, they were cascading onto her new suit that she was so proud of. She ran between the rows of filing cabinets to hide from inquisitive eyes.

She was now crying uncontrollably like a small child while dabbing unsuccessfully at the continual flow of tears. Her legs weakened and she fell to the floor. She tried in vain to get up. She felt like such a failure, and as was in keeping with her character, she had a talk with herself, put a smile on her face, was finally able to get up, brushed herself off, went to her desk, took a mirror out of her purse, looked at her eyes, took out her lipstick and applied it generously. Her lips were beautifully shaped enhanced by the bright color that matched her red suit. She then applied fresh eye shadow and mascara to lengthen her naturally long eye lashes. Next, she took out her comb and hair spray, put a smile on her face, pinched her cheeks, and was ready to go back to work.

She would not give up. Jane was determined that Cliff was the man she was going to marry. She loved him with all her heart. Her next step would be to construct a new plan to get him to the altar, but what would it be? Her thoughts were interrupted by the sound of the buzzer. It was Cliff. He obviously had finished the papers in question and needed to have them completed which meant she would have to work late.

Cliff asked Jane to call him as soon as everything was finished.

She asked if he needed to have reservations made.

He told her he had already made arrangements.

Cliff shaved, showered, dressed in a yellow blazer, white shirt, blue tie, dark slacks, and walked out the door to pick up Claudette. He arrived at Claudette's, knocked on her door, and when it opened--saw a vision.

Claudette was standing in the doorway fashionably dressed in a white ankle length sheath with a slit up the side that showed off her superlative shapely legs and white silk heels. Her violet eyes were sparkling more than usual matched by the sapphire necklace encircling her swan like neck. She tossed her soft reddish dark curls which made her tear drop sapphire earrings swing side-to-side.

Cliff was captivated by her. She looked so beautiful and he became so excited that she was his. She picked up her purse, and with her arm through Cliff's, they walked toward his sleek

Mercedes convertible. He stopped to put up the top, not wanting Claudette's hair to be messed up. He'd put the top down when he was taking her home.

She looked down on the seat and saw a corsage box. "What's this?" she asked smiling at him.

He looked at her and suggested she open it up. It was the most beautiful corsage she had ever seen; three huge purple orchids. She picked them up and pinned the flowers on the left shoulder of her dress. She was so happy that she felt giddy and moved closer to Cliff while telling him how much she loved the flowers.

He smiled down at her, pulled over to the curb, put the car in neutral, and lovingly kissed her while saying in a soft tone, "I love you very much, my darling."

Claudette wanted him to kiss her, but since they were going to his home for dinner, she wanted to look her best and was, therefore, very concerned about her hair and makeup.

Suddenly remembering that a special dinner was being prepared, Cliff reached for the gear shift and pulled away from the curb. He apologized to Claudette for the abruptness, but being a lady, she totally understood. They couldn't disappoint Miss Monique and Grace who were busily preparing a fabulously delicious dinner.

He pulled into the driveway and saw the welcoming committee standing in front of the door. Cliff opened Claudette's door, held out his hand, and she put her hand in his, as she stepped out of the car. Grace came over, hugged Claudette, and said that they were all happy she was joining them for dinner, Ra Ra got so excited when she saw her sand castle friend that she rushed over and put her arms around Claudette's legs then sweet Jacques joined them. She bent down to hug both of them. They were sweet children. She felt an arm around her and looked up to see Grace anxious to introduce her husband, Gordon. They all walked into the house.

Miss Monique came over and reminiscent of how they greet each other in her native France kissed Claudette on each cheek and she in turn returned the kisses in the same way. She had always liked the French custom of people greeting each other.

Dinner wasn't quite ready. It was suggested they sit down in the living room, however, Ra Ra wanted to show off her room. They went to Ra Ra's room wherein she told them the names of all her dolls and plush animals. She was very organized and very proud of her toys. Her small table was set for a tea party. She loved pouring "tea." In the corner was her rocker, a gift from the hotel. She sat down in her rocker, picked up her doll and showed how she loved to rock and sing to her "baby."

Jacques, not wanting to be left out, took Claudette's hand and pulled her to his room which was equally nice with large windows. He showed her his two small chairs and asked if she wanted to hold his favorite toy, "Cuddles, the goose," dressed in a red and white polka dot dress. The goose was adorable complete with wings and so soft that sometimes Jacques liked to put Cuddles on his pillow and lay his head on his beloved goose.

Miss Monique announced that dinner was ready and would everyone please come to the dining room. Mr. and Mrs. Svensen came in and were introduced to Claudette. Cliff wanted everyone in his home to feel part of the family. Mr. Svensen said that he had a gift for Claudette, a potted plant, he felt she'd enjoy. She thanked him. It was very thoughtful.

Miss Monique came in carrying a silver tray with the aperitif, small goblets of burgundy wine for the adults and grape juice for the children.

The table was beautifully set with the finest Wedgwood gold banded china, lead crystal stemware, sterling silver place settings, crystal finger bowls, and fine linen napkins that matched the tablecloth.

The focal point, the center of the table, was a round crystal bowl with a beautifully mixed floral arrangement of yellow tulips, red roses, gardenias, white cymbidium orchids, baby's breath, and assorted greenery from their garden. Mr. Svensen was doing a superlative job with the garden for which they were all pleased.

They enjoyed a traditional dinner of French cuisine, consisting of: Salade Verte a La Vinaigrette, Soupe Villageoise, Combre A La Menthe, Pommes A L'Anglise, Pegits Legumes A La Grecque, Poulet Roti, Salade Des Fruits, and for dessert Miroir Aux Kiwis served with French rolls and coffee. .

Everyone praised Miss Monique and Grace for their creative culinary skills. Ra Ra slid off her chair, walked over to Claudette, and was patting her arm.

Claudette looked down at the darling and smiled while listening. Ra Ra was taking ballet, tap, piano, and wanted to show everyone what she had learned.

They all went into the ballroom. Grace put on a record and Ra Ra started her dance routines. It was an extremely good effort and they all felt she would be great at her first recital they all planned to attend.

Cliff put on some dance music and they all started ballroom dancing. He danced with his daughter, she putting her feet on his shoes as they waltzed around the room. He saw that she was yawning and knew it was time for "night night." Nancy said that she would get the little ones ready for bed and everyone could come up and kiss them good night.

Ra Ra was in bed with her favorite doll, and Jacques with his favorite plush toy, "Cuddles the goose. They all said their good nights with hugs and kisses. The children were so tired that they fell asleep immediately.

The adults quietly went back downstairs and out onto the patio. It was a beautiful night, a full moon, and the stars shone like diamonds in a velvet sky. They decided to wish upon a star and had fun naming the various constellations: Cassiopeia's Chair, Orion, Capricorn, Big Dipper, and the Corona Borealis.

The garden was beautiful all aglow with bright lights and the pool was illuminated adding to the splendor of the garden. They were putting in a fish pond that would be fun for the children to watch and learn about goldfish, frogs, and enjoy looking at the lily pads.

Claudette found it was magical with its manicured gardens, floral displays, and colorful lighting.

Cliff, Claudette, Grace, and Gordon were sitting on period wrought iron furniture that added to the graciousness of the garden. Cliff reminded Claudette that he would be flying to the east coast in a few days on law business to see a man who had been a client of his firm for many years, and since Gordon also had business in New York, they would be going in Gordon's plane.

The flight plan had been filed and arrangements made. They didn't expect to be away for more than a week. Cliff was excited about flying again with Gordon; it had been awhile since they had flown together, Gordon as the pilot and Cliff, copilot. They made a good team and were looking forward to be flying together again.

Cliff reached for Claudette's hand and they both stood announcing that it was getting late and he should be taking Claudette home.

Miss Monique said, "Just a minute, I want Claudette to take home some of the dessert she liked so much," and rushed to the kitchen.

Claudette was smiling as she thanked and hugged everyone. It was wonderful and she was happy to have been invited and hoped she would be included in future family events.

Miss Monique rushed over carrying a cake box and handed it to Claudette who opened it and was surprised when she saw what it contained.

"This is too much," she said, as she saw it also contained other foods.

But, Miss Monique said that they had so much left over and thought Claudette would enjoy taking some home to her roommates.

Claudette was overjoyed and hugged this warm, wonderfully sweet woman who was a real treasure and added so much to the family.

On the way home Cliff said, "I didn't think we'd be ready to go home, so I made reservations at a great place on the beach in La Jolla. The surf pounds against the windows while you're dining and dancing. It also has aquarium tanks stocked with sea horses that are amazing to watch. A unique restaurant with a dance band," he said.

"I would love to go, it sounds intriguing!" she exclaimed, smiling.

It was off the beaten path and after a few wrong turns, and U-turns, they made it. She said, "We're the U-turn experts," and they both laughed. It was fun being together, they laughed, and he told jokes. They enjoyed each other's company.

It was the kind of relationship most crave but few are ever lucky enough to attain--finding that one special person who has all the characteristics, education, personality, good manners, and other attributes that comprise the basis of a sound, enduring marital experience; the kind that was in their future.

Cliff said pretending exhaustion, "We've finally arrived and look how convenient to find a parking place." He opened her door, as always the perfect gentleman, reached for her hand as she alighted, and hand-in-hand they walked toward the restaurant.

She was in awe as they walked toward the dance floor. He couldn't wait to get his arms around her and deftly glide her across the dance floor while whispering love words in her ear and balancing it out with a few tasteful jokes. They were having a wonderful time and the band was willing to play requests.

Suddenly, she said, "Shouldn't we be aware of the clock? I need to get up early; you may recall, I am taking a few classes prior to taking the bar exam." He assured her she would pass with "flying colors." She wasn't confident and felt it would help if she had a few hours sleep.

It didn't take much for the clock to "get out-of-control," her phrase for when they were together, time moved at a rapid pace, therefore, as in times like these, she constantly asked Cliff, "What time is it?" Reluctantly, he looked at his watch and knew it was time for him to take her home.

Cliff always enjoyed driving with Claudette at his side, but was downhearted when he turned down the street where she lived with her roommates. He pulled over to the curb, turned off the ignition, and turned toward her. He couldn't wait to gather her up in his arms that actually ached to hold her.

She shared his powerful desire and turned to look at him intently. He was a handsome man and she loved the fragrance of his coconut scented shampoo. He was clean shaven and had a closely cropped manly hair cut that made him desirable--her style of a man.

They sat cuddling and talked about his pending trip to the east coast. He gave her a list of phone numbers and said she should call whenever she wanted, he would be happy to hear from her regardless of the time. And, when, "I come back there is something very important that I want to ask you. I'd do it now, but I want it to be totally romantic. I love you very much and want everything to be perfect. It might sound like a cliché, but that's how I feel," he said and asked for her thoughts.

She sighed as she snuggled against his chest, her heart beating faster, and the more she kissed him, the more she wanted him. She was stroking his face and running her fingers lightly across his soft lips. She loved to look up at him when he was holding her close. It thrilled her when she looked up and saw him looking down at her, and she would close her eyes as he passionately kissed her. His kisses overwhelmed and left her breathless.

They lost track of time as they sat holding each other. Claudette looked at the star burst clock, put her shoes back on, and softly, while still stroking Cliff's face, reluctantly said, "It's getting late...but before she could finish the sentence, he put one hand on each of her cheeks and with much fervor kissed her soft red lips. The sensations racing throughout his body was spine tingling.

After kissing one more time, they reluctantly said, "Good Night" as he walked back to his car and turned on the ignition. As he was driving home, he loved remembering the hours they spent in his car talking, embracing, kissing, and then dancing in her living room. He loved looking at their reflection in the mirror above the fireplace, seeing her against his broad chest, and the beauty of the moment.

Suddenly, before he realized it, he was home. It was amazing; he never knew how he got home--it was always a miracle.

It was late when Cliff finally arrived at home and once again he wondered how he arrived safely; he didn't remember the drive. He felt as though the car drove him home automatically, smiled inwardly, and was more committed than ever to marry Claudette--he needed sleep.

He went in wondering if anyone was awake. He walked out the patio doors, past the swimming pool and children's playground to Grace and Gordon's Cottage, however all the lights were out; he turned back deciding he should also go to sleep.

CHAPTER SIXTEEN

Jane was at the law office early the next morning more committed than ever to winning Cliff's love. She loved him desperately and needed him to return her love. She contacted Henri and went over to purchase another outfit. She told him it must be a "guy getter," plus hair style, and makeup.

Henri performed more magic than ever and she looked more ravishing in a white two-piece suit with a matching shell and three-inch heels. She was astounded when she saw herself in the mirror; she couldn't believe it was really her image. All she needed now were some accessories--jewelry. She profusely thanked Henri and gave him a huge tip. He hugged her and wished her luck.

It was a beautiful day and she felt elegant as she remembered the jewelry boutique down the street. The same gentleman greeted her royally, told her how beautiful she looked, and how disappointed he was that she hadn't contacted him.

She said, "Hello Pierre," and apologized after telling him she worked in a law office and had been very busy. He said, "I hope you will call, or if you will allow me, I'd be happy to phone you." She smiled and said, "I'm hoping to find something appropriate to accent my new outfit."

Pierre brought out a tray, put down a rectangle of black velvet fabric, and selected an exquisite blue sapphire choker with matching earrings.

She gazed at the pieces in amazement. They were exquisite and asked if he would put the choker around her neck to let her see how it looked with her new suit. She lifted her hair and he placed the jewels around her neck. She gasped at how beautifully it accented her suit and asked him to securely close the clasp. He walked back around the counter, removed the sapphire tear drop earrings from the case, and handed them to her. All she could say was, "Wow! I can't believe it, do you think a small pin might be too much?" she asked.

He said, "No," and selected a small gold entwined pin with mini sapphires. She looked at it, couldn't resist picking it up, faced the mirror, and pinned it on--the finishing touch.

He looked at her admiringly and again asked if she would accompany him to enjoy dinner at a magnificent French roof top restaurant. She smiled, paid for the jewelry, extended her hand as she thanked him for all his assistance, and hurried out the door anxious to get back to work, but more importantly to "charm" Cliff--win him over.

She really liked the jeweler but it was Cliff she loved and wasn't willing to settle for less even though he never noticed her except when it was business. She thought the road trip from Manhattan would have done the "trick," but it hadn't. Why couldn't Cliff look at her like the jeweler? And why couldn't she consider the jeweler? None of it made any sense. "It was a puzzlement," she told herself as she hailed a cab.

She was hoping Cliff would be at his desk. She wanted to make a "grand entrance." However, once again she was disappointed, he wasn't there. She sat down at her desk and was checking the mail when her buzzer went off, indicating Cliff was calling her.

She opened her desk drawer, took out a small mirror, and checked her makeup and hair. Satisfied with her image, she stood up, smoothed her skirt, picked up her pen and pad, and went to Cliff's office.

She had been practicing her smile and phrasing. When she walked in, and in a soft sultry tone said, "Good morning," and hoped he would look up, but he didn't. He acknowledged her greeting and began telling her what needed to be done that morning and gave her instructions as to what had to be completed during his absence. No trials or depositions were scheduled. He planned to return by the end of the week. "I'm going to see a man who has been a client for a number of years and I'll be returning shortly thereafter. You have my cell number and I will be in contact with our Manhattan office. Do you have any questions?" Cliff asked without ever looking up.

Jane felt her self-esteem had been crushed by an eighteen-wheeler. "He didn't even look at me. I went to all the trouble and bothered so many people at the salon and he couldn't even raise his gaze when he addressed me." Now, she could only concentrate on her weak legs. It was uncertain whether she would be able to walk out of his office.

He asked if she had any questions. She replied, "No," and used all her strength to get up and walk out when he called her back to hand her another file; then he looked up, saw her and was puzzled.

"What is she trying to accomplish wearing that combination of white with sapphires? Claudette is stunningly beautiful in that combination, Jane can't even compare. What is she up to?"

Jane couldn't get to her office fast enough. She was hurt and fell into her chair. This time she didn't even care who saw her crying. The tears were overflowing, sliding down her cheeks, and onto her new suit. She was trying to figure out what to do when she was buzzed again; struggling to compose herself she got up and went to his office.

This time he looked up and said that he wanted to go over a few files that needed to be keyed into the computer. "What was wrong with her? Why was she crying? Was someone ill? But he didn't ask her believing it must be very personal, he didn't want to intrude. If she wanted him to know, she'd tell him," he rationalized and his attention was once again focused on the various files before him.

Jane wondered why Cliff was being so callous; didn't he realize how she felt about him? She just sat at her desk trying to focus on the files that needed to be brought up-to-date, his handwritten notes transcribed, and then everything keyed into the computer. She was fast but the way she felt, it would be very time consuming. Then she felt someone come into her office, looked up and saw Cliff, he was carrying more files, apologized for the additional work and said that it all needed to be done a.s.a.p. She cringed.

Then he smiled softly reminding her he would be leaving in the A.M., and did she have any questions. She managed to somehow regain her composure for a few moments and said, "No."

Cliff drove home still wondering what was wrong with Jane but then dismissed the thought as he walked through the magnificent double doors of his home.

He always looked forward to coming home at the end of the day, having his children rush over to inundate him with their happy chatter while jumping into his arms and the other members of his happy home greet him. It would be even more wonderful when Claudette becomes his bride.

He promised himself he would select the perfect engagement ring for her when he was in Manhattan where he had a favorite jeweler. It was where he purchased jewelry for Julia. They were very creative and fashioned one-of-a-kind pieces. He had already contacted them and after reintroducing himself and the usual pleasantries said, "I am looking for the perfect engagement ring for my future bride and I know you are the artisans to create it." They discussed various styles, diamond colors, facets, whether he favored platinum or gold, and had he given any thought to having it engraved.

Cliff hung up the phone and then decided to phone a florist who makes fabulous creations and ordered a special bouquet to be sent to Claudette first thing in the morning. The florist knew exactly what flowers should comprise the bouquet. Cliff told him he wanted it put in a lead crystal vase and the card should read, "To my Sweetheart, I love you very much, My Darling, All My Love, Cliff."

The florist acknowledged the order and promised it would be delivered early the next morning and thanked him. He really liked the florist who was reliable, professional, and could be counted on to select just the right blooms and vases.

Then Cliff thought about Grace and called the florist back to request another bouquet different from the one going to Claudette however equally exquisite and the card should read, "To Grace, A Very Special Lady, I Treasure and Appreciate You, Love, Cliff."

The florist asked if that arrangement should be put in a special vase and Cliff said, "Yes, but please put this bouquet in an antique vase." He was glad that he also thought to send a bouquet to Grace, a very special lady.

He decided to walk over to the cottage to speak with Gordon to finalize their morning flight.

Grace was watching for him, threw her arms around his neck, hugged, and kissed him. Gordon came over and slapped him on the shoulder, a friendly gesture they often exchanged.

Grace excused herself. She went into the kitchen, made a fresh pot of coffee, and arranged individual desserts on a sterling silver three-tier tray she had purchased that afternoon in anticipation of Cliff coming over.

While Grace was preparing the refreshments, Gordon and Cliff were discussing various aspects of their trip. Gordon said that everything was in readiness. He had gone to the airport, spoke with his mechanic, Al, who assured him that everything checked out one-hundred per cent, the oil had been topped off, brakes checked, and the gas tanks would be filled in the morning prior to take-off.

Gordon said, "I have never seen these before referring to the tea cups and dessert plates. Are they a new purchase?"

Grace replied, "Yes, I saw this antique shop near the bakery. They had this tea service in the window. It was just what I had been looking for and knew you wouldn't mind."

Gordon lovingly said, "How could I mind. You don't have to ask my permission, buy whatever you want. I know you have excellent taste and have always made the best choices." Grace placed the dessert plates, forks, and linen napkins on the table. She held the sterling silver cake server ready to put the delicacy of choice on each one's dessert plate.

"All that's left is for us pack our bags and drive to the airport. I have all the necessary papers and a full set of maps is already on the plane. We filed our flight plan with the F.A.A., and are cleared for takeoff. It's approximately 1,500 miles-- three hours non-stop. We won't need to stop and refuel. We will have enough food and two gallons of water on board.

"I'm glad we're flying together again. Incidentally, don't forget to take your passport; I already have mine in my pants pocket. You're the best co-pilot I have ever had," Gordon said, and quickly added, "My very good friend."

Cliff always liked flying with Gordon and was looking forward to the trip.

Gordon said, "I'll need to stop in Colorado at the Air Force Academy for a meeting but it shouldn't take too long. Why don't you come along, I think that you'll find it interesting, and they serve great food. You'll enjoy it."

Cliff was somewhat hesitant, but Gordon assured him that it was all right in fact he had already spoken to the head of the committee. A badge will be at the main gate for you.

Cliff was even more excited about the trip; he always wanted to see the air force academy and this was a great opportunity to go with Gordon who was considered a V.I.P.

"Thanks Gordon, it's a privilege to know you and even better that you are on the upper echelon," Cliff said, patting Gordon on the shoulder while Grace looked at her two fellas with a broad smile. She was a beautiful woman and the three of them enjoyed each other's company.

"I'll put some of these tasty desserts in a box and pack my boys a lunch," Grace said good humouredly, as she picked up the empty dessert dishes and asked, "Anything special you'd like me to put in your lunch box so you won't be hungry during recess?" They were smiling at her. Gordon winked at his wife. He really adored her.

She went into the kitchen and opened the refrigerator while deciding what to make. She took out: a chicken, potatoes, romaine lettuce, tomatoes, and pasta from dinner, mushrooms, and other veggies for the toss green salad. She decided on a menu of fried chicken, French fries, pasta with mushrooms, a tossed green salad, coffee, and the desserts. They were going to be leaving early which meant she would have to hurry. It would have to be chilled before they left.

Suddenly, she heard her guys come into the kitchen. They had sniffed the fried chicken,   and, like all little boys, suddenly were hungry and she knew that she'd have to make three chickens to ensure there would be enough.

They were having so much fun helping Grace while munching the fried chicken that they didn't notice the time and suddenly Gordon looked up and said, "It's twenty-three hundred hours, and if we want to get an early start, we'd better get to sleep." Cliff gave Grace a hug, kiss, and winked at her. They had so much fun together.

Gordon said, "Cliff, I'll wake you up and remember to take your leather jacket. It will be cold at the altitude we'll be flying and remember your passport," he yelled out as Cliff made great strides toward the house.

Grace finished making the lunches, wrapped and packed them and the orange juice in an ice chest with dry ice. If she had used regular ice, it could be a problem. She also packed some chocolate bars, potato chips, pretzels, and gum in a canvas bag with cloth napkins, paper towels, utensils, a few plates, and cups for the coffee that she put in four thermos bottles. Since they both like their coffee black, she didn't bother putting in cream, milk, or sugar. She carried the ice chest, canvas bag, and thermos bottles to the front door ready to be picked up on their way out. Then she remembered the cell phone charger and music c.d.'s that she also put in the canvas bag. She hoped she remembered everything and went to the bedroom to check on what Gordon had packed, she wanted him to have everything he might need.

She opened his bag, shook her head as she took everything out, and packed six pairs of socks, six sets of underwear, four handkerchiefs, six T-shirts, three shirts, a dress shirt, tie, two pairs of pants, his favorite sweater, and a pair of dress shoes for his meeting. She took one of his suits out of the closet, brushed it, put a handkerchief in the breast pocket, then stopped, and went into the living room.

She walked across the room, stopped at their desk, sat down, opened the top right hand drawer, took out a piece of note paper, and proceeded to write a love note to her darling husband, put it in an envelope, went back into the bedroom, and slipped it into his pocket--a little surprise.

She had a thought and went back to the desk, took out the pad, and wrote a short note to Cliff to let him know that his family was thinking of him and were waiting for him to come home and make Claudette a member of their family. She put it in an envelope, wrote Cliff's name on the outside and slipped it in the suit jacket pocket next to Gordon's note. Grace was always as thoughtful as she was beautiful.

She glanced over at her sleeping husband and softly smiled, her eyes twinkling. He looked so angelic. She couldn't wait to change into her nightgown and selected pretty pink semi-sheer chiffon with tiny red rose buds. It was her husband's favorite. She brushed hair and teeth, turned off the light, slid between the sheets, and cuddled up close to her darling. She wondered how she would survive without him, but then rationalized, "It's only a few days a week or two at most," as she too drifted off to sleep.

It seemed as though she had just fallen asleep when the alarm went off. She had to get out of bed and prepare breakfast. She wanted the two of them to eat breakfast together in their little cottage that they loved.

It must have been the smell of bacon wafting through the house that caused Gordon to get up. He never could resist the smell of bacon, she knew that, and it was the ideal way to get him out of the "sack." She looked up and saw him coming in. He was rubbing his eyes in an effort to focus. He came over, extended his arms, and pulled her close to him, as he said, "Good Morning Sweetheart. Love you, love you, love you," smiled and kissed her soft perfectly shaped lips long and passionately taking her breath away. He held her gently and before he could say anything more, loudly said, "I think the bacon is burning." She abruptly turned around, grabbed the spatula, and quickly took out the bacon putting the slices on a plate lined with a paper towel to collect the drippings.

Gordon couldn't wait. He picked up a strip as Grace put the plate of eggs, toast, orange juice, coffee, croissants, and vitamins on the table, smiling as her darling was already serving himself. He picked up his glass of orange juice, handed the other to Grace, they encircled their arms and clinked glasses as they often did. They enjoyed having fun, no matter what they did.

Grace tried not to look at the clock but knew the time was near when Gordon and Cliff would have to go to the airport. She offered to drive them. There was a method to her madness; she just wanted to spend more time with her husband.

They went in to dress, and then headed for the front door where Gordon noted the ice chest, canvas bag, and thermos bottles filled with coffee.

"Oh!" Grace shrieked, "I forgot the gallons of water." She abruptly turned, ran to the kitchen, opened the pantry door, and took out three glass gallon bottles. Gordon was right behind her and took the bottles to the water distiller and filled them. They were very particular about the water they drank. When the gallon bottles were full, Gordon carried them to the front door just as Cliff came up the steps. They greeted each other and picked up the items.

Gordon again reminded Cliff, "Your passport?" Cliff patted his pants pocket to indicate that he had it. He was carrying his briefcase with the legal papers he needed for the appointment with his client and asked Gordon, "Don't you have your briefcase?" Grace who was trying to remember everything ran into the bedroom and came back with it. "I hope you both have everything now, otherwise I'll have to Federal Express it to you, which wouldn't be a problem, unless you need something in a hurry in which case, if it's papers I can fax them to you." They all laughed and walked out the door for the drive to the airport where Al maintained Gordon's plane in between flights.

Cliff said, "I'll drive while you two sit in the back seat and neck." It felt nice to sit in the back seat encircled by Gordon's manly arms. He always held her gently in his strong arms. He was a very strong man, but when he held or touched Grace, he was the epitome of gentleness. She loved the way he held her and brushed his lips first against her ear, then her cheek, and held her closer to him as he passionately kissed her. She loved his kisses, they left her feeling wonderfully breathless and she would gaze at him as though she were star struck.

The drive was ending all too quickly, as Cliff announced he was pulling into the airport.

Gordon walked ahead to talk to his mechanic and ensure all was in readiness. He waved, and walked over, "Hi, Al, how is everything going? Is she ready?" He always referred to his plane in the feminine.

Al said, "She is fueled and ready to take off."
He saw Grace and walked over to say, "Hello." They had known each other for a number of years and she counted on Al to do everything to keep her husband safe by maintaining the plane in empirical condition. She couldn't help asking if he had checked all the hoses, lines, brakes, wheels, and a few other things she had learned about over the years.

Al tried not to laugh. She usually included car parts. She was so sweet. Everyone loved her. Al was part of that group as he replied, "I even checked the oil and filled it with gas," and they all laughed.

Gordon walked over to his Cessna Citation, and proceeded to start checking the exterior to ensure everything was in readiness--no general visible exterior damage, no dents. All those various aspects had to be checked: oil in the two engines hydraulic fluid, reservoir engine fire extinguisher bottles, and some 5,000 pounds of fuel filled the two tanks.

Cliff was also checking the exterior a procedure that pilots were required to follow. They were both satisfied. The plane's exterior was in good condition, and the tanks were filled to capacity.

Grace was watching the procedure she had witnessed a number of times as Gordon came over to give her a huge bear hug as he held her so close to him you wouldn't be able to get a ruler between them. He gave her a long, lingering passionate kiss that left her breathless, and when he let go, she almost lost her balance, and they laughed.

Cliff hugged and kissed her as Al opened the door and the stairs folded down for the pilot and copilot to enter the plane. The mechanic handed Cliff the ice chest, water bottles, and beverage containers filled with coffee.

Al said, "It looks as though you have enough food for an army," and then Grace asked almost hysterically, "You do have your credit cards and some cash don't you?" They both nodded in unison.

Cliff pulled up the stairs, securely closed the door, walked into the cockpit, sat in the co-pilot's seat beside Gordon, and each adjusted his seat belt and shoulder harness.

Gordon had previously filed their flight plan by computer that was electronically transmitted directly to the F.A.A. computer. They checked the weather along their route and as part of the preflight inspection, ensured there was adequate pressure in the cO_2 bottles that would be charged into the engine in the event of a fire.

Gordon was assigned the code, 2467. He would be required to dial it into the transponder when he was in flight and the blip would be seen on the air traffic controller screen. The Code 2467 identified the blip as being Gordon's plane.

After starting the engines, they completed the taxi check list, and checked with the tower that had his flight plan, which had previously been sent to the Flight Service Station Computer. Gordon contacted the ground controller at Lindbergh Field and asked for his A.T.C. Clearance to Colorado Springs, Colorado.

Gordon and Cliff, after receiving A.T.C. clearance, started taxing down the taxi way, contacted the tower for takeoff clearance, moved the lever and flaps to the take off position, set the trim for takeoff, checked the speed brakes ensuring that the thrust reverse worked, as they were moving down to takeoff at the end of the runway.

By the time they were at the end of the runway, all the check lists had been completed, the tower controller said, "Citation 501 Golf Golf you are cleared for takeoff." As soon as they were airborne, they would contact approach, and they would be switched from tower to departure control. Their frequency 1273 was part of the A.T.C. clearance.

They departed from San Diego. The Citation 501 Golf Golf initially climbed to 3,000 feet and would be steered onto the path and away from the area, turning at a 090 heading, climbing, and maintaining 7,000 feet at a cruising altitude until they were approved to climb to a cruising altitude of 37,000 feet.

Grace had been standing by the hangar, smiling and waving continuously as her eyes filled with tears that were flowing down her beautiful cheeks; and even though she was glad he and Cliff were going on this trip, she felt a pang of apprehension as she watched the Cessna transporting the duo's ascent into the sun's rays as the plane's altitude dramatically increased and was enveloped by the bright blue sky, disappearing into a bank of white fluffy cumulus clouds.

Grace momentarily closed her eyes. She could still feel her husband's arms around her and his passionate kiss on her lips. She gently ran her finger tips over her lips as she remembered his sweet kisses. They always had the most enviable perfect love, were truly happy, enjoyed each other's company, and treasured each moment they spent together which was never enough. He was always very loving, attentive, treated her grandly, and always put her on a preverbal pedestal. Their love was envied by all who knew them. Everyone wanted an in-depth relationship with the same caring, loving, and sensitivity.

Loving her husband always filled her with a tremendous feeling of pleasure and delight whether he was sitting at his desk, playing tennis, swimming, playing with their grandchildren, or helping her in the kitchen. They enjoyed cooking together, trying new recipes, or walking on the beach their arms entwined around one another. She loved to think of them dancing together and pausing to kiss, it was fabulous--all the magic was still there--she could feel it.

CHAPTER SEVENTEEN

No sooner had they taken off when they began talking about being hungry and grateful that Grace, being such a caring and loving person, always packed great lunches. They knew she had packed a real feast. Cliff reached over, picked up a thermos of coffee, gave it to Gordon and one for himself as they watched the dials and maintained radio contact.

Now that they were further away from the airport, they had clearance to climb to an altitude of 11,000 feet; and when they passed over Julian, California, they were over the desert and would climb to an altitude of 37,000 feet as they headed toward their Colorado Springs destination. After their meeting at the United States Air Force Academy, they would continue on to New York, their final destination, where Cliff had an important meeting with his client.

They decided to "dig" into the picnic basket and each selected a fried chicken leg and French fries. They began munching while watching the dials. Gordon decided to put the plane on automatic pilot as they enjoyed their lunch. The weather was good, they were right on schedule. Everything was going smoothly as they were approaching the Rocky Mountain chain that extends from Canada, south through seven states: Montana, Wyoming, Idaho, Utah, Colorado, New Mexico, and Texas.

They laughed and joked. The flight was progressing as planned. Then about 180 minutes into their flight, as they were flying over the Rocky Mountains and looking forward to their meeting at the United States Air Force Academy, the weather drastically changed. They had penetrated a thunder cloud, made a conscious decision to take it off automatic pilot, and decrease their altitude to 11,000 feet.

The size and intensity of the rain drops increased dramatically, developing into a storm. Suddenly and without warning ice was beginning to form on the wings. Their main concern was that the deicers would not be sufficient if it iced up too rapidly.

The ice build-up on the skin of the plane was causing them to lose altitude. Realizing that with ice rapidly forming on the wings and other areas of the plane, it would be impossible for them to maintain their altitude; they had to consider the worst case scenario--the plane going down, crashing from an overload of ice.

Gordon instructed Cliff to make radio contact, "Citation 501 Golf Golf. We're going down due to heavy icing making it impossible to maintain altitude," and cited their latitude and longitude. Gordon continually tried in vain to control the plane but the flaps were frozen. In desperation, he attempted to pull up, but the plane failed to respond; they kept going down. All he could do was to glide it down as safely as possible. They were very stressed out

"Hopefully," Gordon said, "We can bypass the 'chain of lakes' and avoid as much as possible the Ponderosa Pine Forest located at the base of the mountains, which could badly damage the plane, possibly resulting in a devastating forest fire, and worst case scenario, they could be badly injured or killed. We have to put it down where we won't crash into anything and do everything possible to come out of this unscathed. We have too many people who depend upon us."

Cliff said enthusiastically, "Look there's a clearing in that small valley; I believe we can set her down on that grassy meadow. It looks as though we'll have sufficient space." They checked to ensure that their harnesses and seat belts were tightened up as much as possible.

Gordon said, "I can bring her in--but it will be touch-and-go. Our landing speed will be about 100 knots. I'll have to make a soft belly landing; in this instance; it's the ideal way to bring her down with a minimum of our being severely injured.

We'll need the shelter of the plane to protect ourselves from the elements," Gordon said.

Cliff agreed. It was a good plan.

Gordon decided that he would glide the plane down on the grassy plain that they had selected as an emergency landing strip.

They made a belly landing, skidding along this meadow, unable to stop. He knew that he had no brakes because the landing gear wasn't down, but he felt that he had to do something, therefore even knowing it would be useless, he continuously applied the brakes with no success.

Cliff and Gordon braced themselves for the inevitable crash as the plane continued rolling forward with no hope of manually stopping it and ultimately crashed into a tree, shearing off the left wing. They hit with such force that they would have been catapulted out of the cockpit had they not tightened their harnesses and seat belts to the maximum.

Simultaneously the Emergency Locator Beacon, ELB, was activated by the crash, and the radio signal was automatically sent out for the controllers to pick up.

The emergency signal was received and a call for help was immediately sent out to the local sheriff who began organizing a search party and arranging for a helicopter to scout the crash area. Their main concern was getting to the crash site to check on the pilot and co-pilot, administer first aid at the site, and transport them to the hospital via helicopter.

The sheriff was given the names of the plane's occupants and the next of kin. When the phone rang, Grace ran to answer, believing it was her husband calling to tell her that he had arrived at the United States Air Force Academy in Colorado and they had a good trip. However, the voice she heard was not familiar and she couldn't understand why he was calling her.

The sheriff was having difficulty with the connection. He decided it would be a tremendous shock if he called Mrs. Gordon Deveaux to advise her that their Cessna plane had crashed and they were in the process of sending out the rescue party.

Instead, he called the San Diego Police Department, introduced himself, and asked to speak with the chief of police. The sheriff explained that it was an urgent matter. 'A Cessna plane owned by a local couple who are residents of your city, General Gordon and Grace Deveaux, took off from Lindbergh field and crashed in Colorado. On board were Gordon Deveaux, pilot, and her son-in-law, Cliff Camden, co-pilot.

"Sir, we don't know the condition of the plane's occupants, a search party is heading out in a helicopter, and we hope to have word soon.
"I was hoping one of your officers would be kind enough to personally go to their home and break the news as gently as possible to Mrs. Gordon Deveaux, the pilot's wife. Her husband, General Deveaux, is a Congressional Medal of Honor Winner. The co-pilot, Cliff Camden, is her son in law," the sheriff said.

The chief of police said that he would have a car go out immediately and requested that the sheriff keep him posted.

The sheriff agreed and was glad he had handled it that way.

The chief of police instructed two of his officers to go over and see Mrs. Deveaux to tell her about the plane crash. It's an unpleasant but necessary task.

Grace was still wondering about the phone call, but rationalized, "It must have been a wrong number" and busied herself in the kitchen with Miss Monique who had just baked a plate of chocolate chip cookies and was pouring milk for the children, Nancy, Grace, Mr. and Mrs. Svensen, and herself. A tradition they all enjoyed as they laughed, while some were busy dunking   their   cookies.

The doorbell rang; Grace excused herself and went to answer it while wondering who would be coming over. She wasn't expecting anyone.

She opened the door and saw the two police officers and had a sinking feeling. Why were they coming to her home? They were somber when they asked to speak with Mrs. Gordon Deveaux. She asked what it was concerning. They didn't answer, instead asked if they could please come in and speak with her.

It brought back that dismal memory when Cliff told her about how two officers came to tell him that Julia had been killed by a drunk driver, but she tried to put that thought aside, not wanting to believe that they came to bring terrible news.

She invited the officers to come in and asked them to please come into the library and be seated as she was desperately trying to remain calm.

They told her that the local sheriff in Colorado Springs called their chief of police requesting that officers come over to advise her that her Cessna plane had gone down and that a helicopter and search party were on their way to the crash site.

Grace was trying desperately to remain calm. How was she going to cope? The officers were starring at her, worried that she would faint. They asked if anyone else lived in the house, but Grace seemed unable to answer. Then the officers observed two small children running into the room and started talking to Grace. One of the officers asked if anyone else was home; Ra Ra nodded and pointed to the kitchen.

The officers walked into the kitchen, introduced themselves, and told them what had transpired. Miss Monique and Mrs. Svensen started to cry, they couldn't help it.

The officers said that they didn't have any more news and were concerned about Mrs. Deveaux.

Miss Monique ran into the library to check on Grace who was sitting on a couch as the children were busy talking to her and patting her leg for attention.

Miss Monique suggested that Nancy take the children outside as she walked over to Grace who was sitting with her head in her hands; her face wet with tears. The cook sat down beside her, extended her arms, encircling her, and gently patted her head that was now on her shoulder.

Grace could not control her tears, she was devastated and Miss Monique was very concerned not only about Gordon and Cliff but also Grace who was so pale that her skin appeared almost translucent.

The officers repeated, "The rescue team has not as yet reached the plane but they would keep her posted."

Miss Monique thanked them and they said that they could show themselves out. It was a very difficult situation as she tried to comfort her beloved employer.

Nancy now appraised of the situation, called Cliff's office and spoke with Jane who said that she would make arrangements for the company jet to fly them to Colorado Springs and call the sheriff for additional details. Jane wanted to know the hospital where they would be transported. Nancy said that she didn't know. They were still waiting for the details.

Miss Monique sat comforting Grace, and asked Nancy to please call their family doctor and ask him to come over.

Fortunately, their doctor was visiting nearby and came over upon receiving the phone call. He had known the family for decades since they all lived in New York and they had always enjoyed each other's company. They took trips together, visited in each other's homes, and took pride in hosting extravagant dinner parties attended by their friends from the art galleries and museums. They had fun enjoying the same things.

He was very concerned both professionally and personally as Nancy opened the door and showed him into the library where Miss Monique was holding and comforting Grace who looked like a beautiful, fragile porcelain doll.

The doctor walked briskly toward them and held out his hand; Grace looked up and tried in vain to focus through tear filled red eyes. She let him hold her hand and he took her pulse. He then said to Miss Monique, "Let's take her to her room where she can lie down and get some rest. I'll give her something to help her sleep and leave some of the prescription and directions with you. It's imperative that you don't give her too many, and if you have any questions at any time day or night, call me, and if you need me to come over, I will."

They helped Grace to her feet, but she was unable to stand. The doctor realizing how weak she had become, asked Miss Monique to show him the way to Grace's room as he carried her up the stairs.

They put her to bed and did everything possible to make her comfortable. The doctor administered the prescription and told Miss Monique that Grace would sleep. He then handed the cook a vial of the prescription and was explicit on how it should be dispensed and not to leave the bottle in the room. He didn't want Grace to reach out and take more of the medication than indicated.

Then they went downstairs to the kitchen and Miss Monique poured each of them a cup of coffee and offered him some of her freshly baked croissants. She was a wonderful cook and it was always a pleasure sitting in her kitchen, enjoying her culinary creations.

Finally, he got up after thanking her profusely for her hospitality, the good food, and said, "I'll go upstairs and check on our patient. Please call. Remember call, you won't be bothering   me."

The rescue team arrived via helicopter at the crash site and began analyzing the situation.

The pilot had successfully brought the plane down. It crashed into a tree. The team was concerned about the gas tanks exploding and causing a possible fire.

They had to be extremely careful prior to approaching the plane to ensure that it was sufficiently stable for them to enter. After close examination, they determined it was as least temporarily safe and cautiously walked into the cockpit.

It was obvious that neither one of them had been in any condition to get out of the plane after it crashed. Cliff had hit his head on the control panel and was rendered unconscious. His father-in-law was in shock and suffered several broken ribs and a fractured arm and leg.

The team carefully removed the pilot and copilot from their seats, secured each to a back board, carried them out of the plane, and into the helicopter that was standing by to transport the injured men to a hospital.

They knew Gordon was a retired United States Air Force officer and the recipient of the Congressional Medal of Honor. Cliff was also an air force veteran; therefore, as soon as the men were stabilized they would be transported to the United States Air Force Hospital.

CHAPTER EIGHTEEN

The rescue team was in constant radio contact with the sheriff who immediately notified the San Diego Chief of Police that the rescue team had arrived at the crash site and were in the process of transporting the injured pilot and co-pilot to the United States Air Force Hospital, and would let him know as soon as they were admitted. He also called Mrs. Deveaux's home and apprised them of the situation.

Shortly thereafter, Jane called the sheriff in Colorado, who said that the search and rescue team had arrived at the crash site and were in the process of transporting both men to the hospital, and if she could please call back, he'd let her know when they had been admitted.

The rescue team called again, this time to tell the sheriff that both men had been admitted to the United States Air Force Hospital and gave him both the telephone number and their room numbers. He thanked them and said, "When you are in the area stop by, I'd like to buy you all a cup of coffee."

The sheriff then called Jane with the information she was so anxiously waiting for. She thanked him profusely telling him how grateful she was. Then she asked him for the name of the hotel closest to the hospital which he willingly provided and offered to call and let them know that she and his wife would be arriving and to reserve two rooms.

Jane corrected him; please make that one room and a suite for his wife, so that she will be more comfortable.

The sheriff asked Jane to call him when she knew when their plane would land and he'd meet her at the airport. She was very grateful and told him how much she appreciated all he had done.

Jane decided not to phone, but drove over to deliver the news in person which was the kinder, gentler way; at least the news wasn't tragically negative. They had been found and the rescue team was transporting them to the hospital. They were alive and to Jane that was all that mattered. She had to get to her beloved Cliff rationalizing that he needed her. She loved him so much and was anxious to be at the hospital to nurse him back to health. This was her opportunity and she was going to make the most of it.

She knocked on the door. Miss Monique answered and invited her in. They were all anxious for news and hoped that Jane had the answers that would be most welcome. She asked about Grace and watched Miss Monique's face that was drained and saw the worried expression, her eyes were red, and her face puffy making it apparent that she had not slept.

"Mrs. Deveaux had been medicated by her doctor. She was distraught because we had no word about her husband or Cliff," Miss. Monique said.

Jane said, "I have news. The sheriff in Colorado called. The plane had been found and both Gordon and Cliff have been rescued and were being transported to the hospital. I have the telephone number and their room numbers. I called the airport and have asked them to get the company jet ready and file a flight plan for Colorado Springs. She also said that she asked the sheriff to make hotel reservations for them, and he offered to meet us at the airport."

Miss Monique felt such a sense of relief. It was as though she had lost a thousand pounds. She now felt everything would be as it should. She found herself singing in French as she usually did when she was happy. She told Jane to make herself comfortable--she would be back shortly.

Miss Monique literally ran up the stairs, she couldn't wait to get to Grace's room and tell her that her precious husband and son-in-law were in the hospital, and the company jet would take them to the hospital as soon as she was ready.

The door was open and she stuck her head in. Grace was sitting on the edge of the bed still in her nightgown. She heard Miss Monique, turned her head and waited for her to come in. She literally ran in, hugged her boss who was more like a friend, and tried to speak slowly, but she was so excited that the words tumbled out in French and she had to try to calm herself and repeat them in English several times to be sure that she said them correctly.

Grace's face was suddenly shining with a broad smile and her eyes although red started to twinkle as they often did.

Then Miss Monique held out her robe and suggested that she might want to take a shower and freshen up as she was certain that Grace would want to leave to see Gordon and Cliff as soon as possible.

Grace nodded and Miss Monique went into her bathroom, turned on the shower and said that she would pack a suitcase. Then Grace turned and asked Miss Monique if she would accompany her.

Miss Monique said excitedly, "I would love to and I will pack a bag for both of us and another for the men," and ran to get the suitcases.

Then suddenly she remembered Claudette and knew that Cliff would want to see her. She checked the phone book and called to relay the events and said that they would be flying there and invited Claudette to go with them, knowing that Cliff would want her there.

Claudette was quiet for a long time and then muffled sniffles could be heard, finally trying to regain her composure, she said that she would very much like to go with them, would pack a suitcase, and drive over to their home. She thanked Miss Monique and said that she would be leaving shortly.

Miss Monique headed for the closet where they stored the suitcases, took out several, and then remembered Jane. She picked up the suitcases and went over to speak with Jane, telling her that she was going to pack and would be ready to leave for the airport within the hour. Jane said that she would be back with a limousine that would be large enough to accommodate them and their luggage, and departed while Miss Monique began packing the suitcases. She decided to pack a separate one for Cliff and another for Gordon with pajamas, robe, slippers, and casual clothes.

She called Nancy to ask for her help and said that they would be leaving soon. "Here is the phone number of the hospital, and I will be using Mrs. Deveaux cell phone. I will call you as soon as we register at the hotel. Please be careful what you tell the children. As soon as I know their father's condition, I will let you know and tell them only the minimum of what they need to know. Now, please help me pack. We need to leave as soon as possible."

They went into Grace's room and Miss Monique opened dresser drawers and started putting articles of clothing on the bed to be packed. Then she opened the closet, selected a number of outfits including a suit, shoes, casual clothes, two jackets, robe and two nightgowns as Nancy carefully folded and packed.

She then opened Gordon's closet, took out casual clothing, two jackets, a suit, dress shirt, casual shirts, shoes, bedroom slippers, pajamas, etc. She then said that she was going to Cliff's room and would be putting articles of his clothing on the bed and would appreciate it if she would pack them in the suitcase that she'd put on the bed.

Next, she went to her room, packed a variety of clothing, and called out to Mr. and Mrs. Svensen advised them of the situation and that she, Grace, Claudette, and Jane would be flying to Colorado to see Gordon and Cliff. "I will call as soon as we have registered at the hotel."

Finally, they were all packed. Claudette arrived her eyes filled with tears spilling down her translucent cheeks. She felt Miss Monique's warm friendship and ran into the older woman's arms to be consoled. At that moment Grace called. Miss Monique excused herself and went upstairs.

Grace said, "I feel a little unsteady would you please help me down the stairs?"

"Of course," Miss Monique said as she put an arm around her and then Nancy was on the other side and the two of them assisted Grace down the stairs.

Jane arrived just as Nancy brought down the other suitcase and they were ready to leave for the airport. Jane was shocked when she saw Claudette with her suitcase. Not at all what Jane had expected. She didn't want Claudette to go with them to Colorado, but there was little she could do but be polite.

Miss Monique said, "I'll be calling to keep you all informed," they hugged, and she said, in a pleading voice, "Please remember to say prayers and call the doctor."

Mr. Svensen carried their luggage out to the limo and assured them that he would take care of everything, not to worry. He helped Grace out to the car and made sure that she was comfortably seated, then Claudette, Miss Monique, and Jane entered the limo and they waved as the vehicle made its way down the driveway and out the gate.

Jane was livid. She sat pursing her lips, gritting her teeth, and digging her fingernails into the palm of her hand ever since she saw Claudette in the house with her suitcase. She wanted to have Cliff all to herself, to make him realize that she is the ideal person for him and would make a great wife. He already appreciated her as a secretary and personal assistant, why then couldn't he see that she was the perfect mate for him. It bewildered her.

Miss Monique was sitting next to Grace very concerned. She didn't look at all well and wondered if she should give her another of the sedatives the doctor had prescribed but thought better of it. They would be at the hospital within a few hours, and once she saw her husband, she would feel one-hundred per cent better.

The limo driver knew the runway where the jet was fueled and ready to take off. He pulled over, got out, opened the door for them to alight, and began taking out their luggage when the plane's attendant came over, introduced himself, although Jane knew him, and began picking up their luggage and taking it to the plane.

Jane and the others thanked the limo driver. They all boarded the plane and tried to make themselves comfortable which was very difficult in view of the circumstances. The pilot came back and informed the group that he was ready to take off and gave them instructions. He said that the trip would take about two hours, and if they needed anything, Steve, the attendant, would do everything possible to attend to their needs, as he turned to go back into the cockpit.

The takeoff was very smooth and Miss Monique did everything possible to make Grace comfortable.

Claudette suggested that perhaps she might want something to drink, water or juice. Grace nodded and Claudette got up and went over to Steve and asked what juice was onboard. He said, "We have tomato, orange, and grape juice." She asked for four glasses of grape juice. He came over with a tray and four glasses of grape juice. Grace and Miss Monique accepted a glass and said that Claudette had made a very good choice. Claudette also accepted a glass but Jane refused. She would accept nothing that Claudette had anything to do with.

Miss Monique noted that Grace looked much better and the three of them chatted while Jane was too busy stewing. Her face was all contorted as she was thinking very negative thoughts about Claudette.

The flight was very smooth, great weather. When the pilot announced that they should fasten their seat belts as they were about to land, they were all amazed that the time had gone by so quickly.

Jane called over the attendant and asked him to call the sheriff, tell him that they were landing, and if he could meet them at the airport.

Steve said, "I'll be happy to call."

They landed and were thrilled that the sheriff was there to greet them. Steve helped load the luggage into the sheriff's car, they thanked him, waved to the pilot, got into the vehicle, and were off.

The sheriff suggested that they first stop at the hotel, register, have their luggage sent up to their rooms, and then he would take them to the hospital.

Jane thanked him and agreed with his plan. Jane went in to register. The bell captain said that the luggage would be placed in their respective rooms.

Then the sheriff drove them to the hospital. They were all excited and yet apprehensive. He took them to the sixth floor and spoke with the floor nurse who came over and said that she was glad they were able to come so quickly.

Miss Monique performed the introductions: Mrs. Deveaux is Gordon's wife and the mother-in-law of Cliff, Claudette is Cliff's girl friend, Jane is Cliff's secretary, and I am their cook and housekeeper.

They asked about Gordon's condition. The nurse said, "The doctor will be in a better position to give you all the details," in the meantime, she put her arm around Grace and offered to take her to her husband's room. They walked down the hall, the nurse opened the door, and Grace had the first glimpse of her husband since that fateful day when he took off in his plane.

She walked over and he looked up at her, smiled, and said, "I am glad you are here. I missed you my love, and if you want to give me something, I would love a nice long kiss." She bent over and kissed her darling husband and was glad that their prayers had been answered. She then reached out and stroked his face. They couldn't get enough of one another. He reached up and stroked her hair and moved his hand down to her arm. The nurse came over with a chair and Grace sat down. She felt as though she would never leave that spot. She didn't need a hotel; all she needed was her precious husband.

Gordon asked her if she had seen Cliff. She said, "No, I came straight to your bedside."

He said that he was worried and asked her if she would go over and see Cliff,

She said that she would and come right back.

He said, "But not without first giving me another kiss." They both smiled and laughed as she bent down and they kissed.

She noted that the nurse was still in the room and asked to see Cliff.

The nurse said, "You are the only medicine your husband needs. It's wonderful to see people who are so much in love."

Grace walked the short distance down the hall, opened the door and went over to the bed, saw Cliff, and began speaking to him.
The nurse called her aside and explained that he had amnesia and probably wouldn't recognize her.

Grace went back to Cliff's bedside and said, "Hi, how are you feeling?" He looked at her strangely seemingly unable to speak. She had expected to hear him say, "Do I know you?" but was uncertain as to how to answer the question and wouldn't until she spoke with his doctor. She asked Cliff how he felt, and he said that his head hurt. Stroking his face, she said, "I am certain that you will be feeling better soon. I'll be back later to visit you."

Grace went back into the hall where Miss Monique, Claudette, and Jane were waiting. "Will the doctor be here soon?" Grace asked. The nurse said that he was on his way. Grace said that they would sit and wait.

The doctor arrived and the nurse introduced the ladies. He was very compassionate and said that he was sorry that they were meeting under such depressing circumstances and wanted to answer all their questions and allay their fears. Dr. Simmons walked over to Grace, extended his hand and held her hand as he proceeded to inform her about her husband's condition.

Considering that he was in a plane crash, he's in very good condition. Your husband has three broken ribs, a fractured upper left arm, and a broken left leg. His prognosis is excellent and he should be able to go home in about ten weeks. However, it is advisable that his leg remain in a suspended position during the initial healing process.

Grace asked about Cliff's condition and prognosis.

Dr. Simmons said that Cliff had suffered a very serious concussion, has short term amnesia, and recommended that he remain in the hospital for ten weeks.

"What a relief," Grace said and the others vehemently said, "Amen" Grace asked to go in and see Cliff and Dr. Simmons accompanied her into his room. He was lying very still as she walked over to his bed. The doctor moved a chair over; she sat down, and held her son-in-law's hand as she said, "Cliff, its Grace. How are you feeling?" knowing full well that he would not recognize her. She smiled, leaned over and kissed him on the cheek. He just looked at her and murmured some unintelligible words.

"Cliff, it is so good to see you," Grace said.

"Where am I," he asked.

"You are in the hospital, and I want you to have a good rest." She spoke softly as she stroked his cheek. He looked into her eyes, a smile crossed his face. She said, "Claudette is here and would like to come in and see you, is that all right?"

He nodded.

She left the room and returned with Claudette who came over to his bedside and kissed him softly on the lips. Puzzled, he gazed at her.

"Who was she?" he wondered.

She began telling him that she was his girl friend, and they were very much in love.

Grace quietly left the room. She was anxious to speak with Miss Monique and Jane who were patiently waiting in the hall. When they saw her approaching, they were very relieved when they saw the happy expression on her face. It was so uplifting. They had all been through so much but it seemed that their prayers had been answered. Both men had been rescued and were getting the best medical attention they needed and would be going home in approximately ten weeks. Great news!!! And they all smiled and hugged.

Jane asked to see Cliff, but Grace said that she would have to wait. Right now he needs his family and those closest to him. He shouldn't be bothered with anything pertaining to business matters.   All that would have to wait until he has his memory back--completely recuperated.

Jane was devastated.   She thought that this would be her chance to make Cliff love her.   "How could she have been so wrong?"   She turned away from the group, hurt, and distraught as she said, "I think that I'll go to the hotel," as she slowly walked down the hall, and into the elevator.

Grace asked Miss Monique to please call Nancy, "Tell her the good news and pass it on to Mr. and Mrs. Svensen. Also, please be sure to give her the telephone numbers of both the hotel and hospital, and that we plan to return in about ten weeks with both Cliff and Gordon."

Grace walked over to Cliff's room and carefully opened the door.   She saw Claudette sitting by his bed, smiling at him, and patting his shoulder.   It was a beautiful picture.   She then went to Gordon's room and was greeted with a very loving smile. He waved her over with his good arm, and as soon as she was close enough, he put his arm around her and kissed her as though he was starved for her.

A nurse came in and asked if there was anything she could do. "Yes, there is," Grace said.

Gordon interrupted her and asked what she was going to ask for: a bed brought in so that his wife could be next to him as she had been from the day they said, "I do."   Before the nurse could respond, he said that with Grace at his side he would get well faster, and his spirits would be ten points plus--off the scale.

The nurse, smiling, said that something could be worked out.   She left the couple and returned with an orderly carrying a cot, pillow, and blanket.

Gordon said, "Whoopee," and "If you come over here, I'll kiss you.   You have made me so happy which will result in my speedy recovery." He was so enthusiastic that the nurse laughed.

She noted that his morale had increased substantially since his wife walked into his room. When the nurse first saw his wife looking so fragile as though she was going to faint from the stress, eyes red, would also end up being a patient. And, now she was the picture of health. It was obvious that the two of them belonged together and were very happily married.

The nurse said that the nutritionist would be in with the menu and they would also be happy to serve his wife. She wondered if they heard what she just said because they were holding hands and looking into each other's eyes. They were very much into each other and oblivious to everything and everyone else.

Miss Monique came to the door and quietly opened it a crack, she was so filled with joy as she saw the two of them so enraptured with each other. She didn't want to interrupt but really wanted to give Gordon her best wishes. They all loved him so much.

She opened the door a bit further and Grace turned, smiled, and welcomed her into the room.

Gordon was happy to see her, waved her over with his good arm, and asked, "Aren't you going to give me one of your delightful bear hugs." She beamed as she bent down and he put his arm around and kissed her on the cheek as she kissed him on his forehead.

How good it felt to have him back. He was a wonderful man and they all loved him dearly; jokingly he said, "What brings you to Colorado, mademoiselle?" She smiled, too full of emotion to speak, and without wanting it to happen, tears of happiness filled her eyes. He reached up with a tissue and patted her cheeks blotting the tears that had overflowed. She was indeed a treasure--a dear member of their family.

Grace told Gordon that she would be back shortly as she followed Miss Monique out of the room. She looked exhausted and suggested that she go back to their hotel suite, take a long hot bubble bath, order dinner, and lie down. The suite is large enough for all three of us--Claudette, Miss Monique, and me. Jane has her own room down the hall.

"I shall be spending all my time here in the hospital with my darling Gordon. They brought in a cot for me, therefore I'll be sleeping here with my husband," Grace said.

As Miss Monique walked toward the elevator, she could hear Grace singing; life was getting back to normal.

Jane left the hospital and went to the hotel. She had a single room; the others would be sharing a suite. She walked into the hotel, stopped at the desk and asked for her key. The clerk told her that the bellman had taken her luggage up to her room and to let them know if she needed anything. She thanked the clerk and a bellman offered to show her to her room. They stepped into the elevator, rode up, and got off when it stopped at her floor. She followed him down the hall; he stopped in front of her door, put the key into the lock, and held the door open for her. She walked in and was left all alone.

She sank down into the nearest chair, feeling very dejected. The hotel manager knew why she and the others had come to Colorado and wanted to do everything possible to make her and the others comfortable. Management placed a huge fresh floral bouquet on the table next to a bowl of fruit and a tray carefully arranged with crackers, cheese, pate, chocolate covered strawberries, and other finger foods.

She had arranged everything for the trip, came all the way from California just to be with Cliff, and felt very unwelcome as though she had been thrown out with the garbage. She hadn't even been allowed to see Cliff, they wouldn't let her. Nothing she had done had any affect. He didn't even notice her. All that time and money she had spent at the hair dresser, the makeup sessions, new expensive wardrobe, accessories, and costly jewelry--all to no avail.

She felt drained as she sat in her room all alone as though mesmerized looking at the fruit bowl and tray of finger goods the hotel had provided, but even though she couldn't remember when she had last eaten, she wasn't hungry. She knew that she should get some rest, but nothing really seemed important. It was all for naught. She just sat like a rag doll.

CHAPTER NINETEEN

It had been ten weeks since Gordon's plane crashed and they were transported to the hospital. Claudette had spent countless hours at Cliff's bed side, talking to him, patting his hand, pushing hair out of his eyes, and singing to him.

He was trying so hard to remember and continually asked her endless questions. He wanted to know everything, especially what the two of them meant to each other, where they had met, what they did, and how long had they known each other.

Claudette carefully and softly answered all his questions and as she did so, she prayed he would remember her. She studied his face as she told him about how he flew to Stanford for her graduation, gave her a beautiful corsage of purple orchids, and the most fabulous gift: a gold engraved locket with their photographs inside and engraved with the words, "Forever My Love."

She also told him about their road trip down the coast after her graduation. The museums they visited, their walks and picnics on the beach, bike rides, sea food dinners, etc. It appeared as though she could see a glimmer of recognition.

Grace came in, saw Claudette, and quietly walked over to his bed. He turned to look at Grace and then Claudette who knew that he wanted to know who she was.

Claudette said, "This is your mother-in-law, Grace Deveaux, her husband, Gordon was in the plane with you."

Cliff looked at Grace, studying her face as she smiled at him and brushed a lock of hair out of his eyes. He suddenly smiled at her and said, "I...I think, I remember you, don't you live in the cottage behind the tennis courts?"

She couldn't control her excitement, and without meaning to said louder than she had planned, "Yes! We all live on the property you purchased."

Cliff remembered her and she bent down to hug and kiss him on the cheek. This was wonderful. She was so excited that she said, "I have to go tell Gordon, he will be so happy. Our prayers have been answered," as she quickly walked out of the room.

Cliff turned his gaze to Claudette; he wanted very much to remember her. She was very beautiful and the way she had been at his bedside, he believed she had to be a very important part of his life.

He asked her to tell him how they met and she relayed the events at the beach when he walked over to where she and Ra Ra, his daughter, were building a sand castle.

Suddenly he squeezed her hand and said, "I remember! I remember!" and reached out to bring her close to him. He wanted more than anything to kiss her. She stood up and leaned over him as he put his hand behind her head, bringing her face close to his and kissed her so passionately that she was left breathless. He really remembered her.

"I am so happy," she said. It was so wonderful. She had missed him much more than she thought. The kiss was perfect. Now instead of her and him, it was us, one of the most beautiful words in the dictionary. She was still leaning over him as they were starring into each other's eyes and he was about to kiss her again when the doctor came in.

He walked over and said, "There doesn't seem to be a need in asking how you feel."

"No," Cliff said, "All of the pieces seem to be coming together and it feels good to know who I am and it feels great to get my memory back. Now, tell me when can I leave this exciting abode?"

The doctor was amused, it always pleased him when his patients were recovering to the point that they wanted to "escape" the confines of the hospital.

Dr. Simmons said, "It's been ten weeks which means you are right on schedule. How are you planning to return to San Diego to complete your full recovery? You'll be able to recuperate at home and go to the VA--Veterans Administration-- in La Jolla, California, where they have medical and hospital facilities for your follow-up checkups."

Grace said that they hadn't even thought about how they would be returning to San Diego. The doctor offered to see what he could find out. Grace asked about her husband and the doctor said that as soon as they know how they will be traveling both men could be released.

Gordon's plane had been removed from the crash site to be repaired. He was an expert pilot and brought the plane down with a minimum amount of damage. It had been expertly brought back to pre-crash days, moved to a nearby airport, and was fueled ready to takeoff.

Grace and Claudette went to their hotel suite to shower, dress, and be ready to depart. They told Miss Monique that they would be leaving later that morning. Grace then went to Jane's room and knocked. No answer. She knocked again, but nothing. She went back to their suite, called the desk, and learned that Jane had checked out. Grace was surprised, but couldn't dwell on that, she needed to call the concierge and arrange for a limo.

Grace suddenly said, "Wait a minute. We need to purchase gifts for the nurses who were so wonderful throughout this ordeal." She called the desk to inquire if they had a gift shop. They all went down to the gift shop, made their selections, and had them gift wrapped.

The bellman carried down their luggage, they thanked the personnel, checked out, and walked out into the sunshine. They stopped at the hospital, distributed the gifts, nurses assisted Gordon into the limo, and Claudette was urging Cliff to lean on her.

How wonderful, they were all in the limo. They arrived at the airport, luggage loaded on board, and everyone settled in. The flight attendant did everything possible to make them comfortable. It was so wonderful to be going home. Grace had her Gordon and was busy fussing over him; Claudette couldn't keep her hands off Cliff, and Miss Monique was so happy her family was going home.

Miss Monique asked the flight attendant if he would call their home and let the others know they would be home in a few hours. He nodded.

The plane landed without incident and a limo was waiting. Their luggage was transferred from the plane to the limo. Grace went in the limo first to assist Gordon who still had his leg and arm in a cast and made him comfortable with a mound pillows. Claudette, despite Cliff's protests, insisted on helping him, and when Miss Monique was in, they were on their way home.

Mr. and Mrs. Svensen, Nancy, Ra Ra, and Jacques were in front awaiting their arrival. It was a glorious homecoming. Miss Monique ran into the kitchen to make one of her famous dinners while Grace was making Gordon comfortable and Claudette was still fussing over Cliff.

No one said anything but they were wondering what had happened to Jane, she just seemed to disappear. Grace decided to call her. She was perplexed; Jane's phone had been disconnected. Then she called Cliff's law office, and before she could ask about Jane, they were anxious to tell her how glad they were that Cliff was home and had regained his memory; they kept going on and on. She had to interrupt to ask about Jane.

The voice at the other end suddenly lost all its enthusiasm and stopped talking. Grace thought that she was having difficulty with the phone and repeated her request, again silence. Finally, she asked to speak with one of the law partners who came on the line and expressed their relief that Cliff was well, back home, and they were looking forward to having him back at his desk.

Again, she repeated the question.

"Finally," he said, "Jane isn't with us any longer." Grace didn't understand, know what to say, or how to react. The voice on the other end was silent. Well, Grace asked, "If she isn't with the law firm in San Diego, did she move back to New York?"

"No."

This whole conversation was unnerving. Grace wondered, "Why can't they tell me where Jane is." Again, losing patience in an emphatic tone, she repeated, "Where is Jane? Did she move? What's her new telephone number? I want to call and thank her for all her help."

"Jane was in an accident," he said.

It seemed as though it was going to take forever to get a complete answer. Why was he being so evasive? "Are you going to tell me? Is she in the hospital?"

"No, it was a fatal accident. She didn't survive. I didn't know how to tell you especially on the phone."

Grace was in a state of shock. She was trying to regain her composure. Her eyes were brimming over with tears spilling down her cheeks. She didn't think that she would ever be able to cry again after she had shed so many tears for her darling husband. She had a multitude of questions she had to ask, took a deep breath and said that she would like to know how such a terrible thing had happened.

He said that it was an automobile accident; she didn't even make it to the hospital.

Grace was wondering how she could tell Cliff. Jane was a great secretary and personal assistant, had helped them all so much after the loss of their daughter Julia, their move across country, and a multitude of other things. How could this have happened?

They would never know what happened. Never know how Jane felt that her efforts weren't appreciated or needed. She arranged everything, but after they arrived, no one seemed to care or need her. She left the hotel, flew back to San Diego, and rented a car. She was really in no condition to drive. She hadn't eaten, was exhausted, and was crying as she drove out of the Lindbergh International Airport. Her eyes were filled with tears making it difficult to see where she was going. She continued driving and went through an intersection against the light. Her car and three others collided. She actually caused the accident. They had to use the "jaws of life" to get her out but she was already gone.

Grace finally said that she was sorry. Jane was a very nice person and very competent. They always appreciated everything she did for them, especially the arrangements to fly to Colorado.

She realized that she was rambling, thanked him for the information, and extended an invitation that when he was in the neighborhood to stop by, he would always be most welcome. Grace was at a loss as to how to handle this information. She decided to wait until after dinner.

Miss Monique announced that dinner was served and everyone said in unison, "Good because we are starving," as they began walking toward the kitchen. They were all offering to help Gordon, but he insisted that he didn't need any help and said, "I am getting to be a pro using these sticks" as he waved one crutch around for emphasis.

Grace was startled and said, "Let's not show off! We all know you are terrific, no matter what you do." He sat down and they lifted his leg onto a pillow on top of a foot stool.

It was wonderful everyone sitting down together at the kitchen table chatting, exchanging ideas, and the children talking incessantly. It was good to be home again to enjoy the fragrance of Miss Monique's cooking that filled the room and beyond.

All through dinner Grace was thinking about what had happened to Jane. She must have been very distraught. Why did she leave Colorado without telling anyone? What was her problem? She arranged the entire trip and then seemingly vanished without saying anything, resulting in a multitude of questions that would never be answered. They said that Jane's eyes were red; her face wet with tears, and believed she had been crying which accounted for her going through the light at the intersection.

Gordon looked at his darling wife and said, "Why are you so pensive? What are you thinking about?" She turned to him and he leaned over and kissed her. It was so wonderful to have things back to normal but what she had to tell them wasn't normal. It would have a very devastating effect.

"You still aren't talking my darling," Gordon said. Then Ra Ra and Jacques came over and crawled onto her lap. What a delight! They were so adorable. She loved "playing" grandma.

Nancy said, "It's getting late and bath time had to be observed.

They looked up at her and groaned. "Let's wait a little longer," they wailed. They wanted more time with the grownups but were losing. They ran to Claudette who dearly loved them as Cliff watched.

He loved watching Claudette interact with his children. She was so kind and caring with them.

Claudette said, "If you go right now with Nancy, you can come back down in your pajamas and join us."

Ra Ra jumped up and down clapping her hands, and Jacques, being a bit of a copycat, joined her. It was so cute.

Nancy held out her hands and they went with her but announced, "We'll be back."

"That's good; we'll be waiting," Claudette said laughing.

They were all noticing that Grace wasn't her perky self. She didn't laugh or join in. She was solemn and they didn't know why.

Finally, Cliff put an arm around her shoulders and asked, "What's wrong? You don't seem happy. What's wrong? Please tell us. We want to see your smiling face."

Grace took a deep breath and they all looked at her. They couldn't image what had upset her. She was so pale that her face had an almost translucent appearance. The silence seemed to go on forever. Grace took another deep breath, moistened her lips, and prayed that she would be able to say it in the nicest way.

I called Jane's apartment today, but no one answered. Then I called Cliff's law office and asked to speak with her and wondered why everyone was being so evasive. Finally, after speaking with a number of personnel, I was told that there had been an accident. Jane had rented a car at the Lindberg Airport and was driving erratically. It is believed that she was crying and her vision was obscured by her tears. She didn't observe the signal, drove through a red light and caused a three-car collision. They had to use the "jaws of life" to get her out. But, it was too late, she was killed instantly. There were sighs, gasps, and words such as, "Oh! My God."

The group acted as though mesmerized. Ultimately, Miss Monique said, "I don't believe it. We didn't even understand why she suddenly checked out of the hotel and left Colorado without a word to any of us."

Claudette was worried about Cliff. Jane had been the most perfect secretary, always on "Top of things." He looked drained which wasn't good for him. He had a concussion and was still recuperating. Miss Monique didn't know what to say. She like the others was in a daze. It was all too terrible.

Mrs. Svensen asked about arrangements.

Grace said, "I'll call tomorrow.

They heard Nancy saying, 'Don't run, walk," to the children who were wearing their pajamas.

Claudette asked, "Would you like me to read you a bed time story?" Ra Ra and Jacques jointly said, "Yes. You come too grandma."

They said "Good night" to everyone, ran over, grabbed Claudette's and grandma's hands, and were pulling them toward the stairs.

Grace said, "I'll read a bedtime story to Ra Ra and you can read one to Jacques."

Claudette agreed and went with Jacques into his room, tucked him in bed, and looked at all the books on his shelves. "What story would you like me to read?" Claudette asked.

Jacques knew exactly what story he wanted and pointed to the red book, but she couldn't find it. He kept pointing and was getting impatient, he really wanted that book.

She kept asking him what is the title, but he just kept repeating Cuddles, Cuddles the goose, <u>Cuddles Helps Santa Claus Save Christmas(c).</u>

"Here it is," she said holding it up. Jacques clapped his little hands, enthusiastically jumped out of bed, picked up his Cuddles plush toy that was on the little chair, and climbed back under the covers in anticipation of hearing his favorite story.

Claudette adjusted his covers and smiled at the little boy holding his favorite toy, Cuddles.

"Let's start," Jacques urged.

But, she said, "It isn't Christmas."

He said, "I know, but it's my favorite story. I like it! I like it!"

Claudette sat down on the edge of the bed and began reading the book, <u>CUDDLES HELPS SANTA CLAUS SAVE CHRISTMAS(c).</u>

"I am not familiar with this story," Claudette said. "What is it about?"

Jacques in his cute little way said that it's the story of how Santa has a really big problem and Cuddles with her magic beak solves it. It has thunder, lightning, a big castle, and "It's soooo cool."

Grace stuck her head in and asked, "How is it going?" Has he fallen asleep?

He really likes this story and look at how cute he is hugging Cuddles, the goose, his favorite toy. Grace came in and sat down.

Claudette began reading and shortly thereafter the adorable boy holding his Cuddles was sound asleep.

The ladies went back downstairs to join the others. It was supposed to be a day of celebration, Gordon and Cliff were back home to recuperate, but it was also turning out to be a day of mourning for Jane. They just couldn't believe the way she had acted leaving Colorado so abruptly; it was as though she was running away.

Numerous unanswered questions. Gordon asked Cliff if he understood any of it.

"No," Cliff said, "It's incomprehensible. She was an excellent secretary, very organized, dedicated, and great with clients. It will be difficult to replace her. She will be missed." By the time that Cliff finished speaking everyone felt even sadder and tears were filling their eyes.

Miss Monique felt that far too many tears had been shed and announced that dessert was being served. "Let's all go into our cozy kitchen and enjoy some ambrosia."

Cliff couldn't resist, "What have you created now?"

Monique wasn't about to divulge, "You'll have to come in and see for yourself."

They walked somberly into the kitchen, seated themselves, and tried to get excited about what confection Miss Monique had whipped up. She was a fabulous chef having mastered French and Italian cuisine. They all loved her creations. The table was already set with cake plates, forks, and cups of coffee as Miss Monique said in a chirpy voice she used when she was getting ready to serve one of her exciting creations.

"Close your eyes and put your hands in your lap." They heard her footsteps as she approached and placed the surprise in the middle of the table, and as she stepped back trying to control her excitement, Miss Monique said, "You can open your eyes," as she waited for the oohs and aahs.

They stared in disbelief at the luscious creation then exclaimed that it looked fabulous and knew it would be delicious.

Miss Monique was smiling as she stood next to them holding a cake knife ready to cut and serve. She cut the slices; Grace passed the plates, sat down, and said, "Bon Appetite!"

Gordon was the first to expound on her delicacy, "This is absolutely delicious. You've been holding out on us," he said laughing. "What other goodies can we expect? We love everything you make," held up his coffee cup and said, "Let's toast our magical chef, Mademoiselle Monique." They raised their coffee cups and clinked.

Grace, unhappy to do so, said, "It's time that we all were in dreamland." They all hugged, thanked Miss Monique, and as they went upstairs, wished everyone a good night and said, "We'll see you all in the morning."

Cliff had a fitful night. He kept dreaming about Jane and wondering if he had done or not done something that caused her to be so downhearted and depressed as to drive when she obviously shouldn't have been behind the wheel.

He wasn't the only one who felt disconcerted about Jane's demise. Miss Monique and Grace always wondered if they could have done something, but they honestly couldn't think of anything that they could or should have handled differently.

Cliff asked Grace if she would please contact Jane's mother.

When Grace called Cliff's law office, she learned that Mrs. Simms had already been contacted and had left precise instructions of what was to be done and emphasized, no public service. It was to be private with only a few selected persons invited. Furthermore, she requested that no one contact her.

Mrs. Simms was deep in mourning and did not want to be disturbed by anyone no matter what their good intentions might be. She also requested that all personal items be donated to a thrift store with the exception of any important papers. She thanked everyone on behalf of her daughter. Also, if any monies were due Jane, they were to be donated to the San Diego and Chula Vista Public Libraries for the purchase of books to benefit children in Jane's name. Mrs. Simms hoped that covered all possible contingencies and reiterated that no one was to contact her and said, "Good bye."

Grace was shocked about what she had been told. She had never heard of anything comparable. Why was Jane's mother so adamant about no one contacting her? A number of people at Cliff's West Coast Law Office would have liked to pay their respects but Mrs. Simms denied them the opportunity. How was she going to tell Cliff, he would be devastated. He was in no position to go to a service, but he would have appreciated the opportunity to speak with Mrs. Simms to offer his condolences. Now, he would just have to forget Jane.

Grace said that Jane's mother instructed that any monies owed to Jane be donated to the San Diego City and Chula Vista Public Libraries for the purchase of books to benefit children. Cliff thought for a moment and then said, "I'll check to see how much she has coming and I'll add a bonus.

"Mrs. Simms has a good idea making that gift to the library in Jane's name. It will be a good tribute to her and will bring pleasure and happiness to children now and for years to come."

It was fun playing with Ra Ra and Jacques. They were such cute kids and he loved spending quality time with them and Claudette. But, Cliff was anxious to get back to the office. Lounging around the house was getting to be monotonous. He loved the law and wanted to get back to seeing clients, etc.

Just then he heard the large door knocker and wondered who would be calling as it was still very early. To his pleasure, it was Claudette and she looked ravishing, her hair beautifully brushed and down around her shoulders, her eyes were sparkling as she enthusiastically rushed over to him, putting her arms around his neck as she slid onto his lap. She had a great figure and looked great in the yellow two-piece dress with matching heels. She always looked fabulous regardless of what she wore.

She put her hand behind his neck as he brought her close to him with his powerful arms and he pressed against her sensual lips in a kiss that left her breathless. They couldn't be satisfied with just one kiss and were still kissing when Grace walked in. Claudette looked somewhat embarrassed,

Grace said, "Just stay in each other's arms. When you're in love sitting on your fiancé's lap is pure ecstasy." They agreed. Grace said that she had come in to ask if they would like to join her and the others for one of Miss Monique's fabulous breakfasts. "Just come in when you're ready," Grace said as she walked toward the kitchen.

She glanced up as she walked past the stairway and saw her darling grandchildren Ra Ra and Jacques coming down the stairs with Nancy.

She asked, "Are you ready for breakfast?"

"Yes," they said and then asked, "Are we having pancakes?"

Grace said, "Let's go ask Miss Monique." The kitchen as usual was warm and cozy with the sun just beginning to stream in through the windows. It was a light airy room perfect to enjoy the morning sunrise.

Miss Monique was smiling. She loved to keep everyone guessing about the menu. The children were not about to give up. They kept asking and asking.

Finally, she asked, "Did you wash your hands?" They held out their hands for her inspection and approval. She leaned over and said, "Hmmmm, looks like you did a really great job washing up. I'm proud of you," and she patted them on top of the head as they put their arms around her legs to hug her. They were so delightful.

"Let's sit down," she said as she heard some of the others coming in. Cliff and Claudette's arms intertwined and looking at each other in that special way reserved for lovers. Her heart warmed when she saw that Cliff looked so much better.

She busied herself making pancakes, eggs, sausage, toast, bacon, pouring fresh squeezed orange juice, piping hot coffee, and milk for the children.

Gordon came in his arm and leg still in a cast. He was becoming quite an expert at using the crutches. He and Grace were happy that today his casts would be removed which would be a relief. It was no fun carrying around all that plaster. They sat down and heard shouts of glee as Miss Monique put the pancakes on the table. Ra Ra and Jacques were thrilled that they were going to have pancakes. Grace put pancakes on their plates, poured them a glass of milk, and waited for them to enjoy their breakfast. But they didn't start eating.

"What's wrong?" their grandmother asked.

"You forgot the maple syrup," they said.

"You are right," and Grace and immediately poured maple syrup on their pancakes and watched them enjoy their favorite breakfast.

Grace said that they would be going to the doctor's office and asked if Miss Monique needed anything.

"No. Everything is fine and the kitchen is well-stocked," she said.

Claudette said that she had some appointments and would call later that afternoon.

Cliff pulled her close to him and passionately kissed her. "Let's go out to dinner tonight and wear something rather festive if you know what I mean. Dressy evening type wear. I'll be wearing a tuxedo. Are you in for an evening of fun, frivolity, and dancing?"

Claudette was pleased at the prospect of going out with him. It had been too long. "Yes and I'll be looking forward to it," she said and "I'll look forward to your phone call. Enjoy your day," and she walked out the door.

After she left, Cliff went to the phone, called Tiffanies, introduced himself and asked for the manager. Cliff said, "I need a superlative engagement ring. I plan to ask her tonight, so I will need the ring this afternoon. Can you come to my home and bring a selection of your most artistic rings, I'm thinking about two or three carats. Do you have any in stock? Do you have any that are one of a kind?"

The manager said that it could be arranged and asked if 3:00 would be a good time. "That's perfect," and gave him the address and telephone number. He told him that he was the managing partner of a west coast law firm.

The manager asked, "Were you recently injured in a plane crash in Colorado?"

Cliff said, "Yes," and that he would be expecting him at 3:00 and if he needed to change the appointment time to please call. Cliff suddenly remembered that one of his law partners had recently become engaged and was extolling the virtues of his beautiful bride and the exquisite one-of-a-kind ring he had purchased at a small eloquent shop. Again, Cliff reached for the phone, called his law office, and asked to speak with Larry.

"Hello Cliff, great to hear from you and that you're doing so well. We miss you here. You know that we are incomplete without you" Larry said.

"Thank you, and it's always nice to hear that one is appreciated," and they both laughed. "Larry, as you know, I'm planning to ask Claudette to marry me," Cliff said as he was interrupted by Larry congratulating him and wishing him the best.

"What can I do for you? Do you want some advice from a newlywed bridegroom?" he asked with his smiling voice.

"Yes, I am in the process of purchasing an engagement ring. I want something she'll love that is not run-of-the-mill. It has to be totally special, hopefully an original, but I know it is short notice. Any suggestions? Where did you purchase the ring for your bride?" Cliff asked.

"I bought mine at a small shop that has exquisite jewelry many of them are the creation of the jeweler and owner of the shop, Pierre Bouchard. He is an old school gentleman with manners many no longer observe, and he is very personable. You'll like him," Larry said, and then asked, "How easy is it for you to get around? Are you able to drive? Or is it too soon?"

Cliff said, "The doctor prefers that I wait another week before I start driving."

Larry was very concerned and offered to pick Cliff up and drive him to the jewelry store. "I'll call to make sure Pierre is in his shop, and I'll be over to pick you up in about twenty minutes. How does that work with your schedule?"

Cliff said that would be perfect and he would be ready. He then called Tiffanys and explained that he needed to cancel the appointment and hoped he hadn't inconvenienced anyone. They were very kind and wished him well with his convalescence.

Right on time, Larry arrived in his new sleek two-seater Rolls white convertible.

"Wow, what a beautiful car! It must be a dream to drive. What is the engine size?" Cliff had a multitude of questions and Larry had all the answers as they talked about the Rolls on the way to the jeweler.

"Here it is," Larry announced. "The owner's name is Pierre Bouchard. You'll like him. He's a highly educated French gentleman whose family is in the French royal line," Larry said, as he led the way and opened the door for Cliff. He noted that Cliff really looked as though he had fully recuperated.

Mr. Bouchard approached the pair and said, "Larry, it's great to see you again and how is the happily married bridegroom?" They all laughed softly and Larry introduced Cliff.

Pierre asked how he could be of service and said he was happy to meet Cliff and humbled that they came to his shop.

Larry said, "Cliff is planning to marry the girl of his dreams, therefore he needs an engagement ring. I told him about your shop and the fabulous pieces you artistically create."

Pierre suggested that they be comfortably seated in front of the glass counter at the side of the room.

He disappeared into the back and returned shortly with a tray of gems, some set in gold and others in platinum, ranging from one-half-carat. Pierre put the tray on the counter and asked Cliff, "Is there anything you like?"

Cliff paused. He really didn't know what to say. He leaned over and asked Larry what he thought. They both seemed bewildered even though Larry had purchased his ring just a few months before.

Pierre said, "Cliff, perhaps I can be of assistance. Do you have a preference as to gold or platinum?"

Cliff said, "I think gold."

"That's a start," Pierre said. "Now let's look at couple of different sizes: this is a one-half carat diamond, this is a one-carat, and here is a two-carat. Do any of these seem to be the size you were thinking of?"

Cliff said, "One-carat would be ideal." He felt that Claudette wouldn't want something too ostentatious; she was not that kind of girl. "A one-carat diamond with three small diamonds on either side, mounted on a yellow gold band would suit his fiancée." Then he asked the jeweler, "What do you think?"

Pierre said that would be a beautiful engagement ring as he again went into the vault for a selection that would fit Cliff's description. Pierre returned a few moments later with two more trays. He said, "All of these are one-carat with small diamonds mounted on either side as a beautiful accent on yellow gold. Do any of these seem right?"

Cliff asked if any of the rings in the tray were one-of-a-kind. "Yes," Pierre said, "I designed several of them," and pointed to the ones that were his original creations.

Cliff kept staring at the rings, and after a few minutes, he was more confused than ever. "Larry, what do you think? How did you choose?" Cliff asked.

Pierre said that he had a suggestion. "I'll take out a few that I think might fit your criteria and put one on each of these velvet fingers that are used for display purposes."

Cliff stared at the displayed rings and asked Larry what he thought.

Larry said that it's really a personal decision, but he favored the one on the left.

Pierre took two more rings and placed each one on a velvet finger display. "Does that help?" he inquired.

Cliff reached over and picked one up and turned it under the light as Pierre handed him a magnifying glass. The ring was breath taking. The cut of the diamond was perfect. "I think this is it," Cliff said and then turned to Larry and asked what he thought. "I think it's perfect. Claudette will love it."

Pierre, smiling, said, "That is one of my favorites. I just finished designing it yesterday. It's a perfect flawless diamond for your perfect bride."

Cliff sat back; it was a challenge but well worth the effort. He had to remember this shop as he planned to come back often and asked Pierre for his card.

"What do you want engraved on the inside," Pierre inquired.

Another decision, he was trying to think. He wanted the inscription to be succinct, poetic, and one that professed his love for her. Pierre, "I would like the inscription to read: 'Forever My Love,'" Cliff said.

Pierre had one more very important question, "What size is her finger?" Cliff said that he anticipated that question, had asked her several weeks ago, and she said that she wears a size five ring.

"Is it possible that it can be inscribed now? I know that it's short notice, but I was planning to ask her tonight," Cliff requested.

"I understand what it's like to be in love and anxious. If you are willing to wait, I will do it for you now," Pierre said.

Cliff was thrilled and told Pierre how much he appreciated it and wanted to give her a special piece of jewelry on their wedding day and wondered what the jeweler might suggest.

Pierre paused as he was giving the request a great deal of thought and then, his eyes shining, said that he could design a bracelet with alternating diamonds, rubies, and sapphires.

Cliff couldn't control his enthusiasm. Pierre's suggestion was perfect. "She has a small wrist," Cliff said.

Pierre said that he had a solution. "I can make it adjustable with the additional stones dangling. If she prefers to have the bracelet fit perfectly, I can make the bracelet smaller to the exact size of her wrist. If you decide to do that, just call and let me know when you and your bride are coming in, I will be expecting you. It will give me an opportunity to congratulate her and see the beautiful ring on her finger.

Pierre finished engraving the engagement ring and handed it to Cliff. It was perfect. Pierre was a genius when it came to jewelry.

Cliff showed it to Larry who wasn't surprised; he knew the kind of work Pierre was capable of. Cliff looked at the ring one more time, paid Pierre, and asked when the bracelet would be ready.

Pierre said that he would call by the end of the week. Pierre handed him the ring in a velvet box.

Cliff thanked Pierre and shook his hand. Cliff said that he planned to give the ring to Claudette that evening.

Cliff thanked Larry on the drive home and said how very much he appreciated the introduction to Pierre. "I will be seeing the doctor tomorrow and plan to be in the office next week. Your car is a fine piece of machinery. When I get ready to purchase another vehicle, I'll call you for an introduction to the salesman."

They arrived at Cliff's home, he opened the car door, ring box in hand, again thanked his friend, Larry, and said that they must get together soon, and reminded him that he was looking forward to seeing him and his bride at his wedding. Cliff closed the car door and quickly walked up the steps and through the door of his home.

Grace was walking toward the door to open it. When Cliff burst in, his face flushed, he grabbed Grace and swung her around.

"What is it?" Grace asked.

"I got it! I got it!" Cliff repeated excitedly.

"You got what?" she asked, a quizzical look on her face.

Cliff held out his hand with the velvet ring box.

Grace picked it up, carefully opened the box and exclaimed, "It's beautiful. Claudette will love it. When are you going to give it to her?"

Cliff replied, "Tonight." They hugged each other in anticipation and excitement of the evening's events.

CHAPTER TWENTY

The excitement of the evening's proposal brought back visions of the day that Gordon proposed to his wife. Grace vividly remembered how very handsome he looked in his United States Air Force uniform as she thought he would be escorting her to the Officers' Club on base.

She remembered how much time she had spent deciding what to wear. She was going through her closet, trying to find the right dress. It was impossible. Nothing seemed to be right. "How could I have ever thought these dresses were appropriate or perfect for a special occasion?"

She remembered taking dress after dress out of her closet and standing in front of her full-length mirror as she held each one up in front of her, and then tossing them aside on the bed. It was impossible. Nothing, absolutely nothing in her closet would do. She grabbed her purse that was on her dresser, ran down the two flights of stairs, opened her car door, slid onto the front seat, put the key in, started the engine, and headed for the mall. She hoped to have ample time to find the perfect dress.

She parked near the entrance and went into the most fashionable store, walked in, and was approached by a sales woman who offered to assist her. When Grace explained that she desperately needed the perfectly stunning dress for a date that night, the sales woman directed her to the designer department.

Grace walked toward the nearest display of evening gowns and reached out to check each one. A sales girl came over and offered to be of assistance. Grace explained that she needed an extra special fabulously sensational dress for that evening. "I'm certain the man that I so dearly love is going to ask me to marry him, and I must find the absolutely perfect dress. I'm sorry; I forgot to ask your name."

The sales clerk said, "My name is Lauren, and I am happy to serve you" as she was busily looking through the racks for the dress that would enhance Grace's figure and make her look ravishing. It didn't look as though she'd find anything appropriate and Grace was quickly becoming disenchanted. She was trying to decide where to go if she couldn't find anything here when suddenly the clerk rushed over to tell her that she had found the greatest creation.

"It's in a box that had been delivered early that morning and put on a shelf because they didn't have time to open it. They had been extremely busy all morning," she said.

Grace looked up and saw the clerk carrying the huge white box.

The clerk put it down on the counter and said to Grace, "Why don't you open it?"

Grace walked over, removed the lid, and saw the most beautiful shade of blue that she had ever seen. It was spectacular. She very carefully took the dress out of the box, walked over to the mirror, and held it up in front of her. It was perfect.

Lauren said, "It's perfect for you. You have the most beautiful velvety blue eyes this dress accents. Your guy will be entranced when he sees you. It looks like your size. Do you want to try it on?"

Lauren showed her to a dressing room and offered to help. She arranged the gown on a hanger and put it up on a hook.

Grace kept looking at the dress. She couldn't believe she had found it. How often does that happen? She slipped the dress on. It was perfect.

The clerk asked, "Do you need anything? I hope that you will let me see you in the dress."

Grace felt obligated since the clerk was so accommodating and stepped out of the dressing room.

Lauren squealed while trying to say softly, "It's perfect. It's you." Suddenly shoppers were clapping as they were looking at Grace in her gown--she was a vision of loveliness. Grace smiled, stepped back into the dressing room, removed the dress, and put on her street clothes.

Lauren came over, carefully folded the dress, and put it back in the box.

Grace thanked her and said, "I will call the store manager and tell him that you are an asset to the store and that you possess excellent customer and public relations skills."

Lauren thanked her and said, "I know that you will have a wonderful time tonight."

Grace was anxious to go home but then realized she needed a pair of shoes and a matching bag.

Lauren asked, "Do you need help with something else?"

Grace said, "I need to purchase a pair of shoes and matching bag."

Let me show you to the shoe department and explained to the shoe clerk what Grace was interested in purchasing.

The shoe clerk came over with a pair of heels and a bag that perfectly matched her dress. She tried on the heels, they were perfect. He then handed her the beaded evening bag and she walked over to the mirror and admired herself.

"I'll take them both," she said as she asked him to please charge her account. Grace was thrilled with her purchases, thanked the clerk as she picked up her dress, shoes, and bag boxes as Lauren came over offering to carry them to her car. "That's very nice of you," Grace said as they walked to her car.

Grace couldn't wait to show her mother the purchases. Her mother was ecstatic when she saw the dress. "It's you, absolutely perfect" she said. "I can't wait to see you in your new finery. Your father and I will be downstairs and we'll let you know when your date arrives," she said as she walked forward to embrace her daughter. "I'll turn on your bath water. Enjoy your bubble bath," her mother, said.

Her mother, in addition to turning on the water for her bubble bath, lit a few candles and turned on soft melodious music.

Grace stepped into the huge tub filled with bubbles and relaxed. Everything was wonderful, and after tonight--all would be perfect.

Grace carefully selected a skin body softening lotion that she applied after towel drying. She felt fabulous as she carefully applied her makeup, combed her blondish red naturally curly hair as it softly cascaded down around her shoulders. She always loved her curly hair and didn't do what so many of the girls did to either straighten or change it.

She put on her new dress, slid into her shoes, then walked over to the floor length mirror. She liked what she saw and hoped that Gordon would. Her jewelry box was open on her dressing table and she deliberated, wanting her selection to properly accessorize her gown. She carefully selected the pearl necklace with matching earrings her parents had given her on her sixteenth birthday.

She stood once again in front of the full length mirror this time clutching her new blue evening purse that matched her shoes. She felt very elegant as she opened her bedroom door and began walking down the stairs. As she approached the main floor, she called to her parents. They liked to see her come down the stairs in a new outfit.

They watched her and she saw by the smiles on their faces, they approved. Her mother had put on dance music and her father was waiting for the first dance. He was an excellent dancer. Her parents often went out dancing.

The door bell rang and her mother said, "Quickly go upstairs and make a grand entrance."

Grace's father answered the door and Gordon extended his hand. He was quite the gentleman and to him a hand shake was a sign of respect. Then he walked over to Grace's mother and handed her a bouquet. He was extremely thoughtful.

Grace's father called her and she started down the stairs as Gordon stared at this beautiful girl whom he so dearly loved. They watched Gordon's face and were pleased with what they saw.

When Grace reached the bottom of the stairs, her mother handed her a beautiful white ermine stole; her father hugged her as he draped it around his daughter's shoulders. Gordon handed her a corsage of three creamy white orchids, the perfect accent for her dress.

They left amid words of good wishes and have a good time. Gordon opened the car door for her, and she easily slid inside. It was a beautiful, expertly maintained cream colored Cadillac, and they were off. Gordon was a real gentleman, very gallant.

The sky was beautiful full of twinkling stars and a full moon. It was a wonderfully warm evening with a soft breeze blowing. She looked even more beautiful in the moonlight, and he was thinking, "I'm a lucky man, she's all mine, and I adore her."

"Are we off to the officers' club?" she asked easily.

"You'll see and do you have a preference?" He asked, smiling while he reached for her hand.

She felt so good with him, it was as though they were two separate entities, but together they were one--complete. She loved him so much and knew in her heart that he felt the same way. She was anticipating an evening they would both remember through the anniversaries they would celebrate together. She suddenly looked up and gazed through the windshield, this was not the way to the officers' club. Where were they going? She became even more excited and filled with more anticipation.

They had been driving for quite a while. She had lost track of time. Nothing was more important than being with Gordon, their hands clasped together, she sat leaning against the soft plush leather seats as the car sped forward.

He remembered how he had come upon a unique French restaurant one day when he made a wrong turn and there it was. He parked and went in. It was totally charming. He sat down and ordered a French pastry, it was delicious, he was delighted when a lady came over, introduced herself as Penelope LeClair, and said that she and her husband, Philippe, had immigrated from France and opened the restaurant to offer authentic French cuisine.

He asked her to sit down. She was charming and had created a marvelous warm and cozy environment. They chatted for while and she inquired if there was anything else she could serve him.

"Yes," he said, as she remained seated. "There is something else," and before he could finish the sentence she got up and asked, "What would you like? I'll get it for you."

"Please sit down Madame LeClair," he said softly and proceeded to explain what he was referring to. "I am planning to ask the most wonderful girl in the world to marry me and originally thought that I would take her to the officers' club at the base, but I think this would be a more perfect setting. It is a charmingly cozy room with the magnificent adjacent gardens in bloom and the flowers perfume filling the air through the French doors is ideal.

"This atmosphere is perfect. We will enjoy: authentic French dinner, dancing, and at some point I'll ask the girl of my dreams to marry me amid the merriment and sound of a violin softly playing our love song, 'I Will Always Love You,' the perfect setting," he concluded.

Madame LeClair was enraptured with what he had said. "How perfectly beautiful," she said her eyes tearing. "We will be honored for you to bring your perspective bride to our humble restaurant," she said as she reached across the table to touch his hand.

"Thank you," he said, "I am most appreciative," and he proceeded to tell her the date and time they would be arriving. "I am remiss with my manners." he said, "My name is Gordon Deveaux, the name of my future wife is Grace, and I am glad to have found the most perfect place to 'pop' the question."

"I am happy to meet you General, and may I call you Gordon?"
"Yes, I would be honored." All of the arrangements were made. He left the menu up to her, he knew that she would make it special including the dessert and told her so.

As he walked out, he said that he hoped the restaurant would be filled to capacity with happy fun loving people enjoying a good time.

Gordon turned the car onto the road paralleling the restaurant, and parked. "Close your eyes," he said in a soft commanding voice.

She was amused as she followed his instructions. He opened her door, helped her out, and felt her brush against him. He wanted to kiss her but decided to wait until later otherwise they might never go inside and have dinner. He guided her toward the door of the quaint French restaurant where he had reservations.

Madame Penelope LeClair, owner of the restaurant, had been watching for them and saw him get out of the car, walk around, and open the door for Grace to alight.

"Are your eyes closed?" he asked excitedly.

"Yes, they are closed." When they were in front of the restaurant, he said softly, "Open your eyes, my love."

Grace opened her eyes and was thrilled with what she saw. There in front of her was an old world style restaurant in all its glory. "How beautiful," she exclaimed, clasping her hands together in front of her. "I love it; how gallantly thoughtful of you to find it. It will always be permanently emblazed in my memory," she said looking at it while endeavoring to memorize every detail.

He tightened his arm around her as he bent down to kiss her and gently guided her toward the open door where Madame LeClair was anxiously waiting to greet them. She and her husband had planned a special menu and the band was eagerly looking forward to playing for the couple.

Madame LeClair was smiling broadly as she said, "Bienvenu" and guided the couple to their table specially set with traditional French china, crystal, silver, and a sparkling white linen table cloth with matching napkins. A bouquet of delicately cut red, white, and blue iris--the colors of the French flag and the national flower of France, iris-- were carefully arranged in a crystal bowl between a matching pair of crystal candlesticks.

Gordon and Grace were breathless as they stared at the table so exquisitely set, awaiting their arrival. Gordon walked over and held the chair for Grace; she sat down and looked up at him lovingly as he arranged her stole on the back of her chair.

He couldn't resist and bent down to kiss her. The more he kissed her, the more she wanted him. He couldn't get enough of her: "How was it possible that he could feel this way. He never thought it would be possible, never thought he would get married, and yet here he was on the brink of asking this gorgeous creature in blue to marry him. It was all so exciting."

He walked around to the other side of the table, pulled out the chair, and sat down. He couldn't take his eyes off her and loved that they were sitting across each other. They sat gazing into each other's eyes.

Madame LeClair came over, lit the candles, and said that she would be back momentarily.

Her husband, Philippe LeClair, came over with two crystal stemware glasses filled with a spectacular burgundy wine, on a small silver tray. He introduced himself and smiled as he picked up one glass and placed it in front of Grace and the other for Gordon.

They didn't even notice that Monsieur LeClair had walked away. They only had eyes for each other. Gordon raised his glass and she raised hers, they clinked glasses, and sipped some of the delicious purple liquid.

The restaurant was crowded exactly as Gordon had hoped it would be. He wanted a crowd to share in their special moment. Grace was saying how very much she appreciated all the arrangements and time Gordon had spent to give her this magical evening. They chatted softly and sipped the superb wine as the band was tuning up.

Gordon was anxious for the band to start playing so that he could hold her in his arms. He wasn't the only one anxious for the music to begin. Grace was also anxiously waiting to hear the music. Their wish was granted when the band began playing. Gordon recognized the tune as one that included a violin solo and anticipated what he felt would happen next and was not disappointed.

The violinist approached their table and soft strains filled the air as he carefully and methodically moved the bow across the strings. It was melodious--very romantic. Gordon and Grace were enchanted as their gaze moved from the violinist to each other. What a magical evening! How perfect.

Madame LeClair, a charming, endearing hostess, was approaching with their salad. She placed the bowl on the table, tossed it, and served them.

"It looks delicious," they said in unison. Mrs. LeClair smiled and left the couple to enjoy their salad. They wanted the evening to last forever; therefore, they ate slowly, while looking at each adoringly.

Gordon couldn't wait to hold his future bride and asked, smiling, "May, I have this dance, my love?" She looked up at him admiringly as he got up, came over to hold her chair as she arose, and they walked the short distance to the dance floor.

They whirled around the dance floor to the soft melodious music. It was indeed a magical night. The band played beautifully and had perfect rhythm making it easy to dance to the musical selections. Gordon couldn't dance unless the rhythm was perfect. He was a superlative dancer and loved whirling her around the floor.

They danced continuously until Gordon suggested that they step into the adjacent garden patio. It was breath taking with the waterfall in the corner adding to the ambiance. The wondrous sound of the waterfall cascading onto the rocks below then flowed ever downward as sprinkles of water were splashing on the plants below. The trees, plants, and fragrance from the roses, gardenias, and other flowers transformed the garden into a magical setting.

It was a marvelously intimate setting. There were white round wrought iron tables, matching wrought iron chairs, and a bouquet of fresh flowers on each table. They sat down on one of the white wrought iron benches with side arms and a back.

Gordon put his arm around her, drew her close to him, and kissed her passionately. "Shall we go in and see what Madame LeClair and her husbands have whipped up for the next course of our dinner," he asked as he helped her to her feet, and with their arms entwined around each other went in to sit down at their table.

Madame LeClair saw the couple come in and immediately went into the kitchen. Her husband also saw the couple come in and began setting up their next course. Madame LeClair picked up the dishes, put them on a tray, and carried it into the dining room.

She carefully put the main course and side dishes in front of each of them. "Would you like to have coffee or tea?" she asked.

Gordon said, "Coffee, please."

Mrs. LeClair nodded and returned with two cups of coffee, a basket of rolls, and two finger bowls that she carefully placed on the table. They thanked her and began enjoying their dinner. It was delicious.

Grace asked Gordon almost apologetically, "What is the name of these marvelous creations?" He reached out to touch her slender, delicate fingers and said, "This is 'omelegte aux tanes herbes;' a fresh herb omelet, here we have 'paves te rumsteak au poivre vert,' sirloin steak with fresh peppercorns, and this," indicating with his fork is 'pommes sautéed a cru,' sauteed potatoes," and laughed as he said again pointing with his fork "is coffee and that, a basket of rolls." They laughed as their eyes met across the table.

The LeClair's were carefully watching the couple, wondering when he would "pop" the question and if they should serve the dessert or wait; they were undecided. She decided that she would approach the table and offer to clear the dishes.

They said, "Yes. The dinner was delicious, enjoyed every bite, and we will be coming back often."

Madame then asked cautiously, "Would you like your dessert now?"
Gordon said, "Yes, that would be perfect."

She nodded and said that she would also be filling their coffee cups and asked, "Is there anything else I can serve you?"

Gordon said, "Yes, but later." Mrs. LeClair retreated to the kitchen.

The band was playing. Gordon said, "I'll be right back, I'm going to ask the band to play a special request."

Grace smiled and nodded.

Gordon saw Mrs. LeClair watching him and he motioned for her to come over. "I'm going to ask her now," he said. "I would appreciate having the violinist come over to our table when I get down on one knee. I'm going to do this traditional style."

She was smiling through tears of happiness and nodded.

As he walked back to their table, he felt for the bulge in his pocket to convince himself that the ring was still there. He sat down when he got to their table and asked, "Do you know how much you mean to me?"

"Yes," she said.

"I love you very much Grace." He watched her velvet blue eyes sparkle as he pushed back his chair and got up.

She looked at him puzzled, and thought, "Why is he getting up?"

He walked over to her and she turned toward him, thinking that he was going to ask her to dance. He got down on one knee just as the violinist was approaching, held her hand, and said, "My dearest darling, you are my life, I love you very much, will you marry me?" and while the violinist was playing their song, Gordon took the velvet ring box out of his pocket, held it in front of her, and opened it.

"He repeated, "I love you. Will you marry me?"

She said, "Yes," bent down beside him and threw her arms around his neck and hugged him.

All the people in the restaurant clapped and cheered.

He took the diamond engagement ring out of the box as she extended her left hand. He slipped the ring on her finger, kissed her hand, brought her close to him and they kissed passionately to the pleasure of everyone in the restaurant but most especially the LeClairs.

While the violinist was still playing, Gordon helped her to her feet and guided her toward the dance floor for their first dance as an engaged couple.

At the conclusion of that dance number, everyone started rushing over wanting to congratulate the couple. It was like a dream that all these people were congratulating them and wishing them a happy future. They felt as though they were in a whirlpool, it was so fabulous, like a dream. She knew that they would treasure every moment forever.

The LeClairs came over and added their congratulations. Madame LeClair couldn't help herself. She had to embrace this beautiful couple who were very much in love.

Gordon and Grace asked the LeClairs to please sit down at their table and enjoy a glass of champagne. They started protesting, but the newly engaged couple wouldn't take "No" for an answer and the two couples sat down to toast the occasion.

Suddenly, Gordon stood up caught up in the emotion of the occasion and said raising his glass of champagne, "Monsieur, please champagne for all our well wishes. I hope that you will all stand and join me in a toast." All the people in the restaurant stood up, raised their glasses and said in loud cheery voices said, "Congratulations! Gordon and Grace, the future General and Mrs. Deveaux." It was glorious. The band started playing and they all danced amid a rush of confetti and balloons.

CHAPTER TWENTY ONE

Cliff was very excited, as he was trying to decide where he should take Claudette for dinner. It had to be extra special. He was sitting at his desk, thinking when Gordon walked in, saw Cliff deep in thought, and asked if he could help.

Cliff said, "I'm trying to decide where to take Claudette tonight as you know I am planning to propose."

Gordon said, "I have the perfect place. It's where I proposed to Grace. It's a charming French restaurant with a dance floor, band complete with violinist, and a patio garden with a waterfall. It's perfect. I took her there when I was stationed here and we go back regularly. The LeClairs, who own the restaurant, are lovely people. I could call and make a reservation for you."

"I would really appreciate that, Gordon. It sounds like the perfect place, very enchanting."

Claudette had been spending the day getting ready for her big date. She was very excited and wanted to look her best and wear the most perfect dress. First, she needed to find a hair dresser and remembered that Jane and others had gone to a first-class hair stylist and make-up artist who had worked wonders. Claudette started going through her notes, found the telephone number, and called Henri.

"Hello, may I please speak with Henri," Claudette requested.

"This is 'enri, how may I help you?"

"I have heard that you can work absolute magic, and I need some expert magic inasmuch as my love is going to ask me to marry him tonight. I know it's short notice. I would be most appreciative if you could fit me in. I could be there is twenty minutes," she said in a pleading childlike voice.

"All right, but not later than twenty minutes."

Claudette hung up the phone, grabbed her purse, and ran out the door. She got in her car, opened her purse, took out the keys, started the engine, and was off. As promised, she arrived at Henri's on time.

She liked his salon. It was very clean and everything was arranged in an orderly manner. The hair stylists were wearing white light weight cotton coats and looked very professional. She introduced herself. Henri came over to greet her, handed her a smock to protect her clothes, and showed her to his work station. She sat down in the chair and asked if he had any immediate ideas about how he was going to proceed.

He paused and said that he did have some ideas. He began what she thought would be a long arduous task. She let herself sink into the chair, closed her eyes, and endeavored to relax while Henri worked his magic.

Several hours later, he asked her if she was ready to look at her reflection?

"I would rather wait until your makeup artist has worked her magic," she replied.

He acknowledged her request.

She relaxed and waited. "It will all be worthwhile," she told herself as she wondered what she was going to wear. Claudette told herself, "I can go to the top fashionable shop in the mall after I leave here. Oh, I should have gone there first. What will I do if my hair gets mussed up? Sometimes, I'm not the greatest planner. But, I must have done something right to have the greatest guy in the world in love with me."

Henri was watching his makeup artist at work and nodded approvingly. "May I ask who is this man you are going to all this trouble to please?"

"He's the love of my life, absolutely wonderful."

"I wonder if I know him; if you don't mind, may I ask what is his name?"

Claudette didn't mind answering his question, "Cliff. He has his own law firm."

Henri was suddenly deep in thought. Where had he heard that name before? I know that name and remembered Jane and what had happened to her. How could he ask that question without providing any information?"

"I think I have heard of him," Henri said pensively while adding, "Some of his personnel have been here. Are you one of his employees?"

"No, I just graduated from Stanford Law School and will be a practicing attorney at law as soon as they send me my bar results."

"That should be a really great day," Henri said, knowing that it would be a wonderful occasion. He was going to say something about Jane but decided it would not be the gentlemanly thing to do. Instead, he asked what she had planned to wear for her big date.

"I was thinking about yellow satin or better yet a gold lame ankle length dress with a slit up the side and off one shoulder. I want it to mold and enhance my figure. Any suggestions?"

Henri replied, "We have some shops nearby; I can ask one of my employees to bring over some selections, and you can try them on."

As he promised, the girl returned with an arm load of dresses, for Claudette. The dresses were put on a rack and Claudette began going through the selections, picturing herself in each one as she pushed the hangars back and forth on the rack. She shook her head, terrified that she wouldn't be able to find that perfect but elusive gold lame ankle length off the shoulder gown with a slit down the side.

Suddenly. there it was right in front of her on the rack. She couldn't believe it. She carefully took the hanger off the rack, hoped it would look as good on her as it did on the hanger, and that it would fit.

She went into the dressing room, closed the curtain, and slipped off her street clothes. She carefully took the treasured dress off the hanger and tried it on. She dared not look in the mirror. It was scary. Did it fit properly?

The girl who had brought the dresses over asked if she would like some help.

"Just a minute," Claudette said as she turned toward the mirror and cautiously lifted her head to view herself in the mirror. She clasped her hand to her mouth. "I look perfect," she thought. The girl inquired again and Claudette repeated, "Just a minute, I will be right out." and stepped out of the dressing room.

The girl gasped, "You look beautiful," and screamed, "Henri, Henri."

He ran over wondering what was wrong. Then he saw Claudette. "You look gorgeous. You are like a dream, a vision of loveliness," Henri said breathlessly. The other salon personnel came over and were astounded when they saw Claudette. "You look beautiful," they exclaimed, "except for your shoes."

Henri said, "Run over and get her a pair of heels with a matching bag." The girl ran out the door and came back with several boxes of shoes and bags. She put the boxes on the counter and opened them up.

"They are all so beautiful," Claudette said as the girl put them down for Claudette to try on. She ultimately selected a gold sandal sling back pair of heels and a matching bag. They were all enchanted by her beauty as she proudly stood in front of them.

She felt like hugging them. They were great. She felt like a princess.

Henri said, "I think it would be a good idea to take off the dress and we'll carefully pack it in a box with tissue to prevent wrinkles."

She went back into the dressing room, carefully slipped out of the gown, and handed it to the girl who was waiting outside the curtain. Claudette quickly dressed anxious to gather her precious purchases, go home to take a long leisurely bubble bath, and dream of the hours to come.

Excitedly, she ran out of the shop to her car, opened the passenger side door, carefully put in her packages, closed the door, went around to the driver's side, slid in, closed the door, put the key in the ignition, and turned on the motor. She glanced to the right and saw the salon personnel waving and broadly smiling. She waved and smiled back.

Henri came over to her car and said that they all wished her luck.

She profusely thanked him and said that she would be a regular at his shop and would be telling all her friends how great he and his staff were, and how much she appreciated them. "Henri, perhaps you know of a great jewelry store nearby? I would like to purchase some accessories."

"Yes, there is a marvelous and very talented jeweler who is very talented and creates many one of kind jewelry pieces. His name is Pierre Bouchard, his shop is in the next block, and you will like him. He's a very distinguished gentleman," and gave her directions.

She thanked him and drove toward the jewelry boutique.

She saw the shop, parked, and went in. True to his word, Henri was right once again. The jewelry store window contained a number of exquisite pieces. She couldn't wait to go in and opened the door.

A very gallant gentleman walked over asking, "Mademoiselle, may I be of assistance?"

She asked, "Pierre Bouchard?"

"Oui," he said.

"Henri recommended your shop and I am so glad that he did. You have so many beautiful pieces that are obviously original creations and are very talented," Claudette said.

"I will have to thank 'enri when I see him. Tell me, how may I assist you?"

Claudette told him that she was looking for something special to accent her new gown. "I think my love is going to ask me to marry him tonight. I just purchased a fabulous gold lame ankle length fitted gown with a slit up the side that is off the shoulder. Do you have a suggestion?"

Pierre Bouchard asked her name as he extended his hand.

She willing accepted his hand and he brought it to his lips and kissed it. Claudette, wanting to be polite, said, "My name is Claudette and my love's name is Cliff."

He said, "Both your names begin with a "C" that will be most advantageous when you put your initials on stationery and other items."

"You know, I never thought about that before. It will be one more thing that we can discuss tonight," she said and thanked him for mentioning it.

Pierre Bouchard became pensive. He now knew who her fiancé was and what a jewel he had and the engagement ring he had designed and Cliff purchased would be perfect on her slender finger.

"You have beautiful violet eyes that would be accented by gold, pearls, rubies, diamonds, or sapphire earrings. Were you thinking of earrings?" he inquired, with a heavy French accent.

"I'm not sure. What do you think? "

"You said that your dress is off one shoulder, therefore a necklace or choker might interfere with the lines of the dress. I think that a pair of earrings would be the perfect accent," he said as he turned around to pick up a black velvet lined tray and placed it on the counter in front of her.

She leaned over to look at the collection but had difficulty deciding; they were all so beautiful! She required screw back earrings. She never had her ears pierced and never would. Pain was not something she was willing to endure. Her mother had always wanted to take her to have her ears pierced and showed her a beautiful pair of earrings that would be hers. But she always refused. She knew that screw back earrings were easier to lose, but that was something she willingly accepted.

"Do you see anything you like?" he asked.

Her eyes brightened as she reached into the box and picked up an exquisite pair of dangling ruby earrings, each stone encircled with tiny diamonds, and saw that were for pierced ears. "My ears aren't pierced, I only wear screw back earrings," she said.

He assured her that he could make the necessary changes if she had a few minutes to wait. She nodded and he saw that her wrists were very small. He was mentally endeavoring to calculate the circumference of her wrist in millimeters for the bracelet Cliff ordered as her wedding gift.

He opened a drawer, removed a few tools, and started making the necessary changes for the transformation to screw back earrings, put them on the velvet cloth, and suggested she try them on.

She carefully picked up one of the earrings, held it up to her left ear lobe and tightened the screw; she picked up the other earring and screwed it to her right ear lobe. She turned to the mirror and was delighted with the affect. "They are the perfect accent for my dress," she said.

He reached under the counter for a velvet box and opened it up for her earrings.

She was pleased. He was a gentleman. She removed the earrings, put them in the box, and he handed it to her. She presented her credit card and thanked him. "I will be coming back," she said and "I will be telling all my friends. Thank you very much. You have made my special night even more special." She waved and he waved back as he held the door for her.

She left smiling, opened her car door, got in, put the special box on the seat beside her, started the engine, and pulled away from the curb on her way home.

She was looking forward to taking a long leisurely bubble bath, spreading on her favorite body lotion, and putting on her scrumptious one-of-a-kind new ball gown. "It will be a really great evening. I just know it."

She took in her packages, opened her gown box, took it out, and hung it up on a padded hanger. How beautiful it looked. How it shimmered with the lights.

She went in, drew her bath, and while the tub was filling carefully put a scarf around her hair. She didn't want it to get wet. She put in a c.d., featuring Jascha Heifetz, her favorite violinist, lit some rose scented candles, opened the cabinet to take out several large fluffy terry towels, removed her robe, and stepped into the tub. "Wow!! How relaxing," she thought as she enjoyed the music and fragrance of the rose scented candles. She also brought in a clock not wanting to lose track of time, be late.

The bath was as glorious as she knew it would be, toweled dry, and put on her fluffy robe and slippers. She looked in the mirror as she took off the scarf. Henri had done a fabulous job. She was very thankful to him, his staff, and Pierre, the jeweler.

She blew out the candles, hung up the damp towels, picked up the clock, c.d. player, and went into her room, the phone was ringing. "Hello," she said. The voice on the other end was the one she dearly loved,

"Hi, what are you doing?" Cliff asked.

"I just finished taking a bubble bath while listening to Jascha Heifetz and enjoying the fragrance of rose scented candles," she replied.

"Sounds as though you've been pampering yourself. Are you getting ready?"

She wanted to get a reaction from him, so she said, "Ready for what?"

He was startled. "She couldn't have forgotten: is she "'playing with me?'"

"Oh that! Yes, I plan to be ready when you arrive," she smilingly said breathlessly being very excited. She wasn't sure but thought, "This is going to be a glorious evening, one to remember 'til eternity."

"Is seven o'clock convenient?"

"I think that I can just manage," trying not to let on how much she was looking forward to seeing him. She couldn't wait for him to wrap his arms around her and make her feel so alive. She stopped herself; if she kept thinking about her dear love, she'd never get dressed.

"I'll see you soon," he couldn't wait. He kept checking to be certain that he still had the engagement ring he purchased that afternoon. He put it in his inside tuxedo pocket. It was a deep pocket and wouldn't fall out if he bent down for any reason.

They concluded their phone call and each began getting dressed. Cliff put on his tuxedo with all the accessories. He didn't know why he had chosen ruby red buttons and cuff links then looked in the mirror as he tied his bow tie, put on his jacket, picked up his wallet, keys, cell phone, and handkerchief. He was ready to go.

Gordon and Grace were sitting in the living room anxious to see him in his fancy attire. Grace exclaimed, "You look so handsome!"

Gordon walked over and nodded in agreement.

Miss Monique came out, she too wanted to see him, and everybody wanted to see the ring. He reached into his inside pocket, took out the velvet box, and opened it. They all said in unison, "It's beautiful. She'll love it."

Gordon turned to Grace and said, "They're going to the same French restaurant we went to when I proposed to you. I spoke with Madame LeClair today and made the reservation."

"That's perfect," Grace said. "You will both love it. They are truly charming people. We go back often. And, remember to walk in the garden. It's fabulous with the waterfall, flowers in bloom, and the wrought furniture. The LeClairs will make your special evening perfect. And, the violinist is fabulous."

Cliff hugged and thanked them. He put the ring box back in his inside pocket, took out his keys, and said, "I love you," waving as he walked out the door.

He was very excited when he opened the car door, put the key in the ignition, and was off for the most wonderful night of his life.

Claudette was preparing to put on her dress as one of her roommates came in and exclaimed "That is a beautiful dress, where did you find it?"

"I'll tell you all about it tomorrow," she said as she slipped into her gown and gold sling back heels. She reached for the velvet box, opened it, put on the ruby earrings, took the top off the box with her new matching bag that she opened to put in her cell phone, change purse, keys, handkerchief, lipstick, and comb. She was ready as she felt her heart beat increasing. .

Her roommate stared, "You look so beautiful. Aren't those earrings new?"

Claudette said, "Yes. I found the most fabulous shops and I want to tell you everything."

The ringing of the doorbell interrupted their conversation. Her roommate offered to answer the door, but wanted to hear all the details. Claudette promised to give her a "play-by-play."

She opened the door, asked Cliff to come in, and said that Claudette would be ready in a minute. He thanked her as he waited anxiously. He couldn't sit down, he was too excited.

He heard a door open and turned as he saw her walk into the room. He stared in disbelief. "You look gorgeous," he said as he handed her the corsage of red rose buds. He couldn't take his eyes off her. The dress beautifully molded her body, she had the perfect figure, and the slit showed off her shapely long legs.

She took the corsage out of the box and he pinned it on her gown. It was the finishing touch to make the picture perfect.

He took her arm and slid it through his as they walked out. He opened the car door; she gathered up her long skirt, and carefully slid onto the seat. He leaned in, kissed her, closed her door, walked around to the driver's side, got in, put the key in the ignition, and as he started the car, he once again complimented her on how beautiful she looked, a real doll.

They drove to the restaurant, listening to the strains of classical symphonic music they both enjoyed. He kept looking at her and smiling.

She asked numerous times, "Where are we going?"

He'd answer, "If I tell you, you won't be surprised," she smiled and tried to be patient.

The weather was perfect. The sky seemed to be lit up and they both thought it was only for them. The stars were twinkling brightly and the full moon enhanced her beauty.

Cliff wanted this night to be just as perfect as the events that unfolded for Gordon the night he asked Grace to marry him. Claudette looked beautiful sitting next to him like a fragile porcelain doll, but she hadn't given up asking him where they were going. It was becoming a fun game. They were getting closer to the restaurant, Gordon had provided excellent directions.

Cliff said to himself, "It must be around the next bend," and there it was. He quickly said to Claudette, "Close your eyes."

He couldn't believe it; there was a parking space right in front. He parked, went around to the passenger side and opened her door. He kept asking, "Are your eyes closed?" When he turned around with Claudette, he saw a lady in the doorway and knew it had to be Madame Penelope LeClair.

When Gordon called to make the reservations, he told her about Cliff and Claudette.

Claudette kept asking "May, I open my eyes now?"

Finally, he said, "Yes."
"Cliff...this is sooo beautiful. I love it and you for thinking of it. And, who is that charming lady in the doorway?"

Cliff explained that it was Madame Penelope LeClair. She and her husband, Philippe, are the owners and were there to welcome them. She held open the door, the couple smiled, and walked through as Cliff made the introductions; and she told them how happy she was to have them choose her restaurant.

Claudette was amazed at how cozy and charming it was.

Madame LeClair showed them to their table and inquired as to whether they would like an aperitif.

Cliff said, "Yes, please, two vintage glasses of Bonaparte '03."

They sat drinking the superb vintage while holding hands across the table. The red rosebud corsage was accented by her diamond and ruby dangling earrings.

"Are those earrings new?" Cliff asked, "I don't believe I have seen you wear them. They are very becoming."

"Yes, I just purchased them this afternoon at the cutest boutique from a very talented jeweler. He creates the majority of the pieces and is quite distinguished. I told him that I would be coming back and telling my friends," she replied.

Cliff said, "How interesting. What is the name of this gentleman?"

"Pierre Bouchard. A true old world French gentleman, he even kissed my hand," she sighed.

Cliff thought how coincidental that she should go to the very shop where Larry took me to purchase her engagement ring. "The earrings are perfect, I like the way they frame your face."

Madame LeClair brought over a silver tray with their aperitif and said, "Bon Appétit." They raised their glasses and said to each other, "Bon Appétit."

Cliff pushed back his chair, got up, walked over to Claudette, held out his hand, and said, "Mademoiselle, may I have this dance?" She smiled, extended her hand, arose, and they walked hand-in-hand on to the dance floor.

The band members were smiling as they watched the couple dance to Johann Strauss' "Blue Danube Waltz." It was glorious whirling her around the floor. Madame LeClair had tears in her eyes as she watched the young lovers, wished them well, and silently said a prayer for them.

The band continually played a variety of dance numbers: rumba, tango, swing, two-step, and the couple kept dancing to the delight of the others enjoying their dinner. At the end of the next tune, Cliff guided his love toward the garden patio. She wondered what he had in mind, and then as they stepped under the arch, she gasped as she saw the magnificent waterfall illuminated by colored lights. The water was tumbling down onto a myriad of colored pebbles surrounded by small water lilies and a fish pond filled with coqui and other gold fish.

Claudette was amazed as she took in the garden with all its beauty. The gardenias, roses, passion fruit, and a multitude of bulb plants were in full bloom filling the air with their special perfume.

She turned to Cliff smiling and said, "How did you ever find this special place? It's fabulous. It takes my breath away and makes me speechless to be in the midst of all this beauty." He suggested that they sit down on one of the wrought iron benches.

"Yes," she said, "Let's take in the wonderment of this moment and add it to our memory book."

The lovers sat down. He put his arm around her, gently put her head on his broad shoulder, and they sat there drinking in the beauty of the night. The stars were also in "bloom," twinkling in the velvety sky, adding to the magic of their night.

He tilted her chin upward as they looked at the "Milky Way" and the other constellations: "Pegasus," "Cassiopeia's Chair," "Big Bear," "Small Bear" and "Orion." He enjoyed astronomy and hoped she would share it with him. "Did you know that the Ursa Major Constellation is known as the "Big Dipper" and is sometimes used to point the way to the North Star?" he informed her.

She turned her gaze toward him. She loved when he got wrapped up in a subject and expounded upon it. She also loved astronomy but didn't have time to research the subject and now could enjoy delving into it with the man; she was deeply in love with, who was well-versed.in astronomy.

"That's all so wonderfully interesting," she said. "I never had time to take courses in astronomy but find it a totally fascinating subject."

"Now, we can enjoy exploring the galaxy together," he said. "I was just thinking that we should purchase a telescope and enjoy looking at the stars. It will be a great learning experience for Ra Ra and Jacques.

"Yes, it will be great for the children. Everyone will benefit. We will all become experts," she said smiling.

She was happier than she had ever been, as he tightened his arms around her and pulled her the few remaining inches closer to him. He couldn't get enough of her. He felt as though he needed to "unzip" his chest, put her inside against his heart, and their hearts would beat together forever making them truly one.

His kisses, still burning on her lips, thrilled her beyond belief. She never thought anyone could make her feel loved. When he said, "I love you," it was so beautifully sincere.

The words that she longed for, and when he again said, "I love you," without thinking, she raised her hand, put it on the back of his neck, and said the words that he longed for, "Cliff, I love you," and the kisses mounted in passion.

Time was going and he felt that they should go back inside and finish their tasty dinner that was building up to the finale.

They reluctantly got up and with their arms entwined around one another, walked back into the restaurant.

Madame LeClair was watching for them, brought over the next course of their dinner, and small warm rolls--a trademark of their restaurant. She placed the salad bowl on the table and with the tongs tossed the salad and put some on each of their plates.

Claudette said, "It looks delicious. Is the salad dressing one of your creations?"

"Yes," Madame LeClair said somewhat self-conscious, blushing profusely, she was always self-conscious when someone complimented her. "It's my husband, Pierre's, creation. He is magical in the kitchen. Just give him condiments, ingredients, and he becomes creative. Everything he makes is sensational."

They enjoyed their salad, and when they were finished, she brought the main dish which was also fabulous. Claudette was very enthusiastic about the restaurant but most especially their hosts, the LeClairs, and the ambiance.

When they finished their main course, Cliff suggested that they dance. "I'm going to ask the band to play a special request," he said as he walked across the dance floor. Mrs. LeClair was watching for her cue and knew that after this dance he was going to propose. She got excited, hot and cold all over; it was going to be a magnificent moment.

He came back to the table, held out his hand, and once again asked her to dance. She willingly took his hand and they walked onto the dance floor. This time he requested a romantic classical tune from decades before, "It's Been A Long Long Time..." and in his beautiful baritone voice sang softly to her as they danced. "Kiss Me Once, Kiss Me Twice, Kiss Me Once Again, It's Been A Long Long Time."

He loved the songs from World War II, they were beautiful love songs written at a very tenuous time when the country was at war. His grandparents and parents had an extensive record collection, played the songs, and would sing them.

"This is a beautiful song," she said, "I always loved the songs from WWII; my grandparents and parents also played the records constantly and sang them."

"That's great. "Just one more thing we have in common," he said, whirling her around the floor.

She loved to dance and was thrilled that he was such a good dancer. They glided effortlessly across the floor.

"Wouldn't you like to have some dessert?" he asked.

"That would be nice," she said as they walked back to their table.

Madame LeClair was watching and knew what she was supposed to do.

He held Claudette's chair, she sat down, and he went around the table and sat down. All evening he had been feeling his pocket to make sure that the ring box was where he had placed it. He couldn't afford for anything to go wrong now.

She looked at him; he suddenly got up. He walked around the table, kissed her, and got down on one knee as the violinist came forward playing softly.

"Claudette," he said as he went down on one knee, "I love you with all my heart, will you marry me?"

She stared at him in disbelief. She felt he was going to ask her to marry him but didn't expect it to be like this. It was perfect.

He reached into his tuxedo pocket, took out the ring box, and repeated, "I love you, sweetheart, will you marry me?"

She said, "Yes! Yes! Yes! I will, darling, marry you!" wrapped her arms around his neck, and kissed him.

He opened the ring box and she saw the most perfectly cut pure white diamond engagement ring. He took it out of the box, she extended her left hand, and he slipped it on her third finger. It fit perfectly.

The others in the restaurant stood up cheering and clapping loudly. But the newly engaged couple didn't hear them. They only had eyes for each other. They stood up embraced and kissed each other. They were suddenly surrounded by the restaurant well-wishes.

Monsieur and Madame LeClair came over to hug and kiss them French style, one kiss on each cheek, and congratulated them.

Cliff raised her hand with the ring on it and said, "Monsieur and Madame LeClair, champagne for all." They clapped and toasted the newly engaged couple.

The band played Cliff's request, "Wonderful One," their love song. They danced as close as possible to the strains of the waltz.

Then they heard the band playing the "Anniversary Waltz." Although it was a bit premature, the couple continued dancing and Cliff invited everyone to join them.

It was a moment that no one would ever forget as balloons and confetti cascaded down from above.

Everyone was dancing. Cliff thought that now everyone being in a jubilant manner, celebrating, that a more peppy number might be appropriate. He asked the band leader if they could play and sing a swing number from the 1940's, "If I knew you Were Coming, I'd Bake a Cake," and said, resoundingly, "Let's all jitterbug!" The floor was filled with happy smiling, laughing dancers.

Claudette said, "You really know how to plan and throw a party."

After a few more dances, Cliff suggested that they sit down at their table and enjoy the dessert the LeClairs had prepared in their honor.

"This is great," she said, "One marvelous surprise after another," and she happily walked to their table on her fiancé's arm. Her fiancé--what a marvelous word--she would always love hearing.

Madame LeClair had relit the candles and smiled as her husband put down a silver tray with the most beautiful dessert she had ever seen. She asked Claudette, "Would you like to cut and serve," as she handed her the silver cake knife."
Claudette took the knife, cut a narrow slice, put it on the plate that Madame LeClair handed her and placed it in front of Cliff. She cut another piece and put it on her plate.

"This is too much for us," she said, "Let's see if we can cut enough slices for all the people enjoying our party and who have become our friends."

Madame LeClair nodded, went back to the kitchen, came back with cake plates, and began slicing pieces for everybody including the staff.

Claudette felt like a hostess at her own party, picked up the dessert laden plates, walked to each table, and put the luscious baked Alaska dessert in front of each person for them to enjoy.

When Claudette returned to their table, Cliff stood up, walked over, and held out her chair like a gentleman. She sat down and he leaned over and kissed her. They were about to enjoy their dessert when Madame. LeClair came over with a box, saying that it was a surprise and it was not to be opened until they were seated in their car after leaving the restaurant.

Claudette reached out to touch the woman's hand. What a wonderful person and a great new friend they would always treasure.

The dessert was just as fabulous as they expected it to be. The LeClairs' they agreed were very talented and knew how to turn their patrons from customers into friends.

Cliff said, "We haven't danced the tango or rhumba." He pushed his chair back and went over to Claudette, held her chair as she got up, and they held hands, walking to the dance floor.

The band seemed to know what they wanted and began playing the tango, "A Media Luz." It was wonderful when others got up to join them on the dance floor. Then they played a rhumba, "Yellow Bird."

Madame LeClair was watching and thought the couple really knows how to move their hips in rhythm to the music. Her husband held out his arms to hold his wife and they danced together as though they were professionals and many thought, "Perhaps they were." The floor cleared as everyone watched the couple looking adoringly with love into each other's eyes as they danced.

When the number concluded, everyone clapped and the LeClairs bowed as they blushed and everyone was chanting, "More, more, more," as the band started to play, "It Had to be You."

Claudette said you know what would be fun to do the Conga, I saw it in a classic movie last week. The band played, Claudette was in front with Cliff's hands on her waist, and the others joined in behind them as they danced the Conga. When the number concluded they all clapped.

Cliff and Claudette appeared to onlookers as though they were thinking, "What the LeClairs have is so wonderful, I want our love to endure and blossom as theirs has. They enjoy working and being together and as a team made their restaurant a success."

They took one more walk in the garden, neither wanting the magical evening to end. It had been absolutely perfect. Claudette especially loved the waterfall and gazing down upon the fish lazily swimming back and forth in their uniquely shaped pond.

Cliff placed his hands on her cheeks, drew her to him, and met those striking sapphire eyes. He knew that he could spend the rest of his life, looking but would never find another girl as perfect as his Claudette. He had the very best and leaned forward anxiously yearning to kiss her perfectly shaped ruby lips. It was the most intense kiss, they ever shared, leaving them both breathless and knowing their engagement was perfect and their future would be blessed, as they stood under the stars twinkling down on them as though showering their future nuptials with blessings from above.

"Shall we leave?" he suggested regretfully. She nodded, unwilling to leave, and break the spell of their enchanted evening.

They returned just as the band was playing its final number for the evening, "Good Night, Sweetheart," as he swept her into his arms and hummed the tune in her ear.

They reluctantly walked toward their table, remembering all that had transpired throughout the night but most importantly their engagement. They picked up the box Madame LeClair had presented to them and walked toward the kitchen to find the LeClairs who came out, hugged the couple, wished them well, and invited them to come back soon and often.

Claudette and Madame LeClair had tears of joy in their eyes. They were both romantics. The engaged couple said that they would be back and thanked them for their many kindnesses, walked toward the door, stopped, turned, and waved prior to going through the door into the night.

The night was magical as they walked toward the car; Cliff opened her door, waited while she arranged her gown, sat down, and he closed her door.

He went around, opened his door, slid in, put the key in the ignition but hesitated before starting the engine. He turned to her, enfolded her in his arms, drew her to him, and they kissed passionately. It had been such a perfect night, neither wanting it to end.

He started the car, and as they drove home, he reached out and held her hand. He didn't want to let her go but it was really getting late as he stopped in front of her apartment. She turned toward Cliff and hugged him as she too did not wanting the evening to end. "Would you like to come in? We can open the box from the LeClairs."

"Yes," he said enthusiastically. He got out, opened her door, walked in and sat down on the couch as she put the box on the coffee table in front of them. She suggested that they start their togetherness and they opened the box.

They looked inside to see a small, round beautifully decorated cake with whip cream spelling out their names, Cliff and Claudette, and one candle in the middle. "What a beautiful thoughtful gift," Claudette said as she reached inside the box, carefully picking up the cake, and putting it down on the coffee table. "I'll get some plates and a cake knife," she said as she hurriedly disappeared into the kitchen.

"Here," she said, as she handed him some matches. Cliff took the plates from her and put them on the table. She put on some music and sat down. He lit the candle; they both made a wish, and blew out the candle together.

She picked up the cake knife and put his hand over hers as they proceeded to cut the cake. They cut a slice and she carefully put it on one of the places, picked up a fork and fed him a piece and he fed her a piece. It was delicious but it needed one ingredient, a glass of milk. She went into the kitchen and returned with two glasses of milk.

They sat eating their special gift and drinking milk while listening to the strains of romantic music. Neither wanted to know what time it was, but the inevitable was that it was really getting late or rather early in the morning. He finally stood up and said that she needed her beauty sleep and they laughed.

She walked him to the door. He drew her into his willing arms and held her gently but firmly kissing and caressing her. She said, "I think you probably need some rest to continue recuperating. I want you well for our really big day although tonight was perfect, and I thank you for each and every moment.

"Tomorrow, I'm going to call the LeClairs and thank them once again. I would like to invite them to our wedding. I feel as though they are now part of our family."

He agreed, just one more caress and kiss, and as he walked out the door said, "I'll call you when I get home."

She replied, "I'll be waiting," as she watched him walk down the steps, across the walk, open his car door, get in, start the motor, and drive off.

True to his word, Cliff called her when he got home. It was late and everyone was asleep. He was in his room, just taking off his tux, and getting comfortable in his pajamas as he said. "Hello, my future bride soon to be Mrs. Cliff Camden."

"I couldn't feel more wonderful. You really know how to be romantic and make me feel as though I am floating in heaven. The evening was perfect. How did you do it?" she asked.

"I will tell you all about it tomorrow. How about meeting me for breakfast, or if you are planning to sleep late inasmuch as it is Sunday, we can make it a brunch. I want you really all to myself all day, and tomorrow night. I'd love for you to come over for dinner. Gordon and Grace are anxious to see you and the ring."

"Then they knew you were going to ask me to marry you tonight?" she asked.

"Yes, they did and made a few suggestions. I'll tell you about it tomorrow."

"What kind of gift are you planning to give the LeClairs? I would like to help you pick it out. It has to be something really special for all they did for us tonight. They are truly wonderful people and I know that you appreciate them as much as I," Cliff reiterated.

Claudette affirmed. I don't know what to get them. Any suggestions?"

"No, but if it's all right with you, perhaps Gordon and Grace will have some ideas."

"I really would like to have their input. They are also very special and dinner tomorrow night with your extended family will be a real treat. I'll be looking forward to it," she said and he felt the excitement in her voice.

They didn't want to end their conversation. It was hard enough being apart, but hanging up now on the night of their engagement seemed to be tearing them apart.

She asked softly, "How are you feeling? Are you totally over the effects of what occurred in Colorado? What does your doctor say about your total recovered?"

She wanted so much for him to fully recuperate. The thought of his being sick was unacceptable; after they were married. She would make certain he remained healthy.

She was already planning that they would have an exercise regimen, eat properly, keep a reasonable work schedule, maintain a positive attitude, and remain focused on what was important. She was going to be the perfect wife.

CHAPTER TWENTY TWO

Gordon and Grace were sitting in the kitchen, chatting while drinking the freshly squeezed orange juice Miss. Monique put before them. They were anxious for Cliff to come down and give them a play-by-play of the events as they unfolded the night before.

When Cliff came down, one look at him and they knew everything went according to plan.

"Come on," Grace said anxiously, "Don't keep us guessing. We're waiting to hear everything."

He bent down, kissed her and patted Gordon on the shoulder prior to sitting down and drinking his orange juice. "Everything was perfect," he said. "It couldn't have been better if I had written the script. You were right, Gordon, the LeClairs are fantastically wonderful, very caring people, and their restaurant, with the garden patio was a perfect setting prior to my proposing. The band and violinist were superb, great musicians who kept perfect rhythm. We had a great time dancing and the other patrons joined in making it a very memorable evening."

Grace said smiling, "Then we have to assume she said, 'Yes.'"

"Yes," Cliff said, "She did and it will be an evening neither of us will ever forget nor didn't want to end. Thanks again, Gordon, for suggesting it and making the reservations. Madame LeClair was as gracious as you said. She met us at the door, made us feel very welcome, and the dinner was beyond reproach. The violinist came forward as I got down on one knee adding to the moment. The garden patio is a work of art; we especially liked the waterfall."

Grace asked, "What was she wearing?"

"A gold lame dress molded to her figure. It was off one shoulder with a slit down the side. I gave her a corsage of red rose buds that were accented by her ruby and diamond earrings she coincidentally purchased that day at the same jewelry store where I purchased her ring. The proprietor is a French gentleman, Pierre Bouchard. He creates one-of-a-kind pieces, each one distinct and unique," Cliff said.

"Don't tell her, but I also purchased a bracelet he is designing with sapphires, diamonds, and rubies that I plan to give her as a wedding present. Let me know if you would like me to take you there. He has beautiful pieces and can make anything you want," Cliff said.

"I would appreciate that, Cliff," Grace said, "I've been looking for the perfect pin to accessorize my new suit."

"Just tell me when you'd like to drive over, or I can give you the directions, and I'll call to tell him to expect you."

Cliff turned his attention to include Miss Monique and said that he had invited Claudette to dinner and hoped it wouldn't be an inconvenience.

Miss Monique said that she was delighted and the sentiment was echoed by Grace and Gordon. They all wanted to see her ring and hear her version of what had transpired the night before, the night of her engagement to their dear Cliff.

Cliff was silent for a few moments, thinking about how very blessed he was. He had two such wonderful friends, his in-laws. They were very special and didn't fault him for falling in love again. He felt further blessed that Grace and Gordon decided to make their stay to San Diego a permanent. move. They loved the cottage, being close to their grandchildren, and members of Cliff's household. He was glad that they decided to make the move to San Diego.

Grace and Gordon knew that Cliff had loved their Julia who was killed by a drunk driver and wanted only the best for him. They didn't want him to mourn her forever. It was God's blessing that he had found someone who made him happy and loved his children. They were a very tightly knit family enjoying each other's company, family activities, and having meals together.

They especially appreciated having their own cottage on the grounds where they had their privacy, occasional intimate dinners, and breakfasts when they chose to sleep in especially on Sundays when she would make pancakes or waffles, eggs, bacon, sausage; and they would sit in front of the fireplace or on their patio, sipping coffee, chatting, and reading the Sunday paper.

The days were even more precious since the plane crash. She was thankful, loved looking at her darling husband, showering him with a multitude of kisses, and doing everything to make him happy and comfortable.

Grace was thinking about the jewelry store where Cliff had purchased Claudette's ring and thought she would like to purchase something special for Gordon, perhaps cuff links, tuxedo shirt studs, or a watch, and wondered about what other pieces she might consider. The jeweler would undoubtedly have some suggestions. She decided to speak with Cliff about going to the store.

Miss Monique was busily arranging things in the kitchen as Grace asked about planning the dinner menu to honor the newly engaged. They got along beautifully enjoying little coffee breaks together, planning menus, and shopping. The cook had become a member of their family and a treasured friend.

Miss Monique pulled a variety of cookbooks off the top shelf and put them on the kitchen table. She refilled their coffee cups, put down a plate of warm croissants and jam, and sat down next to Grace as the two of them started pouring over the cook books anxious to make another of Miss Monique's outstanding delicious dinners.

Gordon and Cliff left the two menu planners and walked outside to take a stroll.

Gordon said, "Cliff, I would like to take you up on your offer to introduce me to Pierre Bouchard, the jeweler. I've been intending to get something special for Grace and I'd like to see some of his creations. You could have a chat with Grace and casually ask if there is a piece of jewelry she would like to have but be careful not to let her know that you are asking for me. I want whatever I choose to be a surprise."

Cliff said, "We can go now."

"I'll get my wallet and meet you out in front," Gordon said,
They drove to the jewelry store. Gordon hadn't been in that section of town, they discussed how quaint it was--more like a village with a multitude of shops.

Cliff had called Monsieur Bouchard in advance that Gordon, his father-in-law, was anxious to visit his shop and inquired whether it would be convenient for them to drop by that afternoon

The jeweler was as always very cordial and said that he would be expecting them. Pierre was somewhat anxious to hear about the previous night's events when Cliff had planned to ask his love to marry him. He didn't know what Gordon might be interested in but, nevertheless, he was busy assembling an assortment of pieces to show them when he heard the door open and saw the pair. .

Cliff walked over, extending his hand eager to shake Pierre's hand and introduce him to Gordon. They shook hands and expressed how grateful they were that he had time to meet with them.

Pierre said, "I hope that I am not being rude, but I am anxious to hear about what transpired last night. From the look on your face Cliff, it had to be all you expected."

Cliff nodded, his smile even broader than before, as he said, "Yes, it was absolutely perfect and I have you to thank for a major portion of it. She loved the ring and I know she will be equally ecstatic about the bracelet you are fashioning for me to give her as a wedding present--a gift she will always treasure."

"The earrings she purchased from you framed her face beautifully and were accented by the red rosebud corsage I gave her."

Pierre enthusiastically said, "You 'ave a gorgeous bride. I knew from what she told me as she was selecting zee earrings that she was going to be the recipient of zee ring. I'm looking forward to meeting 'er. Incidentally, you are right, she does have very small wrists and I was mentally calculating the size."

Cliff filled him in on the events of the night before and again expressed his appreciation for all he had done. A thought suddenly occurred to him, "Why not invite him for dinner to meet Claudette and the rest of his wonderful family. After all, he has become a very special friend.

"How would you like to come to dinner tonight at our home and meet Claudette, my fiancée, and the rest of our family?" Cliff asked adding. "You would be most welcome."

"Yes, zank you. It would be a honeur."

Gordon had been looking at the velvet lined boxes Pierre had put before him.

"These are really beautiful," Gordon said. "It makes it difficult for one to choose. I am not certain as to what I should select. Do you have any suggestions?"

Pierre asked, "Is it a special occasion?"

"Not really. It will be a special gift to compliment her beauty and reinforce how very much I love her."

"What about a diamond necklace with matching earrings?"

"That does sound like a good choice. Do you have any pieces I can see?"

"Yes," he turned to go into the vault and returned with several velvet boxes. He opened each one and carefully put them on the counter."

Gordon bent over to examine each one of the pieces as Pierre put a black velvet covered mannequin designed for displaying a necklace on the counter as he asked, "Is there one you would like me to put on zee mannequin?"

"Yes, I rather like this one," Gordon said as he pointed to one with his index finger.

Pierre carefully picked up the necklace and placed it on the mannequin.
"It's a beautiful piece," Cliff offered and sat back not wanting to unduly influence Gordon's decision.

"Do you have another one of these display units?" Gordon inquired.

"Oui," Pierre said, as he took another one out, put it on the counter, and asked Gordon which necklace he would like displayed. Gordon indicated which necklace he would like put on that display unit.

He sat back trying to decide. Did he really like either one of those or perhaps was there a third that might be a better choice. Then he asked to have a third necklace put on another mannequin. Pierre was only too happy to accommodate, knowing that sometimes it is a difficult decision.

Now Gordon had three necklaces displayed before him on mannequins. He turned to Cliff, "What do you think? Do you have a preference?"

It was a difficult decision. Gordon had chosen the top three, all of which were beautiful. "I kind of think the middle or the one on the left, the first one I chose."

Pierre, do you have a piece of velvet that could be placed on the counter to display the necklace in another position?"

Pierre took out three pieces of velvet: black, burgundy, and white. He placed them side by side on the counter. He then took the middle necklace and placed it on the black velvet, the left necklace on the burgundy, and asked, "Is that helpful?" endeavoring in every way to accommodate his discriminating customer.

Gordon took a deep breath and said that he thought the one displayed on the burgundy velvet fabric, the first one he selected--beautiful brilliant diamond necklace set in platinum-- was ideal "I think that's it," he said as he reached out and picked it up. He held it in his hands, admiring the stones and settings.

"There are fifteen princess cut diamonds, each weighing one-half carat for a total of seven and one-half carats on a platinum rope chain," Pierre said.

"Is this a secure clasp?"

Pierre assured him. "It is a screw clasp, very secure."

"Yes, I think this is the one. Is there any way that it can be engraved?" Gordon asked.

"Not the way I designed it, but I could be creative and add a piece of platinum by the clasp that would hang down and look as though it were an integral part of the necklace," he said.

"Good. Let's do that," Gordon said

.

"All I need is for you to tell me what you would like engraved."

"Decisions, decisions, decisions," Gordon said, and all three men laughed.

Pierre handed him a pen and notepad.

Gordon proceeded to write down what he wanted engraved. When he finished, he asked Pierre how long it would take.

Pierre said, "I can have it for you in a few hours. If you would like, I could bring it with me tonight and find a way to secretly hand it to you when I arrive."

"That sounds perfect," Gordon said

Gordon added, "I would like a matching pair of screw-on earrings. Please let me know what unique designs you can come up with."

He picked up the pen, wrote down their address and phone number, and asked Pierre if he would like directions.

He said, "No, I am very familiar with zat part of town."
Gordon and Cliff got up to leave, they shook hands, said "Dinner is usually served at seven."

"We'll see you this evening," they said, smiled, and waved as they walked out of the shop.

Pierre was thrilled. He had made some new friends who appreciated his talent. It was going to be a great evening. He planned to purchase a bottle of fine wine and a bouquet of red roses for his hostess. "It's going to be a great evening," he thought smiling to himself.

He was from Paris, France, had no family in this country, and many times was very lonely; he only had his shop and his talent for making designer jewelry. He had been fortunate to have kind, considerate customers who appreciated his workmanship, thereby making it all worthwhile.

It had always been his dream to come to America and become a citizen. He received word that next week his dream would come true; he would be an American citizen with all the rights and privileges. It was exciting, but he didn't really have anyone to share it with. It would be nice to have someone to share his big moment. It wasn't easy being all alone. He wasn't sorry he had come and could rejoice in having his greatest dream come true, becoming an American citizen.

He put all that aside, looking at his watch, realizing that he better get started working on Gordon's gift for his wife. He had promised to deliver it tonight when he was going there for dinner.

"What a nice gesture to invite me, a perfect stranger. Well, maybe not perfect," and he laughed at his own joke.

CHAPTER TWENTY THREE

On the way home, Gordon called to tell Grace, I have invited a special guest for dinner."

"Who is he?" Grace asked.

"We'll tell you when he arrives," Gordon said, sounding mysterious.

Grace told Miss Monique one more guest is coming to dinner, a man, but she didn't know who. "Maybe he's single," Grace said with a twinkle in her voice.

Miss Monique didn't respond, she had too many hurtful experiences with men and was no longer interested in any kind of relationship. She was very happy and content with her place in this household and was not at all interested in anything changing. She liked and felt a real part of this family.

Miss Monique said firmly, "I'm not interested."

Grace smiled to herself, trying to recall how many times over the years she had heard those words.

She asked Miss Monique, "Will there be sufficient food to serve one more adult?"

"Yes, no problem," she said as she checked and stirred the numerous pots on the stove and those pans in the oven.

They had discussed which china to select. Grace put a damask table cloth on the dining room table, went to the china cabinet for the place settings, and crystal stemware. It was taking shape when she suddenly realized that they didn't have a floral bouquet for a center piece.

She knew Nancy was busy with the children; therefore, she called Mrs. Svensen to see if she had the time to go out in the garden to pick flowers for their center piece.

She said that she would be delighted, went in the kitchen, picked up the clippers, flower basket, and went outside into the garden.

The table was beginning to look beautiful. Next, Grace opened the silverware drawer, selected the needed pieces and added them to the table place settings. All that was needed were the matching damask napkins and crystal candlesticks.

Mrs. Svensen came in with the flowers, together they arranged, and put them in a large crystal bowl. Grace didn't want anything too tall because then people wouldn't be able to see one another across the table.

Grace told Mrs. Svensen that dinner would be at seven and hoped both she and her husband would be joining them and their guests.

Mrs. Svensen seemed somewhat uncertain.

Grace realizing the woman's discomfort asked what was wrong.

Mrs. Svensen said, "But we are only hired help."

"Nonsense," Grace said, "You are members of our family and are welcome at all family functions. We are asking you because we want and love you both."

Mrs. Svensen, blushing like a young girl tears of happiness in her eyes, thanked Grace and felt so much pent up emotion at being included in family gatherings that she reached out and hugged Grace.

Grace patted her back and said that they would be eating at seven. Mrs. Svensen smiled as she left the room. She was anxious to shower and wash her hair. What would she wear? She rushed outside to find her husband and told him that they had been invited to dinner and to be part of the family.

He was also speechless, let out a whoopee, grabbed his wife, and swung her around. It was a dream come true, they were part of a family. They were from Sweden and wanted so much to belong in this great country and now they did.

Grace stepped back, looking at the table when Nancy came in. She asked Nancy, "How does it look to you? Is there something you think should be added or changed?"

"No," Nancy said, "It's perfect."

"Good. We will be having dinner at seven, and of course, want you and the children to join us," Grace said.

"Are you certain that you want the children at the table?" Nancy asked.

"Yes, definitely. They can be a bit messy but are adorable, and like you, are important members of our family," Grace said, humming as she headed toward the kitchen to help Miss Monique.

Grace loved her life. It was perfect. Her darling husband, whom she loved very much, had recovered. She was very happy living with her extended family and would continue to do everything possible to maintain her happy life style.

Cliff thought that he should call his fiancée and let her know that he would be picking her up about six-forty if that would be convenient, when the phone rang. It was Claudette calling to say, "Hello," to her love and wondering about their dinner date.

Cliff said, "It's all set for seven o'clock. I hope that is convenient. . Miss Monique and Grace have been selecting recipes and cooking all day. And, Grace has been happily choosing the table settings, napkins, etc. It has been a happy fun day."

She said, "I'm not alone. My roommates are here with their dates, I'll look forward to seeing you."

Claudette realized that she had not said the words Cliff wanted to hear, but she was being troubled, not about what he said, but that her father was giving her a hard time. He called that morning and told her that she had to come to Manhattan immediately. He said that he had sent his private jet and demanded that she leave in the morning. The sound of his voice was unfriendly, he was highly agitated. She really didn't want to go, but it seemed that she had no alternative.

She couldn't talk to Cliff, not because others were there, but because she was busy packing and didn't want to tell him on the phone. It would be better to tell him after the party tonight.

She had really been excited about tonight's dinner party with his family, but now she was uncomfortable. How would she be able to avoid saying that her father ordered her to come home in the morning? It was a discomforting prospect she thought. With tears in her eyes she was trying to think clearly about what she was packing. She'd probably arrive with a haphazard wardrobe.

How could her father do this to her? She was so excited when she called to tell him her exciting news that she was engaged and very happy. He didn't seem to care. How could he be so unfeeling? Cliff was bound to know something was wrong when he picked her up. How could she camouflage the fact that she had been crying for hours. Her eyes were red and puffy. She decided to take a bubble bath, towel off, go in the shower and wash her hair. "Hopefully, I will feel better as I stand with the warm water splashing down over me as I wash my hair."

It helped but obviously not enough. She looked in the mirror as she brushed her hair, and as creatively as she could, applied makeup and made a silent promise to herself that she wouldn't cry any more.

Now to decide what to wear. She had planned to wear a black fitted cocktail dress with a matching three-quarter sleeve jacket, but now she wasn't certain that was a good color choice.

Perhaps she should wear something with a little more color. She had a darling pink two piece with a full skirt that would look great with her pink heels, or a yellow two-piece dress. The top was sleeveless, the skirt fitted, and a cute short sleeve jacket that would look good with her yellow heels that had a matching bag.

"That's it," she thought, "I'll wear the yellow dress, and when I get back, I'll wear the black cocktail dress for Cliff. Suddenly the thought struck her like a bolt of lightning when would she be coming back. "I can't think of that now or I'll start crying again," she said softly to herself as she began dressing. It was six thirty and she didn't want to rush. Sometimes she dressed so hurriedly that she felt as though she was being "shot out of a cannon" and didn't want this to be one of those times.

Her roommate knocked on the door and Claudette told her to come in. She looked at Claudette and felt intensely sorry for her. She knew about the call from her father and was sad that it happened after such a wonderful night--her engagement party.

She made a few makeup suggestions as she helped Claudette with the finishing touches. "You look beautiful," she said picking up Claudette's bag to pop in more tissues.

"You'll be fine. Let's see your ring again, it's beautiful. You'll have a wonderful time tonight, I just know it."   She hugged her, just as they heard the door bell ring. She stepped back and went to answer the door.

"It's Cliff." She called out. "Congratulations, I know you both will be very happy. You are the love birds of the century," and gave him a kiss on the cheek.

Cliff heard footsteps, looked up and saw Claudette. He said, "You look more ravishing than ever," as he rushed over to gather her up in his arms and passionately kiss her.

When they were seated in his car, he asked if everything was all right; "You look upset."

She looked at him and said, "I'll explain later. We don't want to be late," as they put on their seat belts and drove off.

It was a short drive and they were silent, listening to symphonic music. When they arrived, it looked as though every light in the house was on.

They were all watching for the newly engaged couple to drive up. Suddenly, the front door flew open and Grace came bounding out unable to contain her enthusiasm. She wanted to be the first to congratulate the couple.

She hugged them and told Claudette how beautiful she looked. They walked in and Gordon came over to offer his congratulations; the others Ra Ra and Jacques were jumping up and down for joy. They were adorable, enjoying the excitement of the moment. Miss Monique and the Svensens also came over to add their good wishes.

The front door knocker sounded. Gordon walked over to open the door, it was Pierre Bouchard, the surprise guest who surreptitiously handed his host the package. Gordon had purposely worn a suit with large inside pockets and put it there until he had a few moments to take it to their cottage.

He introduced Pierre Bouchard to the group.

Claudette stared at him and then somewhat speechless said, "You are the jeweler?"

"Oui, mademoiselle," he said as he kissed her hand.

Cliff came over and said to Claudette, "Monsieur Pierre Bouchard designed your engagement ring and had difficulty not saying anything when he realized who you were when you went into his shop to purchase the earrings."

She smiled and told Pierre how very much she loved the ring and thanked him profusely as she put one hand up to her left ear lobe and said "I thank you for creating such a beautiful pair of earrings. I really like and enjoy wearing them very much."

Grace came over, very much interested in this surprise guest, and was introduced to Pierre Bouchard. She extended her hand and he bent forward, kissing it in traditional French fashion. He handed her the large bouquet of long stem red roses. She was very gracious as she thanked him for his kindness.

Pierre also brought a bottle of rare vintage French wine that he handed to Gordon. "I hope that this vintage will compliment the dinner.
Gordon glanced down at the label and was deeply impressed. "This is truly a very rare vintage," he said, admiring the year of the wine.

Miss Monique came in and was introduced to Pierre Bouchard. They stood rigidly staring at each other in disbelief. Everyone was watching, not understanding what was going on. The silence was thought provoking.

"Is something wrong?" Grace asked, becoming somewhat concerned.

"No," Miss Monique said as she scurried back to the kitchen.

Grace went after her. "What's the matter? You look as though you've seen a ghost."

"I feel as though I have. It's been many years. I can't believe that he's here now and in this house where I live and work," Miss Monique said as she searched in her pocket for a tissue. Grace picked up a box of tissues and extended it.

Miss Monique by this time was so overpowered by tears, it was impossible to understand what she was saying. Grace picked up Miss Monique's hand and put it on top of a tissue extending upward from the box and waited for her to regain her composure, but she just kept crying harder and harder.

Grace was uncertain. What could possibly be so terrible? Why was this woman who was usually so happy without seemingly a care is in such pain? Grace put her arms around the cook and patted her back while waiting for the crying to subside.

Meanwhile, Pierre Bouchard was also visibly shaken. How could he possibly have foreseen this would happen? How could she be here? It had been so many years. Gordon walked over and asked what was wrong. "You look so pale Pierre, what has caused you to be so visibly upset? Can I do something? How about a drink?"

Pierre didn't hear a word. He felt as though the floor was opening up and he was going to be swallowed up.
Gordon was becoming very concerned. He didn't know what to do but knew he had to do something. He reached out and gently touched Pierre's shoulder; suddenly he started to bend over as Cliff ran over just in time to prevent Pierre from falling face down on the floor.

They guided him over to a couch and sat him down on either side of him. Pierre was ash white. Claudette ran over to the bar and came back with a tumbler of brandy. They held it to

Pierre's lips and he sipped a small quantity of the amber liquid then they put pillows behind him and gently pushed him against them.

They stood waiting for Pierre to regain his composure. Cliff asked, "Would you like to lie down for a few minutes?"

Pierre shook his head. He didn't know what to do but lying down was not going to ease the situation. It definitely was not the answer.

Miss Monique was finally able to control herself, dabbed at her eyes with the tissues and suddenly turned toward the stove and began stirring pots and checking the oven contents. She looked at the clock on the stove and noted it was seven thirty. She thought, "Too much time had been lost." She turned to Grace and began to talk about the dinner they had worked long hours to prepare.

Grace knew that this was not the time to ask questions and turned to pour the oil, vinegar and other condiments on the salad, tossed it, and carried it to the table. The salad plates were already in place. After the guests were seated, the salad would be tossed and put on the salad plates.

The relish dishes containing, pickles, olives, and assorted condiments were already on the table. The water glasses were filled, the place cards in position, everything was coming together.

Grace made several trips back and forth to the kitchen, bringing out the platter with the main dish, the vegetable dishes, and several baskets of rolls in a covered dish to keep them warm.

Two glasses of milk were placed on the table. One for Ra Ra and the other for Jacques who would be joining them at the grownup table. This was to be a celebration of Cliff and Claudette's engagement.

Gordon opened the bottle of wine to let it breathe, wrapped a towel around it, and put it in a silver ice bucket. He bent over and lit the candles as he said, "Grace, the table looks beautiful. You out did yourself as you usually do. I am so proud of you," as he bent over and kissed her.

Grace went back into the kitchen to tell Miss Monique that the table was set and everything looks delicious. "You did an admirable job, spectacular. Now, it's time for you to take off your apron and join us to toast Cliff and Claudette on their engagement."

Miss Monique shook her head and murmured in an almost inaudible voice, "No. I can't."

"Yes you can. Whatever the problem, we will take care of it later. You worked very hard on this dinner and I know that you want to toast Cliff and Claudette. It's a special evening and we need you to make it complete," Grace said as she walked to the sink, ripped off a paper towel, put it under the cold water, and handed it to Miss Monique. "Here put this damp paper towel against your eyes for a few moments, take off your apron, put on one of your glorious smiles as we go into the dining room to partake of your delicious repast, and enjoy receiving the high praise that will be yours for perfecting this glorious meal."

Pierre was beginning to regain his composure. He stood up and started making his apologies for leaving early.

Gordon said, "That's nonsense. You are staying. Whatever the problem, we will deal with it later. Pull yourself together man, nothing can be that bad and repeated, we'll work it out later."

Pierre reluctantly agreed and walked with Gordon to the table.

Everyone was assembled in the dining room as Grace said, "Tonight, to make it more elegant, we have place cards. Please find your place and stand behind your chair. Cliff will fill your wine glass and we will drink a toast to our loving couple, Cliff and Claudette, who became engaged last night."

Cliff put his arm around Claudette and they leaned against each other. It was a beautiful picture. Gordon filled the wine glasses for the adults, grape juice for the children, and they held up their glasses as Gordon said, "This is a very happy occasion, to the future Mr. and Mrs. Cliff Camden."

Everyone said, "Hear, hear, turned toward the person next to them, clinked glasses, and took a sip of the aged vintage."

Grace and Gordon seated Ra Ra and Jacques and put a napkin on their laps. They looked so cute with their apple red cheeks, Ra Ra in an adorable red velvet dress with white cuffs, a Peter Pan collar, a narrow red satin bow in the center of the collar, and a red satin ribbon in her hair. Jacques was attired in a suit and tie.

"That is an exceptional wine," Gordon said addressing Pierre and they all agreed. Gordon held out Grace's chair, Cliff, Claudette's chair, Mr. Svensen for Mrs. Svensen, and suddenly Pierre held out Miss Monique's chair.   She looked at him dumbfounded as she accepted his act of courtesy, wondering if she would be able to eat even one bite of food.

Grace felt that it was up to her to keep things light and the conversation moving. Ra Ra and Jacques were helpful in that area with their cute way of expressing themselves and constant chatter. They were always interested in everything and asked a myriad of questions.

Grace asked how they liked the tossed green salad Miss Monique had prepared, using her own recipe. Everyone said that it was delicious and would have seconds but then they wouldn't be able to eat the main dish, etc.

Miss Monique smiled and thanked them. She said, "It is in honor of the newly engaged couple. They raised their glasses to her in tribute and thanks.

They were passing the next course and it seemed Miss Monique and Pierre Bouchard were loosening up a bit and beginning to join in the flow of conversation.

Cliff and Claudette were holding hands under the table and looking into each other's eyes, living for the moment when Mr. and Mrs. Svensen asked again to see her ring, which of course, Claudette was happy to display. She held out her hand for all to see.

Ra Ra was enthralled and asked, "How do I get a ring like that? I'm a good girl. Daddy, can I get a ring like that one, pointing to Claudette's, I'm a good girl, aren't I?"

Everyone laughed. "Yes, my darling daughter, you are a very good girl. Do you want a ring?"

"Yes, Yes, Yes, I do, I really, really do," she said with a broad smile on her face as she banged her spoon up and down for emphasis.

Cliff said, "All right. We'll talk about it later. Is that all right?"

"That's all right daddy," she said satisfied, and put the spoon down on her plate.

Miss Monique agreed, saying that Claudette's ring was truly a beautiful work of art. "Cliff you really have an eye for the beautiful. It's just the right size, not too ostentatious."

Grace was glad that Ra Ra and Jacques were dining with them especially since the incident between Miss Monique and Pierre Bouchard created the stressful atmosphere.

Grace didn't know what the problem was but it had to be something very hurtful for each of them. She wondered what it was and how long ago it had taken place. Would Miss Monique be willing to tell the story of what had happened, how she knew Pierre? Grace was a romantic and concluded it would be an all enveloping story that hopefully included a touch of romance with all the revealing aspects.

.   Pierre suddenly surprised everyone when he complimented Miss Monique for her culinary skills. "You are really a superb chef. I have never tasted anything this delicious. Is it your recipe?"   Miss Monique was startled.   She never expected any kind words out of his mouth as she stared at him incredulously.

"Everyone loves Miss Monique's artistry in the kitchen. She has a knack for taking the simplest of foods and turning them into a culinary delight," Gordon said as he stood up and again lifted his glass saying, "We must all toast Miss Monique for providing this superb repast."

Miss Monique blushed which was quite becoming, then asked if anyone wanted seconds or thirds. No one answered. "Does that mean that we are ready for dessert?" Resulted in a resounding, "Yes," especially from Ra Ra and Jacques who were always ready for anything sugary.

After the table was essentially cleared, Miss Monique came in with a large silver chafing dish, which she carefully placed in front of Gordon, poured Kirsch over the cherries, and gave him a match to ignite the grand presentation.

It was a glorious display resulting in a happy round of hand clapping in anticipation of enjoying the fabulous cherries jubilee dessert originated in honor of Queen Victoria's Diamond Jubilee Originally; the dessert was served over a scoop of vanilla ice cream.

Ra Ra and Jacques couldn't wait for their serving. They were cautioned to eat slowly as there wouldn't be any seconds. The children were awe stuck. They never saw such a superb display, setting their dessert on fire.

Cliff's bright hazel eyes watched Ra Ra and Jacques gaze at the delicious confection with wild delight while   Grace finished serving the scrumptious dessert.

Miss Monique intently watched as all their guests were served and put a spoon full in their mouth, enjoying rich flavors unfold as they tasted the grand dessert. They all had the look of someone eating a superb delicacy unable to believe what their palate was telling them, how fantastically good it was.

The conversation picked up again. This time they were questioning Cliff and Claudette about whether they had set a wedding date. They looked at each other incredulously and each wondered silently, "Why hadn't they talked about a wedding date, especially since they were so much in love?"
Cliff said smiling self-consciously, "As you know, we just got engaged," as he gazed intently at Claudette, anxiously waiting for her to speak, to say something, anything, but she didn't and he wondered why.

After what seemed an interminable period of silence, Claudette said after taking a deep breath, "We'll have to set our wedding date after I get back from New York. My father is demanding that I fly to Manhattan for a visit. He left me no alternative but to acquiesce. I was going to tell you later tonight, it makes me very sad. I really don't want to go but he has left me no choice. He even went so far as to have his private jet flown here to transport me. I'm very sorry. Please forgive me. Cliff, I am deeply in love with you and want more than anything to marry you, be your wife."

Everyone felt as though they were privy to a very private conversation and noted that her beautiful eyes were filling with tears that were cascading down her cheeks. They all sat very still not really sure about what to do.

Finally, Miss Monique asked if anyone would like coffee or more wine and began serving as Gordon suggested that they withdraw to the living room or go outside to their beautiful garden arbor.

Cliff was in somewhat of a state of shock not noticing they were the only two left at the table. Claudette reached across the short distance between them and touched his face. She loved the way he made her feel.   Just touching him created an electrified sensation that quickly traveled throughout her body. It was sensational.

"I'm sorry," she said. "My father called me last night. Remember when you called and I told you my roommates and their dates where there and I couldn't talk? Well, I couldn't talk because I couldn't collect my thoughts. My father was on the other line being relentless with his ruthless demand that I come to New York. It was scary. Please forgive me. Say that you forgive me."

"Yes, off course, I forgive you. I love you very much and can't wait until I see you walk down the aisle toward me in your bridal finery. I will be the proudest fela' ever," Cliff said, trying to reassure her. He didn't like seeing her so distraught as he reached out to gently touch her cheek wet with tears.

"I have a plan. I'll fly to New York with you and be a buffer between you and your father. I'll ask for your hand and make him realize that I am the best thing for you since they colored margarine." He wanted to make her laugh and thought colored margarine would do it. He could have said, "Since sliced bread."

A small smile was visible and suddenly she laughed so loudly that the others were startled and came back in wanting to know what the joke was.

She said, "Cliff also has a degree in history and knows all these minute events that occurred throughout the ages. It's interesting that initially margarine was white; later it was sold with a little packet of coloring that when mixed in the margarine resembled butter."

There were a few small glitches but as a whole they all agreed that the dinner party was a huge success as they sat in the garden under a beautiful moonlit sky amidst the soft strains of Chopin.

Gordon was contemplating when he would give Grace the diamond necklace he had purchased. Cliff was thinking about the reason Claudette's father was insisting on her presence, Miss Monique about Pierre and vice-a-versa. Several members of the household were overwhelmed by what transpired during the dinner party honoring the engaged couple.

CHAPTER TWENTY FOUR

Cliff was remembering, while turning into the airport parking garage, the previous night when he offered to accompany Claudette to New York. He took out their luggage and they began walking toward the terminal to ask directions to her father's family jet.

A clerk came out to guide them and they boarded the plane. The flight attendant, James Harcourt, welcomed them as they seated themselves ready to take off as the pilot, Steve Dunbar, came back to introduce himself which wasn't necessary because Claudette knew him. He had been flying for her father since before she was born.

She introduced him to Cliff.

James said, "Clearance has been granted, the flight plan filed, they would be taking off shortly," and excused himself.

Cliff's arms were gently wrapped around her and they were gazing into each other's eyes when the pilot once again approached them. He cleared his throat because they were so intent on each other that they didn't see him approach.

"When I went back to the cockpit, your father called. I didn't realize that I would be saying the wrong thing when I told him that you were both aboard and we were ready to take off." James continued, "It is with deep regret that I have to tell you," he then paused taking another deep breath, that your father will not permit Cliff to accompany you, to put it bluntly he doesn't want Cliff on the plane with you.

Claudette was appalled. "That's ridiculous," she said, but knew that it was no use protesting. When her father made up his mind, it was set in stone. She turned to Cliff and told him how sorry she was.

"It's all right," he said as he turned his attention to the pilot. "Just give us a few minutes and I'll leave quietly," Cliff said.

He whispered in her ear that he would take his company jet and meet her in New York.

She said, "I'll go with you."

"Won't that make your father angrier?"

"At this moment, I really don't care what my father thinks. Come on let's go. Is your plane at this airport?"

"Yes. I'll contact my pilot."

She said, "Let's go, I'll give a message to James to give to the pilot that I'll be in New York, but am making other arrangements."

They left the plane and walked toward the terminal.

Cliff took out his cell phone and called his pilot who was on the job. "I need to take off immediately for New York. Can you file the flight plan A.S.A.P.?

"Yes. Somehow I felt you would be calling. We're fueled ready to take off. Welcome aboard."

They walked out of the terminal toward the plane. It was a beautiful day. The sun's gently warming rays were inviting as they walked arm-in-arm toward the plane. They suddenly heard footsteps running in their direction. They turned; it was James who stopped in front of them, desperately trying to catch his breath. They waited but he couldn't seem to calm down.

"What wrong," Claudette asked thinking that he needed a glass of water.

"I have to tell you that your father is furious. He was screaming as he said that he was ordering you to fly home in his plane and that Cliff was not to come. He would not be welcome," James said still trying to catch his breath.

Claudette looked from the attendant to Cliff and back to the attendant. "Did my father say anything else? I don't understand what his problem is. He never acted like this before."

Cliff was beginning to feel that it was not safe for Claudette to go. Her father sounded irrational. He was very protective. "I don't want you to go. It doesn't sound safe."

Claudette made a three-quarter turn away from Cliff to face James. "Is there anything else that you haven't told me," she asked almost apologetically.

"Yes," he said as he hesitated, shuffling his feet, bringing his hands to his face, and then shoving them deep into the pockets of his pants. "I didn't want to tell you, but he is furious. I have never seen him like this and neither has the pilot." He took another deep breath and said, "Your father said that if you don't come now without Cliff that you will never be welcome in his home and he will disinherit you."

Claudette was in shock. Her smooth complexion was now drained of all color; she was so pale that they thought she would faint. To keep her from collapsing Cliff tightened his arm around her. She was not steady. Both men were very concerned. Cliff carried her inside the terminal. They were looking for a chair when an airport aide came over offering to help, saw Claudette wasn't feeling well, and guided them to a side room with a couch where she could lie down.

Cliff and the flight attendant were visibly concerned. Cliff told the flight attendant that he should probably go back to the plane. "No sense in angering her father further."

James said, "I'll go but not willingly. Should I tell her father anything?"

"No, we'll have to talk about the best way to handle this. Thanks for all your help and please thank the pilot for us."

James turned and reluctantly went back to her father's plane.

Cliff turned to Claudette, "How do you feel sweetheart?"

An attendant came in concerned, "How is she feeling?" Without even waiting for an answer, he produced a tray with two glasses: one with orange juice, the other, with water."

Cliff asked Claudette to drink the orange juice. He lifted her head and held the glass against her lips. Her hair was disheveled and her mascara smeared. She wasn't quite as pale. Her color was starting to come back.

She finished the orange juice; Cliff put the empty glass on the tray, picked up the glass of water, handed it to Claudette, and encouraged her to drink it.

They sat for what seemed like hours but it was only a few minutes while Cliff waited for Claudette to regain her composure.

The door opened and her father's flight attendant came in. He had been running, and in between trying to breathe and talk, he kept sputtering. It was not a pretty sight. He kept pressing his hand against his chest while trying to get the words out. "Your father wanted me to give you a message and he handed her a folded piece of paper. Do you want me to wait for an answer?"

"Just a minute while we read it," Cliff said cautiously.

"Claudette," the message from her father began, "I was looking forward to your coming to New York alone. I'm disappointed that you chose to ignore my wishes. I'm not interested in meeting Cliff or hearing anything about your so-called engagement. You can't be serious. You know that it was arranged for you marry Hector Fegley, the son of my law partner. You were always in agreement. I am very upset. If you elect not to marry Hector, our relationship is terminated, you will be disinherited."

The note wasn't signed but Claudette knew it was from her father. She recognized his inimitable method of stringing words together to form a sentence. It was quite evident that the message had been written exactly as he had dictated it. She was visibly upset and Cliff was in empathy, pain visibly showed in her violet eyes that had the look of an ocean storm.

James again asked, "Would you like to respond to the message."

They were trying to decide if they did or didn't.

Claudette sat up, "Thank you, James, but there is no message. Don't tell my father that I was upset, just say nothing. If he asks about his note, just say that you delivered it and please say nothing more."

James nodded and apologetically said, "I'm sorry and hope that everything works out for both of you." He shook hands with Cliff, waved, and walked away.

Claudette felt better and turned to Cliff saying, "I love you, really appreciate you, and am anxious to be your wife, Mrs. Cliff Camden."

Cliff was delighted; those were the words he wanted to hear. He couldn't wait for them to be married.

She interrupted his thoughts by adding, "As soon as possible. I have the uneasy feeling that my father will do everything humanly possible to interrupt our ceremony. I don't want to give him any more time than necessary."

"Today is Monday," my darling, "Shall we make Saturday, our special love day?"

"Yes, my love, we can make it happen. Sweetheart, it doesn't have to be a gigantic affair. Grace and Miss Monique will help. It will be glorious," she said.

He helped her up, put his strong arms around her, and drew her to him. They were so close that not even a ruler could be slid between them. He kissed her more passionately than ever leaving her breathless. They had now lost all sense of time as she melted into his arms. This was where she belonged. She felt so loved and secure as she enjoyed and wanted more and more kisses.

Cliff whispered in her ear, "Don't you think that we should be going. There are plans to be made. Where do you want to get married?"

"Initially in church, but now I think that a garden wedding would be more in keeping with this time of year. All the flowers are in bloom and Mr. Svensen has the garden so beautifully manicured.

"What do you think about erecting an arch that could become a permanent part and asset to the garden?" .

"That's a great idea," Cliff said, "We can ask Mr. Svensen to plant concord grapes and passion fruit on either side and trains them to grow up and over the arch. Don't you think that will be a work of art?"

"Yes, it's a wonderful idea. Let's go home and tell everyone," Claudette said enthusiastically. .

Cliff was very concerned. "You know, I have another thought. I think first we should go to your apartment, pack a suitcase, and move you into Camden Manor. There are several rooms with an outside entrance and a balcony. You will be very comfortable. I am concerned that your father may try something. Would you like to do that?"

Claudette was pensive. She didn't want to admit it but she was also scared. "I like it. Yes, let's do it."

Cliff said, "Let's do it now."

While driving, they were rather pensive as there was a lot to think about. She knew her father. He was both ruthless and relentless. She had never known him to give up and had a penchant about her marrying Hector, who, in her opinion, was a "weasel. She had never been able to stomach him. Everything about him was obnoxious."

Cliff broke the silence, asking, "How are you feeling?"

"Better, but we must not underestimate my father. He will never give up."

"Why is he so insistent on your marrying that creep?"

"Hector's father owns property in downtown Manhattan that is worth a fortune plus interest in banks and percentages in a multitude of businesses. He is really very wealthy, owning a dozen plus homes throughout Europe and the United States," she answered.

"Wow! That's quite a portfolio. Your father doesn't have any qualms about your happiness, doesn't care about you, only interest in what you can bring home for him. What a sad commentary." The conversation suddenly ceased as he drove into the driveway adjacent to her apartment.

"Cliff before we go in, perhaps it is time that I tell you about my parents."

"I have a feeling that it is not a pretty story. Are you sure you are up to it?"

"Yes, and you are right. It is not a pretty story. It is even sadder now in view of what my father has done.

"I would like to go back in time to give you a complete picture of my mother, Christine DuBois, a statuesque blonde, hair flowing down around her shoulders, youngish facial features whose modeling career of high level fashions paid for her tuition, was kind, considerate, and loved to have a good time.

"Despite her busy schedule, Christine maintained a 4.0 average, graduated Summa Cum Laude, and was valedictorian of her graduating class."

Claudette adored her mother. Whenever the two "girls" went shopping, the sales clerks would address her mother as "your younger sister." The mother and daughter would graciously smile and thank the personnel. Once they stepped outside the stores, the "girls" would stop for a few minutes and laugh, enjoying the clerks' beautiful remarks.

Following her mother, Claudette started accepting modeling assignments but Claudette's mother was not in favor of her daughter being a model and devised different ways to dissuade her daughter from entering the field. She didn't want her daughter to face the unscrupulous industry individuals who wanted to be granted special "favors" from their models for "false promises." Christine wanted her daughter to stay young, innocent, and virginal until her wedding night.

She would say, "Darling, I think it's a good idea, but I want you to enjoy yourself while you are young. I know that law school has a very demanding curriculum; therefore I want you to concentrate on your studies, not get involved with something that will be a distraction.

"I want you to have a good time dating and going to parties, instead of a boring job." Claudette, being a good girl accepted her mother's explanation and forgot the modeling career.

Claudette's father, a 6' 8" tall blonde handsome man with the girth of a football quarterback, was inflexible, demanding, crude, and unreasonable unlike his wife. Time and money were his obsessions and consumed all his time. He was very dedicated to the law and would rather spend time with a client instead of attending his wife's and daughter's celebrations.

He had no interest in family life and often failed to attend birthdays, anniversaries, special events, and parties.

He would say, "I have no time for parties and such tomfoolery. My clients need me and are very important, therefore I have to help them whenever they want or need me."

To ingratiate himself and become a partner in the prestigious Fegley, Williams, and Jones law firm. He devised a plan whereby Claudette would marry Hector Fegley, Sr.'s son, Hector, who was obese, boorish, crude, and obnoxious. He graduated last in his class from a little known law school influenced by his father's generous donations.

Whenever Hector saw Claudette, he reacted like a boa constrictor
about to catch its prey.

Her father delineated his plan to Christine and Claudette and the benefits therein.

Claudette faced her father and said indignantly, "Father, I will never marry Hector, even if he were the last man on the planet. I can't stand him, and the idea of marrying and spending the rest of my life with him is revolting. He reviles me. I don't care about any benefits. I will never, never, never marry Hector!"

Christine allied herself with her daughter, pointed her index finger at him and angrily said, "I don't want you to pressure our daughter into a loveless marriage so you can be a law firm partner. When she is ready, she will marry the man of her choice, not yours. Do you understand? Furthermore, this matter will never again be discussed!"

However, the arguments continued between husband and wife. She would not agree and he would attempt to influence his wife to change her mind.

A year before Claudette's graduation from Stanford University, Christine suffered a massive stroke. Her demise cheated her daughter from celebrating with her mother this once in a lifetime momentous occasion.

When Claudette finished speaking, Cliff put his index finger under her chin, tilted her head back, and gently kissed her. "I'm sorry your father is making it so rough for you. However, your mother cared deeply for you, I regret not having had the opportunity to meet her and tell her how much I love her beautiful daughter, and that I will do everything in my power to make her happy and love her always."

"My mother would have loved you and I firmly believe that she is looking down on us and giving us her blessing."

Cliff said, "I care very deeply for you my love and shall always be here for you. Today is Monday, my sweetheart, we have already decided to make Saturday our special love day. We can make it happen. It doesn't have to be a gigantic affair; Grace and Miss Monique will be there to help make it happen."

"I believe it will be wonderful with Grace and Miss Monique's help," she said as Cliff put his arms around her, brought her close to him, and passionately kissed her.

"It's getting late. Let's drive over to your apartment and you direct me as to what you want to take. We can always come back later for the rest of your things.

They walked directly into her bedroom. She opened her closet and started taking out a set of matched luggage. Cliff waved her aside as he picked up each suitcase, put it on the bed, and opened each one.

She glanced over the contents of her closet, deciding what she really wanted to pack now, what she would pick up later, and started making a pile of clothes she would take to the local thrift shop.

Claudette then opened her drawers and was just as judicious in choosing what she should take, discard, and donate. Her robe, slippers, and sweaters were jammed in. Jackets would be carried on hangers.

She thought she was finished when Cliff asked about her shoes and handbags. She purchased them as matched sets, liked all of them, and started packing her shoes and bags. Next, she picked up her jewelry box and began packing her cosmetic case with lip gloss, mascara, eye brow pencil, other cosmetics, removers, hair dryer, conditioner, hair spray, etc. She disappeared into the bathroom, picking up her dental hygiene items, electric tooth brush, water pick, combs, hair brushes, shampoo, and other a sundry items. The kitchen was her next stop. She went into the kitchen and selected a few personal utensils.

Fortunately, she had enough luggage to accommodate all the possessions she was taking.

"Cliff, you're building muscles carrying my luggage," and they both laughed. It felt good to laugh. The day had been filled with enough disappointments and dissension.

She took one more look around, walked over and picked up her pillow, electric blanket, and bed spread. She hoped that was it. She left a note for her roommates and walked out.

Cliff looked up to see Claudette carrying her bedding. "You are an adorable picture," he said as he reached out to relieve her of the cumbersome bundle she was having difficulty carrying.

"Thank you," she said. "I didn't realize how heavy it was," as she glanced toward the car loaded down with her possessions. "Is there room for me? Perhaps, I should just walk along side the car."

Cliff said, "That's a good idea. Maybe you should for exercise"

Cliff laughed as he opened the door and said, "There is sufficient space for you," and she slid onto the seat.

"Can you see out the back window," she asked, concerned his vision might be obstructed.

"Yes, no problem," he assured her.

"I was wondering how you are going to explain this to your family," she asked.

"Simple," he said, "I'll just tell the truth. They will be compassionate and anxious to make you feel at home. After all, in just six days we'll be married and it will be your home. How exciting is that?"

"It's very exciting and I believe everyone will be happy and excited for us," she said.

"I most heartedly agree," he said as he reached out to hold her hand.

Cliff thought this would be the ideal time to talk about their honeymoon. "Where would you like to go on our honeymoon?" he inquired.

"I really hadn't given it much thought. Where do you think we should go?"

Cliff had no idea. He hadn't given it much thought either. "I don't think it will matter where we go because we'll most probably spend all our time in the hotel room. We could go to one of the hotels on the bay right here in San Diego, with a balcony and beautiful view. There is also the Hotel Del Coronado that is right on the beach. I plan to show you how much I love you and only stop to eat, shower together, and enjoy the Jacuzzi. We will only have to be concerned about enjoying ourselves, leaving the rest of the world totally shut out. We'll have a wonderful time, and when we're hungry, there is always room service. What do you think?"

"I think it's a wonderful idea. You're a genius for thinking of it," she said lovingly. "You have carte blanche to make the reservations. It will be fun. We won't be spending time traveling. I love it," she said her violet eyes twinkling as she stroked the back of his neck. "Pull over for a minute; I just have to kiss you, my adorable one."

They drove up to see a reception committee awaiting their arrival. Claudette looked up at him quizzically. I called Grace and apprised her of the situation. She wanted to welcome you. Claudette was relieved. She was marrying into a wonderful family.

Grace rushed over with Gordon close behind her. They hugged her and told her how glad they were that the wedding date had been set and excitement filled the air.

Miss Monique, Nancy, and the Svensens were anxious to add their happiness and well wishes.

They were all busily picking up the pieces of luggage and carrying them into the house.

Grace said, "I selected a large bedroom with an adjoining bath that also has a sitting room and balcony. You'll be very comfortable. It's a beautifully decorated room painted in shades of soft pastels and an heirloom canopy bed. If there is anything you want changed, no problem. We want you to be comfortable."

"I'm certain it will be perfect and why should I tamper with perfection," she said, smiling in appreciation. She loved them all and felt the ancient Roman Gods were shining down on her. She said to herself, "I am very blessed."

The room was beautiful just as Claudette anticipated. Grace was very organized and started hanging up her dresses and filling the dresser drawers with her lingerie, sweaters, etc. Everything was rapidly being put away.

Grace opened the bathroom door, walked over, turned on the water in her private Jacuzzi, and threw in lavender scented bubble bath.

Claudette was smiling as she watched Grace hang up her robe and put her slippers by the tub. "It looks wonderful. Thank you so very much. I appreciate everything."

"I have a very important question to ask you and sincerely hope and pray that you will say, 'Yes.' Grace, will you please be my matron of honor?"

Grace was stunned. She didn't expect that. "I consider that a tremendous honor. If you're sure, I would be happy to be your matron of honor."

Claudette really loved this woman and reached out to hug her. "I have another request if I may. Would you please help me select my wedding gown?"

Grace was thrilled beyond belief. She felt as though she had a daughter. It had been difficult losing Julia, her only daughter, but here Claudette had begun to beautifully fill that void.

There were tears in Grace's eyes as she spoke the words that Claudette was anxiously waiting to hear, "I would love to help you pick out your wedding gown. You will be a beautiful bride."

"Could we do some shopping tomorrow and have lunch, just the two of us? I would be most appreciative," Claudette said.

"I would love that," Grace said. We'll make it a fun day checking out the latest in negligees. It will be such fun, just us girls."

"Now, why don't you step into the Jacuzzi and relax. Here, I'll light some fragrance candles and turn on the music. Would you like Beethoven? Come on down when you finish, but don't rush, relax," Grace said.

Claudette disrobed and stepped into the tub. It felt so good and the fragrance of the lavender was very soothing. She sunk down into the tub and thought, "Next week Cliff and I will be enjoying a tub together. How great that will be! The music was very soothing and she relaxed after a very difficult day that was doing a one-eighty."
As Claudette was luxuriating in the lavender scented swirling water, she knew that she had to tell Grace about her father, not a pleasant aspect, but felt that both Grace and Gordon had to know. "I'll tell her tomorrow while we're having lunch."

Fresh from her bath, feeling relaxed, and revitalized, she went downstairs to join the others. Everyone said that she looked radiant. Ra Ra and Jacques came running over, grabbing her legs.

"Ra Ra how would you like to be my flower girl? You will look lovely wearing a beautiful dress down to the floor?"

Ra Ra was delighted and began dancing up and down, telling everyone over and over, "I'm going to be a flower girl. What is a flower girl? When will I see my dress?" she asked.

Claudette loved this adorable child with her red curly hair bouncing up and down and her large expressive blue eyes dancing. "I'm so lucky. Saturday, she will be my daughter and Jacques will be my son.

"We'll be a happy family, Cliff with our two cherubs. I'm so happy."

Dinner was a family affair. They all sat in the warm, cozy kitchen, smiling.

Cliff said, standing up and holding his water glass, "Announcement time. Everyone pick up your water glass and stand up. Claudette and I have set our wedding date."

There were cheers all around.

Ra Ra started jumping up and down with Jacques followed her lead.

"Don't keep us guessing," Miss Monique said a sweet smile on her face.

"Come on man," Gordon said, "When is it?"

"Saturday afternoon," Cliff replied.

"This Saturday!!! Are you kidding? How can you be ready in time? That's awfully quick."

"We are anxious to say our vows and begin our life together and with all of you, our family," Cliff said. "Isn't somebody going to make a toast?"

"Of course," Gordon replied, "To Cliff and Claudette, all our best wishes and happiness. You have a bright future and we will be here to support you in every way possible. Saturday, we will all be there. We love you."

Cliff looked lovingly at Claudette as he put his arm around her and drew her to him. Everyone smiled and cheered anxious to do everything possible to ensure their happiness.

Miss Monique put a basket of freshly baked hot croissants covered with a cloth to keep them warm in the center of the table. The fragrance was intoxicating.

"Let's sit down and enjoy this delicious repast by our epicurean chef," Gordon said. Everyone sat down and picked up their glass of freshly squeezed orange juice.

"Tell us what we can do to help with the wedding? What plans have already been made? Where will the wedding be held?" Miss Monique asked.

"Thus far, we have decided to have the wedding here in the garden," and addressing Mr. Svensen, Cliff continued, "You have done such a fantastic job with the garden, we hope you can add one more feature for our wedding that will become a permanent part of our garden."

"What did you have in mind?"

"We would like an arch built to be symmetrically perfect from all angles and appear to move with the passerby. Let's plant concord grapes on one side, passion fruit on the other side, and train the vines to grow up and over the arch making it a work of art."

Mr. Svensen said, "I like it. We can sink four-by-fours in each corner and nail three-quarter inch red wood lath to the four-by-fours at an angle. For the curved arch, I'll get two pieces of bender board, soak it in the pool to make it pliable, and while wet nail one piece to the front four-by-four and the other to the back four-by-four creating a curved arch. Then I'll nail more lath on the top of the bender board .for the grapes and passion fruit to curl their tentacles around. We'll paint it a very soft pink. It'll make a great addition to the garden, a real work of art. I'll get started on it right away and have it finished for your wedding Saturday. Had you planned to stand under the arch to take your vows?"

"Yes," Cliff replied. "We believe it will be a perfect setting. What do you think?"

"I totally agree," Mr. Svensen said enthusiastically.

Everyone agreed that the arch would make a perfect setting for their wedding.

Mr. Svensen said that he would be checking with the nurseries to order the plants in question, pick up the needed lumber, and cement to set the posts. "The weather is warm, therefore the cement faster will cure faster and in the meantime, I'll paint the lath prior to putting it in place with screws. I prefer screws to nails. It should be ready for your wedding, and an asset to the garden," he said as he pushed away from the table, kissed his wife, reached in his pocket, took out the truck keys, and waved as he walked toward the door.

Grace asked Claudette if she was ready to go shopping.
+
Claudette nodded, kissed Cliff and said, "I'll get my bag and shopping list," as she ran upstairs.

Gordon kissed Grace as he pulled back her chair and she got up to get her things to go shopping with Claudette.

CHAPTER TWENTY FIVE

Gordon, after pondering the subject, got up his courage and drove over to the jewelry boutique. He wanted to know why Pierre reacted as he did, so visibly shaken that he turned white and almost fainted when he saw Miss Monique. What could possibly have caused such a violent reaction? He had been sorry for both of them since the incident.

Miss Monique hadn't been herself since last night. Oh! She performed her duties as chef and was pleasant and cheery but he knew it was all an act. He realized how miserable she was, and liking her as much as he did, he had to find an answer.

Traffic was really thick. It had never taken him this long to get there. "There must be a special event," he theorized. He hadn't called ahead but hoped that Pierre would be in his shop. Gordon thought if he had called ahead, Pierre would be too embarrassed to meet with him.

Gordon turned down the street where the shop was located and found a parking place. He didn't want to park in front because if Pierre saw his car the shop might suddenly be closed. Gordon parked, put some coins in the parking meter, and walked toward the entrance.

He always liked the shop although he had only been there a few times. It had an elegant look with the long rows of clear glass cases housing the many varieties of jewelry. Behind the counter was Pierre who looked up when he heard the door open. Gordon hoped that Pierre would greet him in a friendly, not hostile manner.

"Hello Gordon," Pierre said in a friendly tone as he came forward to shake his friend's hand. Gordon was relieved. He really liked Pierre and was glad to be cordially greeted.

Gordon grasped his friend's hand in a friendly handshake.

Pierre said, "I am so glad that you included me in the celebration of the newly engaged couple. You have a beautiful family and a lovely home. I really enjoyed the dinner, it was delicious.

Gordon said, "We were happy to include you and hope you will attend their wedding."

"I shall be delighted to attend. When is it?" Pierre inquired.

"They decided that it would be this Saturday afternoon. The time hasn't been definitely set inasmuch as they just made the decision yesterday. We won't have time to send out invitations. It might be a good idea to call on Friday, if you haven't heard from us. There is so much to do and not much time," Gordon said.

Pierre was thrilled to be included. He really liked these people and treasured the newly found friendships.

Gordon was reticent to bring up the situation with Miss Monique. How could he ask something that was obviously so personal and private but he decided to forge ahead.

"Pierre, I wonder if we could sit down for a few moments?"

"Yes. Let's sit over here. Would you like a cup of coffee? I just made a fresh pot."

"Yes, it's time for my second cup," and laughed as he watched Pierre go into the small alcove and come out with two cups of coffee that he put down on the small round table in the corner.

They sat down and sipped the dark rich blend. "This is really good," Gordon said. "You make a terrific cup of coffee. It tastes just like Miss Monique's. Perhaps you use the same beans. It's delicious."

Pierre looked down. His facial expression changed dramatically.

Gordon said, "I hope I didn't say anything wrong."

"No. It's all right. We probably do use the same coffee beans and method. We knew each other a long time ago in Paris, France. It's a very long sad story. The engagement party was the first time that I had seen her in many years and it was a shock. I thought that something terrible had happened to her and to see her here in America so far from our home land was a tremendous jolt. I didn't know how to react or what to do and I guess it showed.

"I wanted to call and talk to her but didn't know if I should. It's a very difficult situation.

We were very much in love and engaged to be married. I had to make a trip to find precious gems, gold, and platinum for my jewelry business. I had no choice but to go to another country to make the purchase. I went and what followed was a horrific   nightmare.

"The plane was hijacked and went down. It was reported that I didn't survive when in reality, I was taken prisoner. The hijackers knew that I was on the plane and wanted my money and the precious gems, gold, and platinum. They didn't believe me when I gave them all my money and jewels.

"They put me in solitary. I was beaten and starved because they believed that I had more money and gems that I didn't want to tell them about. I suffered for a number of years and finally through some quirk, I was rescued.

"My rescuers were looking for someone else. I was fortunate they found me just minutes before I was to be executed. All of the other passengers had been executed one at a time and we were forced to watch. It was horrible. I have spent years trying to block out the images but it isn't easy.

"After I was rescued, they transported me via air ambulance to a hospital for medical attention. I was in horrendous pain. My captors kept me in solitary, cut, burned, stomped, and broke my bones without any regard. I had little or nothing to eat.

"My rescuers were shocked when they saw me. I'll never forget the tears in the eyes of those grown men when they saw me. I was a pathetic sight. They had to cautiously pick me up and onto a stretcher. I was essentially skin and bones and unable to walk.

"They were very kind and seemed to know that the slightest jostling would result in my suffering considerably.
"I didn't care about the pain, I was grateful to finally be free. Just two more minutes and I wouldn't have had a chance; my sadistic captors were ready to execute me."

Gordon was shocked as he listened intently to his friend's story. He had theorized what might have happened, but nothing like what he had just heard. He was in empathy with his friend who had suffered such injustices at the hands of those terrorists. He was trying to think about what he could say. No words would be adequate. All he could do now was to be a good friend.

Pierre removed his jacket and rolled up his sleeves. As he did, Gordon saw the deep scars and was shocked that one man could do this to another.

Gordon was at a loss for words and didn't know what to do. He reached across the table and touched the jeweler's hand as a sign of empathy while trying to control the tears welling up in his eyes. He had seen combat as an air force pilot but fortunately did not see or hear anything as horrifying as what he had just heard. It sounded like another horror story from the German World War II concentration camps.

Pierre appreciated Gordon's act of friendship.

This was the first time the jeweler had told anyone about the events leading up to and subsequent to his capture by the terrorists. He was amazed at how much better he felt talking about it. Now, he had someone who knew the facts and details, someone he could speak with about the horrendous heart-wrenching experience.

"You are probably wondering about Monique," Pierre continued. "It took years for me to gain back my strength and learn to walk again. The psychiatrists and psychologists were very astute and caring. I appreciated all they had done to help me move forward. It was a tremendous challenge. I had and still have nightmares but fortunately not as often. But there are times when I wake up screaming.

"After I was released, I tried to find Monique but learned she had immigrated to America but no one knew exactly where.

"I wanted desperately to find her, but it seemed futile. I worked, and after awhile, I made some money, I also booked passage to the United States. I fortunately was able to obtain papers that would allow me to immigrate. I had to leave the area, the devastating memories, and make a new start.

"I am very grateful that America accepted me. I have worked very hard to be a good citizen. I learned this business was for sale and I met with the owner who was ill and needed to retire. He was anxious for a quick sale and helped me to purchase this jewelry shop. He trusted me to pay him and I did plus extra. I am very appreciative to that man and my new country.

"I am excited that next week, I shall become an American citizen that I would like to share with you my new friends. It will be a very exciting day."

Gordon said, "Let us know the date and time and we'll all drive there together. Thank you and it will be an honor to see you sworn in as an American citizen.

"Thank you. I was hoping that you and your family would want to be present."

Gordon, "I had always wanted to find Monique but was thwarted at every turn. I had virtually given up, and when I walked into your home and saw her, it was a tremendous shock.

"I wanted to gather her up in my arms but was uncertain when I saw her facial expression, then she lost all facial color, and looked as though she was going to faint as she ran out of the room. I, too, was trying to regain my composure. It was a very difficult situation.

"I am still at a loss as to what to do. I want to tell her what had happened and that I didn't desert her. I've always loved her and I believe in my heart she loves me. I've never given up the dream of making her my wife."

Gordon for the first time in his life felt as though he was in a vacuum. It would take some time to absorb what Pierre had just related.

Pierre drew a deep breath and asked, "What do you think I should do? How do you think I should proceed? I want desperately to meet with Monique and let her know that I didn't walk out or abandon her. I don't know what she's thinking. I want her to know the truth. I never stopped loving her that what happened was not of my doing."

Gordon tried to take in all he had heard. It was like listening to a horror story that was pure fiction, but he knew in his gut it wasn't. This man had been brutalized through no fault of his own and the irony of his living in the same city as his beloved from whom he has been separated for years, trying in vain to find. It was all too unbelievable the two lovers were living just a few miles apart, totally incredulous.

"Pierre would you like me to relay the story to Monique? You could come home with me now, I will hide you in another room where upon you will be able to hear the entire conversation, and when I think it's the right time; I will tell her that you love her very much and would like to come to her. She will not even know you are on the premises unless I tell her or you come out. Is that something you would like to do?"

Pierre hesitated. It was a tremendously important decision. Should he do it? He never gambled and this sounded like a tremendous gamble. He couldn't afford to lose.

Gordon said that it was a calculated risk and then quoted that old adage, "Nothing ventured, nothing gained."

Pierre continued to deliberate as to what he should do. Ultimately, he knew that he would acquiesce. It was the only viable solution. He drew in a deep breath as he clenched his fists and emphatically exclaimed, "Let's give it a try!"

Gordon was pleased. He felt as though it was the only solution. "Let's do it tonight. The more you think about it, the more apprehensive you will be."

"All right. I trust your judgment."

Gordon reached for his cell phone and fortunately Grace answered. He didn't want to say too much because Grace's answers might possibly alert Miss Monique. "Hello Sweetheart. Are you home already from your shopping trip?"

"Yes, we got home a few minutes ago."

"I'm bringing a guest for dinner. I will fill you in when I get home. Please try to keep Miss Monique occupied, I don't want her to see me drive up or see our guest in advance. When I get everything set, I'll call you and you'll understand."

Grace acknowledged his request.

Gordon said, "Love you, Darling," and concluded the call.

"It's all set. When would you like to leave?"

"We can go now," Pierre said as he got up to start closing the jewelry store by putting gems in the vault.

Grace, remembering the conversation with her husband, sent Miss Monique out to the greenhouse to get fresh parsley, a variety of herbs for dinner, and pick some fresh vegetables from the garden: radishes, romaine lettuce, tomatoes, and green onions. She felt that would keep her busy and away from the house for awhile.

She saw him drive up, went out to greet him, and saw Pierre Bouchard. She greeted him warmly and he kissed her hand which seemed to leave her somewhat flustered. Gordon hurried both of them into the house and stationed Pierre in a small room off the living room.

Grace asked if he would like a cup of coffee or a drink. Pierre declined. Gordon said, "Make yourself comfortable and try to be quiet."

He guided Grace out of the room and asked where Miss Monique was.

"She's outside getting some herbs and vegetables from the greenhouse and garden. She should be in soon. I'll go outside and check; in the meantime can you please tell me what is going on?" She wanted desperately to be enlightened.

Gordon said that he didn't have much time but gave her the main points, and Grace, being a romantic, seemed to swoon.

She was smiling, reached up to kiss her husband, and ran out to find Miss Monique.

A short time later, he heard the kitchen door close and saw her coming in with a basket of freshly gathered herbs and vegetables.

Gordon said, "Miss Monique could you come into the living room, please?"

She came in and he asked her to sit down. She sat down on the couch and he, in an arm chair across from her. She looked at him quizzically. He had never acted like this before. She was worried that she had done something wrong, and was trying to think what it could possibly be, but couldn't. Then she decided she would just give a blanket apology and promise never to do it again. She took a deep breath, sat up very straight and said, "Gordon, I deeply apologize."

Gordon asked, "What are you apologizing for?"

"I don't know but I must have done something terrible. You look very serious."

"You haven't done anything wrong, if anything you are perfect, and we love you.

Miss Monique sighed a breath of relief. She really adored this family and didn't want to alienate anyone, cause anyone pain, or discomfort.

Miss Monique, he haltingly began, his hands clasped as he leaned toward her, "I have taken it upon myself to broach a subject that is deeply personal, and I hope you will appreciate my position. We are very fond of you and your happiness is very important to us.

"I'm certain that you recall the dinner party to congratulate Cliff and Claudette on their engagement."

She nodded.

"You also recall that the surprise guest was Pierre Bouchard who fashioned her unique engagement ring?"

Again, she nodded, but now had moved forward her apprehension was very visible. She bit her bottom lip and intermittently was wringing her hands and running her fingers through her hair.

Gordon thought, "I hope she doesn't cry or faint." He glanced to the left and saw Grace and with a wave of his hand invited her to join them. She sat down on the couch next to Miss Monique who welcomed her.

Grace put her arm around the woman and held her hand.

Gordon once again endeavored to get the words out in an eloquent fashion. "I went over to Pierre's shop this afternoon and I asked him why there was such a strong reaction when you two saw each other and he took me into his confidence. There are certain aspects you don't know about that will end your anxiety."

Miss Monique said, "I am not sure I want to know. After all what could he say? He left me. He told me he loved me, asked me to marry him, and then disappeared. I'm not sure I'm interested."

Grace patted her hand in an effort to calm her down.

"When you know the facts of what happened, you will feel very differently."

"I...I don't see how that's possible," she said.

"Please bear with me. Let me tell you what really happened."

Reluctantly, wringing her hands, she agreed. Her lip was now bleeding because she had been biting it.

"Would you like a drink of water or a cup of coffee?" Grace asked.

"No, thank you. You're very kind, but I don't want anything," she said as she burst into tears and moaned. Grace was patting her back and speaking softly as she looked at Gordon urging him to hurry. The woman was in so much pain, and once she knew the truth about what happened, there would be a change in her behavior.

"You didn't know that Pierre took a trip to purchase jewels, gold, and platinum for his jewelry store. Unfortunately, what happened next was totally unexpected. His plane was hijacked."

Miss Monique gasped, "Hijacked, hijacked!" she gasped and repeated questioningly.

"Yes, the hijackers were terrorists and very ruthless. All of the other passengers had been executed one-at-a-time in front of the other captives. Pierre was the last and was to be executed in two minutes, but it was thwarted when he was rescued. The rescuers were there to rescue someone else. Pierre was spared. They transported him via air ambulance to a hospital where he was treated both medically and psychiatrically.

"He was tortured mercilessly. He had very severe wounds. They had used him as a battering ram. He was burned, broke his bones, and beat him into unconsciousness."

"Why did they torture him? She asked almost unable to talk.

"They believed he had vast amounts of money, precious jewels, gold, and platinum they needed to finance their terrorist activities. He had none and repeatedly told them, but they wouldn't listen.

"When he finally regained his strength and could walk again, he went to look for you but suffered another setback when he learned you had immigrated to America. He was heartbroken. He still loved you as he always has and wanted more than anything to marry you. The only choice he had was to start working and earn some much needed money to also immigrate to the United States. "He didn't know where you were but hoped he would be able to find you. He never gave up hope. When he came here the other night, he wanted to talk to you but was concerned that you were too upset and wouldn't want him."

Miss Monique suddenly regained her composure, stood up, and in the loudest voice they had ever heard out of her mouth, said, "Of course, I forgive him. I love him, I have always loved him and nothing would make me happier than to be Madame Pierre Bouchard. I would love more than anything else to have his arms around me, and have him tell me that he still loves and wants me."

At that moment Pierre walked into the room toward his beloved. He said, "Ma Petite," which was what he always called her. She whirled around so fast they thought she would fall, but suddenly there was Pierre, his arms outstretched, running to embrace his beloved. Pierre wrapped his arms around her, kissed her hair, and their lips met in a very passionate kiss.

"Ma Cherie', it's been a long time, I missed you very much," she said. They were both crying and their tears mixed as they kissed again and again their arms entwined around each other.

Then she moved her head back to look at him. "I can't believe it," she said. "I have dreamed about this moment forever. You're here, you're really here, my darling," she said.

Pierre couldn't believe his good fortune. He had his beloved. "You are as beautiful as ever, Ma Petite," he said with love in his eyes, Je t'aime."

Gordon and Grace were enthralled. They were happy for both of them.

CHAPTER TWENTY SIX

Grace and Gordon were busy in the kitchen when they heard approaching footsteps and turned around to see Pierre and Miss Monique their arms entwined, looking blissfully in love.

They rushed in to thank them profusely. "Thank you hardly seems adequate," Miss Monique said desperately clinging to her Pierre. "We are very appreciative. To have my love back is a dream come true. I never thought I would see him again, and to think of what he went through at the hands of those animals."

She wanted to hug and kiss them but that meant she'd have to let go of Pierre and she couldn't bear to do that. She had been without him too long and wasn't going to let him out of her grasp or sight. How could she ever have doubted his love for her? The thought repulsed her but now she had her love back and nothing would ever interfere again. Their dreams of being together had come true.

Gordon and Grace loved looking at them. Pierre was looking up at his beloved with love and tenderness. It was a beautiful sight. And, Miss Monique looking down admiringly at him, and as their eyes met, one could see the immense amount of magnetism moving back and forth between them, as he tenderly moved her chin downward and kissed her. He was not a tall man being of European descent. She was taller and would have to bend down when they kissed.

Gordon and Grace were transfixed as they observed the couple. Grace's eyes filled with tears as she and Gordon smiled. They were ecstatically happy. The magic of love was everywhere.

They finally walked the few steps to Pierre and Miss Monique expressing their joy as they hugged the pair and their tears intermixed.

After an interlude, Grace stepped around to pick up the coffee pot, poured four cups, put a tray of French coffee cakes on the table, and waited. She was very happy for the couple and wanted to do everything possible to make their life beautiful. They had suffered at no fault of their own and deserved blissful happiness.

Grace softly asked, "Why don't we all sit down and enjoy a cup of coffee and some pastry?" They smiled. Pierre held the chair for his Monique, moved his chair as close as possible to hers, and held her hand. It was evident that nothing was ever again going to separate them again.

Gordon held Grace's chair and the four of them sat in the cozy kitchen, enjoying the moment. After a short time, they quietly pushed their chairs back and walked out of the kitchen. The newly reunited couple needed to be alone, together.

Gordon and his wife walked out into the garden. Everything was in bloom. The bright colors and the perfume from the flowers filled the air. It was breathtaking. They walked hand-in-hand, reliving the events leading up to and concluding with the newly reunited couple being together.

One of their favorite places to sit was on the family swing under its canopy. It was like an outside couch, soft, and comfortable. They sank into the soft pillows and cuddled up romantically.

They were very happy for Pierre and Miss Monique. They deserved happiness. "I wonder when he'll ask her to marry him again," Grace said wistfully. "You know, I have an idea, of course, we'll need to talk it over with Cliff and Claudette, but you know that other cottage being used for storage, it would make a great home for Miss Monique and Pierre. It's far enough away from the main house for them to have privacy and yet be a part of our wonderful family. What do you think? Are you in favor?"

Gordon enthusiastically said, "Yes, it's a great idea."

They were so intently involved with one another that they didn't notice the two figures coming toward them until they were standing directly in front of them.

"Hello, you two love birds," Claudette said lovingly.

Grace and Gordon looked up. They were still somewhat embarrassed when caught in the act of being passionate.

They moved over and suggested Claudette and Cliff join them. They sat, putting their feet down on the grass as they pushed the swing back and forth.

"This is fun," Claudette said.

Gordon looked at Cliff and jokingly said, "Why is it girls always think it is fun to swing?"

Cliff said, "I don't know but they decidedly do and always look happy like a small child."

The four of them sat swinging, each holding his beloved.

Grace was the first to speak. "There is a subject we would like to broach with the two of you"

"Wait a minute," Gordon said. "You're getting ahead of yourself. They don't know what transpired prior to their coming home."

"That's right," Grace said.

By this time Cliff and Claudette were somewhat excited. "Is it good news?" she inquired. "I hope so. It must be good by the look on your faces. Come on tell us. Don't keep us in suspense," she laughingly urged.

Grace looked at Gordon. He said, "You tell them, you like this kind of story. In fact, I'd say you thrive on it," and everybody laughed.

Claudette was anxious to hear what had transpired that afternoon. She turned her gaze pleadingly at the pair who looked as though they had the most wonderful secret and when would they divulge it. She didn't know how long she could stand the suspense.

Her curiosity overwhelmed, she finally stood up and faced the pair, "Well," she said, and starting laughing, "When are you going to tell us?" It was becoming a fun game and they started laughing. Claudette sat down and said demurely, "All right if you want to keep the secret to yourselves," but she couldn't finish the sentence without laughing.

Gordon looked at Grace and said, "You are going to love this. Go ahead Grace tell them before Claudette bursts. A broad smile crossed his face. He was having fun, enjoying all of this.

Grace began, "You recall Pierre was invited to be a guest at your engagement dinner party, the encounter he had with Miss Monique, and how flustered the two were when they saw each other almost to the point of passing out. Miss Monique's fair skin paled when she saw Pierre. He was in a state of shock and would have collapsed on the floor if it hadn't been for Gordon and Cliff. They intervened, thereby preventing Pierre from falling down on his face."

Cliff and Claudette nodded, indicating that they recalled the entire incident.

"We've been very concerned. Gordon went to Pierre's boutique this afternoon and was taken into his confidence, relaying what had transpired during the intervening years when he and Miss Monique were separated.

"It's a tragic story of what occurred when the plane he was traveling on was hijacked and he was held captive by ruthless terrorists who took great pleasure in beating him, breaking his bones, burning, starving him, and forcing Pierre and the others to watch as one by one the captives were executed. Two more minutes and he would have been mercilessly murdered.

"He was rescued by men who were searching for another prisoner. He couldn't walk and was badly malnourished. They air lifted him to a hospital where he began the recuperation process. When he returned to Paris, he learned Miss Monique had immigrated to America.

"Pierre immigrated to the United States, determined to find his true love. It was coincidental or maybe it wasn't. It could have been divine providence that we met him, and he was here that night.

"Their love is strong. It's beautiful."

Grace upon bringing them up-to-date said she and Gordon had a suggestion that requires your input.

"We have felt from the beginning that Miss Monique was part of our family and now we are feeling the same way about her Pierre. We're certain they will be married. We thought since neither of them has any blood relatives, and in reality are members of our family, we can refurbish the cottage at the other end of the property being used for storage.

"It will be perfect for them. First, I thought they could participate in the remodeling, but, and this is my idea, I think it would be great as a surprise. What do you think?"

"It's a great idea!" they all agreed.

"Let's go over now and check it out," Cliff urged.

The quaint cottage was complementary to Gordon and Grace's cottage surrounded by blooming flower beds and fruit trees. From the exterior, it didn't seem to be in need of repairs.

They entered, and although it was very dusty and needed a good cleaning, it seemed to be in good condition. Grace said that perhaps a few of the walls could use a new coat of paint. It wasn't peeling but could be freshened up.

The living room had a wood burning fireplace and large windows that would brighten the room with the morning sunlight. The French doors leading out onto the terrace would be perfect for morning coffee or a moonlight drink of wine as they gaze out over the grounds of green grass, succulents, rose beds, flowers, and fruit trees.

"Let's look at the kitchen, The appliances could be updated and walls painted a nice bright yellow enamel and perhaps put in one of those windows for growing herbs, etc.," Grace said

"I agree," Cliff said as he examined the table and chairs and determined they were in good condition; their natural wood vintage added to the cottage's charm. "The cabinets can be sanded and refinished; applying two coats of varnish will enhance the ash wood." He liked natural wood as opposed to painted. "The drawers of course should also be refinished that will result in the kitchen having a bright cheery look," he said turning to Gordon for his evaluation.

"I agree," Gordon said, looking at the floor. "Giving the floor a good scrubbing and coat of wax will be the finishing touch, it shouldn't take too long."

Claudette was conferring with Grace and suggested that the utensils might need a good cleaning since the cottage hadn't been occupied for a number of years, and began checking the two bedrooms, bathroom, and dining area. The room with a fireplace and French doors leading to an outside patio would be a perfect den for Pierre.

Gordon said, "The bathrooms should be freshened up with a new coat of paint." Grace checked the linen closet noting that the contents should be laundered. The bedrooms also needed freshening. They would check with Mr. Svensen and give him the option of bringing in the appropriate cleaning crews. He was very knowledgeable in number of areas, would assess, and know exactly to do.

"I'm so excited," Grace said and Claudette was in total agreement.

Cliff asked Gordon if he wanted to touch base with Mr. Svensen and set everything in motion. Gordon was only too happy to work with Mr. Svensen and possibly even join in the restoration project.

They walked back to Camden Manor, the main house, laughing and talking about how exciting it was going to be having the happy couple living on the premises.

Pierre and Miss Monique were sitting at the table in the cozy kitchen gazing into each other's eyes, couldn't get enough of one another. All they wanted to do was to be close; having Pierre's arms around her was pure ambrosia.

He couldn't believe his good luck. Just a few hours before, he was still missing her so much that it felt as though someone had stomped on his chest. He never dreamed that she was living right here in San Diego just a few miles from his shop. How incredible that he was invited to dinner in this home and there she was, his Monique, the love of his life, the woman he adored, and dreamed about for years. How could he know that when Gordon came in his whole world would be changed and for the best.

Pierre lifted his hand and stroked her cheek. It was soft and beautiful. She was so lovely that he adored every inch of her from her toes to the tip of her adorable nose. His beloved. He wanted to close his eyes when he kissed her, but he couldn't because he needed to see her beautiful face. If he closed his eyes, she might not be there when he opened them. He still couldn't get used to the fact that she was here, he was here, and they were here together at last.

Miss Monique was "floating on a cloud." She never thought it would happen. It occurred all the time in her dreams, whether asleep or awake. She was very lucky. Her prayers, although doubted, had been answered.

Here he was--her love. It was impossible and yet here they were together again. All the old feelings were there; their love was stronger than ever.

She remembered him a handsome young man in his twenties, bright red hair, happy disposition, smooth face, muscular body, and broad shoulders.

His jewelry was worn around the necks, wrists, and fingers of nobility, world leaders, and the wealthy.

And she had had a very exclusive famous Parisian restaurant, serving the most delicious foods made with the best ingredients and fresh herbs to clients from all over the world.

They had a wonderful time walking down the Champs-Elysees, visiting museums, Notre Dame Cathedral, climbing the Eiffel Tower, picnics in the beautiful parks, and shopping in the many quaint stores.

She felt regretful that he had suffered so interminably at the hands of those terrorists without her being aware of his trials and tribulations. The thought was abhorrent. His temples had grayed and streaks of white ran through his hair. His face had some wrinkles and he had lost considerable weight but he was as handsome as ever. She wouldn't do anything to change it and had to put it out of her thoughts, the only solution. She couldn't dwell on those aspects. "He looks great and seems to have fully recovered for which I am most grateful," she thought.

They were oblivious that the sun was going down below the horizon as they clung to each other still sitting at the kitchen table. Neither wanted to move. They were afraid that even the slightest movement and their dream of being together would vanish leaving each alone.

CHAPTER TWENTY SEVEN

The foursome were excited and continued talking about how great it was going to be having Monique and Pierre occupying the other cottage.

As they were walking toward the house, Mr. and Mrs. Svensen were coming toward them which was convenient as they wanted to speak with them about the restorations. Gordon began explaining what they wanted to accomplish in as short a time as possible.

Mr. Svensen looked puzzled as to why it was being renovated. Gorden then realized that they didn't know what had transpired that afternoon. He suggested that they sit down at the patio table and learn about the day's events.

The Svensen's were initialed shocked to hear about Pierre's ordeal, but when they heard the entire story, were in total empathy and wanted to do all they could to make the couple happy. They had only met Pierre once, but liked him, and were surprised to learn that the two were engaged in France. Mrs. Svensen who loves her husband very much was intrigued by their romantic love story; it sounded unbelievable, yet true.

"Do we know anything about their immediate plans? Any word about their wedding plans?" Mrs. Svensen inquired.

Grace said, "Nothing yet. They're sitting in the kitchen lost in each other. We're anxious to know if they have made any plans but hesitate to intrude. I'm sure we must all be hungry. Let's walk over to our cottage and have a snack." They all agreed.

They were a harmonious group. It was pleasurable being together to enjoy a variety of activities. The cottage loomed in the distance and they started walking faster as they realized how hungry they were.

Pierre and Monique were still sitting so close together that they could feel each other's hearts beating, their arms remained entwined. They were still unwilling to move because the bond might be broken but their muscles were beginning to ache from sitting in one position for so many hours.

Pierre peered into Monique's eyes as he put his index finger under her chin, and brought her lips closer to him and he kissed her passionately.

They both felt they belonged together but knew they would have to move because their legs were aching, their feet falling asleep. The cramping intensified causing out of necessity, for them to push back their chairs and stand up while still embracing each other.

They were wondering what was next. What would they do now? But neither was willing to say or do anything. Finally, Monique asked, "You must be hungry. I can make us something to eat. Would you like that?"

"I would like anything with you. I just want to be close to you. Being with you is a dream come true. I never want to be separated from you again." He reached out the short distance between them, bringing her to him, as he wrapped his arms around her.

When Gordon came to his shop that afternoon, he never dreamed that he would be standing here holding his beloved. He felt blessed. The bulge in his pocket was feeling heavier with each passing moment. This had to be the moment he thought would never happen, but it did. He suddenly took one step backward, got down on one knee while still holding her hand; he looked up at her beautiful face.

"Monique, I feel as though I have loved you all my life. You're the one shining star on my horizon. I want us to spend our lives together, never to part."

Reaching into his pocket, he took out a velvet jeweler's box and opened it revealing an exquisite engagement ring set in platinum. The look on her face was one of disbelief. How could this be happening? Her facial expression was one of amazement.

Pierre said in a very emotional voice, "I love you, will you do me the honor of marrying me."

She stood transfixed as he waited for her reply.

He asked again, and this time, her eyes shone, and her lips parted as she said the words that he was waiting for, "Oui, ma cheri, Oui, Je t'aime beaucoup. I will marry you. I love you very much."

He took the ring out of the velvet box, put it on the third finger of her left hand, and kissed it as he arose.

Again, he said, "I love you and will do everything possible to make you happy." They stood as the moonlight was shining through the window illuminating the happy couple.

She was so excited that she wanted to jump up and down, run around and scream out to the world, "I am in love and getting married to the most wonderful man in the world."

The three couples had returned from the cottage to hear Miss Monique's voice and they wondered what was happening. They gingerly walked over and peered into the kitchen.

Pierre was standing and Miss Monique was waving her arms and squealing. It was rather perplexing and then the couple saw them by the kitchen door.

Miss Monique said, "Come in, come in and join in our happiness," as she held out her hand sporting the most magnificent four-carat diamond ring. There were more squeals of joy as they looked at her ring and began wishing them well. It was a truly happy moment.

The men were patting Pierre on the back and telling him that he had a gem in Monique. Pierre never thought he could be this happy again. He felt wonderful and was enjoying the happy feelings that were surging throughout his body. He felt as he though no man had ever felt before, he wanted to remember every second of this day.

Everyone congratulated them. They wanted to hear every detail. It was a truly joyous occasion. "Have you set a date," Gordon asked.

"We haven't gotten that far. I want it to be soon," Pierre said and turned to Monique, asking her how much time she needed to get ready for their wedding.

"I don't know. Right now as you know we're planning Cliff and Claudette's wedding."

Cliff said, "How would it be if you were married a couple of days before the day of our wedding. That way you would have your special day and could rejoice as you attend our wedding."

Pierre and Monique thought that was a great idea, and they all sat down to plan not just one but two weddings.

Pierre said, "My apartment will not be adequate. It is very small. We'll need to find a place to begin our married life."

"Not to worry," Cliff assured him.

They were excited to tell the newly engaged pair about the cottage. They said, "Grace, why don't you do the honors?"

Gordon said, "Just a minute," as he went into the dining room, reached into a cabinet, took out a vintage bottle of champagne and the silver ice bucket.

Grace went to the refrigerator and pulled out several trays of ice to put in the ice bucket. Gordon put in a cork screw and 'pop' the cork was extracted while Cliff opened the china cabinet, selected eight crystal champagne glasses, and put them on a silver serving tray.

Claudette started creating a few hors d'oeuvres to make everything more festive. Each had a glass of champagne. Gordon made the first toast, followed by Cliff, and the others all of whom wanted to voice their happy acknowledgment of the occasion.

Then each started looking at the other trying to decide who should tell the couple about the gift they were preparing. There were sly glances between Gordon and Cliff about who should give the exciting news and then Cliff motioned to Gordon to go ahead and do the honors.

Gordon stood up, raising his glass and asked the others to join him. He said, addressing Pierre and Monique, "This is a momentous occasion and we want you to know that we consider ourselves your family and want you to know that you will always have a place here in your own cottage."

Surprised Miss Monique gasped. "What do you mean?"

Gordon said, "You recall that cottage at the far end that has been used for storage, we have decided to refurbish it for the two of you. The appliances will be replaced with new ones. Walls will be painted, floors scrubbed and waxed, fixtures upgraded, linens, draperies, rugs, and curtains replaced. But you must make us a promise that you won't go there until it's ready for you to occupy. In the interim, the two of you can occupy that suite of rooms on the top floor."

Pierre and Monique were speechless. "That's so good of you," Pierre said. You are so good to us and I pledge that you won't regret it. I am honored, monsieur, to be a member of your family, and will do everything possible to make Monique happy and be a true and valued friend to all of you."

"We'll see you in the morning and begin planning your wedding and a dress for your beautiful bride," Claudette said.

They hugged prior to adjourning to their respective rooms.

When they had left the kitchen, Pierre looked at Monique. "What do you want me to do?" he asked.

She said, "I would rather wait until our wedding night, but I can't let you go. We can occupy the same bed, kiss, and fall asleep in each other's arms, but I'd like to wait for the intimacy until we are married. Is that all right with you?"

"It's more than all right with me. We will spend our honeymoon in the cottage. It will be perfect and very romantic," he said. She took his hand and they walked upstairs.

Cliff shouted, "Pierre can you come here a minute, please." He was somewhat perplexed as he walked toward Cliff.

Cliff handed him a pair of pajamas, robe, slippers, toothbrush, comb, and shaver.

Pierre was grateful and emotional as Cliff noted that his eyes were filled with tears. This man had gone through so much and they were happy to make his days extra special. He patted him on the shoulder and said, "Sleep well, my friend, you are with your family."

Pierre was so overwhelmed that he reached out, hugged Cliff, and turned to follow his fiancée to their suite of rooms.

Monique paused outside the door of their suite, waiting for Pierre. She wanted them to walk into the room together hand-in-hand.

The room was beautifully decorated. Pierre stood back in awe at the furnishings and again felt very lucky. He took his fiancée in his arms, pulling her gently to him and held her as he whispered in her ear, "Shall we get ready for bed so that we can go to sleep in each other's arms? And, I promise that we will wait until we're married and in our cottage to be intimate."

She smiled, glancing down at her ring, and walked into the bathroom to get ready for bed.

CHAPTER TWENTY EIGHT

Claudette and Grace were in the kitchen preparing breakfast as they discussed plans for Monique and Pierre's wedding.

"Let's go downtown and look for her wedding gown and other clothes. She has never dressed up and now she has a reason to look her best." They talked about the caterer and other calls to make in preparation.

The Svensen's came in. They were talking about plans for the cottage. Mr. Svensen said that he was going to purchase the necessary items and Mrs. Svensen was going to start cleaning. Everyone was excited.

Pierre woke up, went into the bathroom, shaved, and showered. He wanted to be fresh for when Monique woke up.

He got back into bed and laid there watching her sleep. She looked so beautiful lying there and when she awoke and looked at him, it was in disbelief. They were really together. He held her and enjoyed the scent of her violet perfume. She always loved violets.

"Good morning sweetheart, love you, love you, love you," he said.

"Good mooring darling, I love you," she said.

They laid there in a loving embrace enjoying each other and thanking God and their friends. It was too good to be true. "Guess we better get up. Remember in a few days you will be my beautiful bride, Mrs. Pierre Bouchard. It will be the greatest day of my life," Pierre said as the gently caressed her face.

They joined the others in the cheery kitchen. It was wonderful seeing all those smiling faces. They all sat at the table ready to enjoy breakfast when Nancy came in with Ra Ra and Jacques.

Miss Monique looked at Ra Ra and asked her, "How would you like to be a flower girl at two weddings and have a different dress for each one?"

Ra Ra exploded with squeals of joy and rapture. "Really. Really. Will both dresses be down to the floor with bows?"

"Yes, they will."

"I'm ready. Where are my dresses? I want to get dressed up now for the parties."

Everyone laughed. They all loved her adorable antics.

"We'll leave right after breakfast," Grace said.

Claudette reminded the newly engaged couple, "Remember, no peeking at your honeymoon cottage?"

Monique looked at Pierre and they smiled at each other promising that they wouldn't go in that direction. They too wanted to be surprised. It was all too wonderful. How in a few hours life can be so totally transformed

Mr. Svensen came back with a truck load of materials while his wives with helpers were taking down the curtains and drapes. The floors were being stripped to be sanded, varnished, and waxed, while the walls were being washed for the painters. Progress was being made.

Later that afternoon Mrs. Svensen asked Cliff and Gordon about dinner. Should she start making dinner or should she call to have it brought in. They wanted to go out to dinner, however shopping all day could be tiring and maybe the ladies would rather just sit down at home and relax.

"Why don't you call our usual caterer? They know what we like that way everyone can relax and ask the caterer to come back after dinner to clean up please. We don't want to be washing dishes when we have so many plans to make," Cliff said.

Mrs. Svensen called the caterer and as usual they were very flexible and said that they would arrive at seven o'clock, and she went back to the cottage to help oversee everything.

The ladies were having a great time watching Monique try on wedding gowns. She kept protesting that she couldn't afford it, but Grace kept reassuring her that it was their gift to her. She did look lovely and after trudging to numerous stores the perfect gown was finally found much to the relief of all.

They also found the perfect gown for Grace whom she wanted to be her matron of honor and a darling dress for Ra Ra who would probably be so excited that she'd never want to take it off.

Other outfits, shoes, bags, a coat, negligees, etc., were also purchased for Monique despite her objections about them spending too much money.

The ladies arrived home exhilarated from their shopping but also tired. There were three pairs of feet aching to be massaged and their fellows were only too happy to oblige.

Cliff and Gordon were glad they had called the caterer to relieve everyone from having to prepare their repast.

They all went upstairs to shower and refresh themselves.

Dinner was splendid and laughter filled the dining room. Ra Ra was repeatedly asking about her dress and they promised her she'd see it right after dinner. When she was excited, she'd pick up her spoon, bang the handle on the table, and jump up and down.

After dinner as promised, Ra Ra saw her dress, and was delighted. It was white organdy with puffed sleeves, pink and red rose buds with green leaves and short stems scattered at various intervals throughout the dress. She of course had to try it on and looked like a doll.

They planned to cut some fresh red rose buds from the garden to put in her hair. Also, the florist would be bringing extra flowers for the hair dresser to weave into the coiffeurs.
It looked as though everything was in readiness. Miss Monique couldn't seem to contain herself. In between smiles, she was crying. It would take her awhile to adjust but happiness was on her doorstep.

It was the day of the wedding for Pierre and Monique. All was in readiness. Pierre looked very elegant and handsome in his tuxedo, as did Cliff, Gordon, Mr. Svensen, and Jacques.

The caterers had arrived and had everything under control while upstairs the ladies were having a field day running around getting everyone dressed in their finery. Ra Ra was ready to go. She would have slept in her dress, if they had let her.

Grace looked lovely as the matron of honor; Claudette and Mrs. Svensen were ready and now for the bride. The hair dresser had done an excellent job on everyone's coiffeur and makeup.

They helped Monique into her gown and put her veil in place. She was a vision of loveliness as she put on her white satin bridal gloves embellished with faux pearls to match her gown. She asked, "How do I look?"

"Beautiful they all said," as she turned to look at herself in the full length mirror.

There was a knock at the door, Claudette said, "I think that's the photographer."

She opened the door a crack and saw that it was the photographer. He came in, began snapping photos, and left.

We're all ready. Shall we have the organist start playing the wedding march? Monique nodded. This was her day and she wanted to remember every minute detail.

They started walking to the top of the staircase. Gordon would be at the bottom to escort Monique and "give her away."

Down the stairs went Mrs. Svensen, Claudette, Ra Ra, Grace, and then Monique, the bride who would be on Gordon's arm.

She looked up through her veil to see her Pierre standing at the altar and next to him Cliff, the best man, Jacques the ring bearer, and the judge Cliff had asked to preside.

She was anxious to be Mrs. Pierre Bouchard, but at the same time didn't want it to go too fast as she wanted to savor every delicious moment.

Gordon smiled as he bent over to kiss her and transferred her arm to Pierre's.

The couple stood there looking at each other. The judge patiently waited while repeatedly requesting that they turn and face him. They smiled, turned to face the judge, and apologized.

As the judge began the ceremony, the air was suddenly filled with the fragrance of the pastel cut flowers that were fashioned in unique floral arrangements.

When the judge asked the couple to repeat their vows, Gordon holding hands with Grace listened intently and they in turn repeated the vows they had said years before and the LeClairs looked at each other and were grateful they had been included.

Cliff with his arm around Claudette was thinking about how happy he was going to be upon reciting their vows in a few days.

The judge was now saying upon completion of the spoken vows, "You may kiss your bride." It was a stirring moment for this special couple. Pierre lifted Monique's veil, and he kissed her. They turned, and started walking back down the aisle to the traditional wedding music as man and wife.

Everyone was anxious to congratulate the happy couple.

The caterers had done a magnificent job amidst the photographer taking photos; waiters were weaving in and out with champagne in crystal stemware on a silver tray.

Cliff picked up his glass of champagne and invited everyone to join him as the best man to give the first toast, "To our dear and treasured friends, Monique and Pierre, may all your days be filled with love and happiness. We are happy to have both of you as members of our family and will always be here for you--all our best wishes for a wonderfully happy future."

Everyone cheered and joined in raising their glasses in a toast to the newlyweds.

Cliff walked over to the Svensen's and inquired as to whether the cottage was ready.

"Yes," he said, "All systems go."

Mrs. Svensen echoed her husband's agreement and added that she had purchased all the necessary items for the linen closet, new curtains and draperies had been hung, and their bed had been made with a soft down comforter and pillows. All was in readiness down to a well-stocked refrigerator, candles, and fresh flowers. "I even put a new negligee and pajamas on the bed."

Cliff hugged her and profusely thanked them both for all their hard work. "It wasn't hard work, we enjoyed doing it. Our greatest thanks will be the look on their faces," she said.

Gordon walked over to Monique who was looking radiant on the arm of her new husband. He said, "I would like you to meet the LeClairs. They operate the most fabulous French restaurant and the band that will be playing at your reception is featured at their establishment.

The newlyweds thanked the LeClairs for coming and upon hearing their French accent the foursome began speaking in French. All the other members of the bridal party were watching and pleased for the newlyweds as this was the beginning of another wonderful friendship.

Gordon and Grace joined Cliff and Claudette as they were deciding how to proceed. The caterers had arrived and set everything up awaiting the bridal party and guests. They all sat down and enjoyed a fabulous repast complete with numerous toasts and gifts that embarrassed the couple who felt that enough had been done for them, but graciously thanked everyone.

The band and violinist featured at the LeClair's French Restaurant began playing the first dance, "Wonderful One." The music was intoxicating and they were all enjoying the frivolity of the occasion including Ra Ra and Jacques who were also dancing.

The newlyweds, bridal party, and guests danced continuously pausing occasionally to have another sip of champagne and wedding cake.

Claudette, Cliff, Gordon, and Grace were off to the side trying to decide when it would be appropriate to walk the newlyweds over to their honeymoon cottage. Claudette said, "It will be timely when we observe they are ready. It won't be that difficult."

Suddenly, they realized that the festivities were winding down and it was time for the newlyweds to begin their honeymoon. Cliff suggested that Gordon make the announcement and they all follow the couple to their cottage.

Claudette quickly walked forward with the top layer of the wedding cake and a bottle of champagne in a silver ice bucket for the couple to enjoy when they're alone. Grace passed out rice for everyone to throw just before Pierre carries Monique over the threshold.

Gordon started gathering everyone together and walked over to the bride and groom asking if they were ready to begin their honeymoon. Monique blushed unabashedly as she nodded and Pierre looking very proud and handsome smiled and nodded while holding his bride as close to him as possible.

CHAPTER TWENTY NINE

They all started walking toward the cottage followed by the violinist who was playing softly. It was a beautiful night. A full moon was shining down as though giving its approval in a velvety sky full of twinkling stars.

Rice was raining down on the couple as Pierre gently picked up his bride and carried her across the threshold of their cottage to cheers from the group as the door closed on the happy couple.

On the walk back, Claudette and Gordon were jubilant. It was a beautiful wedding and made them even more anxious for their wedding day. All the arrangements had been made thanks to Grace and Gordon. Claudette had her dress and Cliff had made the reservations.

The excitement was growing. They paused in the garden as he gently pulled her close to him and passionately kissed her. He pulled back to look at her beautiful face bathed in the silvery moon light to drink in the exquisiteness of her eyes that were sparkling like the stars above, when they witnessed a shooting star and each like children made a wish.

They just stood there enjoying the warmth of each other and the beauty of the moment when they heard footsteps running in their direction. Confused and concerned as to who it might be, they turned and saw Grace rushing toward them with a worried look on her face.

She had to pause and catch her breath. It had been awhile since she had run with such intensity knowing that the matter was urgent. They looked at her, perplexed. Cliff put his arm around her as he steered her to the nearest bench. They sat with her waiting as patiently as possible under the circumstances.

She tried to speak but was still breathless and Cliff asked if she would like a glass of water.

She shook her head and again endeavored to speak.

Finally, with her hand pressed against her chest, she said, "I have some bad news, but it's not all that bad. Your father has been in an accident and it is serious."

Now, Cliff was worried about what the news would do to Claudette.

She asked, "How is he?"

"He's doing very well and frankly did not want you to know. The prognosis is guarded but good. He told his law partner not to call and that he was not interested in attending your wedding. Furthermore, he had written a new will prior to the accident disinheriting you and never wants to see you again. He was very emphatic that you were not to come to see or communicate with him in anyway whatsoever."

Claudette was devastated. She knew that the situation between them was strained because he adamantly insisted that she marry Hector Fegley and when she told him that she had fallen in love with Cliff, her father cut off all lines of communication and disowned her. He was extremely antagonistic. When she tried to talk to him and invite him to the wedding, he screamed so loudly that she had to hold the phone at arm's length as he was still hurting her ear drums.

She kept trying to calm him down but to no avail. He had his mind made up and told her that if she married Cliff, she was not his daughter and banged down the phone.

Claudette was desolate. How could the father she loved, respected and with whom she had thought loved and protected her be so tyrannical? She sat there shaking her head as the tears filled her violet eyes and tumbled down her cheeks.

Grace was patting her hand while Cliff was doing his best to console her. He was desperately trying to rationalize how could he console someone whose father had behaved so abominably. He shook his head in desperation.

The deafening stillness was only broken by Claudette's uncontrollable sobs. Grace and Cliff were in a quandary as to how to handle this delicate situation. They loved Claudette. It was virtually tearing them apart seeing her like this, as they were endeavoring to rationalize how a man could be a loving father and then turn against his one and only loving daughter because she refused to succumb to his irrational demands.

Her father didn't come to her graduation, didn't send her a gift or call to congratulate her, therefore, he didn't care. He was only interested in the monetary gains if his daughter married Hector Fegley.

Pierre with pride, carried his bride across the threshold, walked forward with her still in his arms, lifted his foot hooking it behind the door to close it, while continuing to encircle her in his arms. He didn't want to put her down. He couldn't believe his luck.

Just a few years ago he was being held against his will by terrorists and now here he was with his beautiful bride, Monique, in his arms. She was all his and he all hers," he thought as he brought her even closer to him and kissed her. The newlyweds were excited and filled with anticipation as they stood in the foyer of their honeymoon cottage.

Pierre glanced around the room for the old fashioned record player. He had asked Gordon if there was one in the cottage and he nodded. Pierre had given him some records from his extensive collection and asked Gordon if he would put them next to the unit and one especially to put on ready to be played.

He reached out and started the music as he asked his bride for this dance. Their song, "Wonderful One," was being played and they enjoyed it as they waltzed around the room in each other's arms.

The moonlight was streaming in through the windows and seemed to dance on Monique's hair. It was all so enchanting. At the conclusion of the dance, they started walking toward their bridal chamber and noted the top layer of their wedding and a bottle of champagne on the night stand.

Pierre said, "Let change and then enjoy a repast of the goodies."

She smiled in acknowledgment, picked up her negligee, and turned to ask Pierre to please unzip her. She couldn't believe that her new husband was unzipping her bridal gown. It was all so wonderful. She turned and he kissed her as she walked in to the dressing room adjacent to their bedroom.

She slipped off her gown and suddenly heard music.

"He must have brought the record player into the bedroom and was playing soft romantic music for them both to enjoy."

He changed into the pair of new silk pajamas that Mrs. Svensen had put on the bed, put on his robe and slippers, and opened the bottle of champagne.

The anticipation of starting their life together was filling him with so much love.

Monique came out in her soft pink chiffon negligee. He stood in awe gazing at this vision standing before him.

He stood mesmerized as he saw the slim lines of her figure through the transparency of her peignoir. He was so anxious to hold, kiss, and bathe himself in her beauty.

He extended his arms toward her and she walked into them to be held and caressed. He tightened his arms around her and she responded in kind. He picked her up in arms and gingerly laid her on their bed and they made mad passionate love.

Their love making was like floating in paradise, a dream come true. They fell asleep.   Shortly thereafter, Pierre started thrashing around and screaming. The traumatic experience of a hostage seeing all those people being massacred by the terrorists filtered into his dreams.

She didn't immediately understand what was causing his nightmare, all she knew was that she wanted to hold and make him feel safe. She put her arms around him and kissed him in an effort to comfort and block out the terrible nightmare. He woke up not realizing he had been reliving a terrifying experience.
They were holding, caressing, and kissing each other when once again she felt him tightly against her, and they began making love.

It was hours later as the sunlight slowly streamed in through the windows that the couple began waking up to a beautiful honeymoon day.

They looked at each other, smiled, and kissed each other good morning.

Pierre said, "I know it's not romantic, but I am really hungry, how about you?"

"Yes, I am ravenous. Let's enjoy some more of our wedding cake."

He handed her the cake knife and she cut a slice of their wedding cake as he poured two glasses of champagne handing one to his bride, and they encircled each other's arm as they toasted and drank to each other.

Pierre put on another record and came back to their bed as she held up a piece of cake. He ate from one side, and she from the other. They were laughing while feeding each other in between sips of champagne.

He said, "You look even more adorable with frosting on your face," and they both laughed.

Suddenly they were surprised to hear a knock at the door; he put on his robe, and walked over to open the door. No one was there but he did hear running footsteps fading away as he opened the door and was surprised to see a wrought iron tea cart with flowers and a full breakfast.

He wheeled the cart into their bedroom; they sat on the bed, and began uncovering the dishes. They were enjoying the aroma of coffee that filled the room.

Monique poured one cup that they both drank from it at intervals. It was so wonderful sharing everything. She tore a piece off one of the croissants, fed it to him, and poured maple syrup on the waffles that they relished with bacon, eggs, and sausage.

Pierre began profusely apologizing.

She couldn't understand why. She held his hand and said, "You have nothing to be sorry for. You are perfect."

He interrupted her, "I thought I had a nightmare."

"Yes, you did but it's not important. I'm here and whenever you have a nightmare my arms will tighten around you, I will kiss you, and whisper how much I love you."

CHAPTER THIRTY

Everyone was in a dither, time was of the essence, as they were all rushing around preparing for Claudette and Cliff's wedding the next day.

Claudette was still downhearted and tried desperately not to think about her father who wouldn't come to her wedding and wondered how he could be so cruel but she kept telling herself that was his decision and she shouldn't dwell on what she couldn't change. Tomorrow was her big day, the most exciting day of her life, actually the real beginning of her life with the man of her dreams.

Cliff was the love of her life, a truly wonderful man. She somehow knew that he would never disappoint her. He was always attentive, the perfect gentleman opening doors, holding her chair, assisting her with her coat or stole, and always stepping aside to allow her to precede him.

She considered herself a very fortunate lady to have a man totally committed to her. If only...but she stopped herself. She had to put aside, out of her mind anything regarding her father. She didn't understand it, but he made it vividly clear that he didn't want to be a part of her life, nor did he care about her. It had to be a closed book, she said to herself, and started to pack her suitcases and cosmetic bag for their honeymoon.

Grace had helped her select a beautiful trousseau compete with accessories.

Claudette was wondering why she was taking any clothes in view of the fact that they probably wouldn't even leave their hotel room but being style conscious, she couldn't go without taking casual, street, and cocktail clothes even though she didn't believe they would be worn.

The phone rang, Claudette welcomed the interruption. It was Cliff calling because he was concerned.

"Hello sweetheart. I just had to call and tell you how much I love you and am looking forward to our special day. How are you? What are you doing?"

"I'm packing to be ready for our great adventure."

"How many suitcases are you taking? Shall I rent a bus or moving van to handle it all?" and laughed.

"You really think you're funny, don't you? You know that I need everything in my suitcases. Just because you can put everything you need in your pocket, you find my packing a subject for amusement."

"Sorry. I know that you need all that stuff and I should be grateful because it will help me keep in shape, building muscles, as I'm carrying it all, and I will be able to cancel my gym membership."

"If you were here, I'd throw a pillow in your direction. You really think you're funny."

"Yes, I am funny," and they both laughed. He liked the sound of her laughter. She sounded as though she wasn't dwelling on her father and his mistreatment. "Can I interest you in a walk and moonlight snack?"

"Sounds good, I'll come down and we'll pack the picnic basket together. It'll be fun."

"I'll meet you in the kitchen," he said.

She felt so much better. He had that affect on her. She looked in the mirror, combed her hair, applied fresh lipstick, mascara, eye shadow, blush to her cheeks, and ran down the stairs for an exciting rendezvous with her beloved.

Cliff was already in the kitchen. She silently wondered what he was putting in the picnic basket and decided to poke around inside the basket when he put his hand on top of the basket and said with a smile that she loved. "If you look, you won't be surprised." He looked like a little boy with a really big secret.

She stepped back laughing. "You certainly are a culinary expert. Is there something I can do to help the Great Clifford?"

He bowed pointing to the cucumbers, radishes, tomatoes, carrots, and broccoli.

"You can wash the veggies and peel the cucumbers."

She opened the drawer taking out the peeler.

Cliff was telling jokes that kept the atmosphere light.

They put all the goodies in the basket, picked up a blanket, and headed for the French doors that led to the patio and garden beyond.

It was a beautiful night very clear, you could count the stars while watching them twinkle like diamonds on a black velvet blanket.

Claudette said, "What a beautifully bright night," while walking along the path to their favorite spot. The white wrought iron furniture surrounded by beds of blooming roses, hyacinth, gardenias, tulips, daffodils, and other colorful blooms all added to the garden's beauty.

Their favorite tree surrounded by soft green grass was up ahead. Cliff walked ahead and bent down to spread the blanket down on the grass. He joyfully reached out extending his arms and playfully grabbed her to him. He was so strong but always very gentle with her and she loved the way he held her close to him and passionately kissed her.

They were both thinking, "In a matter of hours we will be married, starting the adventure that will bring us even closer, sharing everything, and learning about each other. It will all be very exciting." She was enjoying all kinds of marvelous feelings, vibrations surging up and down throughout her body.

Cliff gently lowered her down on the blanket and they enjoyed the closeness of their bodies as they sat on the blanket. It was a glorious feeling and she thought tomorrow night, our wedding night, "I will be wearing the most fabulous pink chiffon negligee embroidered with tiny red rosebuds surrounded by green leaves with my new husband, and she inwardly gasped at the words "my new husband" who will be caressing me.

"His arms will be ever so gently wrapped around me as he passionately kisses me while methodically removing my negligee. I will be all his. We will be one. The thoughts made her tingle all over making her toes curl. It will be pure ecstasy as she thought about how great it is going to be sleeping in the same bed, under the same covers, going to sleep in his arms, and waking up together as they kiss good morning. "I can't wait," she thought filled with excitement; her thoughts were interrupted as Cliff suggested that they dig into their picnic basket.

Cliff asked, "What are you in the mood for first?"

"I would really like to munch some veggies: radishes, cucumbers, tomatoes, carrots, broccoli, and by the way what else did you bring?"

He "dove" into the picnic basket and brought out a pizza with sausage, meat balls, and olives, her favorite.

She reached for a slice but being in a playful mood, just as she put out her hand to pick up a piece, he moved it out of her reach.

They were having so much fun.

"What did you bring to drink?"

"I brought Raspberry tea."

The repast was enjoyed under the blanket of stars.

Suddenly, Cliff shouted, "Look a shooting star. Quick make a wish!"

It was as though the planets were blessing their forthcoming marriage.

"Did you make a wish," she asked while running her fingers through his hair.

"Yes, and you're not going to get me to tell you what I wished for."

With that, she started tickling him and they rolled around on the blanket enjoying the crisp night air.

"Are you still hungry?" he asked.

"Yes, any more 'rabbits' you can pull out of that basket?"

They were having so much fun, he thought as he reached into the basket and extricated a huge banana split--a dish from yesteryear.

"Wow," she said, "You did that all by yourself? Let me see it up close."

Cliff held out the creation containing a banana half on each side of the dish, in the center three scoops of ice cream, drenched with chocolate sauce, smothered with whip cream, sprinkled with chopped nuts, and topped with three cherries.

"It's a real work of art. What made you think of it?"

"I was passing a retro corner drug store that had huge posters of ice cream creations from the fifties, I was so transfixed that I stopped and when I looked in saw girls dressed in poodle skirts and saddle oxfords. I walked in, the juke box was playing, kids dancing, and I went to the counter. I couldn't resist but ordered a banana split. It was mesmerizing as I sat there perched on a stool intently watching the soda jerk using the ice cream scoop, swirling on the whip cream, sprinkling on the nuts topping it with 3 cherries, and smiling put the dish in front of me with a spoon.

"I turned around to see what the others were eating and was amazed at the hot fudge sundaes, more banana splits, ice cream sodas, and something called a devil's delight with enough ice cream, toppings, and whip cream to feed a small tribe."

"It sounds like a fun place," she said. "Why don't we plan on going there?"

"Good idea. Let's hope I can find it again. I'll try to recall where it was and we'll go. It'll be fun," he said as he took out two spoons and they started enjoying his creation.

Suddenly, they heard footsteps and saw two figures approaching in the distance. As the figures grew closer they realized that it was the newlyweds also out for a romantic evening.

Claudette called out, "Monique and Pierre come on over."

They were surprised to see Cliff and Claudette.

"Come join us. There's plenty of room on the blanket and you can taste Cliff's fabulous ice cream creation."

They hesitated not wanting to intrude but realized they were being urged to join them.

Claudette handed each of them a spoon and soon all four were enjoying the ice cream dessert as Cliff again told the story.

They were surprised when they saw Grace and Gordon approaching. It looked as though a twosome was going to be enlarged even further. Soon all six of them with their spoons were enjoying Cliff's creation.

It turned out to be a party as they sat on the blanket laughing and joking.

CHAPTER THIRTY ONE

The house was alive with excitement as everyone except the bride and groom were rushing around checking all the details. Everyone wanted the day to be perfect for the couple. It was turning out to be a project of gargantuan proportions.

Flowers were arriving and set in place amidst the ribbons, chairs set up, and the caterers had arrived and were busy in the kitchen.

It seemed as though all was in readiness.

Gordon went over to Grace and suggested that they go to their room to get ready. She had some other things to do, but he was insistent. She took his hand and together hand-in-hand they went to their cottage.

He said, "We have enough time, let's hop in our tub and take a bubble bath together. She looked at him, it was the first time in months he had suggested they bathe together, and she was thrilled. It was great having such a huge tub that they had enjoyed on so many occasions.

The fragrance of roses from the soft glow of the flickering candles permeated the bathroom while the soft highly piled bubbles created a relaxing and romantic atmosphere as they enjoyed lying in each other's arms. It was wonderful, but they had to be cognizant of the time otherwise as it always did when they were together, minutes and hours passed by far too rapidly. They still had to get dressed to attend Cliff and Claudette's wedding.

Gordon looked so handsome in his tux as he turned to zip up Grace's gown. She was a vision in her matron of honor dress. Gordon thought how very lucky he was to have this remarkable woman for his wife. "She's perfection," he said to himself.

He asked her to come over and sit down beside him on the love seat. She was perplexed as to why he was asking her to sit down when they had to go to the main house for the wedding. . Gordon was going to be escorting Claudette down the aisle and here he was asking her to sit down. Not understanding, but anxious to please, she sat down beside him when he suddenly got up, bent down on one knee, and took her hand. He said, "I am proposing to you once again. I want you to know how very much I love you and I'm asking you again, will you marry me?" He was so gallant that she smiled and emphatically said, 'Yes!"

He reached into his pocket, took out the large velvet box, and opened it. She put her hands to her face and sighed as she saw the contents of the white satin lined box that contained the most beautiful diamond necklace she had ever seen.

He removed the necklace from the box, opened the clasp, and fastened it around her well-defined ivory throat. She was speechless as she reached down and touched the necklace. "It's beautiful, thank you."

"No, don't thank me, you are truly worth it, and much more as he took her in his arms and kissed her passionately, then reaching into another pocket he took out another box that matched the first but was several sizes smaller. He opened it as he held it in front of her. She shook her head and said, "Oh! Gordon, this is too much."

"No," he said, "It's not enough."

She took the earrings out of the box and fastened them to her ear lobes. He turned her toward the mirror where she stood in awe of how spectacular they looked.

"They are beautiful," she said.

"You make them beautiful. Do you know how very much I love you and how very much you mean to me? You are my world."

She nodded and lifted her lips as she pressed them against his in a kiss that sent magical feelings throughout her body. The magic was still there.

CHAPTER THIRTY TWO

Grace, Monique, Mrs. Svensen, and Nancy were busy helping Claudette get dressed. Her gown was spectacular. She had gifts for each of them, and their gifts for her made her day even more special.

The hair dresser and makeup artist arrived and were busy working their magic. Ra Ra walked in. She looked adorable in her flower girl dress and said, "I want some makeup, I want to be beautiful, too!"

Claudette asked the makeup artist to apply a very pale pink lip gloss and a dash of powder on the girl's delicate pink cheeks.

Ra Ra walked over to the mirror and said, "I am beautiful, aren't I?"

"Yes, you are," they all agreed.

There was a knock at the door, they screamed, "Don't come in."

"I won't come in. How is everything progressing?"

"Just fine, we need a little more time. Come back in about twelve minutes."

They handed Claudette the traditional blue garter and she slid it up her leg. She had all the traditional requirements: something old, something new, something borrowed, and something blue.

They held out her gown, she stepped into it, and they zipped her up. They ooed and awed. She looked gorgeous in her designer bridal gown with the seed pearls sewn throughout.

Grace picked up the exquisite veil and helped her put it on. It was equally spectacular. It was beyond floor length. They arranged her train and handed her the wedding bouquet comprised of white orchids, gardenias, lily of the valley, and white camellias bound with long white ribbons tied to a small white Holy Bible. They all had their bouquets, and Ra Ra was proudly holding her basket of rose petals.

Once again there was a knock on the door, it was Gordon asking, "Are you ready?" They said they were and Gordon said, "I'll inform the organist."

They heard the wedding march, opened the door, and the bridal party preceding the bride as they started walking down the stairs. It was a procession of beautiful gowns and lovely ladies.

Gordon walked forward and held out his arm for Claudette; they started down the stairs, and then down the aisle as the bridal march was being played.

Cliff was standing by the altar, looking very handsome in his tuxedo and next to him his best man, Pierre, also in a tuxedo.

Cliff was staring at his bride at the top of the stairs and saw her radiant face, a beauty he had never before witnessed in life; she was a picture of loveliness just like an angel from heaven. She looked beautiful, the way a bride should look, as she was coming down the stairs toward him on Gordon's arm.

As they approached the altar Gordon kissed Claudette and put her arm through Cliff's.

The minister was asking Cliff to repeat his part of the wedding vows when they heard some murmuring in the back and wondered what was going on. The bride and groom turned around and heard a man's voice getting louder and louder as he approached the altar.

Everyone gasped as they realized it was Claudette's father and were silently wondering why he had come.

One of the guest whispered to another, did you know that he had abandoned, disowned, and disinterred his daughter? They knew that he wanted her to marry the son of one of his law partner, Hector Fegley, when she refused her father didn't want her in his life, and didn't want to be part of her life.

Why had he come? What had he hoped to accomplish? Was he here to disrupt the proceedings? The guests were staring in disbelief at his presence.

What were Cliff and Claudette going to do?

They all stood looking at this man who at one time was the ideal loving father until she, to quote him, disobeyed by refusing to marry the wealthy man he had chosen for her.

She had continually told him that she didn't love Hector, never liked him. There was nothing neither he nor anyone else could do to make her marry a man she detested, and now he was here to ruin the most important day of her life. She stood there transfixed--her heart racing.

Everyone objected to her father's intrusion.

Gordon stood up not knowing what to do. Was her father here to stop the wedding? What was his purpose? Mr. Svensen also arose anxious to help in any way he could.

Cliff was doing his best to steady Claudette. She was pale and he was concerned she would faint. Everyone was concerned about her and what her father might do. They were at a loss as to what to do. How do you handle this kind of situation?

She noted that her father was having difficulty walking as he approached her. He looked tired, old, and pathetic. Evidently, the automobile accident had taken its toll.

They all waited in silence even Ra Ra was frightened and shaking.

"Claudette," her father hesitated and haltingly said as he paused and took several more deep breaths, "I am very sorry. It is very difficult to say this because, as you know, I am a very proud man, but I have been wrong. I am sorry. You are my daughter, and I love you very much. I want you back in my life, and not just you but also this man you have chosen to be your husband.

I was very wrong. Cliff must be a wonderful man and again repeated, I want to be part of your lives. I have changed my will, you are no longer disinherited. I want to be back in your life. Will you please give me a chance to make it all up to you? I promise I will be different. I will change.

"Can you ever forgive me?"

Claudette didn't know how to respond. Here he was interrupting the ceremony, the most important day of her life, and for what? He could say something now, and tomorrow change his mind.

He took several deep breaths as he held on to his cane and repeated, "Please, can you ever forgive me?"

She looked at him, wavered, and her legs almost gave way. Cliff held her even more tightly, hoping that soon she would be able to regain her composure. She looked at Cliff wanting to know what she should do.

"He's your father, he's old, sick, and came here to make amends. Do you want to forgive him? It might make you feel better. He lives in Manhattan, and we, in San Diego. The cities are three thousand miles apart; he won't be coming here that often. You might never forgive yourself or have another chance like this. He has essentially come begging for your forgiveness which was difficult for him. He's a very proud man and will be our children's grandfather. Shall we give him a chance? I will be here to support you, no matter what you choose to do."

Claudette turned to her father and asked, "Do you mean it? Will you accept Cliff as your son-in-law?"

Her father said, "Yes. Yes, I will. I promise here before God and all these witnesses, I shall be an exemplary father you will once again be proud of me. You fell in love and chose Cliff; therefore, he's my choice for you."

He timidly asked, "After the ceremony could we talk and will you allow me to hug and kiss you? I also want to apologize to your husband, Cliff, shake his hand, and give your marriage my blessing. I would also love to hold my two wonderful grandchildren."

She looked at Cliff who nodded.

She said, "Yes, after the ceremony."

An usher showed her father to a seat and the ceremony continued without further incident. The couple repeated their vows, exchanged rings, and said, "I do."

The minister pronounced them "Man and Wife," and said to Cliff, "You may kiss your bride."

She said to herself, "We are now Mr. and Mrs. Cliff Camden. My dreams have come true."

Cliff lifted Claudette's veil, put his arms around her, kissed his wife, and said to her, "My darling, every day, I am with you will be like a holiday, You will always be Forever My Love."

###

www.ingramcontent.com/pod-product-compliance
Lightning Source LLC
Chambersburg PA
CBHW062018170626
46813CB00001B/212